ANNE WORBOYS was [...] established British au[...] novels, many of whic[...] written short stories for women's [magazines?]. [...] reviewed for The Society of Women Writers and Journalists. Her many interests include theatre and travel and spending hours in her garden.

You Can't Sing Without Me

Anne Worboys

PIATKUS

First published in Great Britain in 1996 by
Judy Piatkus (Publishers) Ltd of
5 Windmill Street, London W1

First published in paperback in 1997

*A catalogue record for this book is available
from the British Library*

ISBN 0-7499-3012-8

Set in Times by
Phoenix Photosetting, Lordswood, Chatham, Kent
Printed and bound in Great Britain by
Mackays of Chatham PLC, Chatham, Kent

To Margaret Gause-Shuman
who introduced me to the Valle

Chapter One

Four o'clock on a hot Wednesday in August. The twins had their pocket money. Claire came into the house through the conservatory, idly swinging her tennis racquet. The thick velvet curtains of the drawing room held the heat at bay, conferring an impression of dusk on the low-ceilinged, oak-beamed room.

Charlotte, leaning against the rails of the galleried landing, saw her come and ran down the wide staircase. 'Let's go to the village and get some sweets.'

Claire dropped her racquet on the hall floor and sagged at the knees. 'I want a swim.'

'I want a Mars Bar.'

'Sweets are bad for your teeth.'

'One little Mars Bar? Pooh!' Charlotte dived out of the front doorway. Her bicycle was leaning on the wisteria vine. Impatiently, she lifted it and bounced the front wheel up and down. Heat shimmered on the gravel. 'You should've known it was hot,' she said. 'You shouldn't have been playing tennis.'

'I wasn't playing, I was practising. Mr Sefton said my service was poor.' Mr Sefton was the coach at Hillcrest School.

'Come to the shops with me, then we'll go to the Bubbly Hole.' Charlotte leaned forwards across her handlebars, gazing intently at her twin, wheedling.

'You won't. You'll stop and read the comics.'

Charlotte jerked upright and tossed her head. 'Go by yourself then.'

'You know I'm not allowed.'

'You should learn to swim.'

As if she didn't know. But she never would.

The twins came from a disadvantaged background, whatever that meant. Somewhere in their past there was a faceless, shadowy birth mother, unendowed with flesh and blood. She could not 'manage' two of them, they had been told, and twins couldn't be split up. So the glamorous Godfreys, rich inheritors of Folly Hill farmhouse, became their parents – their real parents, the twins felt, just as they regarded Kenneth and Yolande as their real sister and brother.

'I'm going,' said Charlotte, giving the bike a forward lurch.

'Pig,' Claire muttered without malice.

'Little birds in their nest agree.' Vivien Godfrey, the best-dressed woman in Forge Green, came breezily into the hall, swinging an Italian leather shoulder bag. Her crisp two-piece was cinnamon-coloured, her cut-away sandals a perfect match. Her hair was blonde and expensively cared for, her nails well manicured, her legs brown and shapely. People thought her beautiful as well as elegant, not seeing that her beauty was all in her radiance and her proud carriage. Vivien Godfrey was lovely because she was loved.

She paused to admire her twins in their clean white T-shirts and jeans: every mother's dream children. Claire struggled up from the floor; Charlotte laid her bicycle on the gravel and ran inside. Wild-rose cheeks in their angel faces. Apricot-coloured curls. A shared defiance.

'We always agree,' they said in chorus.

It could choke Vivien with emotion to see the twins spring together in mutual self-defence at a rub from the outside world, even though they quarrelled as often as Kenneth quarrelled with Yolande.

Vivien thought God had been reckless in handing out such beauty. And talent, for they had the sweetest of singing voices. They belonged to the Forge Green village church choir, and they sang duets at their school. Yolande said they must have their voices trained. She pictured them becoming great opera stars.

Vivien feared losing the twins. The young student who had given them up in order that she might finish her education would be a woman now, in her late twenties. Independent. Or married, with an understanding husband. She imagined him saying, 'The Godfrey girls are on TV tonight, darling. You must see them.

2

They bear an uncanny resemblance to you.' Maybe the mother had the same apricot-coloured curls.

It didn't bear thinking about.

Kenneth said they would have more fun in pop. He saw them in black leather, gyrating to beat music as part of a group.

His father was sharp with him, seeing black leather as a violation of their purity and innocence.

Yolande was envious of their hair and the green eyes that they pretended had come down from a great-grandmother on their father's side. Yolande had inherited the lady's long legs, Kenneth her beaked nose, or so they said. The family lived easily with the fiction of common ancestors. They imbued the twins with Godfrey flesh and Godfrey blood. Only when some unusual trait arose, like Claire's refusal to swim, it was remembered that they came from an office, ready made, in their own carrycots.

Vivien looked round for her car keys.

'Behind that.' Claire pointed to a lacquered box standing on a Georgian table. Vivien peeped behind it and found the keys in a letter tray. She rattled them on their ring. 'Now, who could have put them there?'

'You did,' they chorused, paying her out for poking her nose into their private world. Then Claire spotted the new bracelet. 'Muum!' She grabbed Vivien's wrist. 'Where *did* you get this?'

'Yesterday's present.' Vivien glowed.

'Did Daddy give it to you?'

'Doesn't he spoil me?'

Claire spun it round on her mother's arm. 'Oh, I do like that,' she purred. 'Can we borrow it?'

'It's not suitable for little girls.'

'Painted roses! It looks more suitable for us than you. Look, Charlotte! Roses.'

Charlotte fingered the raised enamel. 'Can we have it when you die, then?'

Vivien gently extricated her wrist from their little fingers. 'No one's going to die, you naughty thing.' She stepped smartly out of the door, smiling, and crossed the gravel forecourt trailing musky perfume.

As she opened the door of her highly polished Riley (the gardener doubled as odd-job man), she heard Charlotte say, 'Why shouldn't you go by yourself? You don't have to get into the water till I come.'

Vivien swung round. The twins were not allowed to go to the Bubbly Hole alone. Then Claire said, 'You know I can't.'

Vivien slid into the driving seat and started the engine.

Later, she thought she remembered experiencing a quiver of uncertainty as she nosed into the road. She could have returned and spoken to the housekeeper. That was hindsight. What she always remembered, always, was that the little gold watch on her wrist pointed to four fifteen. Stella Bloomingdale, proprietress of an exclusive boutique in Wylie-under-Lyne, had promised to give her first option on a rather special dress, provided she came before half past four.

She let out the clutch. The Riley moved forwards, carrying her to her date with a dress she did not need. That was what she remembered afterwards, how unnecessary it was. And she remembered the sky, chequered with black thunderclouds. She thought at the time, They won't go anywhere if it rains.

Charlotte darted outside again and picked up her bicycle. 'I'm off,' she said, straddling the saddle, one foot resting on a pedal.

Mrs Fuller waddled through the hall in her crossover apron, smelling of beeswax polish and carrying a watering can. 'Going down to the river, are you?' she asked.

'I can't because Charlotte's going to the village for sweets,' Claire replied, pouting.

'It's a day for a dip and no mistake. Swimming yet, love?' Mrs Fuller looked sideways, teasing.

Claire tossed her head. Everybody knew perfectly well she couldn't swim, would never be able to swim.

'Why don't you go down on your own, duckie, if your heart's set on it? In this heat,' Mrs Fuller suggested dangerously, 'there's bound to be others there.'

'Bound to be,' Charlotte echoed, recognising a way out of the dilemma. 'I'll go to the village and you go on to the Bubbly Hole. I'll catch you up.'

She pushed her foot down on the outside pedal. Claire delivered a lethargic kick at her back tyre. 'Bring my bathers,' Charlotte shouted over her shoulder as she sped away.

'Mind that road!' called the housekeeper.

The roar of a tractor engine juddered in from the adjoining

4

field. 'Mr Abrahams is rushing through his haymaking,' Mrs Fuller remarked. 'It's them black clouds got him worried.' She went outside and looked up at the sky. Abrahams was the farmer who had bought the fields behind the house when the farm was sold. 'But it's not going to rain, is it, ducks? Never does. Though the garden could do with it. Go and get your things,' she said, indulgent and kind. 'You'll feel better down there looking at the water. She won't be long.'

Claire wandered back inside.

Mrs Fuller stood, watering can in hand, admiring the view. Having worked at Folly Hill since she was sixteen, she was more at home within these mellow brick walls and symmetrical yew hedges than in her own tiny cottage in Forge Green High Street. The roses were into their second summer flowering; climbers red as raspberry jam had taken over the plum tree. She watered the zinnias, then wandered round to the back of the house. Here, herbs nestling in their beds nudged up to brick paths. Beyond, a cobblestone yard fronted the stables. My, but it was hot! She emptied the dregs of the watering can on the self-seeded marigolds, put it by the garden shed and returned inside.

Claire had disappeared.

Chapter Two

Face lifted, eyes shining, ponytail flying, Charlotte sped recklessly along the green lane, singing.

> 'Salvation Army, free from sin,
> All went to heaven in a sardine tin.'

A pheasant crept out of a tangle of grasses and scuttled across
in front of her. She dived, missing its tail by inches.

> 'Tin caught fire on a telegraph wire,
> And they all went to hell—'

her voice shot up, touching high C – 'with their sh-ir-r-rts on
fi-i-i-r-c.'

Down the long hill between the frothy hawthorn bushes she
raced. Out in front, half a dozen spotted deer, escaped from
Dornford Manor park, were trapped between the high banks. She
watched them bouncing off on dainty hooves, heads high. They
leaped up on the grass and she sped on.

At the bottom of the hill she swung round Travers's corner and
there was another cyclist hurtling out of a side lane. Max Fosse
swept up beside her, shouting piratically, 'Nearly got you that
time!' then snatched at her nearside handlebar, capturing her.

'Where's Claire?' He rarely saw one of the twins alone.

'Gone to the Bubbly Hole.'

'Where are you off to?'

'The shops.'

'What for? What are you going to buy?'

6

Charlotte pertly tossed her ponytail. 'Nothing,' she said, free-wheeling, enjoying the sensation of being propelled. 'Did you get your Sony?'

'Nearly.'

Noting his hesitation, she looked at him curiously. 'What do you mean, nearly?' He had been saving for ages.

His voice became gruff and unsteady.

'I didn't get my pocket money today.'

'What did you do?' she asked with that air of fascination reserved for other people's misdemeanours.

He released his grip, throwing her with startling suddenness on her own resources. They curved in towards the pavement. Ahead lay the village shops, dissimilar in style and age, yet blending harmoniously, weatherboard with brick, tile with stone. The sun gleamed on their redness, their whiteness, their lovely hanging tiles.

'You must've done something,' Charlotte said, though not without sympathy. 'Otherwise it wouldn't have been stopped.' She knew how unkind Max's father could be. He called it strict.

'I'll have it next week.' He reacted to her offensive curiosity by pretending not to care.

Charlotte leaned her bicycle against a lamppost. She stood facing him, head up, feet apart, her fingers caressing the coins in her back pocket. She knew how desperate Max was for his radio, and how hard he had saved. 'I could lend you some,' she volunteered. 'How much do you need?'

'Only a pound.' His navy-blue eyes shone with warmth and hope.

Only all her week's pocket money! Charlotte managed to hide her dismay. 'I forgot,' she said. 'I'm not s'posed to lend.' She swung round and strutted off towards the newsagents, exuding a defiant mixture of embarrassment and guilt.

Jerking his bicycle upright, Max swung a leg over the seat. 'Girls!' he muttered as he raced furiously back the way he had come. Once out of sight beyond the first corner, he brushed tears from his cheeks with the back of his hand. Everybody had a Sony but him. He was the only boy he knew who had to save up for everything. 'That's how you learn the value of money,' his father said.

7

Max didn't see why he should know the value of money if his friends didn't. Fifty yards ahead he saw little Louisa Waite leading her dog Pip. Putting on an extra burst of speed, he swerved round her, missing her by a whisker. She let out a shriek and leaped to the verge. Max pedalled on his way, his good humour partially restored.

Claire came out into the side garden, carrying the swimming gear. Sasha the corgi, hunched over a bone in the shade of the sycamore tree, glanced up, then resumed her attack on the bone.

'Walkies.'

The dog ignored her.

'Walkies!' This time she used the urgent voice Sasha understood. The dog grabbed the bone in her teeth and scampered for the wooden gate.

Mr Abrahams waved from his high seat on the tractor. Claire waved back. A broad sweep of land ran down into a wooded valley where a stream, a tributary of the Wylie River, ran between overgrown banks. The curve of green fields on the opposite side was prettily dotted with white sheep. To the left at the bottom of the hill the river proper broke away from Puddle Lane, ran for several hundred yards through Farmer Derwent's meadow, hit a slate escarpment, then hurtled over a rock ledge to drop foaming and bubbling into a deep pool. Dick Derwent and his friends who swam there called this pool the Bubbly Hole.

Claire wandered slowly on, looking without much hope for the four-leaf clovers that Charlotte found so easily. Sasha dropped her bone. Claire bent down to pick it up, wiped it on the grass and put it in her pocket.

Max saw them coming. Swiftly he pushed his bicycle up the grassy slope, tucked it out of sight under the hawthorn, and slipped through the gap into the meadow. He lay in wait.

Claire staggered across the road with the dog pinioned awkwardly against her front. Sasha was a fool about cars. She liked to dive at their tyres, snapping.

Max leaped out. 'Boo!'

'Can't scare me.' Claire tried not to show how pleased she was to see him. People teased you if you were nice to boys. Huffing importantly, Sasha trotted off across the familiar meadow with the children following.

Away in the distance, thunder rolled.

'Lightning!' Max exclaimed, gazing up at the sky, eyes bright. 'Lightning can kill you dead.'

'Pooh,' Claire jeered. 'A tiny bit of lightning like that couldn't kill anyone.'

'It could, if it came close. It could get bigger. It could turn into forked lightning. That would kill you.'

She took the bone out of her pocket. 'Sash!' The dog dashed to retrieve it.

'Race you,' shouted Max.

They tore across the meadow, collided in the gap between the bushes and fell face downwards on the grassy bank beside the pool.

'Let's get her to swim.' Max reached out a hand. 'Here, Sash. Gimme.' Sasha snapped, defending her property. She picked up the bone in her teeth and settled among the wild poppies, blood red in the summer grass.

'You should never try to take a bone from a dog,' Claire said.

Max glowered at her. They sat in silence watching the sunlight on the flying spray.

'I'm going to climb right to the top of that bank,' Max announced. 'To the very top.'

'I bet you don't.' No one ever had. There were few footholds and the dry little rock plants easily gave way in their hands. The good swimmers all tried. They would climb until they lost their footing, then with a yell of excitement fall back into the deep water. Splash! Claire never tried because she would be bound to lose her water wings.

Max looked pointedly at her towel roll, hers and Charlotte's. 'Aren't you going in?'

She gazed longingly at the water, waiting for the sight of it to make her feel better, as Mrs Fuller had said. 'I'm not allowed, not without Char. She's gone to the village to buy a Mars Bar.'

'A Mars Bar!' repeated Max scornfully, hating Charlotte. They could have brought the Sony down here and listened to it together.

'If you weren't spending your pocket money, would you lend it to someone?' He tugged at a tuft of grass, giving all his attention to it, jerking it this way and that, pretending he wasn't interested in her reply.

9

'We're not allowed to lend money.' Impatient and disconsolate, Claire went to the gap in the bushes and gazed out towards Puddle Lane, willing Charlotte to come.

Max saw the coins in her back pocket, outlined where the jeans were tight against her rounded bottom. He jumped to his feet. 'Why don't we go into the village and get my Sony?' He gave her a warm smile, winning, anxious, hopeful and a little desperate.

'I haven't got my bike.'

'I'll take you on my bar.'

'What about Sasha?'

'She could run.'

'She'd snap at the wheels and we'd fall off. You haven't got your trunks,' Claire said, suddenly noticing.

His glum face brightened. 'Course I have.' He inserted a thumb at the waist of his jeans, pushing the band away. 'I've got them on,' he said in the manner of one who has only now remembered. 'Go and get undressed. Your mother only means you shouldn't go in when there's no one here, but I'm here. Anyway, Charlotte couldn't save you if you fell off your silly water wings. I could. Go on,' he said persuasively with his lovely smile. 'I'll look after you. Go and get changed.'

She swung indecisively from one foot to the other, looking at the water. 'They're not silly.'

'Go *on*,' said Max and she gave in.

Behind the thorn bushes she rolled up her jeans so the money wouldn't fall out, before tucking the bundle under the cow parsley. Max was standing on the bank, still in his clothes. She slid the yellow water wings round her chest, felt the water with her toes and stepped in at the shallow end, slipping and sliding on the smooth pebbles and stones that lined the pool. 'Aren't you coming?' She disliked being in the pool alone. She stood with the water up to her knees, looking back at him.

He hauled off his T-shirt and unzipped his jeans. 'Race you,' he shouted.

She flopped into the water, dog-paddled fast to the opposite bank and hauled herself up on the ledge. Max came up behind her, but stayed in the water. Claire looked down.

He had nothing on! His willy floated upwards like a little white animal with a life of its own.

10

'Gimme a go on your water wings,' said Max, enjoying her consternation.

She thrust them at him in self-defence, terrified he would bring his nakedness up on the ledge beside her. He slipped them under his arms and threshed across the pool, shrieking softly, pretending he was a nonswimmer like her. At the foot of the waterfall where it was most bubbly and turbulent he headed through the overspill and emerged gasping. Rolling over, he played at being a dolphin. Claire huddled on the rock shelf, tight with apprehension. After a while he swam slowly back, stood up in the shallows and headed towards the bank.

'Hey! Max!'

'You can swim if you want to,' he said, tossing her wings on the grass. 'In Africa and places like that, black people throw their children in when they're babies. They swim,' he said, smiling engagingly, encouraging her. 'They never get drowned.' He picked up her towel and began to dry himself.

'Max!' she shrieked, leaning out over the water, stretching her arms towards him, beseeching. 'Max! Bring my water wings back!'

He turned, full frontal, and she saw his willy, a tiny, unthreatening appendage on his strong body. She knew then he was not teasing, that the exposure of this, his most private part, was a symbol of the wickedness he was about to enact. Dry-mouthed with fear, she watched while he pulled on his clothes, picked up her water wings and prepared to walk away.

'Max! Bring them back!'

'I can't now,' he said. 'My clothes would get wet.'

Sasha came out of the long grass. She looked across at Claire, then up at Max. Her stump of a tail jerked spasmodically, as though she knew of the mischief and wanted it to stop.

'It's all right, Sash.' He bent down to pat her silky head. 'Claire can swim if she wants to.'

'I can't,' sobbed Claire. 'You know I can't.'

He turned and disappeared behind the bushes, where she had left her clothes then emerged with a hand in his pocket.

'Max!' screamed Claire, but he had gone.

Max hurried back across the meadow, dropped the water wings in a ditch at the roadside and pedalled into the village. Franklin's

Electrical was at the far end of the High Street. He leaned his bike against a lamp standard, fished in his jeans pocket for the money he had just stolen, and pushed the door open. The bell above jangled, bringing the proprietor hurrying from the back of the shop.

'Hello, young man,' he greeted Max genially. 'You're just the chap I was expecting. Pocket-money day, eh?'

Max mutely held out the coins, not meeting Mr Franklin's eyes. He knew only too well that grown-ups had a particular ability to recognise guilt. Conscience drove the blood into his cheeks.

'Good Lord! That's a bit close for comfort!' Franklin exclaimed as a flash of lightning lit the shop and thunder cracked overhead. He lifted the flap of the counter, went to the door and peered out, frowning. Rain lashed the windows. 'You can't go out in this, young feller,' he said, turning. 'Better sit down. I'll get your Sony.' He winked. 'Been looking after it well for you.' He went back behind the counter and disappeared down the narrow passageway between shelves stacked with boxes.

Watching the water streaming down the glass, Max thought of Claire. He wouldn't have done what he did if he had known this would happen. He wished now he hadn't. Of course, she was already wet from swimming across the pool, but all the same . . . In his mind's eye he saw her huddled against the rock, cold and scared. Lightning could kill you dead. He hadn't been thinking about himself when he said that – or her. He must go back.

As he put a hand on the latch, another flash of lightning lit up the sky and immediately a further crack of thunder sounded overhead. Mr Franklin, returning from the back of the shop with the Sony in his hand, said authoritatively, 'Hey, you can't go out in that!'

Max's shoulders slumped. 'I've got to go,' he muttered.

'It'll be over in a few minutes. Don't be so impatient, young man. Here's your radio.'

Max eagerly approached, hands extended.

'You'll need batteries. They're extra.'

His arms fell limply to his sides.

The shopkeeper looked hard at him. 'What's the matter, boy? Haven't you got the money for the batteries?'

He shook his head.

'Don't worry. I'll keep it for another week.' He put the radio on a shelf.

Max made blindly for the door, bearing his grief towards the greater privacy of the street.

'Hey, Max! Didn't you hear what I said? You can't ride your bike when there's lightning around. Not with chrome handlebars, you can't. Sit down there.' Franklin pointed to a chair.

Max stood quite still, lips trembling.

'I'll tell you what,' said the shopkeeper, relenting. 'I'll throw in the batteries.' He took the Sony down again, reached for a box on a high shelf and began to rip the plastic cover off. 'You can take it home as soon as the rain's over. OK?' He took out the batteries and began to fit them.

'Thank you,' muttered Max and surreptitiously wiped his eyes. It was a beautiful radio, dark red with shiny chrome fittings. He backed into the chair. Franklin reached over the counter and gave the precious object to him. Max took it with eager hands and switched it on. The Bay City Rollers blared out.

'Hey, not so loud, if you don't mind.'

Max grinned. Elation surged through him, driving Claire from his mind. Lovingly, he placed the radio on his knee, encircled it with his arms, dreaming.

Claire sat still as a mouse for a long time, waiting for someone to come. Her bathing suit dried. The water splashed merrily over the rock fall, catching the sunlight. Then the sun went behind the hill. Hours passed – it seemed like hours. Sasha gazed at her from the opposite bank.

In the distance there was another rumble of thunder. Sasha leaped to her feet, heading for the gap in the bushes. Claire looked fearfully up at the sky. Black clouds were rolling in from the horizon. Sasha trotted back to the riverbank, barked anxiously and waited for Claire to respond. Barked again. Made encouraging forays in the direction of the road, turned, trotted back again. Barked. Claire knew what she was saying: that she wanted to be taken home where she could hide under the bed until the storm was over.

'Go by yourself,' Claire whispered, afraid to call out in case she disturbed the waiting nightmare in the water. 'Get Mummy.'

Sasha stood still, intently watching her, then with a little sigh, half a groan, sank to the ground with her chin between her paws.

Lightning. In blinding flashes it leaped across the sky. Thunder roared after it. Great fat raindrops fell. Dozens of little fountains sprang up across the pool. Sasha dashed away, then crept back, pleading in her doggy way for Claire to come. Clouds thundered forward, obliterating the sun. Golden wires juddered through the air, the lightning Max said could kill you. It came in forks, like the roots of a tree, blazing. Claire tucked her feet tightly up against her bottom, hugged her knees, tried to make herself smaller so the darting, searching light would not find her.

Sasha took a flying leap into the water and began frantically to swim.

Claire screamed, 'No, Sasha! Go home!'

Bewildered by the rejection, Sasha turned back. She paddled to the bank, clambered up on the grass and, without pausing to shake herself, dashed through the gap in the bushes.

A moment's relief. Then Claire remembered there was no one at home. Her father was at work, her mother in Wylie-under-Lyne, Charlotte in the village. Mrs Fuller would have locked up and gone.

She looked down. Darkness seemed to rise up out of the water, painting it black as tar.

She lifted her head and examined the cliff behind her. With hopeless hope she saw little ledges, and tufts of grass for hand-holds.

Another crack of thunder, sharp as a pistol shot. She waited, breath held, eyes screwed tightly shut, for the streak of lightning that would kill her dead. Finding herself still alive, she stood up. Balancing herself with one hand against the rock face, she went to the end of the ledge and began to climb.

Chapter Three

The storm had settled the dust, little more. Now it had taken its
unresolved rumblings and threats elsewhere, leaving the bluest of
blue evening skies over Forge Green village. Charlotte came ped-
alling along the lane. Hauling her bicycle up the grassy bank, she
came face to face with Louisa Waite, a Barbie doll in the making.

'Hello,' she said in the offhand manner reserved for younger
girls. 'Hello, Pip.' She bent down to pat the dog.

Pip wagged his tail. Louisa gazed at her in silence, big-eyed
and cautious.

Charlotte laid her bicycle down in the grass. 'D'you want a
toffee?' she asked kindly.

Louisa kicked at the grasses with one sandalled foot, absorbing
herself in the seed heads that caught in her bare toes. Saying 'Yes
please' when there were no parents present didn't guarantee you
were going to be given a toffee.

'Cat got your tongue?' Charlotte quoted Mrs Fuller. 'Hold out
your hand.' She tipped a wrapped sweet into Louisa's hesitantly
proffered palm.

Louisa searched her mind for something that would impress.
'My aunty's gone to Singapore,' she said.

Charlotte riposted, 'I've got a godmother in the Canaries.'

Louisa bent her curly head and concentrated on unwrapping
the toffee.

The dog cocked his ears and dived through the gap in the
hedge. Charlotte raced in pursuit, shouting. He was already
halfway across the meadow, chasing a rabbit, his lead bouncing
behind him.

Louisa emerged from the gap, one cheek bulging. The rabbit

swung round at right angles, heading for the wire fence that separated the field from common land and the woods. The terrier came to a halt, panting. Charlotte snatched up his lead. Louisa trotted across the intervening space.

'You'd better get through the fence,' Charlotte said, pointing up the fact that Louisa, being too young to swim in the Bubbly Hole, should not be on the Derwent property. She pushed the protesting dog between the wires, helped Louisa after him, then with a careless wave made her way upstream through a bed of young larches.

'Claire!' she called.

The pool lay in shadow now, dark and still outside the laughing waterfall. Claire's towel, distinguishable by its elephant print, lay on the grass. Charlotte picked it up and flung it over her shoulder.

'Claire!' She stood listening in the silence, then wandered away through the gap in the thorn bushes.

With his Sony carefully strapped to his carrier, Max sped along the lane. By the hedge he stopped to retrieve the water wings.

Where were they? He stood staring down into the empty ditch, baffled. The only explanation he could think of was that Claire must have taken them. So she did swim in! He felt a surge of delight that he had done this for her. She would never have taken off if he hadn't removed her wings. As he said, anyone can swim if they have to.

He pedalled home whistling cheerfully, thinking how much more fun they were going to have at the Bubbly Hole now that Claire could swim.

Margot Waite was standing at the window behind the sink when her daughter came up the path. She saw the yellow plastic band clamped across her child's T-shirt, and glimpsed the bulges behind.

Louisa pushed the door open.

Her mother was waiting. 'Where did you get them?' she asked distinctly.

Louisa's smile of happy concentration drained away. 'Aunty Maud gave them to me.'

'What!'

Louisa sidled along the wall in search of help. Margot wiped her hands on the kitchen towel and went with small quick steps in pursuit.

Her husband, flaked out with the heat, was sprawled on the sofa in the sitting room.

'Daddy,' Louisa howled, rushing at him. 'Daddy, Daddy, they're mine!'

'Maud!' said his wife from the doorway, striking an attitude, pointing a finger at the wings.

George puffed out his cheeks, shrugged his shoulders and looked lost.

'Well, say something!'

'Just because Claire Godfrey hasn't learned to swim, it doesn't mean water wings should be withdrawn from the market.'

'That's not the point. I made it absolutely clear before Maud went off to Singapore that she could not give Louisa water wings. Anything, I said. Anything at all but water wings. I'm going to ring her. I'm hopping mad.'

'Come on, Margot.' George was easy-going. 'It's not worth having a row with Maud.'

She strode off to look up the Singapore telephone number.

Gently pushing Louisa away, her father looked into her pretty, tear-wet face. He drew a handkerchief from his pocket and wiped her eyes. 'You want to learn to swim, don't you, darling?'

'I can learn to swim with water wings,' she said.

Such big blue eyes. So beseeching.

'Truly. I can learn tomorrow if I have the water wings. I can, Daddy.'

'Are you sure?' He was already halfway on her side, adoring her for her girly prettiness and her trust in him.

'I'm sure.'

'We'll have to talk your mother round, then. My, what a mess you're in.' He picked at the leaves caught in her curls. 'What have you been doing?'

'Walking in the woods.'

'Walking in the woods wearing water wings! What a funny little thing you are.'

'Daddy!' Louisa was solemn. 'Crispin Derwent says when he's a big boy he'll be allowed to swim at the Bubbly Hole, and he'll invite me.'

'What it is to have friends!' He kissed her on the forehead.

'Now, you run along and put those things out of sight. I'll talk to your mother.'

Vivien Godfrey took the dress from its box. The tissue wafted lazily to the floor, buckling into strange shapes on the rich carpet. The silk whispered and shimmered as she shook out its folds. Paeans of praise for Stella Bloomingdale flurried through her mind as she lovingly draped the garment over a padded hanger and found a place for it in her crowded wardrobe.

She floated down the staircase and across the hall, feeling anointed with the precious oils of love and prosperity, embraced by the good will of the mellow old house. Her heels clicked on the kitchen tiles as she walked across the expensive temple to eating and drinking that was absolutely right for elegant Mrs Godfrey, who had everything.

The dog looked up from her basket with sad eyes, rose halfway to her feet and sagged down again.

'Poor darling,' she said, 'Your dinner's late.' She took a tin of dog meat out of the larder and spooned it into a dish marked DOG. Sasha dragged herself to her feet and sniffed at the meat, returned to her basket, pawed agitatedly at the blanket.

'What's the matter?' Vivien looked concerned.

Sasha gazed mutely up. Vivien shrugged. O'Brien the gardener had left a pile of beans on the table. She tossed them into the sink and turned on the tap.

Charlotte, chewing a jelly baby and carrying a *Bunty* comic, wandered in. 'Mum, where's Claire?'

'She's somewhere round. Her towel's by the front door. I'd be glad if you'd hang it up to dry, darling. And do put your bike in the shed.'

Charlotte said, 'I brought Claire's towel home. I found it at the Bubbly Hole.'

Vivien's hand that held the bean slicer stopped in mid-air. 'What do you mean, "found it"?' She rotated on one heel, frowning.

'She wasn't there. Only her towel. I found her towel lying on the grass.'

'Where were you?'

'I went to the village to get sweets. And my comic.'

'And what did Claire do?'

18

'I don't know. Maybe,' Charlotte said, looking away to hide the guilt, 'she might've gone to the Bubbly Hole.'

'Not on her own!'

'Mrs Fuller said it'd be all right. She said there'd be other children there.'

'And were there?'

'I don't know.'

'What?'

'There was thunder and lightning when I was in the shop so Mr Jones said I could stay for a while and read the comics. He said you shouldn't ride a bike when there's lightning around. He *said* you shouldn't,' Charlotte repeated, recognising trouble, shifting the blame. 'But I did go to the Bubbly Hole after the lightning was over. I took her a Mars Bar, but she wasn't there. There was no one there.'

Sasha whined. Charlotte knelt down to pat her. The dog licked her wrist, frantic little licks of love and helpless distress. Charlotte moved her fingers over the dog's chest and back. 'She's wet, Mummy. Sasha's been in the water. That's why she's whining. No one's dried her.'

Vivien snatched at the strings of her apron, tossed it on the table and hurried into the hall. With one hand gripping the impressive oak banister, she called, 'Claire! Claire, dear.'

'She's not there,' said Charlotte, behind her. 'I looked. Maybe she went home with someone.'

The telephone gleamed whitely on the hall table. Vivien swung round, lifted the receiver and dialled hastily.

'Penny, is Claire with you?' She listened for a moment. 'Sorry to trouble you.'

Dialled again. 'Betty, have you seen Claire?'

Charlotte came to stand beside her, watching the changing expressions on her face, the hope that rose each time she dialled; the controlled fear.

'Charlotte, bring Claire's towel.' Vivien's fingertips sped across the table and back, tap, tap, tapped on the wood.

Charlotte brought the towel. 'It's only a little bit wet,' she said. 'Like somebody might have used it. But Claire wouldn't go in the water. Not on her own.'

'Hello? Noël, is Claire with your children?' Vivien clutched at the towel, feeling the damp, saying 'Thank you' into the receiver, flicking through her address book and dialling feverishly. Unconsciously she kept clutching the towel.

'Ray, have you seen Claire this afternoon?'

'Jessica . . . You're sure? Thanks. Sorry to bother—'

'Peter . . .'

'John . . .'

'Harriet . . .'

In the end there was no one left to ring.

Words came echoing back from the afternoon: 'Why shouldn't you go by yourself?'

She sank down on the nearest chair and took Charlotte's hands in hers. 'Darling—'

'She wouldn't go in, Mummy, not on her own. She's much too scared.'

'Her water wings? Were they there?'

'No.'

'Did you look for them?'

Charlotte hadn't looked, but even so they weren't there. Could not have been. Unnerved by what she saw in her mother's face, Charlotte began to cry.

The dog came and stood in the doorway, looking at them. Vivien felt her coat and knew what Charlotte had said was true. Sasha had been in the water.

They did not hear the crunch of car tyres in the drive; their senses were numbed with doom. With the weight of things past that cannot be changed.

'Robert.' Vivien looked up pitifully as her husband appeared at the front door.

He came forward asking, 'What's happened?'

And then they were in the car, doors banging, the warm engine bursting easily into life. They swung round the circle of lawn that enclosed the vulgar, shrieking faces of the zinnias, raced down the hill and skidded dangerously round the corner into Puddle Lane. They leaped out of the car, ran up the bank, ducked through the gap in the hedge, running, running.

They saw the scrap of yellow among the reeds. Robert jumped down into the shallows, floundering through the water. The reeds cradled her, rocking her gently in the water's flow, waiting for him to come.

* * *

20

At Poplar Cottage, Puddle Lane, one of the smaller des res that flanked the river, Laurence Fosse was mowing the lawn. He turned off the motor and went to the back door. His wife Jessica, her dark, curly hair tied up on top of her head, was singing softly to herself as she prepared the supper. She wore a new apron with KISS THE COOK written in large red letters across the bib.

He stepped inside and kissed her greedily.

'Carnivorous beast!'

'I hope you're not going to wear that when we've got dinner guests?' She looked at him sideways, flirting. 'Especially when we've got dinner guests.'

He kissed her again to shut her up. 'Be an angel and send Max out to trim the edges.'

She went happily to the foot of the stairs, flicking the skirt of her apron, making it dance. Strange voices? She listened, head at an angle. Who could be with Max in his bedroom? She went on up to find out.

He was sitting on his bed surrounded by the precious clutter of his private life: a model aeroplane; a slab of wood, vaguely boat-shaped; delicately curved wood shavings; a wicked-looking knife; a pencil box; a roll of string. Jessica had long since given up asking him to keep his room tidy. The voice came from a radio balanced on his knee.

'Max!'

His dreamy look went.

'Where did you get that?' She stepped forward, frowning.

He read the words on her new apron and looked away, embarrassed. 'You wouldn't give me my pocket money, so I got a loan,' he said defiantly.

She sat on the end of his bed. 'Turn it down, please. A loan?' she repeated.

The blood beat up in his face. 'Somebody gave me the money. That's what a loan is.'

She ignored his deliberate rudeness. 'You're not allowed to borrow,' she said. 'You know that.'

'Sometimes I have to,' Max returned, his arms protectively encircling the Sony, eyes on the pictures on the wall: astronauts, racing cars and a poster for a cowboy film.

'Max, dear, you have to take punishment for disobedience. You were swimming when you had a job to do.'

21

'I wasn't disobedient. I forgot. You forget things. You forgot the mushrooms for the steak-and-kidney pie.'

She smiled, showing weakness for her darling boy, her husband would have said.

'And he forgets, too. He forgot his briefcase one day last week. He should have had his salary stopped,' said Max vengefully.

'Daddy remembered, and came back for it.'

'I'd have come back, if I'd remembered.'

'Who lent you the money, dear?'

He looked up at the ceiling where a giant rubber spider hung from a cord, moving with sinister resolution in the hot breeze that crept through the window. 'Jim,' he mumbled.

'Jim who?'

'You don't know him.' He flicked the radio controls, hard. The announcer's voice rose to a shout.

'Turn it down.' She waited. 'Now, tell me Jim's surname. He must be paid back.'

'I don't know people's surnames.' He was surly now, looking out of the window, pretending interest in the shriek of a tormented bird. 'That's puss on the rampage. Hadn't you better go and save it? You're always going on about cats getting the birds.'

'Where does this boy called Jim live?' she asked patiently.

'I don't know. How should I know?'

She rose and turned towards the door. 'Your father wants you to cut the edges. Bring the radio with you.' She added sorrowfully, 'You must know he'll confiscate it.'

'It's his fault I had to break his silly rules,' shouted Max. 'If he hadn't stopped my pocket money, I wouldn't have had to.'

She wanted to put an arm round him but then he would have known she agreed. The sin of going off to the Bubbly Hole when he had been asked to clear up the garage was comparatively small. But parents must stand together.

As she reached the hall, the telephone rang.

They were ringing all over Forge Green village, bringing together the parents of the children who swam in the Bubbly Hole.

'Her father found her face downwards in the reeds.' Jessica Fosse whispered the news, though Max, who had returned to his room when her attention was taken by the call, could not possibly overhear them in the garden. 'You know, the channel on the rock

22

side is deep.' They did all know the Bubbly Hole, had inspected it and pronounced it safe. 'Poor little mite! What a dreadful thing! Dreadful . . .' She took a tissue out of her apron pocket and wiped her eyes. Her husband, gripping the mower bar, was silent, stunned.

'For once I'm going to tell you what to do.' She recounted Max's borrowing, then added, 'You must let him keep the radio. There must be no punishment. I'll find out who this boy Jim is and repay him. We'll have to tell Max about Claire. The radio will be a comfort to him.'

Chapter Four

Charlotte, struck dumb, was rigid, dry-eyed, chalk white. They were in the drawing room. A Turkey carpet, family photos in silver frames, horse brasses, a burnished copper hunting horn – trophies of a happy and productive life in a world that had smiled on them.

Until now.

Kenneth, awkward in grief, pulled a handkerchief out of his pocket and blew his nose.

Vivien sat huddled, wretched, instinctively fingering a damp patch on her skirt that was part of, the last of, Claire. Charlotte wriggled out of Yolande's arms and left the room. Sasha lay in her basket in the kitchen, crumple-faced, staring.

'Sash.' They went together into the dusky garden.

Later, Yolande found her at the bottom of the orchard beneath the Bramley apple tree, arms encircling the dog.

'It's getting dark, Char.'

Charlotte's arms tightened round Sasha, clinging to something more than the dog, something of Claire.

'Please, darling,' said Yolande, she who never called her siblings that, 'come inside.'

Charlotte did not hear. She was listening to Claire's breathing, waiting for her to speak, to say she had not gone alone to the Bubbly Hole and therefore . . .

'Charlotte,' Yolande pleaded, 'Mummy's worried about you. You can't stay here alone.'

I am not alone, said Charlotte in her mind. Claire is with me.

Yolande gave up and went back to the house. 'She won't come.'

Vivien half rose, sank down. 'Try again in a little while.'

24

Kenneth mumbled, 'Mind if I go out?'

Vivien wanted to protest, Where to? And why? The family should be together, finding their comfort in each other, not in dogs and teenage friends and – where was Robert? He too had disappeared. She had forgotten he was with the police. Listening to the crunch of Kenneth's bicycle wheels on the gravel, to Yolande's footsteps as she dragged herself up the stairs to her room, though only in search of a box of tissues, Vivien felt abandoned.

Robert came in, conveying his misery in hunched shoulders and heavy steps, he who was so brisk by nature. So in charge. He did not look in charge now. He had changed into a cotton shirt and light trousers when he returned to the house, soaked to the skin from his plunge into the channel in his city suit.

'How did it happen?' he asked again. 'How did she come to be at the Bubbly Hole alone?'

'Knowing won't bring her back,' Vivien said, as yet unready to accept her guilt. She rose and waited for him to put his arms round her, to comfort her.

'What could have become of her water wings? They've got to be somewhere,' he said, absorbed in ferreting for answers, unaware of her need. 'The police are asking. She wouldn't have gone in the water without them.'

'No.' But she didn't want the mysteries solved. If this hadn't happened or that . . . Nothing would bring Claire back.

'She couldn't have been alone, Viv.' He scratched at her with the long forks of his desperation. If he could only make her think a bit harder, his eyes said, she would produce their child.

Inside of her a painful knowledge accrued: you have to say it now. Later would be better, but you have to say it now because he will not wait until the time is right. He has to know.

She moved back a step, self-protectively. She said, 'They were quarrelling when I left. Claire wanted to swim. Charlotte insisted on going to the village for sweets. Sweets!' she said, retreating into her own anguish. 'And a comic!' She started to think, in the madness of her grief, that she had exchanged her child for that. For sweets and a comic!

'And Claire went in alone? Is that what you're saying? I don't believe it. She was so very scared of the water. She would never have gone in alone!' said Robert, obdurate in his refusal to accept.

'Not to swim. Oh no, Robert. No. As you said, she wouldn't get into the water. Nobody expected she would get in the water.'

'Expected!' he repeated softly. He closed the gap between them so that he was looking down at her. 'What do you mean, expected? You knew Claire was going alone?'

She found some breath, enough to say what had to be said. 'I was getting into the car. I was in a hurry.' She told him why. She could have lied, but the lie would have tormented her into eternity. Light-headed she thought that another kind of pain, her husband's condemnation, might blot out the one she could not bear.

'A dress!' Robert's voice rose, carrying his disbelief, his censure, out of the drawing room, across the hall and up the stairs so that Yolande, crying in her room, knew they were quarrelling. 'Knowing that, hearing what was being said, you left and went – to – buy – a – dress!'

He was going to hit her. She flinched. Froze.

'May God forgive you, Vivien.' His whisper was far more damning than a shout, more painful than a blow. 'For I shan't.'

'I will never forgive myself,' she cried. 'Help me, Robert!' Help me to bear it, she meant.

'You went to look at a dress!' He kept repeating the words, over and over, until her head was full of them, bursting with them. The anger had gone out of his face, replaced by something colder, harder, more permanent. She could see he hated her now, he who had been a loving husband for twenty years.

Yolande came downstairs, eyes red from crying. 'Mother?' She peered into the gloom.

'Don't turn on the light.' Vivien could not bear, just then, to have her wounds exposed. 'Fetch Charlotte,' she said pitifully, 'she must come in. It's dark now.'

'I'll get her. Where's Dad?'

'Get Charlotte. Please, Yolande, get Charlotte.' Vivien collapsed in the lonely room, weeping.

Charlotte was in the long grass with her arms encircling the dog. Yolande brought her back, half-asleep, with Sasha following. Hearing the two pairs of footsteps, Vivien dragged herself to her feet, mopped her eyes and met them in the hall. They climbed the stairs.

At the door to the twins' bedroom they both realized with stunning shock that Charlotte could not be put to sleep there tonight by herself, with Claire's belongings – Claire's bed with its faded blue cover; the scatter cushions with their smug animal faces; the shabby rocking horse, prancing into eternity, smiling its painted wooden smile.

Yolande, taking over, said, 'You'd better sleep with me tonight.' She went busily back across the landing. Vivien, holding Charlotte, followed. Yolande was folding back the covers. Sasha crept under the bed.

Vivien smoothed the curling tendrils on Charlotte's forehead. 'Do you want me to undress you, dear?'

'I'll get her pyjamas.' Yolande hurried back to the twins' room.

'Come, darling,' said Vivien tenderly, 'speak to us.'

Charlotte could not. She was holding on with all her strength. If she loosened her mind's grip, Claire could slip away. She pulled her T-shirt over her head and eased herself out of her jeans. As Yolande finished buttoning her pyjama jacket, Charlotte headed for the door. The dog crept out from under the bed and followed her.

Claire's jeans and T-shirt, which had been found beneath the thorn bushes, lay folded at the foot of the bed. She picked them up, went back to Yolande's room, lifted the dog on to the bed, then crept under the sheet clutching Claire's clothes in her arms. Sasha inched forward and settled against her shoulder, breathing into her neck.

When word of the missing water wings swept round the village, Margot Waite told her husband.

'Holy Moses!' he breathed

She had come straight from the telephone. He was in the garden shed mending the hose.

'I suppose we'll have to —' he began.

'Why would she say Maud gave them to her if . . .? Besides, she would never go to the Bubbly Hole. Never,' Margot said passionately. 'She knows she's not allowed.' Already protectiveness was taking over, greater now than the need for truth.

'They could have floated down the river,' he pointed out, expediently forgetting the reeds. 'She could have seen them from the towpath.'

'Even so, she couldn't have taken them out of the water. The bank's steep. For a long way,' said Margot. 'Further than Louisa would go, I'm sure.'

'Somebody might have fished them out and left them on the path. Could have happened.' George gave the metal clip on the hose a vicious tug. 'She could have found them – simply come across them. We're going to have to ask her.'

'I will. I'll ask her.' His wife put her hands up, palms facing him, as if holding him at bay.

In the far corner of the garden, in the shade of the weeping willow, Louisa was throwing a ball to the dog.

Margot went down the path between the lilac bushes. Louisa looked up into the face so like her own. 'Watch, Mummy! Watch Pip bring it back.' She threw the ball. The dog sank down at her feet, ignoring it.

'He's too hot. Let him rest. Louisa, darling, where are your water wings?'

Louisa eyed her suspiciously.

'I'm not going to take them away. I just want to see them.' She was thinking there might be some mark on them. A name, or some initials that were not C.G.

'You saw them yesterday.' Louisa ran after the ball, picked it up, dropped it, captured it again, dawdled back looking at the flowers, paused irresolutely by the pond and dropped the ball in. 'Oh, look,' she said, blue eyes wide and innocent, 'it's gone in the water.'

Margot picked the ball out. 'Wouldn't you let me see them again, dear?'

Louisa shook her head.

'Why not?'

She refused to say.

Margot did not want to ask her any more questions. She went back to the kitchen.

'Louisa wouldn't go to the Bubbly Hole,' she said, not looking up at the sound of her husband's footsteps. She pulled out the silver drawer, selecting two large forks and a small one. 'She does understand she can't go wandering on the Derwents' land.'

'Yes.' George waited for clarification. 'No, I mean. No.'

'You'd better put something on. I know it's hot but I think you might make an effort to be decently dressed for supper.'

'Yes. All right.' He remained standing, watching her, reading fear and guilt into her unaccustomed criticism.

'Nothing will bring Claire back,' she said.

'Well, no.'

'Of course it would satisfy the police if we . . .' Her movements were swift and jerky. She turned the forks in her fingers, squinting at them. Picking up a tea towel, she gave them a rub. She jerked the tablecloth until the ironed crease lay dead centre and patted it flat.

'Yes?'

'They like to have all the ends tied up. That's what I was going to say. But nothing will bring Claire back.' She took the electric kettle and filled it at the tap. 'Charity begins at home,' she said. 'Imagine someone saying to Louisa, "You took Claire Godfrey's water wings and she drowned."' She replaced the kettle on the bench and shoved the plug in.

'Lucky I talked you out of ringing Maud.' There was a bite to his words.

She turned to face him, eyes flashing. 'So what do you want to do?' She dared him to give the wrong answer.

He went off to get decently dressed, as she had said, for supper.

That night fragments of her parents' discussion drifted Louisa's way.

'Since you're not going to ring Maud, I'll ask Louisa just once. I've thought about it, and I'll do that. Just once. If she admits to having found the water wings, we must produce them.'

Margot closed her eyes.

In the dark Louisa crept out of bed and crawled beneath it. The plug in the water wings was tight. She pushed it this way and that until the air escaped with a tired whoosh. She folded up the flat plastic and laid it at the bottom of her toy box.

In the morning George asked.

Wide-eyed and innocent, Louisa replied, 'Auntie Maud gave them to me.' It was the truth now, for nothing exists but what is in the mind and Louisa had convinced herself that Auntie Maud, who knew she wanted water wings, had left them in the woods for her to find.

The day after his child's death, Robert could not go to work. Neither did he wish to share the house with the guilty and the weak. The guilty who were also weak, for whom a new gown meant more than the safety of his child. Now, responding to the new person that had possessed him in the night and walked with him today, he dragged out of his memory his mother's words when he proudly brought Vivien home.

'She's pretty, but it's what's underneath that counts. She will have to prove herself.'

Now Robert recognised that hard streak in himself. He saw Vivien's weakness for pretty things as second-rate. Had she any of the virtues expected of a Godfrey wife as chatelaine of the big house on the hill? Had she taken on the chairmanship of the WI? Organised the church flower rota? Driven for the sick and needy? All these things his family had done. But Vivien had been merely a cheerful companion and, until now, a good mother to his children. He forgot that was all he had ever asked of her.

'I have to admit the gal's never put a foot out of place,' his mother had admitted in old age.

Well, she had done so now.

If Claire had been her own child, would she have acted more responsibly?

He recalled her happiness that day they brought the twins home. Was it mere relief that she was no longer obliged to bear more children? He was being unfair, he knew it. Vivien adored the twins.

Adored them, but did not deserve them. She didn't deserve Charlotte now, the one who was left. Robert recognised that he was a little mad. Looking for sanity and comfort, he went to the garage and began tinkering with the Rover's engine.

Footsteps on the cobblestones. He looked up. Vivien was emerging from the back door with a garment draped over her arm. He put the spanner down and wiped his hands on his overalls. He was aware of cruelty gathering in him, tightening his stomach muscles, hardening his mouth.

Glancing up, she saw him coming and paused.

'This is it?' he asked bleakly, pointing.

'Robert. Oh, Robert!' Her face was ugly this morning, her hair disordered and somehow less golden, her face puffed from weeping.

He thought dispassionately that she looked a mess. 'But for this, my daughter would still be alive.'

30

'Our daughter, Robert. Oh, please don't be like this.'

He took the gown from her and held it out, despising it with his glance. 'How much did it cost?'

She told him.

'Don't you think someone could use it? A dress like that? Such a waste. There has been enough waste,' he said, striking her with word blows designed to exorcise his own pain. 'Take it to the Oxfam shop.'

There was no Oxfam shop in Forge Green village. Vivien drove to Wylie-under-Lyne.

A big-bosomed woman standing behind the counter took the dress out of the box. When she held it up the light from the window caught the heavy silk folds, tucking rich shadows inside them, hints of brown and gold. Her businesslike manner went. She slid a forefinger delicately, covetously, along a sleeve.

'You haven't worn it,' she said in a puzzled voice.

'No.'

'Why not take it back to the shop?' Her eyes were all at once sharp and suspicious.

To Stella Bloomingdale? She who had offered exclusive rights provided Vivien came in that afternoon, leaving her child to drown? 'I can't,' she said, and stopped breathing.

The woman waited, head at an angle. Vivien watched the pouter-pigeon bosom moving up and down. Waited for the lecturing voice to release her for she could not release herself. Could not speak. Could scarcely run away leaving the dress on the counter, though she might have to if the silence didn't end soon. Mrs Vivien Godfrey seen running, sobbing, down the main street of Wylie-under-Lyne. Poor thing. They lost one of the twins, you know.

'People come here for a bargain,' the woman said. 'We can't give it away at the price one of our customers would be prepared to pay. Not a dress like that. You should advertise it.'

'Yes, of course.' Vivien became glassy-eyed as her brain filled up with the implications of advertising. Telephone calls. Viewing. Ooh-ing and aah-ing. Questions. She folded the gown, returned it to its box.

She smiled. The smile stayed with her as she hurried along the street. She caught a glimpse of it in a shop window, glued to her face.

There was a deep gutter at the edge of the car park. The hand holding the box lifted, the arm reached out. Her fingers relaxed on the string.

Voices. She jerked round. A group of people erupted from a side lane. The arm withdrew its box and sank to her side. She ran to the car, wobbly-kneed in her tight skirt, thinking busybodies were running after her, accusing her of the intention to deposit litter. She threw the box on the back seat and fell behind the wheel, then edged out of the car park and drove like a demon, carrying the dress with her to some sort of destruction.

A patch of woodland reared up at the side of the road. There was a lay-by where the river curved close to the road. She pulled in, switched off the engine, turned round and snatched the dress out of its box. Ignoring the spear thistles that pricked her ankles and tore at her tights, she ran across the wasteland and looked down over a steepish drop. Where water had eroded the bank, dry little channels offered footholds.

She flung the dress down on the cracked mud below. Then she kicked off her sandals and clambered down after it. The burning August sun had reduced the width of the river, exposing a yard or two of clay, pitted with stones. She rocked a large stone back and forth until it came loose. Placing it on the dress, she made it into a bundle, like a pudding, swung it back and forth, and let go.

It went down with only the smallest splash, and sank out of sight.

She felt there was a rightness about this act of wilful destruction. The river that had taken her child should be made to swallow its share of guilt.

Chapter Five

Sylvia Mendoza, the twins' godmother, came from the Canaries. Vivien met her at Gatwick.

They had been at school together. Afterwards, Vivien went to exotic, foreign Florence to learn Italian. 'God knows why,' she would say, laughing. 'I never used it. It was one of my parents' indulgences.' She had enjoyed so many indulgences like this in her life, making her into the person she was.

Sylvia went to Madrid, to bullfights and fiery flamencos. She fell in love with the handsome, dashing Carlos Mendoza. When he died, spectacularly driving a Ferrari in the Monte Carlo rally, she went on a spiritual quest to La Gomera. There she found comfort. She stayed, acquired a villa, and became an important member of the community. They said of her that she was like a tree whose sturdy roots spread through the *pueblo*, embracing the community, holding it together.

Sylvia's features were bold, strongly fleshed in a noble face, the skin velvety – Spanish skin, now. Her lips were carmine, her eyes mink brown. Her hips had widened to Spanish dimensions, and she had a bosom to cry on, as Vivien had not.

She had many attributes, but the greatest was her perception.

What she perceived on her arrival at Folly Hill was a house divided by bitterness and blame. No one said that Vivien could have stopped Claire going to the Bubbly Hole, had she not been hurrying to acquire a piece of finery before it could be offered elsewhere. Nor that Charlotte had dashed off for sweets, advising Claire to go alone. No one said Mrs Fuller encouraged her, though they knew, for she too had been impelled to scourge herself with confession. Even without this

33

knowledge, Sylvia experienced their silent, impotent anger in her heart.

She knew how the twins had lived, tightly coiled one within the other. She saw, as the family did not, that Charlotte had to sit hour after hour under the apple tree with her arms round the dog. Sasha had stopped eating, lost interest in bones, refused Yolande's offers of walkies. Sylvia sat with the girl and the dog for long periods, respecting their silence, merging with it. Others came once and left, feeling rebuffed.

'I'm thinking of calling in Dr Stevenson,' said Vivien, at her wits' end.

Sylvia asked gently, 'What could a doctor do? He has no pills for this.'

'She hasn't cried. She needs to cry. Crying gets grief out of the system,' said Vivien, knowing it did not, for she cried all the time.

'Grief is not her problem. Her problem is how to let go. She has to come to terms with being half a twin. That's what it's about.'

The picture was too terrible for Vivien's mind's eye. Half a girl. Half of both girls. Half of what had been a whole. Which half, and how separated? She drove the illusion from her mind. 'I feel I've lost both of them now,' she said pitifully.

Sylvia comforted her. She understood that Vivien had never struck adversity before and didn't know how to deal with it.

She talked to Charlotte, sitting beside her on the grass with her arms encircling her knees, big skirts bunched behind her. About Valle San Angelo, where she lived on her Spanish island. About Carlos. About her friends in the pueblo. Juan, who played the Spanish guitar on the white steps and sang sweet love songs; who saw ghosts in the streets, walking. Carmina, her maid, who sang also as she swept the terrace and scolded the gypsies who came up to beg. Nikki, the shaman, who for a fee would tell you what decisions you made at soul level.

'You may have decided, for this lifetime, to learn the lesson of living alone,' Sylvia told Charlotte. 'Think about that.'

Charlotte looked at her with eyes lost in a swirl of greenness. 'I did not,' she said.

At least she had spoken.

Alec Rattray, the vicar, arrived. Charlotte would not come in.

He went to the orchard. He considered he had a way with children. Knew how to draw them out. 'Claire is with God,' he said. 'He takes those He loves best.'

Charlotte turned on him, white-faced. 'He'd no right.'

'To take her? Or to love her better than you?'

Charlotte was not to be drawn on that.

When he had waited long enough, he said, half stern, 'You'd feel better if you would only talk, my dear. Talk to your mother. Talk to me. Talk works wonders.'

Charlotte buried her head in Sasha's neck.

'The vicar said it was God's fault. He loved Claire best,' she told Sylvia afterwards. 'Why would He?'

'There's no understanding God. Don't even try. It's the mystery of life and death that we have to come to terms with.'

'Why should He make us twins, if He was going to take one of us back again?'

'I told you, I don't know about God, but I do know Alec Rattray is an old fool.'

'Anyone who makes two twins, then takes one back, is an old fool,' said Charlotte blasphemously.

Sylvia took books to the orchard. Read aloud from *Alice in Wonderland* and the Grimm Brothers' fairy tales. She sat on Charlotte's bed at night and talked, or read while they waited for sleep. She prayed in her Catholic way that Vivien and Robert might allow her to take the child back to Valle San Angelo. There were still a few weeks left of the holiday.

Max was behaving out of character. He stayed in his room all day, listening to the radio. His mother gave him the previous week's pocket money.

'Now you can repay Jim,' she said. They were all gentle with their children now, loving them more, grateful that if there had to be a drowning, their own had been spared.

'It wasn't Jim I got it from.'

'Then who, dear?'

'Claire.'

Jessica caught her breath. 'Claire?'

'She wasn't going to spend it.' Max turned his full attention to the radio, fiddling with the knobs, turning the sound up, filling the room with the wail of a violin. 'Radio Three,' he said, damning it.

He moved the knob again and found Radio One; '*Mrs Elstead of Sutton Coldfield has sent a request for the* —'.

'Turn it off, Max,' Jessica said unsteadily. 'I want to talk to you.'

'I can't pay it back,' said Max. 'Not now she's dead.'

'He's right,' said Laurence when Jessica told him. 'He can't pay it back. And what's more, I wouldn't want the Godfreys, or anyone else for that matter, to know. It's not as though he's done anything wrong. It's just . . . bloody bad timing. We'd better try to forget it.'

Jessica closed her eyes and prayed that Max had indeed done nothing wrong. She remembered how cute he had been when he was small, casting aside crowding memories of the naughtinesses. 'Boys will be boys,' people said.

Laurence took his pipe from the mantelpiece, pressed down the tobacco, struck a match and wandered into his study. Facing the book-lined wall, he stood frowning.

Jessica came to stand in the doorway. He had gone away, somewhere where she could not follow him. He had dealt with the matter in his own way. With half of her mind, the critical half, she condemned him. 'I can't live with this uncertainty,' she said, folding her arms across her chest, holding in the fear. 'I should have asked him then, but I was so shocked. Will you?'

He put the pipe down in an ashtray on his desk. He was more the university lecturer now, than the husband. 'You may find the truth a damn sight less palatable than uncertainty. Have you considered that?'

Her mind was jagged with unfinished sentences too dangerous to hammer out.

'All right. I'll deal with it,' he said, looking at her with compassion. 'My way,' he added, softly emphasising.

Now she felt safe, but without grace.

He went into the hall and shouted up the stairs. Returning to his study, he picked up his pipe again. With feet apart, he stood and waited, contemplating his polished shoes.

Jessica went hurriedly through the side door into the garden.

Max came thumping down, taking two stairs at a time. In the doorway he stopped, arms spread, hands pressed up against the frame. 'What do you want?'

Laurence took the pipe out of his mouth and stared at it. 'Your mother's worried about your having borrowed money from Claire.'

Max looked down at his bare feet. He kicked the toes of his left foot against his right heel and grimaced. 'Ouch.'

'I wouldn't talk about it if I were you. People might get the wrong impression.'

Max swung backwards and forwards in the doorway, staring down at the hurt toe, which had gone faintly pink.

'Know anything about the water wings?' As he asked the question, Laurence turned to look out of the window. The clematis had broken away from its support. He made a mental note to cut it back. 'Huh?'

'No,' mumbled Max.

His father had the answer he needed, the one the circumstances called for. 'That's all right, then. You know, I'm not very pleased with the way you cut these edges. Tomorrow, I'm going to stand over you and show you how they should be done.'

'All right,' said Max meekly. 'Can I go now?'

Laurence nodded. He went outside and looped the clematis up over the nails he had driven into the mortar. Jessica, snatching randomly at weeds in the rockery, came to join him.

'I was thinking,' he said, speaking directly to the plant, 'we might take a run up to Suffolk tomorrow. This damned vine, it's running wild. I'll cut it back in the autumn. We haven't seen your mother for ages. We could leave Max there for a few days. We should send him more often. She likes to have him, and he likes the sea.'

Decisions. Hymns to be chosen. "All Things Bright and Beautiful",' the vicar suggested, and nobody dissented. 'And "Loving Shepherd of Thy Sheep"?'

'All right,' said Robert, who only wanted to get it over with. He had arranged for the Order of Service to be printed in a hurry. The waiting had become intolerable.

Children who had not gone away for their holidays were summoned to the school. They came bearing flowers from their parents' gardens. Under the guidance of Miss Hurst, stoically holding back her own tears while comforting them, they sorted the blooms. Red rosebuds, pink and mauve phlox, waxy carnations, dwarf asters. A great armful of verbascum, whose deep

37

yellow flowers reminded Miss Hurst poignantly of sunshine on the twins' beautiful hair. The children fashioned posies, tied them together with ribbon, laid them on the grass at either side of the path from lychgate to church door.

The village poured in: children's parents, parents' friends, uncles and aunts, business partners and associates. They packed the pews. Charlotte, a small angel in a white dress with a white bow in her hair, walked between Vivien and Robert, her hands held tightly in theirs. Sylvia followed with Kenneth and Yolande.

They paused by the front pew. Robert let go of Charlotte's hand and stood aside. Vivien slipped in, also letting go. Quick as a flash Charlotte joined Sylvia in the row behind. Vivien swung round, her lips parting on a silent protest: *Come to me.*

Robert's pleading hand extended over the back of the pew. Charlotte pressed up against Sylvia. Sylvia, distressed for them, apologetic but making the best of things, put an arm round her. Robert's hand fell to his side. Yolande slid in beside her mother. Robert and Kenneth followed. They stared in front of them, pretending it hadn't happened.

The organ began to play. The tiny coffin was carried up the aisle. Sylvia whispered, 'Look up, darling,' wanting to spare Charlotte the sight.

Charlotte, who anyway could not conceive of Claire in a box, was aware only of drifting perfume from a bouquet of lavender lying on the coffin. Sylvia had told her Claire's spirit was soaring with the birds, and that if Charlotte wished it she might pause, as in a stained-glass window.

'If you believe something hard enough,' Sylvia said, 'it will be true.'

Charlotte's gaze moved over the flower-strewn altar and the depleted front row of the choir where she and Claire had sat. After a while, there Claire was, in the east window between the heads of Mary and the Baby Jesus.

'Sit down, dear,' whispered Sylvia. And, 'Stand up.' And, 'Kneel.' Charlotte obeyed, never taking her eyes off Claire's image in the stained glass, smiling up at her, tremulous and aware. She did not tell Sylvia. It was too private, too spiritual, too holy an experience to share. Besides, she wasn't sure it was happening.

The last strains of the hymn died away. The coffin was lifted

38

and began its journey back down the aisle. The family fell in behind. People saw the smile on Charlotte's lifted face and were startled. Startled, too, by the unearthly quality of it. With Claire insubstantial as a dream beside her, with the organ music surging round them and the scent of lavender in the air, Charlotte drifted towards the door.

Then Claire left and Charlotte experienced a loss like an upward sigh, as of her own soul leaving her body. She swung round.

They were more at home with her scream than they had been with the smile. They closed round her.

'Charlotte! Hush, darling! Charlotte!'

The congregation moved out through the porch, picking their way across the grass between the tombstones.

'Shall I take her home?' Sylvia mouthed the words.

'Yes,' said Yolande firmly, taking charge. 'Yes, Mummy. Let Sylvia take her home. Go quickly,' she said, for Charlotte seemed unable to stop screaming.

'Who can drive you?' Vivien, stirred to panic, looked round blindly for help.

'We can walk.' Glad, anyway, to be spared the intolerable graveside formalities, Sylvia led her away. Out of sight behind the building she slapped her, hard.

It was like turning off a tap. Charlotte said meekly, 'I couldn't stop.'

Sylvia lifted her hand and kissed it.

The children, conspicuous in their blue and grey school uniforms, little white ankle socks and buttoned shoes (the head had thought it a good idea to show solidarity by wearing school uniform), were shepherded away by Miss Hurst.

The wife of Robert's partner, Humphrey Devine, asked, 'Don't we know that woman with the mop of dark hair?'

He lifted his head. 'She's one of the teachers, isn't she?' he said, and forgot.

Louisa's mother stood alone at the back of the crowd, a memory of yellow water wings floating before her eyes, her mind clutching at rehearsed excuses. 'Pressure of business,' for George. For Louisa: 'We didn't think the little ones would be expected to come. My daily's looking after her.' In the event, nobody spoke, for she wore an expression that did not invite them in.

Max's mother also stood alone.

The formalities over, tears poured down Vivien's cheeks in an uncontrolled rush of emotion. People coming towards them turned back, condolences dying on their lips. 'Pull yourself together,' Robert said, judging her, remembering, though he had been only nine at the time, his mother's calm dignity as she had stood erect beside his father's grave.

'I can't.' She scrubbed at her eyes with a soaked tissue. Mutely, she accepted his big handkerchief and used it to hide from the people, from Robert's cruelty, from the emptiness that had overwhelmed her as they lowered Claire into her grave.

The mourners filed off down the lane, climbed into their cars and drove away. Hermione and Jack Card, accompanied by their son William, who had somewhat surprisingly taken time off work to be there, were the last to leave. Hermione, a large woman of character and opinions, had been exchanging low-voiced comments with all and sundry:

'Such a dreadful thing.'

'How will that poor child cope?'

William, walking beside her, said, 'I'm going to marry Charlotte.'

His mother stopped dead. His father, who had not heard, walked slowly on, head down.

William looked away, muttering, 'Sorry. I didn't mean to shock you.'

She found the use of her legs again. 'I dare say,' she said, hurrying to catch up, anxious to excuse this intolerable lapse of taste, 'you were touched by that little upset. We all were.' She added graciously, 'Yolande would be nearer the mark.'

'I never cared for Yolande,' William said.

Because it wouldn't go away, she repeated the exchange to her husband that night.

'Something fired his imagination.' He was dryly amused.

'The child is ten, Jack. Ten! William is twenty-two!'

He shrugged. 'Forget it.'

All over the village they were talking of the tragedy, of the funeral, of the inquest, of how a surviving identical twin could cope. There was no other subject. None of the children went to the Bubbly Hole; perhaps they never would again.

Charlotte was thin as a sparrow, insubstantial. Vivien and Robert, Ken and Yolande were hurt because her love for them seemed to have dissolved. On some level they could not reach, she and Sylvia were together.

'Spiritually,' said Sylvia, and Vivien remembered that was why she had summoned her friend: because she possessed this special insight.

Sylvia then broached the subject of taking Charlotte to Valle San Angelo.

'Perhaps she can help her,' Vivien said to Robert that evening. Although not wanting to lose Charlotte, she was wondering whether, in the absence of the child's poignant oneness, Robert might open himself to healing. Even bestow forgiveness.

'Sylvia won't help her to live as an individual, that's certain.' Robert, like most of Sylvia's English friends, was suspicious of her motives in retiring to a remote island to live among Spanish peasants. She had told him she felt close to the gods in her canyon, and the gentle dead. 'Baloney,' he said, repeating what she had said to Vivien, unamused.

'Perhaps you should go with her,' he said now.

There was a profound silence while Vivien faced the fact that in agreeing she might be choosing between her husband and her child. What might Robert do in her absence? Look elsewhere for the comfort he could not accept from her?

'Well?' He spoke in that hard voice he had taken to using on her. 'Well?'

'I suggest we let Charlotte make the decision.' She averted her eyes, fearing to see a flicker of hope in his.

Charlotte nodded.

'Would you like me to go with you, darling?'

She shook her head.

Vivien hid her searing disappointment, and her relief. Emotions were tearing her apart. 'Come with me to the attic, dear, and we'll find a suitcase.' She was trembling and awkward, climbing the stairs.

Charlotte was detached on the journey to Gatwick, sitting bolt upright in the car, not talking. At the departure gate she threw her arms round Vivien's neck and could not be prised away, though Robert tried. Her face was chalk white and drenched with tears.

41

Vivien waited with hope and apprehension for Charlotte to say that after all she would not go.

Then Sylvia took her hand and they headed for passport control.

Vivien and Robert waited in wretched silence as the two of them shuffled with the queue. As they disappeared through the barrier, Vivien burst into tears.

'She's got Claire's jeans and T-shirt in her bag,' she sobbed, dredging up a small worry because she was unable to say what was in her heart, that Sylvia had taken her child and she could not bear it.

Chapter Six

The plane reversed from the loading bay, sped out to the runway and in a minute was airborne.

'Oh!' Charlotte cried, coming to life. 'My tummy! It's been left behind!'

'I expect they'll post it on.'

'Oh, you are funny. Look at the clouds!' Charlotte squealed. 'We're on top of the clouds!'

'Children are resilient,' Sylvia had said to Vivien. Now, seeing animation in Charlotte's face, she thought, Something has lifted. Please, God, keep it going.

At Tenerife Airport they boarded a bus. Sylvia normally used a taxi but, 'You'll see more by bus,' she said, 'and there's no hurry.'

The road looped and curled through rocky hills, writhed down into valleys dry as sandpaper, and snaked up again. Ahead, a snow-capped mountain, its base blackened by shadows, thrust up magnificently through clouds. 'Look!' Charlotte's voice disappeared in the roar of the engine. 'I never saw a mountain wearing a white collar before!'

And so they came to the little town of Los Cristianos, and the sea.

'This is a ferry?' Charlotte looked up at the ocean-going vessel that towered above them, all black hull and white superstructure. 'It's a ship, Sylvia! A ferry is a little boat.'

'It's a Spanish ferry.' Sylvia hustled her up the steep gangway to the passenger deck. 'Watch your feet. Take my hand. Tread on those struts, they'll stop you from slipping.'

The Spanish ferry moved slowly out to sea.

They went up a companionway to the sky and the gulls and

43

sooty black smoke belching out of an orange funnel, trailing back to the land. Charlotte hung over the stern rail, smelling the salt air, gazing into the churning foam. Sylvia settled on a slatted seat, tied a scarf round her hair and lifted her face to the sun and breeze. Later they went down to a dark panelled saloon smelling of cigarettes. Both of them drank Coca-Cola, and ate foreign-looking biscuits, dry as dust.

'Don't they have tea for ladies?' Charlotte was amazed that Sylvia should drink Coke.

'Grown-ups are different in Spain.' She swallowed the last of it, putting the glass down. 'Let's go back on deck. Any moment now my island will come into view.'

It began as a speck on the horizon. Growing taller, it split into a group of sharp peaks and rocky promontories. A town appeared, white droppings at the mountain's foot. As the ferry swung round, the peaks drew together, one edifice now, touching the clouds.

'I never saw a mountain like that,' breathed Charlotte, awed. 'It's not like Scotland, is it?'

'Quite different,' Sylvia agreed. 'No heather.'

Charlotte sent her a wary, green-eyed glance from under her lashes. Sylvia laughed and gave her a hug. 'Tomorrow, in the bus, we'll drive through those clouds.'

'You're teasing.'

'Wait and see.'

They went to a little hotel in the Ruiz de Padrón. A bare, tiled floor, heavy, foreign-looking furniture.

'Black beds!'

'Spanish furniture is darker than you're accustomed to. It's nice, though, in its way. Don't you think?'

An enormous picture hung above and between the beds: Christ, suffering on the Cross. Charlotte crept close to Sylvia, pressing against the soft, comforting flesh of her thigh. 'Is this a church?'

'No, dear. We're in a Catholic country now. Catholics like to be reminded of their Saviour.'

'I don't like all that bleeding over my bed.'

Sylvia kicked off her shoes to stand awkwardly on the bouncy mattress. She took the picture down and re-hung it facing the wall. 'Let's go down and get an ice cream. Spanish ice cream is wonderful.' She replaced her shoes and Charlotte was whisked through the door.

They ate the ice cream sitting on sun-warmed stones, part of the harbour wall. Little boats were swinging at anchor on a wind-ruffled sea. Afterwards they wandered back into the town for dinner.

'What are all those chairs and tables doing in the street?'

'That's where we eat.'

'In the street!' Charlotte's voice rose an octave. 'Are all their dining rooms flooded?' She remembered the floods in Puddle Lane: Bridge Cottage, Stream Cottage, Corner Pond. Wooden floors buckling, chairs floating like boats, wallpaper peeling away. Max, exultant, paddling a canoe in his garden.

'This is what we do in Spain, eat in the street. Such a lot you have to learn! Would you like to try this restaurant, or that one over there?'

Charlotte made her decision and slipped into the nearest chair. A thin, mangy dog and two sharp-faced cats prowled round her feet. A waiter handed Sylvia a menu, then chased the animals away.

'The dog's hiding behind that pillar!' Charlotte was taking everything in. 'There's a donkey coming. A donkey, Sylvia! It's going to walk past our table!' She was doubled up with laughter. Daringly, she patted its rump. When she turned, the waiter was pouring wine into her glass. She waited for Sylvia to tell him she was only ten. Sylvia merely smiled.

'You can get drunk on wine.' Charlotte was awed by what Sylvia had allowed to happen.

'Maybe you will.'

She bounced up and down on her chair, laughing. Great peals of laughter. The waiters smiled indulgently.

Sylvia swallowed, blinked, and held the menu in front of her face. She blew her nose. 'Let's order, shall we?'

'Is this soup in Spain?' Charlotte asked. 'It looks more like a pie to me.' She frowningly contemplated the crust, tapping it with her spoon.

'This is the way they make soup in Spain. What tales you'll have to tell when you go home: ladies drinking Coke; soup pretending it's a pie; donkeys in the dining room!'

Charlotte thought secretly that her parents would not approve. More likely they'd think she was making it up. She dipped her spoon experimentally, rolled the mixture over her tongue, pronounced her verdict.

45

'Of course you like it. It's good.'

Sylvia paid the bill and they wandered off up the narrow street. Tall buildings. Dark, glassy shops with heavy wooden doors. The guardian mountain loomed above them, foreshadowing night. A flight of wide stone steps.

'Up there,' said Sylvia, 'is the Parish Church of the Ascension, where Christopher Columbus attended Mass—'

'What's Mass?'

'Holy Communion – before setting out to discover the New World.'

'America. "In fourteen hundred and ninety-two Columbus sailed the ocean blue." Miss Hurst tells us rhymes for dates.'

'Lucky old you to have Miss Hurst. Is she nice?'

'Yes.'

'Pretty?'

'Well.' Charlotte considered. 'She's old, you know.'

'How old?'

'Just old. Grown-up.'

'Like twenty?'

'Maybe.'

'Thirty? Or forty?'

'You're teasing.'

'You're laughing. That's what I want.' Sylvia ruffled her hair.

They climbed the steps then paused outside the door. 'Shall we go in and light a candle for Claire?'

'Why? Can't she see? Is it dark where she is?' Charlotte looked apprehensively back the way they had come. Night was falling. The street was filling up with soft gloom.

'For the repose of her soul.' Sylvia led the way. They started down the aisle. Charlotte's Protestant eyes saw another Christ looming up on His Cross, haunting the church with His suffering. She stopped.

Black-clad women passed them on silent feet, slipping into the pews to pray. Sylvia took her hand and drew her forwards. She allowed herself to go, keeping her eyes averted. Sylvia made the Sign of the Cross. Charlotte moved a hand uncertainly across her chest. Sylvia put some coins in a box, picked up two candles and lit them. She handed one to Charlotte. 'Place it there,' she said, pointing. 'Do you know what repose means, dear?'

46

'Yes, but –' Charlotte's voice rose, shrill and impassioned. 'She won't be reposed. Not without me.'

'Hush, dear.'

In the pews faces lifted, frowning. An old man clutching his black cap to his chest spoke severely to Sylvia, blaming her. Charlotte snatched Sylvia's candle and blew them both out.

Murmurs of shock and disapproval. An old woman addressed Sylvia with a flood of low-voiced invective.

'Quickly, dear. Quickly.' Charlotte was hustled back up the aisle.

Outside on the steps she feverishly explained, 'Her soul can't repose without – I mean, it's my soul, too, and I'm here.'

'Darling, what on earth gave you that idea? You and Claire each have a soul of your own, like everyone else,' Sylvia said, emotional and distressed.

'We're not like everyone else!' Charlotte cried. 'We're twins. Twins aren't like ones. And children don't repose. Only at night, in bed. Claire's not in bed. Claire's an angel. You said so. She's flying.'

'Charlotte, dear. Hush!' Some more of those black-clad women were climbing the steps, looking at them askance. Sylvia hastily propelled her down. 'Walk carefully. Watch how you go.' Her voice momentarily wobbled off-key. 'There's a little path along here that will take us to the terrace of the Torre del Conde where—'

'You said –' Charlotte's voice was still demonstrably out of control.

'Hush, dear, we'll talk later.'

They went in silence up a narrow path cut in the rock wall of the mountain, guided by little golden lights set at intervals on the path. A fresh night breeze off the sea drifted among the bougainvillaea blossoms, purple and pink and gold.

'This is a fifteenth-century tower. The fort was used in repelling assaults by the British and the Dutch. There's a bit of history for you.' Sylvia presented it like a gift, wrapped with loving care.

But Charlotte was not listening. She was gazing with peculiar concentration over the tops of the palm trees to where the little yachts and bigger fishing boats rocked gently on the moonlit water. Lamps burning on prows moved up and down in the swell. The air was full of sea smells: flotsam, fish and salt. She spoke.

47

'What did you say, dear?'

'I'm sorry about the screaming.'

'It was my fault,' Sylvia told her kindly, laying a hand over hers on rock that in the darkness still held the warmth of the sun. 'I should have explained before we went inside.'

'At the funeral,' Charlotte said with soft impatience, 'I saw her in the window.'

'You didn't tell me, dear.'

'That's why I screamed. She went away when we came to the door. She didn't want to go out into the churchyard to get buried. She wanted to go up to the sky. She's there now. I think she's a star. That big one, perhaps. Sylvia,' Charlotte whispered, absorbed, 'it's coming towards us.'

'Hang on to your dreams.' Sylvia observed the enchantment in her eyes. 'There's precious little else.'

'Will she come to Valle San Angelo?'

'Who knows? Juan who keeps the grocery says the *pueblo*'s full of the souls of those that have gone on ahead.'

'Do you see them?' Charlotte breathed. 'Is Carlos there?'

Sylvia's smile went into the darkness. 'I sense them,' she said. 'It is enough.'

At Folly Hill they searched for Sasha. O'Brien had not seen her, nor had Mrs Fuller. On a macabre hunch Vivien went to the twins' room. Lifting the cover of Claire's bed, she looked underneath. The dog was there, chin on paws, cast down in despair. When Vivien reached for her collar, Sasha growled dangerously.

Downstairs, Robert was moving about. She heard his slow footsteps in the conservatory, and the sound of a door opening. She looked out of the landing window that had a view of the side garden. He was standing by the pond now. He took a packet of cigarettes out of his pocket, and lit one. That's the third, she thought. He should not be smoking so much. The doctor had told him after last winter's attack of bronchitis that he should give up.

He wandered to the elm tree and back to the pond, pausing by the water lilies to look down into the water. A light breeze had dishevelled his brown hair. He appeared wounded, as indeed he was, for she had wounded him. She remembered that there had been a time when she would have called with confidence, 'Robert, I'd like a bit of help. Could you come up?'

48

She shivered and turned away.

Kenneth came in later, a newly leggy Kenneth, his jeans hanging loose at the waist. He couldn't have lost that much weight! He didn't say, 'Hi, Mum,' with his usual smile, merely walked past her towards the stairs. The gossamer thread with which she had effectively drawn her children to her was deficient now, depleted by wanton overspending and lack of responsibility.

'Sasha's under Claire's bed,' she said, addressing his back, 'and won't come out.'

'I'll get her.'

'Be careful. She growled at me.'

Moments later she heard a shriek. Kenneth came running, white-faced, right arm extended. Blood pouring.

'She bit me. She's gone mad!' His eyes were wide with shock. Vivien found a bandage. 'We'll have to put her down,' he said.

'We can't. She belongs to Charlotte, now.'

Vivien drove him to the surgery, where the doctor said the same. 'You can't keep a dangerous dog. This is bad. I'll have to stitch it.' He gave Kenneth an antitetanus injection.

When they returned to the house the dangerous dog was lying in her basket with tears rolling down her little foxy nose, and they knew there was another reason for putting her down. Her heart was broken.

Vivien tentatively extended a hand. Sasha licked her wrist. She ran her fingers down the long body. There was so little flesh now, covering the ribs. 'I can't,' she said to Kenneth, her voice breaking. It broke easily these days for it had drawn its strength from the love and admiration conferred upon her by Robert. 'She'll get over it. It may take time. Surely a dog wouldn't starve itself to death, would it?'

Kenneth flinched from the pain in his wrist. 'Who knows?'

Yolande came in. 'There you are. I wondered where – what on earth?' She noticed the bandage. Heard Kenneth's explanation in bleak silence. 'You can't put her down,' she said.

'She'll pick up when Charlotte comes home.' Robert had come in quietly, in time to hear.

Yolande knelt down and smoothed Sasha's head. 'You'd no right to let Sylvia take her away.'

'It was Charlotte's choice, dear.'

Yolande heard clearly the guilt in her mother's voice and felt

49

certain Vivien had wanted Charlotte to go, though without knowing why.

'Sylvia had no right to ask. Charlotte wasn't in her right mind. She shouldn't have had to decide. You should have said no. You,' she reiterated, damning them. 'It's your fault Sasha's . . . If she dies it'll be your . . .' She burst into tears, floundered clumsily to her feet and fled.

'Go after her,' said Robert curtly. He immediately regretted his tone, but all the same didn't want to apologise. He was thinking that he could have stopped Charlotte going, but the need to punish his wife had been greater than the sum of all the advantages of keeping her near them.

Vivien did not go after Yolande. If Robert would only put his arms round her and fill her up with comfort, she might have some to spare, to hand on to the children. But his footsteps were going in the opposite direction, towards the front door.

Chapter Seven

The bus was packed. Squat, black-clad women in headscarves clutched baskets bulging into mysterious shapes. Crusty brown faces cracked with smiles exposing stumps of teeth like little tombstones, with gaps between. And gold teeth, too. Charlotte thought they must be very rich, these poor-looking people in their shapeless black garments.

The bus sped through the flat streets of the town and began to climb the mountainside. Gears groaned down, the engine roared. Behind and below, if Charlotte dared to turn her head, lay the little white town of San Sebastian, miniaturised. 'Look!' she shouted. 'A toy town!'

Sylvia mouthed that she could not hear over the clamour of the engine.

Charlotte jumped excitedly around in her seat, eyes shining. She craned her neck over black-clad shoulders, holding her breath, watching great rocks coming dangerously nearer. The bus crawled round them, hovering over space. Where was the road? She went rigid, screwed up her eyes, waited in blank intensity for the bus to hurtle down the mountainside. Dared to peep. They faced the mountain. Faced the sea. In. Out. Zig. Zag. The terror became less spiky. After a while it planed down to a sense of awe.

And still they climbed.

An hour later (Sylvia had said it would take an hour) the bus dragged itself over the final rise and with a huff of triumph went racketing into a brown landscape strewn with boulders.

They could speak now. 'Is this where you live? In the desert?'

'Have you forgotten? My villa is near the sea. There's no sea

51

up here. Not that I've noticed,' Sylvia said, searching with her teasing eyes, making Charlotte laugh.

They leapt into clouds. So they had got to the sky! Charlotte was struck dumb. The clouds thinned. Glittering white villages crept out of the distance. They stopped. Passengers gathered their belongings and descended the steps to be kissed on both cheeks.

'Why do they kiss each other twice?' Charlotte asked, wide-eyed.

'Two of everything is better than one,' said Sylvia.

The driver fetched a bucket of water for the steaming engine. Empty seats filled up. Baskets came aboard stuffed with green produce and exotic-looking fruits. An old man in a dusty black suit came up the steps into the bus and looked round. Gravely he held out his hand to Sylvia.

'*Buenos días, señora.*'

'*Buenos días, Manuel.*'

'Manuel is my friend. He brings me fresh vegetables from his garden. Look,' Sylvia said, pointing. There, tucked between little white dwellings decorated with creeper and vine, was a tidy little vegetable patch. 'That's where he grows them.'

'Don't you have veggies?' Charlotte thought of the abundant gardens at Folly Hill.

'It's too dry and rocky where I live.'

'You live in rocks! In a cave in rocks!'

'You'll see.'

She squirmed with excitement and dread.

They ate fruit and chocolate, drank milk through a straw. The bus bounced and rattled across the roof of the island, swooping into forests and out on grassy tablelands. Chocolate melting over her fingers dripped down the front of Charlotte's T-shirt.

'Look at the mess! Oh dear, look!'

'Carmina will deal with that.' Sylvia glanced out over the driver's head. 'We're going down. Hang on to your hat.'

'It's in the bag. Do I have to get it out?'

'No, dear. I'm quoting one of Carlos's sayings. He drove fast cars, often with the roof down. Mostly I didn't have a hat, either, but there you are.' She was whimsical, remembering.

'I like hearing about Carlos.' What Charlotte liked was the silky tone that came into Sylvia's voice, and the way her face glowed when she spoke of him.

'This is where he is. In Valle San Angelo.'

'But dead?' Charlotte asked cautiously, thinking of Claire, who had been in the sky last night.

'No, dear. He's dead in Barcelona where his body was buried. Here, he lives.' A secret look came into Sylvia's eyes, as though she could see something not offered to other mortals. Charlotte felt a ripple of apprehension, then Sylvia smiled and the moment passed.

The bus ground down into low gear, headed for a dip in the road. A chasm opened below them, plunging for thousands of feet.

Charlotte shrieked, 'We're going over the edge!'

'If we go over today, it'll be the first time,' Sylvia observed.

'You're awfully brave,' Charlotte breathed.

'And so are you, you'll find. Don't crouch down there. Sit up and admire the view. Scares are good for you. They keep you on your toes.'

They entered a dark tunnel. A bright circle of light appeared ahead. They were going to fly across the ravine! She grasped the back of the seat and held on tight. They ground round a tight bend, hugging the cliff.

'I think I'll die of fright!' Charlotte spoke exultantly, embracing the panic now, loving Sylvia for providing it. Across the chasm, orange and brown ribbons of rock strata glittered metallically in the sun's rays. 'I never saw a striped cliff before.'

'Tuck it into your memory for rainy days.'

Charlotte tried to visualise herself on a rainy day at home but home had gone, driven out by the magnificence of foreign Spain.

They descended to the upper valley, passing through flower-decked villages and on to the foot of the ravine. The bus stopped. Ahead lay the silver sea. To their right, a blue-and-white striped awning shaded a bar from the sun. A young Spaniard came running, black eyes flashing, all smiles. He shook Sylvia's hand, then greeted Charlotte in Spanish, with a formal little bow.

Overwhelmed, she edged shyly behind Sylvia. 'Does he think I'm the Queen?'

'No. He'd expect you to be taller if you were the Queen. Jesús is my great friend.' Sylvia looked at him fondly.

'Doesn't he talk English?'

'Why should he? He's Spanish.'

Charlotte felt matters falling into place.

Jesús picked up their bags. A flight of white steps rose nearby; beyond, rough ground enclosed by a low wall.

'Are you the only one who speaks English here, then?'

'Oh, no. There's you.'

Charlotte looked at Sylvia from under her lashes. She skipped ahead to peep over the wall, and met the disconcerting gaze of two dusty goats.

'Why are they shut up in this tiny pen?' She was indignant.

'Because they're Spanish goats. Now this is where we start to climb.'

'Haven't you got a road?' Her eyes roved with awe up the steep mountainside. Villas clinging, tangerine roof tiles bright in the sun. Palm trees erect as sentinels. Great purple beards of bougainvillaea drooping over grey stone.

'Yes, but it's a long way round. Now you've learned three things about Spain. They speak Spanish, they shut goats in pens, and steps can be more convenient than roads. You've learned all that in three minutes!' Sylvia paused to gaze upon Charlotte, amazed.

'Oh, you!' She took the worn stone steps at a run, then called from the first landing, 'Hey, there's another flight going that way. It's a zigzag, like the road.'

'That's the way you get up mountains. In zigzags.'

Babble, babble, babble went Jesús' chatter. Charlotte leaned against the stone wall, hiding her pique at the way this great friend had taken Sylvia's attention.

'He's telling me what's happened while I've been away.' Sylvia reached the landing, puffing. 'It's important I should know.' She was smiling, including Charlotte in a secret joke. 'Señora Fernandez has hurt her ankle and her daughter has had to move in to cook for her. Luis Gómez and his friend Paquita, who were to be married, have had a tiff.'

'He talks so fast I'm surprised you can understand any of it,' said Charlotte, only partially mollified. She dashed up another flight of steps. Drawing in her stomach muscles, she fitted herself into the thin shadow of a palm. The sun was fire on her face.

A heavy wooden door opened, and a woman came out from behind the retaining wall. She looked at Charlotte in surprise, and greeted Sylvia warmly. '*Buenas días, señora.*'

54

'*Buenas días, señora,*' muttered Charlotte experimentally. 'Why do the people live in doorways?'

'Their villas are there, behind the wall.' Sylvia put a hand to her breast, breathing slowly. 'I shall have to go on a diet.'

'I like you fat.' Charlotte skipped on again. Behind her Sylvia translated and Jesús laughed.

Heads came out of windows high up in the wall. Hands waved greetings down to them. An old woman tramping by paused to pat Charlotte on the head. She touched her pink cheeks and marvelled at her hair.

'She says you're pretty, and she's very glad you've come. You could say thank you: *muchas gracias.*'

'*Muchas gracias,*' Charlotte managed self-consciously. Jesús suggested she would be chattering in Spanish before the week was out.

She danced ahead, going up, up and on to another flight of steps, in and out of the shadows thrown by buildings, the palms and the scented plants. Sylvia's rests came more frequently.

'How many steps to your villa?' Charlotte called down from her high stand. 'A million?'

That was something for her to do tomorrow. Count the steps.

A flat lane running between high white walls. Another blue-and-white striped awning. Boxes of bananas, oranges, papaya, gigantic cabbages, a green sea of spinach. A tall, thin man with a huge moustache emerged from the doorway.

'*Buenas días, señorita.*'

'*Buenas días,*' replied Charlotte boldly, and he hurried forward to shake her by the hand.

'Juan,' he said, and she remembered it was he who saw ghosts in the streets, all the time. Ahead, a wrought-iron gate in a tall white wall, green strands of creeper trailing. 'This,' said Sylvia, flinging wide her arms in a proud, encompassing gesture, 'is the Casa Alegre.'

They went up a narrow stone stairway and there was Carmina, brown-skinned, big-bosomed, wide-hipped and smiling, singing softly to herself as she swept the terrace with a big straw broom.

'I'll tell you what I think,' said Charlotte, stamping around on her enormous bed, taking in the ornately carved wooden furniture and the white walls, not seeing the peeling paint on the ceiling. 'I

55

think your villa's a palace. I never saw a bedroom so big. I never saw a bedroom that had a sofa and armchairs. Golly!' said Charlotte, overwhelmed. And then, 'There's a lizard climbing up the wall! And one on the ceiling, upside down. Wow! I've got lizards in my bedroom.'

'Geckos.'

'Geckos? I s'pose they're all right? I s'pose they won't come into my bed?' She paused, head on one side.

'They like walls and ceilings better than beds. I'm going to have a shower. I'll leave you to settle in.'

'Settle in to what? I know, I'll settle into this sofa.' She took a flying leap and sank into a nest of cushions and cool brown leather.

After Sylvia had left, Carmina came into the room, her plump face and warm brown eyes glowing with the pleasure of having a child in the villa. Sandalled feet planted wide apart, hands on hips, she addressed Charlotte in a stream of Spanish. Charlotte shook her head in bewilderment. After a while, good-naturedly shrugging, Carmina left. '*No comprendes*.'

Charlotte leaned her head against the sofa back, feet on an old Moroccan rug, absorbing the magic of the place, not dreaming, just being there, in the dream.

Footsteps in the passage and a fresh burst of Spanish. She jumped up. Carmina was standing by the bathroom door, holding cleaning materials. Sylvia emerged with a white towel wrapped round her head, smelling of warm body dampness and violets.

'You have to tell me what she says.' Charlotte was jealous of them in their secret world behind the language barrier.

'She says she'd like to bring her children to play with you.'

'How old are they?'

Sylvia undid the towel. Carmina put her bottles and cloths down on the tiles, took the towel and began to rub Sylvia's hair. Charlotte, awed, tried to imagine Mrs Fuller drying her mother's hair.

'All ages.'

'If there's a boy about twelve . . .' Charlotte was thinking of Max.

They agreed Fernando would come. 'You'll soon pick up the language, playing with him.'

She followed Sylvia into her bedroom. Bookcases, photographs and the ornaments other people keep in living rooms: big

56

pottery vases, an unlikely brass Buddha Carlos had brought back from a drive through India, a Kurdestan rug strung across a wall.

'You see,' said Sylvia, 'there are no public rooms in the villa.' There was a dining room that joined the kitchen, but it was never used. 'We have breakfast on the terrace before the sun comes round the mountain. Supper after it goes down into the sea.'

'Lunch?'

'In your bedsit.'

'Where do you have your drinks parties?'

'Oh, those,' said Sylvia, dismissing them.

When her hair was arranged, they went on a tour. A narrow flight of stone steps led from the kitchen to the upper garden where avocados and lemons grew. They crossed a rickety bridge to the flat roof where Carmina hung her washing, Sylvia said. A stylish and graceful papaya tree rose beside the building here, its clusters of golden fruit at head height. 'Its roots are in the garden below the terrace,' Sylvia said.

Charlotte looked across the canyon to the vast mountain opposite, then swung round. Behind her and above, white villas with their orange roofs rose out of sight. Breathlessly, she saw they were clinging, 'like flies', Sylvia agreed, to the mountainside. She was awe-struck. 'If I toppled . . .'

'You won't,' said Sylvia.

That evening they ate goat stew with red and green peppers, at a little round table made of stone.

'I never ate a goat before.'

'Poor you.' Sylvia was a past master at rendering the strangeness acceptable. As chatelaine of this magnificent residence, she was gracious and proud. The quiet and helpful guest of Folly Hill had gone. Like a queen, Charlotte thought she was, dressed in an exotic kaftan Carlos had brought from Zanzibar.

The sound of tinkling bells drifted across the ravine. The goatherd was bringing his flock in for the night. So they didn't all live in pens!

'There's not much food on the mountain,' Sylvia said. 'Those may not be the lucky ones.'

Across the ravine the last rays of the sun bathed the crest of the mountain in gold. Little sharp-winged birds dived and swooped, jet black against the eggshell sky.

'How still it is!' All evening Charlotte had been aware of the stillness.

'The wind can race down the valley like a tornado. Never leave swimsuits out at night. They could end up in Africa.'

'My swimsuit, in Africa!' It could happen, she was sure. Anything could happen, here.

Carmina brought fruit plates and knives with a dangerous-looking serrated edge. She walked with a shushing sound, big thighs swinging behind the red skirt, plaited leather sandals flapping on the tiles. She smiled indulgently at Charlotte and said to Sylvia, 'She is happy. Tonight I will give thanks to Our Lady, and light a candle for the other one.'

'What does she say?'

'She says she's pleased you seem to like it here.'

'Oh, yes!' Charlotte reached behind her and lifted a mango off its stem. 'I never got my pud out of a tree before.' She proceeded to peel it, looking with interest at the golden juice trickling down her arm.

'That's the marvellous thing about life. There's always another first time. You're allowed to lick your arm at the table, in Spain.' Sylvia rose and flicked a switch in the wall. Lights hidden among the dark mango leaves brought greenness and goldness to the tree.

'I'll have two friends,' said Charlotte happily. 'Fernando and Hay – what was the name of the man who carried our bags?'

'Jesús.' She pronounced it the Spanish way, 'Hey-soos,' then added, 'Jesus, in English.'

'Jesus is here!' Charlotte breathed. 'In Valle San Angelo?'

'Jesús.'

'You call him that in Spanish?'

'That's the way we say it, in Spain.'

No wonder Carlos came. Charlotte thought of Claire drifting among the stars the previous night. Of Juan from the grocery who saw ghosts in the *pueblo*. She supposed they were allowed to come to the valley because Jesus was here. Golly!

That night she drifted off to sleep listening to music from the *pueblo*. Rich, spicy aromas danced through her senses. Francisco's restaurant was hidden away at the end of a vine-covered path off the steps below. Everything opened off them. They were the spine of the village.

58

Claire came to her in the night, dancing to the music of a guitar. In Charlotte's dream they went hand in hand down to the bottom of the mountain with bougainvillaea blossoms drooping in their faces and trailing through their hair. Old women in black stood in doorways clapping to the music, smiling their gap-toothed smiles. A crowd of gypsies in red shirts and tight black trousers had gathered outside Pepe's bar. On their heads they wore absurdly high-crowned hats. Claire led her in among them and they danced to the gypsy band. Then a boy who looked familiar whirled Claire off through the crowd.

Charlotte screamed.

'She's not here,' the gypsies told her, shrugging and holding wide their arms in empty gestures, palms upturned. 'You won't find her now.'

She wakened with tears streaming down her face. Sylvia, dressed in a long, white cotton nightdress, was standing by her bed. 'What's the matter, darling? Did you have a bad dream?'

'I dreamed Claire went away,' she sobbed. 'Max took her.'

Sylvia held her comfortingly against her soft bosom, stroking her hair. 'She had to go, dear. Who is Max?'

'Our friend.' Charlotte blinked the tears away.

'Come into my bed.'

She gladly slid her feet to the cool marble tiles.

'Just this once,' said Sylvia, 'until you get used to things.'

Chapter Eight

The Bryant boys were sent by their parents to make contact with Yolande and Kenneth. They headed down Puddle Lane.

'What are we going to talk about?' one shouted to the other as they raced their bicycles, dangerously practising S-bends on blind corners.

'Anything but Claire, Mum said.'

They swerved in at the gateway to the Wheat Sheaf, wheels wobbling and crunching in loose gravel.

Yolande and Kenneth were already there, lounging against a slatted table in the beer garden.

'Hi.'

'Hi.'

They leaned their cycles among roses trailing over the boundary wall, verdant and sweet-smelling; they crossed the grass walking like cowboys in their leather boots and jeans.

'There's that creep William Card.' Yolande leaned forward, shaking her hair over her face, closely studying a knot in the table. 'Don't look up, anyone, or he'll come over.'

William hesitated at the door coming out of the saloon bar, then made up his mind. 'Hello there,' he said, standing tall and awkward, waiting for an invitation to join them.

'Hello,' they said, studiously avoiding eye contact.

'How's Charlotte making out?' That was for Yolande.

She tossed back her hair. 'Charlotte's gone away.'

'Away?' He looked astonished.

'To her godmother,' said Yolande, glancing down at her hands.

'Oh,' said William.

Yolande's boyfriend Oliver returned from the bar with a tray of cold bottles and glasses misting in the warm air. 'Hello, William,' he said politely. 'Want to join us?'

'Er . . .'

'Meeting someone, are you?' A Bryant smiled at him, encouragingly.

'Well . . .' A cloak of rejection had begun to drape itself over William's thin frame.

'Oh, right,' they chorused, waving him away. 'Don't let's keep you.'

He went, fingering his spectacles, looking depressed.

Kenneth said, 'Shame.'

They burst into loud, cruel laughter to cover their guilt.

'Yuk,' said Yolande, reaching across the table for her Coke. 'He gives me the creeps.'

'He's all right. Just boring,' Kenneth said.

'Anyway,' Yolande effectively closed the subject, 'he's twenty-two.'

That night she told her mother, 'William Card came up to us at the pub this afternoon and asked about Charlotte.'

Vivien looked concerned. 'You know I don't like you going to the pub, dear. I hope you're not drinking.'

'We were in the beer garden. And I only have Coke.'

'That's a good girl. Who did you say asked?'

'William Card. You know his parents.'

'Hermione and Jack. Yes, that's right. How kind! I don't remember the son.'

'He's that kind of chap,' said Yolande, wandering off. 'Just reporting. I don't s'pose Charlotte would remember him, either.'

Fernando came, a bumblebee of a boy in horizontal stripes and black cotton shorts. Charlotte looked at him first shyly, then critically, comparing him with Max. She found him wanting.

'Ask him if he can swim, Sylvia.'

'I know he does. He swims very well.'

'Can we go down to the beach then?'

He taught her to catch a breaker and swing up, up like a gull, then spin in on its crest to the sand. They played ball, ran races, splashed each other in the shallows, shrieking. His inadequacies faded.

He came sometimes when Sylvia was having her siesta.

'Sleeping!' Charlotte demonstrated, eyes closed, head dropping sideways, resting on her hands. 'In the afternoon!'

Fernando was not surprised. That was what people did in Spain. '*Aquí todos duermen por la tarde,*' he said. They wandered round the *pueblo*, cajoled Juan into giving them carrot and turnip tops for the goats, disturbing his vegetable display. '*Vete,*' he cried. 'Away with you!' Charlotte, growing more fluent every day in sign language, grinned at him.

Next day Fernando led her down the steps and along the vine-shrouded path to Francisco's restaurant. They sat in the shade of a big umbrella and Francisco brought them cartons of fruit juice with a straw. Next day he gave them a mango each, with a warning. Fernando translated his message, shrugging. Charlotte understood Francisco was not going to give them any more.

But it was not so. He tapped their noses, shook his head, tut-tutted to show how amazed he was at their cheek. They smiled at him.

'The Spanish love children,' Sylvia said.

Charlotte did not dream of Claire again but sometimes she would experience a sense of loss, like an echo in her mind. For a short time then she would be desolate until Sylvia said something funny, or Carmina came rushing, waving tea towels, shouting at the cats.

It was nearly ten o'clock in the morning before the sun, 'a slow riser', Sylvia said, surmounted the great peak opposite and sent its burning rays to their east-facing mountainside. Sylvia and Charlotte set out to climb.

Fernando could not come that day. He had to help in his father's transport business. Herman had a truck and trailer which, Carmina told Sylvia proudly, would be paid for in two years' time.

Behind the topmost dwelling in the *pueblo* a narrow track zigzagged upwards, in and out of the boulders.

'Mind the cactus. Watch those loose stones, you can skid on them. It's a long way down,' Sylvia said.

'Are we going to the top?'

'That would take half a day.' They were to follow a track that led to the top of the cliffs behind the Playa Torres. 'I think that's far enough for us,' said Sylvia.

Charlotte led the way. 'Zig, zag. Zig, zag. Hey! It's not so high. We're at the top already!' They came round a ridge. Above them brown and gold rock strata lifted to the sky.

'Caught!' said Sylvia, clapping her hands. 'These mountains are alive. Don't trust them for they play tricks. When we get to the next level you'll find another phantom summit behind it. Round that and there's another. Now I need a rest.' She settled down on a rock. 'We won't need to be too long, though.' A pink light had appeared behind the twin mountain opposite. The sun was coming.

'Phantoms are ghosts.' Charlotte looked sideways at her.

'That's right.'

'Is Carlos a ghost?'

Sylvia's face gentled. 'I like to think of him as a free spirit. We'd better get going,' she added, standing up, moving ahead. 'We're about level with the top of the cliffs now. Look over there and you'll see a track going off to the left. We'll take that.'

Two Germans in heavy boots, packs on their backs, went past them. '*Morgen,*' they said, and Charlotte retorted, bright-faced, '*Morgen.*' To Sylvia she said, 'I expect that's good morning, don't you think?'

'You're multilingual now.'

Sylvia's compliments flowed over her like a warm, bright cloak. She danced along the path. After a while it wound round the headland and there was the sea spread out before them, glittering.

Charlotte went to the cliff edge, timorous yet feeling compelled. She crept nearer and nearer. Hundreds of feet below lay the beach. She could hear the surf roaring, see its white foam flying. She gazed until it seemed she was part of it, rising, crashing, rolling. A fresh breeze fluttered by and she experienced a lifting. She felt as though she was going over the edge, and beyond. Behind her a disembodied voice, warning and anxious, grew fainter. Charlotte was red and gold with the sun. She was in the rock strata. She was blue in the limitless sky, taking off like a rocket now. She was aware of someone tugging, swinging her up and away.

'Claire!' she shrieked.

A hand grasped her arm and swung her violently round. She hurtled to the ground and lay there, blinking up into Sylvia's terrified eyes. 'What on earth?'

Sylvia jerked her to her feet and dragged her back, sobbing, along the path. Sylvia was sobbing, too. Their sobs came in great gusts. Charlotte stumbled and fell. Sylvia's arms came protectively round her and held her tight, grounding her among the dust and stones. Charlotte had a feeling of having been hauled back from a long, long way.

'Vertigo?' Sylvia said, her voice trembling.

'What's that?'

'It's what you have when you think you're falling off heights.'

'When a phantom pulls you?'

Sylvia's face went still. After a while she said, 'Shall we go back?' A frown had taken her over, locking itself in behind the tears and dust. She rested her hands on Charlotte's shoulders, then ran her palms down both arms as though checking that all of her was there, flesh and blood. 'Your poor knees,' she said, crying over them. 'They're bleeding. Oh, Charlotte, your poor knees!' She made much of the scratches, clinging to them as to something she understood.

'My hands, too.' Charlotte held them out, palms up. Sylvia had done that, throwing her down. Saving her from the vertigo, which was Claire.

They came carefully down the track. The sun, a circular ball, fiercely vermilion now, had lifted itself triumphantly above the mountain opposite. It scorched their faces and arms, heated the rocks around them, pitilessly drove them on their way. They did not speak again until they reached the steps that ran down through the *pueblo*.

'Ah! The joy of shade,' said Sylvia in her brightest voice, as though nothing at all had happened; laughing, she flapped a hand across her burning face; 'We left that a bit late, didn't we?'

Back at the villa, she tenderly bathed Charlotte's wounds. Carmina brought leaves from the aloe vera plant.

'They'll cure you in no time at all. You'll see,' Sylvia said. 'Everyone comes for my aloe vera.' She broke the thick leaves open to spread the sap over Charlotte's grazes and cuts. 'Cured!' she said.

Sasha disappeared. They called through the orchard and across the fields. Taking a friend with him, for comfort or safety, or both, Kenneth went to the Bubbly Hole.

It was nearly dark when a stranger came up the drive, cradling Sasha in his arms. At the sight of the family, a doggy foolishness came over her. She wriggled, yelped, broke the man's grip and dived between their legs.

'She was sitting in the wheel tracks,' the caller said. 'Luckily, I was going slowly.'

They stared at him in stunned silence. Sasha would never allow a stranger to pick her up!

He said, defensively, 'I assure you . . .'

Robert thanked him, offered him a drink. 'No? We're very grateful.'

They trooped into the kitchen. The corgi was curled up in her basket. She seemed to have recovered from the embarrassment of being caught behaving like an idiot.

'Weird,' said Yolande. She opened a tin of dog food. Sasha ate ravenously, then threw up.

'I ran into the Card boy down at the pub,' said Robert. 'What's's name? William. Odd fellow. He asked after Charlotte. I thought that was decent of him.'

'I expect he asked on behalf of his parents,' Vivien said. 'Hermione's a nice woman.'

Yolande overheard. 'He's a creep,' she said. 'Remember I told you he asked me about Charlotte, too. Weird.'

Next morning the dog basket was empty. Vivien went searching. Yolande's door was open, her body supine, the one blanket tumbled, indicating a restless night. Her mother bent down to look under the bed. Sweet wrappers, magazines, a great deal of dust. She thought she must speak to Mrs Fuller about the dust. The door to the twins' room was kept shut now. They were training themselves to call it the spare room. She looked under Kenneth's bed. A turmoil of socks, a spill from a haversack, pencils, trainers. She shook his shoulder.

He rolled over, rubbing his eyes.

'Did you see Sasha when you came in?'

He mumbled, still mostly asleep, 'I didn't go to the kitchen.'

She went back downstairs, thinking with dread that a dog wilfully determined to go could slip past a boy coming in. She opened the front door. O'Brien, walking awkwardly, carrying Sasha in his arms, was coming up the drive. He laid her down on the step. But for a small lump on the side of her head, she was unmarked. Her eyes were open, lifeless, opaque, but her features were serene.

Vivien put trembling hands to her face. The trembling went through her. 'We shouldn't have let Charlotte go,' she said.

'Wouldn't've made no difference,' the gardener said. 'She were Claire's dog, in a manner of speaking. Not that she didn't care for t'other one. But it were Claire she follered. When they walked, the dog was allus on Claire's side. I saw it 'appen. A car come fastish up the hill. She must've been waiting behind the gatepost. She shot out like greased lightning. The back wheel just touched her. The driver wouldn't've seen. 'E went 'appily on 'is way. 'Tweren't 'is fault. Dogs will do themselves in, you know. I've 'eard tell of it.'

A picture came into Vivien's mind of Charlotte running, happy to be home, calling, 'Sasha!' Falling silent again.

Vivien went automatically about the task of getting Robert's breakfast, worrying at the problem.

'I'm going to ring Sylvia,' she said to him when she had thought it through. She was anxious to protect what they had left.

Robert looked up, coffee cup halfway to his lips. He never discussed suggestions now. Damned them, more often than not.

'I'm sure it's best.' She pleaded with her anguished eyes.

'If you say so.' He rose and went out to the car leaving her with doubt, with inexplicable guilt, anyway in the wrong.

That evening Kenneth and Yolande, smoking at the bottom of the orchard, saw O'Brien come through the garden gate carrying a sack.

'He's going to bury Sash. Yuk! I can't bear it. I'm going in.' Yolande jumped up, carefully stubbing out the fag end of her cigarette with her sandal before she ran. On the edge of the vegetable garden she paused to pick a tomato and stuff it into her mouth. They believed it would take the scent of smoke from their breath. In the hall she met Vivien carrying a box.

'What's that?' she asked, coming forward curiously. She was newly sensitive to change.

'There's a man coming from the Salvation Army to pick up Claire's clothes.'

Yolande went past, shedding a skein of anger and disapproval. Her bedroom door slammed with a bang that echoed down into

66

the hall. It set Vivien quivering with uncertainty. Why couldn't they talk? Why was everyone flinging judgements on the air, then running away?

Robert came in from the back of the house. 'John Halloran's looking for a pony for young Shirley,' he said, not asking her opinion. Waiting. For what?

She thought he wanted her to share the responsibility. She grasped it with both hands, for it was a sharing, at last, of a kind. 'Yes, send him Posy. Let's get it over with before Charlotte comes back. Everything,' she said, 'everything,' – wanting to keep it all, the pony, the clothes, the twins' bedroom just as it was. But they must put Charlotte's interests first. Make a new start for her. They had decided it was right.

Robert picked up the phone.

Sylvia was embroidering a tablecloth. She made them for a tourist shop in Tenerife.

'It keeps the wolf from the door,' she said.

'Wolves!' Charlotte was dismissive, knowing there were no wolves in the *pueblo*, only cats. 'I hear footsteps.' She skipped across the marble tiles and peeped round the doorframe, looking across the study to the terrace. 'It's Fernando.'

Sylvia put her needlework down and called to him, *'Venga, chico.'*

He came in holding out his hand, offering on his palm a piece of rock crystal.

Charlotte took it and pressed its silky smoothness to her cheek, smelling in it the scents of the mountain. 'Thank you. *Gracias*, I mean.'

Sylvia heaved herself off the sofa. She shook back her heavy hair and straightened her kaftan, brown, orange and gold, the mountain colours that had come to be part of her, a flag of her strength. She looked down at the stone in Charlotte's hand. 'How kind! Do you know, dear, white crystals are considered to be sacred.' She spoke to Fernando in Spanish.

Charlotte listened hard. She was beginning to pick up the odd word.

'He found it on a mountain path,' Sylvia said. 'It has been his most precious possession. Look, dear, how he's polished it.' Taking the stone between finger and thumb, she went to the door

67

and held it out so that the bright sunlight came upon it, setting it glowing like a pale jewel. 'He's had it since he was four years old. He says it's magic. He says when he loses it, it finds its way back. *Es algo magico*.' She looked down at Charlotte, smiling.

'It's beautiful. *Muchas gracias*, Fernando. I shall *transportar* it everywhere with me,' Charlotte promised. 'For the rest of my life.' She polished the stone lovingly with her fingers. She felt it was magic, too.

Chapter Nine

They caught Charlotte as she fell forward, missing her plate of seafood by inches.

'She can sleep in her clothes.' That was Carmina whisking off the little sandals. '*Tanto de correr*.' So much running and swimming. Fernando *mio* was exhausted, too. They left her in her jeans and Mickey Mouse T-shirt, and covered her bare feet with the sheet.

Hours later, wakening, she slid a hand sleepily beneath her pillow, then sat up, anguished. Where was her crystal? Why was she dressed?

A ghostly whisper came through the silent night like a rustle of tissue or silk. 'Who's there?' She slipped her feet to the floor, into the shaft of moonlight that joined the bedroom to the terrace, terrace to mountain, mountain to sky.

Pinch yourself. Pinch. But I am awake! she said to herself. She stole on silent feet to the doorway. The mountain, shrouded in its own darkness, crept close. She could scarcely breathe for its nearness. 'Who's there?' She felt an insubstantial presence. It moved across the terrace, into Carmina's kitchen and beyond.

She followed, feeling impelled, as though in the silence someone was calling. She drifted up the steps past the smelly bins where the cats had been scavenging – greaseproof paper and fruit stones, mango skins, bones too big for a cat to take away. The lemon and avocado trees huddled together on their terrace holding the moonlight at bay. She crossed the rickety wooden bridge on to the villa's roof, and leaned on the parapet facing the mountain. Two skinny cats padded towards her, then paused, alert and suspicious. Slowly their backs arched, their fur bristled. A moment later they were racing away into the sheltering darkness of the lemon trees.

Starry-eyed, Charlotte waited. She knew now who had taken her crystal. 'Claire!' she whispered. 'Claire!'

A breeze came in, faint at first, caressing her face and lifting her hair. She was aware of Claire in the gentleness, Claire saying, 'I'm here with you.' Charlotte held out her arms. She became part of the breeze as it swept up, around and down. She felt whole, a twin in this strange landscape of love and belonging. 'Claire,' she whispered. 'Please stay.'

An eerie stillness lay over the *pueblo*. Something was creeping through the canyon, coming from the mountains. A sound, a rising purr that built up gradually until it became a roar. Leaves swept out of the secret darkness where the aloe vera grew, jerked high, leaped over the parapet. Flap, flap went Claire's jeans and T-shirt, which had been hanging still and lifeless on the clothesline. Now they were dragging at the pegs. Suddenly Charlotte was in a maelstrom, hair flying, propelled by the wind. She was going to be blown over the edge! This had to be the wind that Sylvia had said came suddenly and could take her swimsuit to Africa. Charlotte fought her way to a corner where, with the wall at her back, it could not get her.

The T-shirt jerked free of the line and swept by. Forgetting the danger, Charlotte leaped out of her shelter. Snatching, she missed it by a finger length. It rose high in the air. 'You can get it,' said a voice, gentle, beguiling. 'Reach up. Reach up!' She felt herself being lifted. It was the clifftop all over again. Vertigo, as Sylvia said. She backed once more into the corner, trembling, looking for safety. The jeans came in on a down draught, moved close, teasing. Again she snatched at them but they jerked away, danced out of reach on the wind. They gave themselves up to it, allowing it to toss them over the parapet.

Charlotte leaped out of her safe corner and took to her heels. Over the bridge, down the cluttered steps. She skidded on a mango skin and almost fell into the kitchen, but rebalanced, arms flailing, and sped out on to the terrace. There were Claire's clothes, come to rest by the mango tree.

She dashed forward. Like dancing moths they lifted, taunting her, and fluttered over the wall.

She raced down the outside staircase, striking in a frenzy at the bougainvillaea blossoms, and burst through the gate. There was the lane, and there was Claire, with her hair floating on the wind. She beckoned, calling softly, 'Come.'

The white steps curved away below her.

Sylvia jumped out of bed, hauled on a robe and stumbled, still more than half asleep, through the door. The terrace was empty, wild with a chaos of dead leaves. She looked in at Charlotte's room, and uttered a shout of alarm. 'Charlotte! Where are you?'

The girl was leaping down the white steps, swinging left, swinging right. She swerved to avoid a man coming up and in the moon's shadow lost her footing. A pair of strong arms caught her.

'Lemme go! Lemme go!' she shrieked. The arms turned her round and she saw by the light of the moon it was Juan from the grocery. 'Lemme go, Juan!'

'*Lo siento, señorita.*'

He was saying he was sorry but still he held on, hugging her like a mountain bear while she punched him fiercely with her fists. She heard Sylvia call, '*Gracias, Juan. Muchas gracias.*'

'Sylvia! Sylvia, make him let me go.' Charlotte collapsed inside Juan's restraining hug, sobbing. She heard a gabble of Spanish, and cries of alarm from Sylvia. Then Juan swung her round and they were going back, up the steps, across the lane. Juan manhandled her through the little wrought-iron gate and slammed it behind her. She sped indignantly up to the terrace.

'That'll teach me to put you to bed in your clothes,' Sylvia said wryly, collapsing into one of the white iron chairs, brushing her tangled hair away from her face, pulling at loose strands that had blown into her mouth. 'Oh, my dear child! What have you been up to?'

Charlotte wiped away the tears with the back of her hand.

'What on earth were you doing down at Pepe's bar?'

'I didn't go to Pepe's bar.'

'Juan says he saw you there.'

'Juan sees ghosts,' she said.

'You're not a ghost.' Sylvia's face was gentle with loving concern. 'Don't cry, dear. I'm sorry, I shouldn't have chastised you. But I was upset. You never know who could be down there in the middle of the night.'

Charlotte sniffled quietly and stared at her godmother. 'Juan saw someone else.'

'How many little English girls do you suppose are here in jeans and a Mickey Mouse T-shirt?' Sylvia spoke indulgently now. She tightened the silk cord of her scarlet robe and leaned forward, reaching for Charlotte's hand.

She was afraid to say it, but she said it all the same. 'He saw Claire. She came and took her jeans and T-shirt. She never did like me wearing her clothes. And –' Charlotte felt again in her pocket just to make sure, because Fernando had said sometimes her crystal might disappear, but it would come back – 'she took my crystal, too.'

A stunned silence.

'What can I say? I'm glad Carmina washed them for her.'

The wind had dropped. When did it drop? Moonlight spread gold over the tiles, showing up the debris that had been left. Charlotte went to Sylvia, into her arms. Sylvia held her, not speaking. The clock with the tiled face began softly to strike the hour. There was a rustling in the mango tree and one of the starving cats peered out at them.

Charlotte said, 'Ghosts come out at midnight.'

Sylvia's face went still, the way it had done on the mountain.

Next morning Charlotte wakened to the sound of swishing water. She kicked off her hot sheet and lay drawing the threads of the night back into her mind. The sun came in from the terrace through the wrought-iron shutters, forming patterns on her bare feet. She climbed out of bed and went to the door. Sylvia, dressed in jeans and a voluminous cotton shirt decorated with orange sunbursts, was clearing away with a hose the debris the night wind had brought.

Carmina emerged from the kitchen, smiling and chattering.

'What did she say?'

'That she can see you have had a good sleep.'

'What is she saying now?'

'She has brought you the biggest papaya in the world for your breakfast and she's sorry, but she forgot to bring in the washing last night and the gale took your jeans and T-shirt.' Sylvia was quizzical and smiling.

'I had the most amazing dream,' said Charlotte, gazing at the mountain.

A voice in her head said, 'It wasn't a dream.'

She swung round to Sylvia, meeting her mink-brown, watchful eyes. 'You know,' she said passionately. 'You know, Sylvia. Tell her.'

Carmina, hands on hips with a waiting smile, asked, '¿*Que es esto*?'

Charlotte knew, not from the words but from her tone, that she was asking what was going on. 'Tell her,' she said again. 'Tell her they were Claire's jeans. Tell her what happened.'

She watched Carmina's face as Sylvia talked to her, gesturing in the Spanish way.

Carmina listened gravely. '*Juan ve unos aparecidos.*'

'What does she say?'

'Only that Juan sees ghosts, as you said.'

Carmina wandered off. 'So! I will fetch the papaya.'

Thieving cats. Carmina had only to turn her head and they would appear from nowhere, snatch a bit of fish or chicken, and scatter. Where did they go? Charlotte went in their wake down the narrow, vine-hung steps that led off the terrace into the lower garden where the papaya and mango trees were rooted. They eyed her from a patch of dead leaves, spitting.

She understood that Spaniards did not feel as the English do about animals. If cats did not steal they would starve. She had tried to befriend stray dogs but, 'Don't touch them,' Sylvia said sharply. Rabies, fleas, dirt – there were plenty of reasons why. Charlotte thought they looked unloved, like the cats.

She was about to retrace her steps when all four of them rose from their crouched positions, backs arched, fur standing on end. She followed the direction of their eyes and there was an old stone fountain, grand and mysterious in the shadows. Beside it stood Claire, incandescent in a white robe with her long hair drifting. Mischievously, she touched the fountain and a spray of water flew high in the air and fell on the dark-green leaves, like pearls.

'The fountain's dry,' said Charlotte, horrified. She foresaw chaos. The T-shirt and jeans were Claire's anyway, but now she considered Sylvia's possessions – the villa rolling down the mountainside if Claire wished it. She said again, 'The fountain's dry,' but Claire had gone.

That afternoon Carmina's husband Herman, with his clothes hanging all ways, black beret askew, hurried to the villa carrying a bag of tools. A little later he emerged from the lower garden saying there was no leak. *'La señora debe que imaginarlo.'* He grumbled that in the heat of the day he might have been left to enjoy his siesta in peace.

'I saw it,' said Sylvia, looking upset. 'How can you say I imagined it? There was water all over the place.'

Carmina came from the kitchen, adding her shrill concord.

Herman shook his head, stabbing at his forehead with a forefinger. *'Loca,'* he muttered as he hurried away.

A moment later his head reappeared, heavy brows beetling down over dark eyes. He spoke angrily to Carmina, gesturing. Carmina shouted back. Sylvia joined in. A Spanish row erupted, of the kind they heard frequently coming from the *pueblo.* 'It is nothing,' Sylvia would say, smiling. 'The Spanish don't believe in bottling things up. In a moment it will be forgotten.'

'What's the matter?' Charlotte asked as Herman stormed off.

'He said he heard one of us laughing, dear. As if we would!'

Charlotte took her secrets down the steps and peered round the shadowed garden, but Claire was not there. She turned to see Sylvia looking down across the riot of vine, watching her with sombre eyes.

Sylvia lay awake at night worrying about the ability of a child to unloose forces that might not be contained. She knew the villa was haunted these last few days, that Claire, who had come with the wind down the valley, had not gone away. She sensed her mischievous presence, and glimpsed her in the dreaming night.

'Leave us alone,' she whispered into the stillness, afraid, as she was not afraid of Carlos, who came with love, and acceptance for the lot that had been dealt him. But then, he had had such a slice of life; Claire, scarcely a taste.

The holiday took on a different dimension. When the children ran down to the beach now, Claire ran with them, bobbing along at Charlotte's side.

'You laugh? Reason? Is that right? Reason?' Fernando had decided he wanted to learn English.

Charlotte and Claire jumped, once forwards, twice back. 'Because I'm happy.'

The twins dashed down the pathway that divided the banana

plantation, hair flying, dry palm leaves crackling beneath their sandals. Water from the wells that irrigated the land gushed noisily along its open channels. Fernando, who was not so fleet of foot, pounded after them. Picking up Charlotte's hat, Sylvia dusted it down, sighed, and hurried to catch up.

Pink and breathless, they crossed the breakwater, slipping and sliding on pebbles and stones that were already hot from the sun, shedding their outer garments as they went.

'Spanish girl,' said Fernando, pointing a finger at Charlotte's collarbone. 'Brown skin. Hair ...' He screwed up his eyes. 'What?'

'Blonde,' said Charlotte helpfully. She rather liked the change the sun had wrought, liked being blonde. 'Come on, Fernando.' She dashed for the water with Claire at her side. Claire's hair had also lost its apricot colour, and she was equally tanned.

They swam out beyond the turbulence to where the sea rocked gently. For a while they lay cradled in its arms. 'Don't go any further,' Sylvia shouted, hands cupped at her mouth.

'Come,' said Claire. She was skimming through the water, heading away from the shore. Now she was fearless in her swimming. 'Follow me.' Her voice sang over the murmur of the sea.

Charlotte rolled on to her front and started to swim.

'Come back,' Sylvia shouted from the edge of the foam. 'Charlotte! You mustn't go out so far.'

'Back,' repeated Fernando, thinking Charlotte had not heard, though she had.

She paused, treading water with her back to the shore. She felt unbearably restless. Claire, the free spirit, had reached the far horizon. Now she was out of the water, suspended between sea and sky. 'Follow me,' she sang. 'Follow me.'

Sylvia again funnelled her shout with her hands. 'Come in!'

Fernando, who had caught up with Charlotte, pleaded, 'She say in. Please, in.'

Charlotte flung herself forwards, away from him and away from the shore. She swam fast, faster than she had ever swum, racing for the horizon. Fernando raced after her, caught her and pushed her under. She surfaced coughing, salt water hurting her nose. Her limbs were heavy now, too earthbound to float or fly. Slowly, she followed him to shore.

Sylvia, holding her skirts above her knees, waded in to meet

75

them. She took Charlotte's dripping hand in hers and led her hastily up to where the hot stones of the breakwater met the dry sand.

Charlotte, wanting to comfort her, tried to say, 'I couldn't get drowned,' but the words stayed in her throat. Something was tugging at her mind.

Something that said she could.

The children were out playing when the call came from Folly Hill.

'I hate to do this to you,' Vivien said, 'but we don't think it's a good idea for her to come back expecting to see Sasha, and be told . . . I mean, we want her to get off to a fresh start. Do you understand? If she could come to terms with Sasha's death while she's away . . . Are you there, Sylvia?'

'Yes.'

'Do you know what I mean?'

'Yes. Yes, I do.' Sylvia could see it would be better for Vivien and Robert that way.

She paced through the study, out to the terrace, where the sun had set up a furnace, then swiftly back into her big, cool bedsitting room. In front of the portrait of Carlos, she implored, 'Help me,' knowing he would not. Carlos the racing driver had helped her with decisions. Carlos the disembodied spirit comforted her when the decisions she now had to make alone, proved wrong.

When the children came galloping noisily up the steps and she saw their radiant faces, she knew what she would do. We will not take in Sasha's death, she decided. That is for Folly Hill. Nikki the shaman, who called on occasion when the child was in bed, had informed her that Charlotte was going to have to bear a great deal; Claire's going was only the beginning. Sylvia thought she detected a hint of steel in Charlotte. Not tempered steel that would see her through, but steel that stands unrelenting when the soft breezes turn to gales.

She reiterated her vow. Valle San Angelo will be her refuge.

On the last day of the holiday there were reports on the radio of storms at sea. 'The water will be rough and full of sand on the main beach. Unpleasant for swimming,' Sylvia said. 'Let's walk round to the Playa Torres. It's quite a sight after a storm.'

The bay was in uproar. Beyond the headland aquamarine water

rose higher and higher. A vortex of foam, brown with the sand it had displaced, smashed up against the rocks, raging.

Charlotte climbed on to a boulder.

'Careful!' Sylvia cried over the sound of the sea.

Careful? Her feet took her leaping on to the rock in front, and the one in front of that, scrambling, jumping, faster and faster. She knew the danger and was exalted by it. She was part of the drenching white water that threshed below her, part of the foam and the salt spray above. She was weightless, ecstatic, one of the blessed. The white turmoil hit the rock on which she stood with a deafening crash and leaped in the air. It cascaded over her sandals, engulfed her ankles, reached to her thighs. It was everywhere now, rolling, diving, pounding. She had a feeling of having left all she knew behind. That she was starting out on something joyous, uplifting, grand.

Sylvia shrieked, 'Charlotte, come back! Come back!'

'Come to us,' called Claire, rising like a siren in the sea. 'Come to us!' Charlotte saw that Sasha was there too, ears pricked, all set for a run.

The water rose, crawled back, gathered strength, lifted as high as her head – even higher. It was surrounding her, capturing her, taking her in. 'I'm coming,' she cried and the waves roared back, 'Now! Now!'

But the wave that was to sweep her up hesitated, and was sucked by the sea into a hollow. The hollow grew deeper and deeper, then, while it held its breath, she felt an arm encircling her waist, a hard, encompassing, earthbound arm, and she was swung off her feet. There was no water below now, only rocks. She was being carried across them, bumping, swinging, hurting.

'*Idiota!*'

Now Sylvia's arms were round her, Sylvia's warm tears were on her cold face. 'Darling! What possessed you?'

A man, dark-skinned and stalwart, gripped Sylvia's shoulder. He flooded Charlotte in a spate of abuse, shaking his fist in her face.

'Quickly,' Sylvia cried, running, dragging Charlotte with her as though the sea would come after them and snatch her away. Where the sand gave way to a rough track she leaned against the standing rock, still clinging to Charlotte, holding her against her heart, cherishing her, crying.

77

'I'm sorry,' Charlotte said, meaning she was sorry Sylvia was upset and out of breath, only that.

Neither spoke for the length of time it took for them to come to terms with what had happened. In their different ways.

Then Charlotte cried piteously, 'She's taken my crystal, and now she's got Sasha, too. They were there, in the sea.' She was so lonely, she might have been the only person left on earth.

There was a sound like a sigh, as though all the breath was draining out of Sylvia's lungs.

In a little while they began the walk back. Another track led to the village. They followed it and there ahead lay the little white *pueblo* clinging to its mountainside, orange roofs burning in the sun. Above, the two guardian mountains reared majestically on either side of the canyon. 'Keep her safe,' Sylvia said, speaking within her heart, not only to Carlos but to all the good spirits that dwelt in Valle San Angelo.

That night, when Charlotte had been safely tucked up in bed – safely? – Sylvia returned to the terrace. The mountain seemed especially alive tonight, as though blood ran through its veins. She wished she had someone to talk to, someone from the real world. She had never thought of the canyon as that. Carmina, on her way home, came from the kitchen carrying her rolled-up apron under one arm.

'*Está bien, señora*?' Are you all right?

Sylvia raised her eyes. 'Have you any experience of twins, Carmina?'

'Oh, yes,' Carmina replied, 'but it is a sad story.'

'Perhaps you had better tell me.'

Carmina reached into the dark leaves of the mango tree and thoughtfully fingered a golden fruit. 'This is ripe.' She broke the stem and placed the mango on the table.

'Come, Carmina,' Sylvia said, compelling her. 'Tell me the sad story of the twins.'

'You're worried about the little one, of course. But what's to be will be. She is young. These boys were older. It was different,' Carmina said, dismissing the question. 'Besides, they were identical.'

'Charlotte and Claire were identical, except for a dimple in Claire's chin.'

78

'I must go home and get my man his supper.' Carmina moved towards the steps.

'Stay!'

She sighed, turning back. 'Yes, señora, I will tell you, if you must know. But it is a sad story and I would prefer not.'

'Tell me.'

'The wife of Jaime Martínez, who lives next door to José, had twins. It was a long time ago. Fine boys they were. When they grew up, Federico went to South America. He was killed there in a car crash. On the same day –' Carmina hesitated, then continued, 'his twin, Antonio, here in Valle San Angelo, died of a fever. And they hadn't seen each other for ten years! So! You made me tell you. It would have been better not.'

Sylvia shivered.

'The little Charlotte has survived. What are you worrying about?'

'About whether twins have a life of their own, or one between the two of them.'

It was not something Carmina could answer. 'Twins!' she said, casting her glance towards the mountain as though the solution lay there, as indeed she believed it did. '*Adios, señora.*' She heaved a great sigh, encompassing and underlining the mystery of the universe. 'Try to sleep and not to worry.'

'*Adios.*'

Sylvia lay back in her chair. The mountain crept close until it was scarcely a hair's breadth away. She saw in her mind's eye Carlos coming down, looking across the ravine, waiting, as he always did, for an invitation. 'Come in,' her heart said, and then his shadowy presence was there, hovering by her chair, spreading serenity round her like a cloak of silk. She drifted in memory.

From the steps below came one, two, three notes as Juan tuned the strings of his guitar.

Charlotte wakened early on the morning of her departure, with desolation in her heart. She lay a moment gazing at the awkward black outlines of friendly geckos on the ceiling. Then the dream came back.

She had been standing on the villa roof, imprisoned there. A man, dark-haired, taller than a Spaniard, with a paler skin, stood on a terrace above and behind, looking down. He made no move but she knew he represented danger. That destruction in some as yet unformed way would come from him.

'Help,' she shouted. The shout stayed in her throat. The man did not move. A half-experienced recognition came, then faded. In her dream she crossed the roof and looked down into the *pueblo*, seeking aid. People came and went, busy about their affairs.

'We can't help you,' they said. 'We've things to do, and anyway . . .' They disappeared one by one without finishing their sentences. She knew what they were saying: This is your problem.

She tried to shake the dream away, but the essence of it lingered, filling the room with the dark portent of matters beyond her control. She clambered out of bed. The mountain was a black outline against the primrose morning sky. She waited until she had absorbed its calm, then went down the stairway into the lower garden. She said goodbye to the little white statue on the sleeping fountain. One of the prowling cats looked up at her with slitted, hungry eyes and bared its teeth.

She came back to the terrace and said goodbye to the mango tree, caressing its thick, dark leaves with her fingers. Raising her eyes to rooftop level, she said goodbye to the elegant papaya. A small breeze came through the valley, lifting its long leaves in a gesture of farewell.

'Come back,' said the scarlet geraniums in their tubs. 'Come back when you need us.'

She went through Carmina's kitchen and climbed the steep steps to the terrace where the oranges, lemons and avocados grew. The silence here was dark and heavy, the bushes drawn together, guarding their secrets. She crossed the rickety bridge to the rooftop and, turning, saw above her, with a sense of shock, the terrace on which the man in her dream had stood.

She ran back across the bridge and down the steps, taking her spirit warning with her. In the silent kitchen a cockroach stood motionless, black against the white tiles, then scuttled into a cranny between the cupboards. Out on the terrace she leaned against the stone parapet, gazing at the mountain.

'I'm going home,' she said into the silence, though the mountain knew that, as it knew everything.

'You are alone now,' it said. 'Alone.'

80

At breakfast she looked up into Sylvia's eyes with a kind of desperation. 'Claire could come home with me, if she wanted to.' Before Sylvia could reply, Charlotte added, 'She was there. You know, I saw her in the stained-glass window, watching her funeral. She has been in the village.'

Sylvia pressed down within her the seed of dread Carmina had planted the night before. 'She was already there, then. Perhaps you hadn't let her go.'

'She will come, I'm sure.' Charlotte spoke feverishly. 'I'm sure she will. She'll want Posy, her pony, and the rest of her clothes.'

They went back over the mountains, stayed a night in San Sebastian and caught the early ferry. Charlotte was subdued now, and pale beneath her new tan. Sylvia was already regretting giving in to Vivien, who had thought it unnecessary for her to escort the child all the way.

'It's kind of you to offer, but there's no point. You put her on the plane, we take her off. It can't go wrong.'

Sylvia edged towards the check-in counter. Charlotte was glancing round, surprised by the chatter of English voices, the pale hues of English clothes. She had a feeling of change, of disorientation. She felt the island was releasing her before she was ready.

As they approached the counter, a woman in a navy and white uniform took their passports. 'You're Charlotte,' she said. She was slim, neat and very English. She had long legs, a pink and white complexion, fair hair.

Charlotte stared at this alien being, knowing she would have seemed normal once. She waited for something in her mind to readjust.

'I'm in charge of you,' the woman said, then briskly to Sylvia, 'Would you like to give me her papers? You'd better say goodbye. We're boarding.'

'Goodbye, darling.' Blinded by tears, Sylvia bent down and hugged her, so hard she took Charlotte's breath away. Then she was gone, lost in the crowd.

Charlotte panicked. 'Sylvia!' she shrieked, darting forwards, back, sideways among the tall figures.

'It's all right, little one.' The stewardess came swiftly after her and grasped her hand. 'Sometimes it's better to say goodbye in a hurry.'

Eyes brimming, Charlotte thrust a hand into her pocket for a tissue. Her fingers closed round something cool, hard and smooth. She pulled it out, stared at it, blinked and stared again.

'What's that? A stone you found? Everyone brings a stone home from the mountains,' said the stewardess, deftly slicing away the magic. 'It's a nice one.'

Charlotte held it in her palm, caressing it with her fingers, feeling its hardness and smoothness. She remembered what Fernando had said, that sometimes it went away, but it always came back again.

She moved towards passport control feeling comforted.

Chapter Ten

England. How strange it was! Charlotte sat in the back of the Rover
clutching her crystal with Yolande and Kenneth on either side.
Great oaks in flat green fields. Chestnuts big as houses. Bigger than.
Smug fat cats sunning themselves in windows. Sleek, well-fed dogs.

No one had hugged her at the airport. Another matter she had
forgotten was that they weren't a hugging family. Her mother
kissed her on the cheek, straightened and stepped aside. Her
father kissed her also, patted her cheek, handed her to Yolande,
then Kenneth. A parcel, passed along a line. Stamped: one, two,
three, four. How tall they were, and how thin! Had they been as
thin as that, and as tall, when she went away?

'What happened to your hair?' they asked.

Yolande lifted an end of her own hair and squinted at it, comparing it with Charlotte's. Yolande hated her hair.

Charlotte felt wretched. 'Don't you like me now?' she asked,
hunch-shouldered and timid.

'Silly!' They laughed.

'What are you staring at?' asked Kenneth.

'I forgot what you look like.'

They hooted. 'In two weeks! What a memory!'

She shrank down between them. 'I wish Claire was here,' she
said. A tear she had not known was coming slid off the end of her
nose. The car went silent.

Charlotte wiped the tear away. 'I saw her at the villa.'

Nobody spoke.

'You don't believe me, do you?'

'Oh, yes. Sure,' said Kenneth kindly. 'I believe you.' She
could see he didn't.

'Claire was there,' Charlotte said defiantly. 'Swimming. She can swim now.'

Robert took his eyes off the road to glance at Vivien. To apportion blame. Sylvia was her friend.

Charlotte produced the crystal. 'Claire took this.'

Vivien turned round from the front seat to look. 'You seem to have got it back,' she said indulgently.

She told them it had suddenly manifested itself at Tenerife Airport.

'I expect it was in your pocket all the time.'

Their hammers of common sense beat her into a hollow curve. She waited for understanding to round her out.

'Sylvia told me you made a friend. Fernando, is that right?' Her mother smiled brightly between the headrests.

'Yes. And I met Jesus. He hasn't got a beard now.'

Robert made an explosive sound through his teeth.

Puddle Lane. The Bubbly Hole on their right. The car filled with noisy, fast chatter. They turned into Folly Hill. The chatter faded.

'So here we are,' said Robert heartily, swinging the car round the zinnia bed.

Charlotte looked out and up at the casement windows, the red hanging tiles. The house looked empty and cold. She descended with reluctance.

Mrs Fuller was standing in the doorway, wearing her crossover apron with the pink flowers. 'Hello, love,' she said. 'We've missed you.'

'Here's her bag.' Robert dumped it by the door. 'I'll put the car away.'

Charlotte went into the hall. She dashed upstairs, bearing a desperate hope. 'She has gone,' the house whispered from the depths of its cold shell. 'She is not here.'

'Charlotte!' Yolande yelled, slipping past Mrs Fuller, taking the stairs two at a time.

Charlotte opened the door to the bedroom she and Claire had shared. A strange double bed! Yellow curtains! A dressing table with triple mirrors! She sensed she was turning to stone.

Behind her, Yolande said breathlessly, 'You're sleeping in the little room next to me, Char. We've moved your things.'

Charlotte was staring at a framed photograph of Claire, laughing. Standing alone. She snatched the photo up and swung round. 'You cut her out! We were all in that picture! Yolande and Kenneth and Daddy and you and me! Why did you cut her out?'

'We wanted a photo of her by herself,' said Vivien, coming up behind Yolande, looking distressed.

'Why? Why does she have to be by herself? She doesn't want to be by herself,' shouted Charlotte. 'Where's our beds and dressing table? And where's Dobbin?'

'We put him in the attic. There isn't room for him in your new room. And this is a spare room, now.' Vivien came forward, arms uncertainly reaching. Charlotte looked at the hands on the ends of the thin arms that came from a thin body and thought with unbearable pain of Sylvia's warm bosom, her enveloping softness. She pushed the hands roughly away.

Yolande said, 'Your bed and things are still here. In the little room next to me, like I said. We thought you'd be better there . . . now.'

Now Claire is dead. Now Claire is dead. The words chanted their way through Charlotte's brain.

'There was a photo of us on the piano,' Charlotte cried, irrational in her grief. 'I s'pose you've taken her out of that.' She could not bear this separation. She was raw with it.

'No, of course we haven't,' Yolande snapped, unnerved. 'Come and see your new room. You'll like it, I promise.'

'Claire will never come back now,' Charlotte cried in despair. 'Never! Not now you've taken her bed.'

'Darling.' Vivien reached out again.

Charlotte backed into a corner, crouching like an animal avoiding a lash.

'Claire can't come back, darling. You know that.'

'She can!' Charlotte mewed out of her twisted, suffering mouth. 'I told you she did. She was at the villa, and in the sea.'

Robert appeared behind the others in the doorway, looking stern.

'She came and got her clothes. Her jeans and T-shirt. And my crystal.'

'Come now, my dear,' said Robert. 'Don't be silly.'

His down-to-earthness broke the dream, and Charlotte crumpled. Yolande moved forward to take Charlotte's limp hand in hers. 'Come and see what we've done for your room.' She led Charlotte across the landing.

Robert said in his hearty man's voice, 'Here's your bag,' and dumped it inside the door.

'Mummy's going to have them cut down,' Yolande said, indicating bunched curtains overwhelming the small window. 'It's nice, don't you think? Nice carpet. Mum and I chose it at Waites.'

A lump rose in Charlotte's throat. A wail came up from her heart, found its way over the lump and escaped into the room. Yolande turned and swiftly shut the door.

'Stop it, Char. Stop it!'

She could not. She was out of control with grief and loss, with rootlessness and despair. She stood stiff as a stick at the end of the bed, howling like a dog.

Yolande shook her by the shoulders. 'Stop! Stop!'

The door opened. Vivien rushed in. 'Darling, stop. Please stop. I can't bear it.' She drew Charlotte down beside her on the bed.

Kenneth came through from the back of the house, saw Robert standing in the hall, frowning up at the galleried landing. 'What's going on?'

Robert put a hand to his forehead, shook his head, turned and disappeared into his study. Kenneth crept away through the door leading to the kitchen.

Mrs Fuller was hanging up her apron. She said, 'Tell your mother I've gone home, Kenny. I can't stand it. Tell 'er I'm sorry—' She broke off and wiped her eyes.

Kenneth remembered what his mother had said, that everyone was running away. He wished he could run away while they sorted Charlotte out. He stood hunch-shouldered at the kitchen door, fingering a spot on his chin. Then he went off to the orchard for a smoke.

They calmed her down. Vivien washed her face and brought her downstairs. 'Would you like to help me get the tea, darling?'

'In a minute.' Charlotte went down the passage to the big cupboard. Looking in, she saw Kenneth's cricket bat, her father's golf clubs, garden hats and her own tennis racquet.

Claire's racquet had gone.

She fled out of the back door and down the brick path to the shed. She flung the door open. Her bike was leaning against the wall, and someone had polished it.

Claire's had gone.

Robert was standing before the drinks cupboard in the study, looking moodily in. He turned as Vivien appeared.

'Where's Charlotte? I thought she must be with you.'

'No.'

Vivien's hand went to her mouth. 'Oh, Robert! The stables! We haven't told her about Posy! It's all gone wrong,' she cried distractedly. 'You shouldn't have sent Posy away.'

'This is a fine time to start recriminations!' He gave her a bleak look as he strode out of the room.

Charlotte was running across the yard.

O'Brien, tidying tack, heard the light footsteps. He looked up. 'My! You got a suntan,' he said.

Charlotte looked in Posy's stall. She swung round, eyes enormous.

'Here's your father.' O'Brien grasped the handles of his wheelbarrow and rattled it noisily off across the cobblestones. It wasn't his job to break the news. Nobody had asked his opinion. If they had, he'd have said no. He knew something about children, having five of his own.

Charlotte waited, quivering, for Robert to cross the yard.

'I've sent Posy to the Hallorans,' he said before she could speak. 'Their little girl needs—'

There was a sensation of having slipped erroneously into another world. Of looking back across a vacuum, too spent to readjust. Then clarity came. 'Why does she suddenly need Posy? She didn't need her when Claire was here.'

'Now, now. Be reasonable, darling. You can't ride two ponies.' Robert stopped himself saying, 'She's only on trial.' They had decided to make a clean sweep. They couldn't go back now. Could they?

Bonnie poked her nose over her stall, whinnied a greeting. Charlotte slipped the bolt and went inside to bury her head in the chestnut mane.

Robert said ineptly, 'We could get a donkey, I suppose, to keep her company.' He put a hand on Charlotte's shoulder.

She shook herself free, turning on him. 'What did you do with her bike, then? And her tennis racquet? And her – her—' She tried to say 'hat' and couldn't. Her throat wouldn't work any more.

Robert said beseechingly, 'Charlotte! Charlotte!'

87

She turned her back on him and went dejectedly towards the house. By the back door she changed her mind and took the path that led to the orchard.

Robert thought, Hell's teeth! Not the orchard and the silences. Not again! Then he remembered Sasha's grave.

Kenneth, sitting beside the old plum tree smoking his cigarette, watched Charlotte come. She walked within a dozen feet of him without seeing him, heading for the corner where the pet cemetery lay. Eight crosses stood in the long grass, white sentinels among the brown seed stalks; one for each of the pets who had lived their lives out at Folly Hill.

She stood looking down at the patch of newly turned soil and the cross, two rough pieces of wood joined with a nail. Someone had written with a black crayon, 'SASHA 28.8.75', across the horizontal bar.

Kenneth rubbed his cigarette into the ground and went to stand beside her. 'Dad's having a proper one made,' he said.

Charlotte shrugged and turned away. 'She was Claire's dog.'

Yolande, sent posthaste by her father, hurried across the grass. 'It wasn't our fault,' she said defensively. 'We looked after her. It was nobody's fault. Mr O'Brien says dogs do that. Commit suicide.'

'It was Claire,' said Charlotte with terrible resignation. 'Claire wanted her. She would've called her. That's what she does. Calls.'

'You've got to stop talking like that, Char.' Yolande sounded unnerved.

'I saw them together in the waves. I did! I did!' Charlotte cried recklessly.

'You can't say things like that.'

'It's true! It's true!' She stamped her foot.

'OK. But shut up in front of the parents, will you? They're worried enough about you, without thinking you've gone off your trolley.'

'What's that?'

'Oh, you know. Like Sylvia. I mean, let's face it, she's stark ravers where Carlos is concerned. You don't want to put her in their bad books, do you? Dad already thinks she's a bad influence. And I'd chuck that stone away if I were you. It's a bit voodoo.' Her shiver was ostentatious, meant to convey their disquiet about everything that had happened today.

'What's voodoo?' Charlotte's fingers tightened round the crystal in her pocket.

'Witches go in for voodoo.' Yolande took a deep breath, then said heartily, 'So, how did you enjoy your hol? You didn't say if it was fun.'

'Yes, it was fun.' Charlotte turned towards the house.

'What did you do?'

'Nothing.'

'Oh, well . . .' Yolande shrugged. 'Mrs Fuller's gone home. We'd better go and help Mum with the tea.'

They went in through the conservatory. Kenneth lagged behind. Yolande swiped viciously at a trailing vine that had drifted away from its anchoring hooks on the house wall. Charlotte looked critically at the black grapes neatly suspended among their green leaves. Her eyes roved to the miniature cactus plants in tiny trays. She was seeing in her mind's eye the wide sweep of Sylvia's terrace in a blaze of sunlight. Geraniums rioting over their great stone troughs; the generous mango tree. And the friendly mountain. The loneliness was dark and dreadful, stretching ahead.

She went into the hall. Halfway upstairs she remembered with anguish the dismantling of her room and turned back, dispossessed. The door of the coat cupboard stood ajar. She dived in, pulling it close, and collapsed in a refuge of darkness on a row of shoes.

Her father's voice butted through the crack, cold and hard as stone: '. . . decision. Now it's over to you to choose the right school. Get in touch with those people – what's their name? There's an organisation that provides a list of boarding schools. A smallish one, I thought. One that's hot on music. Singing.'

They were sending her away!

'We didn't want a single girl,' her mother had always said. 'We chose you and Claire because you were twins.'

Now that she was no longer a twin, they were going to get rid of her. Then they would get rid of Bonnie, her tennis racquet, her toys. They would cut her out of family photos.

Charlotte rocked dementedly backwards and forwards on the shoes, forehead against her knees, ears muffled by the hanging coats.

Vivien's cry of protest went unheard.

Charlotte wakened to a troubled dawn. Outside her window in the big elm tree some unfamiliar bird was screeching, 'Awk, awk.' It sounded like a warning. She slipped out of bed, crossed to the door and stood listening, then tiptoed to the top of the stairs. From her parents' room came the long, slow, rasping sound of Robert's snores. She went quietly down.

The drawing-room door was ajar, the room itself in darkness. She felt her way along the wall to the window and drew the heavy curtains, letting the pale morning in. Lifting the photograph albums from their shelf to the floor, she went through them, page by page, searching out the snapshots in which Claire featured. Charlotte extracted every one of them before returning the albums to their shelf.

Back in her new bedroom, she removed some of the books from the bottom shelf of the bookcase, slid the bundle in against the wall, returned the books to their places and went back to bed.

Now Claire, at least, was safe.

Chapter Eleven

He went down to the Bubbly Hole, not knowing why. Something to do with Vivien's accusing eyes and guilt for what he had put her through that day? Loneliness, too, perhaps. He ached with the need to be himself again.

He came through the gap in the thorn bushes and saw a woman in a yellow summer dress, kneeling by the water. She raised her arm and tossed a rose. It fell among bubbles where they fanned out below the waterfall, then sailed in with the current towards the bank, lifted on its rosy edge, turned face downwards and lay still, exactly where he had found Claire, trapped by the reeds.

His held breath exploded.

She turned her head. 'Hello,' she said. 'Hello, Robert.'

An echo drifted across his mind. He strode forwards and stood looking down at her, frowning. 'You're . . .' He was staring at the dark hair.

'Alison,' she said. Her face took on a pinched look. 'Had you really forgotten my name?'

He closed his eyes, opened them again. She was still there. He knelt beside her and touched her wrist – flesh and blood. 'How did you know?' he asked, then remembered the notice he had put in the *Telegraph*: 'Claire, dearly beloved twin daughter . . . aged ten.' His eyes returned, puzzled, to her hair.

'Dyed,' she said.

'Why?' She had such lovely hair, the soft apricot shade that the twins had inherited.

Her mouth turned down wryly at the corners. 'Have you heard them mention their history teacher?'

'Miss Hurst? That's you?' His voice rose an octave with the shock.

'Yes.' Soft-edged triumph lit her eyes. 'I've been at Hillcrest School for four years.'

'What's this Hurst?' he asked roughly. 'Hurst! You followed them! Under an assumed name!'

'It's my name,' she replied. 'I married a man called Leo Hurst.' Her voice trembled. 'I was so lonely. You must know.'

He hadn't known. He had lifted that bit of his past out of his life, concealed it deep and, in the concealing, lost all memory of her.

'Why did you send Charlotte away to school? I heard she went today.'

He stared bleakly at the red splotch among the reeds that was the rose, waterlogged now. 'She needed a new start,' he muttered.

'Was it your wife's wish? No, it wasn't. It couldn't have been. No mother, losing one child, would send the other away. I nearly went to see her about it.'

'You nearly went to see *my wife*! Why, in God's name?'

'I thought it must be her decision. Only because I couldn't believe you would do it.' Her eyes softened and a sweetness came into her face. A remembering. 'But of course I don't know you. Haven't seen you for ten years. Maybe you've changed.' She waited for him to deny it. 'Anyway, it was a mad idea. She would have looked hard at me, and guessed. See!' Alison brushed the dark hair back with her pale hands.

The resemblance to the twins was stunning. Claire's dimple. The same eyes, mysteriously, for they were not the same colour. The sea green of the twins' eyes came from his grandmother. Adopted children grow to be like their adoptive families. How thin that story was, how open to challenge!

She let the dark hair fall. 'Well?' She spoke sardonically. 'It's a good disguise, isn't it?'

He was nervously unsure.

'So long as I'm careful to keep it close round my face,' she said. 'The wife of one of your partners recognised me at the funeral, or thought she did. Celia Devine? Do I remember correctly?'

He thought she was taunting him. His fear hardened.

'They haven't mentioned it?'

'No.'

She picked up a twig that lay in the grass. 'I remember your words that last night when we made the decision – you made the decision – that we wouldn't meet again. "I love my wife," you said. Do you still love her?'

He looked across the water at the drowning rose, then looked quickly away. 'What happened to the man Hurst?'

'The man Hurst?' she repeated, faint mockery in the tilt of her head, the glint of those bluish hazel eyes. 'You dodged my question but I'll answer yours. I went into marriage looking for a cure. Leo soon found out he couldn't atone for my blunders, nor cure my loneliness. He left.' She tried to push the twig into the hard ground. Failing, she dropped it in the grass.

'I'm sorry.' And so he was. Happily married, she wouldn't be here, rocking the boat.

'So I trained as a teacher.' She looked up into his frown.

'We'd better talk,' he said abruptly. The implications of her appearance at this moment were stunning, never mind that she had been around for years. He had to know what she was up to. Charlotte was vulnerable, unpredictable. He imagined Alison stepping in; 'I am your real mother . . .' He looked at her as though she was a bomb about to explode.

She said, and he could see from the wry twist to her mouth that she knew what he was thinking, 'You don't have to worry.' She picked up the twig again, held it between finger and thumb, stared at it. 'I promised. You'll remember that. I promised.'

Ignoring his proffered hand, she leaped lightly to her feet.

He glanced anxiously across the meadow in the direction of Puddle Lane. There was no one in sight.

'I shan't go back that way,' she said. 'I came up the towpath and through the fence. My car's in the lay-by on the other side of the wood.'

He looked relieved. 'Where do you live?'

'You don't have to worry,' she said again.

'We've got to talk, Alison. And we can't talk here.'

She gave him her address, with reluctance. 'You'll see my car outside. A red Mini.' She swung the strap of her bag over her shoulder, then walked away through the silver birches and the dusk.

He climbed the long hill where Claire had searched for four-leaf clovers that might have brought her luck. As he let himself in through the white gate and crossed the lawn, the cat leaped out of the shadows to accompany him. He passed by the front of the house, his footsteps crunching in the gravel. He ought to tell Vivien he was going out; it was late, nearly nine. Twilight. If he had been able to face her ... But Vivien did not belong in the world that had erupted round him. He went to the garage, settled behind the wheel of the Rover and drove away. At the bottom of Folly Hill he turned right, heading along Puddle Lane in the direction of Wylie-under-Lyne.

Remembering.

Covent Garden, Fonteyn and Nureyev in *Romeo and Juliet.* Five of them; his two partners with their wives, and he unaccompanied. Vivien had forgotten and had made an alternative appointment. He remembered with shock that it had been for Stella Bloomingdale's fashion show. How bloody bizarre!

The B-road to Wylie. Switch on the headlights. They flooded a sign saying CAUTION! DEER. In rutting season the Dornford Manor fallow deer had been known to venture as far as the outskirts of Wylie.

He had taken Vivien's ticket with him to Covent Garden. Someone was bound to be there, hoping against hope for a last-minute return. *She* was. Young, anxious, eager, she scanned the faces of those coming in.

Such pretty hair, he had thought, smiling at her. He had never seen hair that colour before: apricots in cream. She darted up to him, face lifted, eyes shining. 'You've got a return! I can tell.'

He handed the ticket to her, still smiling. 'How can you tell?'

'You looked –' She glanced down, stepping back a pace, and her face clouded with disappointment. One hand extended to pass the ticket back. 'I can't afford – Not that seat.'

'My treat,' he said. 'Come on.' He took her arm. An innocent indulgence.

His companions chuckled. He was unfamiliar to them in this mood.

Afterwards, because they knew her now – she had been easy to get to know, moving from stranger to friend in a couple of hours – they took her with them to the restaurant where they had booked a table for six. They were enjoying her. Her age group lay in a period lost to them, between their children and themselves. They overcame her diffidence, convinced her of their total respectability. He winced, remembering that.

94

She had been up at Oxford reading English. Now she worked in a wine bar while looking for a job. In publishing, she thought. They could not help her there. Her parents lived in Devon. She had a brother and a sister.

He would not have driven her home, except that Richmond was not much out of his way. A friend had gone to Austria for two weeks and lent her his flat. Diffidently, she asked Robert in. He remembered the diffidence. She had been granted a favour by an older man and she offered a small one in return. Coffee.

And he had taken advantage.

'I mustn't come again,' he said after the third visit, or was it the fourth? He truly had not meant to return. It was folly. 'I love my wife. You're sweet and desirable. But you must find someone of your own age.'

He asked her not to get in touch. He extracted the promise lightly, playfully, but he did it all the same. Earlier, in the restaurant, he had talked carelessly of his home, Folly Hill, near Wylie-under-Lyne, so there was the danger she could contact him, if she'd a notion to. She also knew the name of their company, Godfrey, Burgess and Devine, as well as its location in Moorgate.

So, 'I love my wife,' he said, shutting her out, locking the door.

Now he knew why he had been so protective of the twins who had her lovely hair and winsome ways. He had to guard them from predators such as himself.

The May following, nine months later – no, ten – the call came to his office. He went to that awful room in Brixton. 'Twins,' she had said on the phone. 'I can't cope. I simply cannot cope. I need your help.'

He remembered going back down the dark stairs into the street, his mind agitatedly searching for answers. They came like a revelation as he drove back across Westminster Bridge. Vivien saying after Yolande's birth, six years earlier, 'I can't go through that again. Honestly, Robert, you've no idea how awful it was. They say if a wife had the first baby and the husband the second, there wouldn't be a third.'

Now fate had offered him the family of four that they had originally planned. He thought, If I could pull it off . . . If only they don't resemble me . . . Even now their little heads were crowned with a downy fluff of apricot gold. He had been born dark and remained so. It was then he remembered hearing that adopted children grew to look like their adoptive parents. He'd keep that up his sleeve in case, later, they came to resemble him.

The red Mini was parked outside a square Victorian house. He went along a path and climbed an outside iron staircase. She was standing in the doorway, waiting, and when their eyes met, she smiled. They could have jumped back eleven years, but for the dyed hair. The flat in Richmond had had an outside staircase too.

She led him down a short passage into a sitting room. Opposite was a narrow kitchen; ahead, an open door with the foot of a bed, brass-railed, in view.

'Sit down,' she said. 'I'll get some coffee.'

He shook his shoulders back, lifted his head, delved into his pockets and rattled some coins. Looking round the room, he noticed a piano. She had said she was musical – she sang, he remembered now. His gaze sought other clues to her life, but found none. A Victorian grate with Dutch tile surround, an old television set, a sofa with a high back and cover of faded chintz, a worn Turkey carpet on ugly floorboards. In a corner stood a beautiful little desk, Georgian, he thought. He transferred his weight from the left foot to the right. His fingers rattled the coins again. He drew in a slow breath and exhaled it through his teeth.

She came in, carrying the tray. 'It's lovely, isn't it?' she said, noting his eyes on the desk. 'I got it when my father died.'

His mind sharpened. Got? Inherited?

She put the tray down and handed him a mug. 'I've sugared it,' she said. 'I remember. You took one and a half.'

He looked up, so startled that he sloshed coffee on the table. He put the mug down and wiped the spill with his fingers before sitting down on the lumpy sofa. This is ridiculous, he said to himself brusquely. Get yourself in hand.

'It's all I had from him,' she said, speaking of the desk. 'And only because my mother gave it to me. Gave it up for me. My father died that year.'

'What year?'

'You know, when I cut myself off from the family and moved into – you remember that squalid room in Brixton? You came there.'

He edged forward on his seat, ready to say there was no point in dredging through the past. They must talk about the present.

96

She hadn't kept her promise, not the essence of it. She lifted a hand to stop him.

'I just want to say, Robert, since you insist on coming here to talk, as you said –' she rested her own mug on top of the television – 'you can. But let me say something, first.'

He nodded.

'My father knew he was dying. They tried to find me. The Salvation Army hand on messages but they won't disclose addresses. So he knew I'd received the message that he was dying. I couldn't go to him because I was eight months pregnant. I was always his favourite,' she said sadly. 'It's even more hurtful when it's the favourite who lets you down.'

He fiddled with his coffee mug, keeping his eyes cast down, waiting.

She continued, 'And so, at the eleventh hour, when I hadn't come, he changed his will. He left everything to my mother for her lifetime – which turned out to be only three more years – and tied it up to go to my sister and brother. They kept it. People do, you know,' she said.

When she paused, he looked up. There was no bitterness in her expression that he could see. Rather a calm, sad acceptance of the fallibility of the human race.

'I just wanted you to know,' she said, 'what you did to me. You isolated me. I think you've come here to ask why I trained as a teacher and got a job at the twins' school. Well, that's why.' Her voice trembled, then broke. 'Because I haven't got anyone of my own. Guilt keeps my brother and sister away. Don't blame me for following my babies. It's not only that you took a piece of my heart when you took them away. I've been so unbearably lonely. You know about loss now,' she said, in a harder voice.

He cleared his throat and shifted in his seat, frowning. 'My dear, there's one thing you've got to get straight. I didn't take them from you. You gave them to me because you wouldn't tell your parents and you couldn't cope alone.'

'Yes.' The shadows beneath her eyes darkened. 'I gave them to you. And if I hadn't,' she said with heart-rending despair, 'Claire would still be alive.'

Outside a child shouted in the street. There was the sound of a car horn in the distance. He began painfully, 'This isn't getting us

97

anywhere –' but stopped when he saw her face was wet with flowing tears.

She emitted a long-drawn-out cry of anguish. 'I've had no one to share the grief with, then or now. No one! Everyone knows you've lost a child, but I can't tell anyone I've lost my baby. And you've got your family, but there's no one to comfort me.'

'Alison!' He struggled to his feet, moved towards her.

She backed away from him. 'Charlotte could have gone on to Yolande's school. I would have gone there, too. I had it all planned. I'd seen the Head and told her I'd be interested if there was a vacancy in a couple of years' time.'

She was standing by the window, crushing her fingers together. He stood a yard away, wanting to come closer but not daring. 'You said Charlotte needed a new start. She didn't. She needed closeness. Family closeness, love and a very particular understanding. Twins . . .' she said. 'A twin, left alone, would be terribly vulnerable.' Outside it had begun to rain, a thin, insistent drizzle, full of sadness.

'We all make mistakes,' he said ineptly.

'Oh, yes. Don't we! I've bitterly regretted not going to my family when I was pregnant. How do I know the twins weren't sent as some sort of challenge for my parents? They were pretty short on compassion.' She sucked in her breath. 'If I hadn't been such a stupid coward, everything would have been different. If I'd had the guts to go home, I'd still have a brother and sister now, and what's more –' her voice cracked again – 'Claire would still be alive.'

'Alison, it does no good to blame me.' He found himself holding the burden of Vivien's guilt. 'You're tearing yourself to pieces.'

'You'd better go back to your wife,' she said. 'I can see you just thought of me as a bitch who got into whelp by chance and serve her right.' She dashed a hand across her eyes. 'It's said bitches have forgotten their pups within hours of their being taken away. I suppose you believe it was like that for me.' She swallowed. 'Every evening I used to look at the time . . .'

His eyes followed hers to the Victorian clock on the mantel.

'I would think – six. She's feeding them now, that wife of his. Seven. She's putting them to bed.' The skin was drawn tight over her cheekbones. 'I went through all this, thinking I'd done right by them.' Her voice rose. 'And you let her die.'

One of Sylvia's aphorisms came to him, and he offered it to her though he didn't believe it himself. 'Maybe it was meant to happen this way. Would it comfort you to think it had to happen?'

'No,' she said. 'We've got free will. I didn't have to get into bed with you. But I loved you. I've never loved anyone else.'

It was a moment of exquisite shock. He stepped tentatively towards her and this time she did not back away. He put two fingers beneath her chin, looked into her eyes. It was as though the years had fled away except that she was no longer a symbol of beautiful, virginal youth and he a randy businessman on a night out. She loved him still, he thought, and she was offering him the solace he so desperately needed, that he could not accept from his wife.

He felt there was a rightness about their mourning their child together. *Their* child, hers and his. Claire had never belonged to Vivien as she had to him.

Alison made a panicky little move. 'Robert! Oh, Robert!'

He reacted with soft violence. 'Don't talk. Don't say anything.' Tenderly, he picked her up in his arms, remembering how he had done exactly this, before.

Alison was leaning up on one elbow, gazing into his face. She gently stroked his cheek. 'You have to go,' she said softly. 'We fell asleep. It's nearly two o'clock.'

The room was filled with moonlight and sweetness and the softness of her flesh. He cupped one hand round her breast, trying to draw her to him with the other.

'No, Robert! You must go.'

She slipped out of bed to show that she meant it.

'Must I?' He began to ask, 'May I come again,' then stopped, knowing he would, and not wanting to put the onus on to her.

As he drove in off Folly Hill Lane Robert saw the light was on over the front door. Another light showed in his study window. Entering, he saw Yolande, wearing her dressing gown, crouched at the bottom of the staircase. At her feet lay a body partly covered with a rug. 'Where have you been?' she cried shrilly.

'What happened?' he asked simultaneously. For a moment, as he recognized his wife, he feared she was dead.

'She got drunk. I s'pose she couldn't climb the stairs.' Her anger dissolved in a rain of tears. 'Where have you been?'

'I'll carry her,' he said grimly, looking down at the unconscious figure of his wife.

'I've been so frightened. It's half past two!'

'Go to bed,' he said, brisk and curt. It was all he could think of to say in the appalling circumstances and the tone, which was not one he would have chosen, came with the words.

Chapter Twelve

'I expect you've got a father of a hangover,' said Robert. He crossed the room to place a cup of tea on the antique mahogany bedside table. 'The room stinks!' Ostentatiously he opened both windows, pushing them wide. 'I've done what I can with the carpet. You'll find the bedcover on the bathroom floor. You were sick on it,' he said, enunciating his words distinctly. 'I've told Mrs Fuller not to disturb you. Food poisoning, I said.'

Fresh, cool air drifted in. Vivien dragged it into her stale lungs and tried to form words. Her thoughts split into what she wanted to say and what she could say. What she wanted to say was, 'Where did you go last night after creeping across the gravel and sneaking away in the car?' What she could say was, 'Thank you for the tea', but his thoughtfulness was outweighed by his deceit. So she said nothing. At least while drunk she had not had to think.

'We'll talk tonight,' he said, and left the room, walking briskly.

She turned back the embroidered sheet and propped herself up on pillows fat with goose down. She reached for the tea cup. Two aspirins lay in the saucer. Two? Had she become the kind of woman who could not be trusted with a whole packet? She gulped them down with the tea, tentatively put one foot to the floor then followed with the other. She had to concentrate on holding her head still. Her skull was egg-shell thin this morning.

She crept into the bathroom, a pastel exotica, a shrine to beauty. Coloured tissues protruded from frilled boxes. Cosy, fluffy mats surrounding the handbasin, the bidet, the lavatory. She opened the door that led into the room opposite. Closed it quickly for she could see by the neatly made bed that Robert had not slept here.

She piled toothpaste on her brush, scrubbed her teeth, rinsed her mouth spreading the peppermint flavour into all the nooks and crannies, refreshing it.

She ran a deep bath, dribbled Gel Pur by Christian Dior into the water, stepped in and scrubbed arms, neck, back, getting the stink out of her skin. Stink, as Robert said. The word despoiled her, dragging her spirits lower, into shame. She lay in the bath for ages giving the perfume time to invade her pores.

She rubbed herself dry with a fluffy towel, smoothed Yves Saint Laurent body cream all over herself. The fresh scents brought a faint lifting of her spirits. She sprinkled dusting powder under her arms and between her toes, then straightened carefully, so as not to jar her head.

It's only a matter of time, she told herself, conscious of being brave. We'll get over this. She would 'pull herself together', as Robert had ordered her yesterday, the day he sent her child away.

Misery flooded back as the scene returned to her. They had said goodbye to Charlotte, who was being led off by a woman called Quant. Vivien got back into the car but still gazed after her, yearning for her, thinking how small she looked, how vulnerable with her hand in a stranger's hand. When Robert started the car, Charlotte turned and Vivien saw panic, not in her eyes, for there was too great a distance between them now, but in the backward jerk of her body. A trapped child, seeing her chance of escape receding with the car.

She grasped the doorhandle crying, 'Let me out, Robert! I can't leave her like this.'

That was when he said it. 'Pull yourself together.' It might have been that harsh mother of his speaking.

They drove home in silence. He put the car away, then disappeared. She thought he was taking his guilt to some safe haven where it would not be vulnerable to her suffering. She waited for his return. Things will improve, she told herself. He is at heart a sensible man. He must see we can't live at loggerheads.

And then, from his study window, she saw him striding purposefully past the house, eyes looking neither left nor right. She heard the car reversing out of the garage and saw it disappear down the drive. Something had happened. Was he going towards something, or was he in retreat?

Fear sent her to the drinks cabinet, to oblivion.

Now, avoiding Mrs Fuller, she crept down the back stairs with the bedcover held under one arm, carefully folded with the disgusting smell inside. She put it in the washing machine and crept silently back, clutching carpet shampoo.

Later she went on a search and found, with a sense of relief equal to her dismay, a rumpled bed in the bedroom situated furthest from hers. She straightened the covers and took the damp towel back where it belonged.

Charlotte's school lay on a small plateau. There were gardens divided by low box hedges. Well-tended lawns ran down an easy slope to grass tennis courts. Beyond lay a wood and beyond that, the sea.

Isabel Quant, tall, slender and just twenty-three, stood behind her desk, smiling at the new class. Her flaxen hair drifted as she looked this way and that, examining the new faces. The class smiled back.

'I want you to write an essay about your holidays,' she said as soon as her introductory talk was over. She glanced at the wall clock. 'You've got three-quarters of an hour.'

Eager fingers set pens to paper, disclosing secrets that would help her understand her pupils. Exposing the rich. The less rich. (You did not attend Mountfield Manor if your parents were poor.) There was much she needed to know about their backgrounds and their interests. And their problems. Isabel's inborn curiosity had made her wise for her age. People had always given her their stories because they trusted her.

One girl sat gazing forlornly into space. Isabel came down the aisle and stopped by her desk. 'You must have done something in the holidays,' she said.

'No,' said Charlotte.

'If you haven't been anywhere –' Isabel thought of the hurdle of rising school fees, though the Godfreys had looked prosperous to her – 'write about what you would have liked to do.'

Hesitantly, Charlotte picked up her pen.

'I would have liked to have a twin,' she wrote.

> I would not have spent my pocket money on sweets. We
> would have flown to Valle San Angelo together to visit our
> godmother and gone to the Church of the Ascension but not

103

lit a candle, except for Christopher Columbus for the repose of his soul because he was a Catholic and went there for Mass which is like Communion in 1492 before he sailed the ocean blue. He would have liked repose after all the discovering.

Then we would have climbed the rock mountains above the ravine and stood on the cliff and I wouldn't have been frightened because Claire would have been standing there with me. And we would have swum together in the sea. Claire would be a champion swimmer. She would swim right to the horizon where the sun went down. Then she would come back fast, not a bit tired. She wouldn't need any repose. We would have eaten mangoes because they grow on our godmother's tree.

Pages and pages later, after she had told of how they raced together up and down hundreds of steep, white washed steps and played with the thin kittens that proliferated in the *pueblo*, when Miss Quant said, 'All right, girls. Time's up,' she heaved an enormous sigh and finished, 'It would have been a wonderful, wonderful holiday.'

Handing back the work next day, Isabel paused by Charlotte's desk. 'You have a tiptop imagination,' she said. 'That was a splendid essay. I've given you nine out of ten.'

'Thank you, Miss Quant.'

'Are you an only child?'

'No, there's Yolande and Kenneth.'

'Really? Are they much younger than you?'

'My sister is sixteen and my brother's eighteen.'

Isabel recognised that six years' difference might be too many for a ten-year-old. 'I've made only one comment.'

Charlotte opened the exercise book. A thick pencil line had been drawn through the words 'I would not have spent my pocket money on sweets'. 'Irrelevant' was written in the margin.

'Do you know what "irrelevant" means?'

Charlotte burst into tears.

When break-time came, she ran off by herself across the lawn. Behind a low brick wall she found a pond half hidden by giant rhubarb. Hunch-shouldered and hurting, she sat down on a stone seat decorated with gargoyles. Grasses drooping over the edge of the pond sent black reflections across the water. Something drifted on the surface, like a shadow receding, and there was Claire by the bulrushes. In her hand was Charlotte's crystal, glowing in the sunlight.

'What are you doing with that? It's mine,' Charlotte said.

Claire turned it over in her hand. A beam of sunlight caught it, striking rays of green, blue and gold, like a rainbow. 'I was there on the island with you,' she said.

'I'm not allowed to talk about it,' Charlotte explained. 'That's why I had to write it like pretending. I'm not allowed to talk about you at all. You're not supposed to be here. They don't like it.'

'Pooh!' said Claire. 'I'll come if I want to. And the Mars Bar was not irrelevant, and nor were the comics – you forgot about the comics. If you hadn't read the comics—'

Charlotte could not bear to hear the rest. She shut the voice out.

A green frog climbed up on a water-lily leaf and looked at Charlotte. The lavender scent grew stronger until it caught at her throat. She wiped a tear away. When she looked again, Claire was fading.

'I'm sorry,' she whispered. 'I'm sorry about the Mars Bar and the comics. You can have my crystal if you want it.'

But Claire had gone, leaving her unforgiven.

A girl wearing a prefect's badge came searching. 'Charlotte! What on earth are you doing here?'

Charlotte looked hard at the frog. 'Nothing.'

'Do you like being by yourself?' the girl asked.

'Sometimes.' Charlotte spoke without taking her eyes off the frog.

'I wouldn't do it too often or people will think you're peculiar,' the prefect advised.

'Off my trolley?'

'I didn't say that.' The prefect was defensive. 'Don't put words into my mouth. I've been searching all over the place for you. You're to go to the music room for an audition at four o'clock.'

'What's an audition?' It sounded like a punishment. Her insides tightened with apprehension. Had her parents, abandoning her, left instructions that she should also be punished?

'What an ignoramus you are,' said the prefect. 'You're s'posed to be able to sing. Miss Leslie's sorting out the junior choir.'

'You can't sing without me.' Claire's voice erupted in her head.

'I can't sing by myself,' said Charlotte, panic-stricken.

The girl shrugged. 'That's what an audition is: singing by yourself. You'll have to.'

'You won't,' said the voice, fierce now. 'Not without me.'

'I won't,' said Charlotte.

'What a funny kid you are,' said the prefect. 'Anyway, I'm marking you down as having been told, so you'd better turn up.' She crossed Charlotte's name off the list and went on her way.

At four o'clock the group to be auditioned set off down the corridor heading for the music room. Charlotte positioned herself at the back so no one would see her slip away. A yew hedge bordered the drive, cutting off a vegetable patch that was out of bounds to the pupils. She had peeped behind the hedge and seen that a strip of grass ran its length to the front gate, where the woods began.

She dived out of the side door, slipped behind the hedge, sprinted across the grass between cabbages and yew, then crept through the gap between hedge and gate. From here she looked nervously back at the school building. Its windows gleamed sightlessly. She fled across the drive and dived into the woods.

Charlotte was at home among trees. She found a hollow trunk and crept into it. There was room here to sit down. This was where she would come, she decided, when the other girls went home for the holidays, for she couldn't stay in that great building all on her own. She would skip out of her tree trunk with the first light and wander all day, then return to the tree to sleep. Perhaps someone would find her and take her home to live with them. Someone who didn't mind a single girl.

A path led deeper into the woods, running downhill. She followed it, sniffing the musty woodland smells, looking round in the green gloom. A red squirrel with a high, fluffy tail came jumping. She stood still as a mouse so as not to frighten it. Birds rustled and twittered in the branches. The squirrel scrabbled with its sharp little claws in the leaf mould, surveying her with its beady black eyes, then scuttled up a tree.

Here, the track widened. She paused, looking round, wondering at the eerie silence that had settled on the woodland.

'Claire?' she said tentatively.

'I'm here with you,' said Claire in her head.

There she was, skipping away, laughing, racing down the

106

slope. Charlotte raced after her, slipping and skidding on the leaves. Claire disappeared behind a tree, darted out, dashed on. 'Follow me,' she called. 'Follow me!'

They raced through the woods, right down to the bottom of the slope. Here the trees were smaller, growing more sparsely. The track became dappled with sunlight, then the sun came right in and the woods were left behind them.

'Follow me,' cried Claire, sprinting up the grassy slope ahead. Charlotte pelted after her.

They stood on a clifftop looking out on a great emptiness of sea and sky. One lone fishing boat lay at anchor in a patch of cloud shadow. The cloud moved and the sun gleamed on its white hull. Seagulls rose on air currents, mewed and cried.

'Follow me,' called Claire again, scrambling down a steep path to the beach below. Charlotte hurriedly removed her socks and shoes before dashing after her, slipping and sliding, losing her balance and regaining it in a whirl of arms. The tide was curling in among the stones, reaching out with white fingers to the boulders, backing off to make another run. Claire had gone into the water. Charlotte joined her, kicking and splashing, holding her skirt high with both hands so it would not get wet.

'Now you can sing,' said Claire. 'Sing with me. I'll audition you.' She laughed merrily. ' "Jerusalem" is what you were to sing for that Miss Leslie. "Jerusalem"!'

> 'And did those feet in ancient time
>   Walk upon England's mountains green?
> And was the holy Lamb of God
>   On England's pleasant pastures seen?'

They sang at the tops of their voices so they could hear over the noise of the water. It was wonderful being with Claire again, singing with her, playing with her. They lifted their faces to the sun.

Suddenly a black-and-white collie-type dog leaped boisterously past, showering them with spray. Charlotte floundered inshore, shaking the splashes from her skirt. The dog, no longer playful, crouched a few yards away from her, emitting a low growl. Charlotte said gently, 'It's all right,' but the dog backed towards the cliff, hair bristling.

Where was Claire? Charlotte swung round, looking for her. Her twin had disappeared.

Moving slowly so that the dog would not think she was afraid, Charlotte turned to go back up the cliff path. A figure was walking along the sand towards her, and as he came closer she could make out a strong-looking man, unshaven, dressed in ragged clothes. Under his arm he carried a gun.

'Hello,' she said politely.

He came right up to her, then stopped, feet apart, staring. Seen close to, his face was like that of a woodland animal, sharp-featured, with boot-black eyes. And he smelled like an animal, too, musty, unwashed.

'I seen you in the woods,' he said. 'You from that school?' He jerked his head towards the cliffs.

She nodded.

'Pretty one, aren't you?' Fast as a rat, he reached out and grasped her wrist.

'Let me go,' she said, her voice high and frightened.

He pulled her up against him. 'Sure I'll let you go when I seen what you got under that skirt,' he said, leering. 'Lemme see, and I'll let you go.'

With her free hand Charlotte obediently flicked up her skirt. 'There's only my knickers,' she said scornfully. The gun, taking on a life of its own, swung round, pointing its barrel into her face, then swung away again. She screamed. The dog crept forward, crouching low. It jumped up and pawed at the gun so that the butt stabbed into her hip and the cold metal of the barrel struck the side of her face.

'Don't shoot me!' she shrieked.

'Get off, Joss,' the man ordered. The dog settled on its haunches, alert, ready to spring.

'I'm not gunner shoot yer,' the man said. 'Why would I want ter shoot yer? I only want to know what you got under them knickers. That's what I want ter know.'

'That's rude! Let me go! Let me go or I'll scream,' Charlotte cried.

The dog jumped. 'Get down, Joss,' he said roughly, then, turning back to Charlotte, 'You scream and I'll have them knickers off you in a trice.' He addressed the dog. 'What's the matter with you, Joss?'

108

'Let me go!' Charlotte shrieked.

The dog sprang at her. The man released his grip on her wrist to swing the butt of the gun round. 'Get off!' he shouted. 'Leave 'er alone!'

Charlotte took a flying leap backwards, or thought she did. She seemed to be suspended in mid-air, staring down the gun barrel. In the ring of light at the end stood Claire in her Mickey Mouse T-shirt and jeans, smiling sweetly, beckoning, holding the crystal in her hand.

'No!' Charlotte screamed. The noise began in her throat, travelled slowly through her mouth and dispersed. She was turning, tripping on a stone, losing her balance, flying through the air, arms flung wide. The man lunged after her, equally slowly, also tripping and falling. Everything was in slow motion.

As he hit the ground, a great sigh rose and seemed to fill the universe. Then the gun went off with a bang that set the gulls screaming.

Chapter Thirteen

Charlotte sped up the steps. Where had she left her shoes and socks? She looked round frantically and snatched them up before hurtling down the grassy slope. Diving into the woods, she felt a little safer, but where was the track? This way? That way? She searched, growing more anxious by the minute.

'Claire!' she screamed.

There was an angry crackling as though dry twigs were being snapped underfoot. Thumps and violent crashes.

'Claire! Help me! Help me!' she implored. 'Please!'

There was the track now, right in front of her, as though someone, relenting, had graciously unrolled it on the ground. She raced along it, uphill, stopping only at a fork. Which way? She chose at random, and sped on. A stitch developed in her side. She slapped a hand over the pain. She seemed to have been running for ever with the pain in her side when all at once there were beams of sunlight in front of her like splinters of glass on the dead leaves. A sward of green in an oasis of sunlight. Sobbing, she threw herself into it.

A dozen girls came flying down the slope, their light, high voices calling, 'Charlotte!' and 'Here she is!' and 'Don't you know the woods are out of bounds?' They clustered round her, flinging anxious questions, picking up her shoes and socks from the grass. 'Don't you know you could be expelled for going there?'

She fell in among the soft bodies with a scream in her throat, hiding in the safety of their arms.

They called Matron. She was put in the sick bay.

'Now, Charlotte.' Matron seated herself upright on a wooden

chair beside the bed, a sergeant major of a woman in a blue uniform with white collar and cuffs. 'You had better tell me what you've been up to,' she said.

Charlotte closed her lips tightly against the scream.

'Don't sulk. You girls may get away with sulking at home, but we don't allow it here.' She readjusted her hips. The small chair complained.

Charlotte opened her mouth, remembered how she had been slapped once before for screaming, and closed it again.

'Where did you go? You must understand that we're responsible for your safety,' Matron said severely.

She knew she couldn't tell the truth, that Claire had been with her. Matron would think she was off her trolley. Nor that a rude man had asked to see her bottom. What could she say? Her head spun with the need to produce some story that would satisfy this frightening person. She thought of the gun, but Claire was the gun and it would blow her head off if she mentioned it.

Hard little lines fanned out, like spider's legs, into Matron's upper lip. She rose from her chair, smoothed the uniform over her jutting bosom, and said in the manner of dealing out punishment, 'I will leave you to rest. Perhaps when you have been alone for a while, you will feel like talking.' Her eyes wandered round the walls, showing Charlotte how big the room was, how bare; how isolated she would be until she talked. Then she left, closing the door behind her quietly, as if no one must know she had a child in there. The five empty beds whispered to Charlotte that the girls who had slept in them were dead. They threatened her.

Fearful, she flung the bedclothes back and crossed the polished boards to look out. She saw the mullioned windows and decorative arches of the main school building, so she must be in a separate annexe behind it.

She looked round agitatedly for her clothes. There were no wardrobes, only little cupboards. She sped from one cupboard to another, frantically unlatching doors. She found her blue slippers, hastily put them on, and carefully opened the door. Peered out. The corridor stretched darkly into the distance, full of shadows and the sort of things that hid in shadows, waiting. Live things, dead things. Things with long creepy arms to grab her. She ran like a hare, right to the end: stairs. She hurtled down and out the door. Across the lawn. Into the main building. She heaved a sobbing sigh.

She heard footsteps and a buzz of voices. Warily, she crept along the wall until she came to an alcove lined with overcoats. Below the coats was a bench and shoe cupboards. Opposite, a classroom window opened on to the corridor. She could see girls standing at easels. A teacher was setting a bowl of flowers on a table. She absorbed their nearness with hungry relief. More footsteps, coming nearer. She curled up on the bench and carefully drew one of the hanging coats round her.

It was Isabel Quant who spotted the pair of legs in blue pyjamas sticking out from under a coat. Tentatively, she drew the coat aside and looked down into Charlotte's face, white as a snowdrop with huge green eyes.

'Well!' she said. 'Fancy finding Charlotte Godfrey under a coat!'

Uncertain how to reply though she could have, for the scream had gone away, Charlotte offered a tentative smile.

'Miss Leslie was looking for you,' Isabel said. 'Didn't you want to audition for her?'

Charlotte said, 'No.'

'Come and get dressed.' Isabel held out a hand. They went along the corridor, up the stairs, across the landing and into B dormitory, where Charlotte slept. 'Funny idea,' said Isabel, 'wearing pyjamas in the daytime.'

Charlotte's lips trembled. 'I was in the sick bay. I couldn't find my clothes.'

'Wasn't there anyone to ask?'

'No.'

'Nobody?' Isabel's voice went quiet.

'Matron was. But she went away. I couldn't stay there by myself,' said Charlotte. 'I couldn't, Miss Quant.'

'Of course you couldn't.' Miss Quant perfectly understood. 'Now, put on something else and come down. It's nearly supper time.'

Matron, supervising the preparation of a tray for Charlotte, looked up as Isabel Quant came through the swing door.

'Don't bother with that, Matron. Charlotte is having supper in the dining room,' she said.

112

Matron's round face turned puce. 'I beg your pardon, Miss Quant?'

The kitchen staff stopped work and covertly stared.

Isabel's eyes changed to a steelier blue. 'You cannot shut up a little girl in an empty wing, Matron. Especially when she's perfectly well.'

Matron was at a disadvantage, five foot two and square as a tank, looking up at slender five foot eight. 'How dare you interfere, Miss Quant!' she blustered. 'Charlotte was put there because she was hysterical.'

Isabel drew herself up. 'Did you find out why she was hysterical?'

'Kindly do not tell me how to do my job.'

'I have already done your job. I've moved her back to her dormitory.'

'Well! Of all the —! How dare you? I shall report you to the Head.'

Isabel turned and left, meaning to get there first.

'I am sorry you've discovered this,' said the Head.

'Guessed, rather than discovered, Miss Wedderburn. When I thought about the essay, it made sense.'

'It was her father's wish. He thought, and up to a point I agree with him, that it should be left to Charlotte to talk about her twin, should she wish to do so. But he feels she'll forget more quickly if no one mentions it.'

'Forget!' Isabel blinked.

'She could so easily, you understand, be made into a tragic figure.'

'She is a tragic figure!' Isabel kept the indignation at bay. 'Don't you think it would be better if the teachers knew, so that they could exercise compassion when matters arise that they may not understand? I think I know why she ran away.'

'Oh?'

'Miss Leslie wanted to audition her for the choir. I'd guess she's been in the habit of singing with her twin and there's a memory there that she can't surmount. Maybe she needs to talk.'

'I'm sure she has talked at length to her family,' Miss Wedderburn said in her cool voice. 'She is, after all, only ten. It's early days. I wouldn't worry, Miss Quant. She has been put down as a singer. Carry on as though nothing has happened.'

June Leslie, the music mistress, was sitting at her desk working out the music timetable. She looked up as Isabel opened the door.

'I came to tell you not to make Charlotte sing if she doesn't want to.'

'What's the matter? Can't she sing, after all?'

'Maybe that's it.'

June Leslie grimaced. 'Parents!' she said. 'Ah well, I'll find someone else.'

The grandfather clock in the corner of the Head's study sombrely struck eight. She switched on the radio to get the local weather report.

'. . . Fisherman's Point last night.'

Her secretary came in, lips parted, ready to speak.

Miss Wedderburn raised a hand. 'There's something about Fisherman's—' They both listened.

'A man, who has not been named, was found drowned on Fisherman's Beach this morning. Police fear his gun may have gone off accidentally, wounding him before the tide came in. His dog was found guarding the body.'

The Head switched the radio off.

'How very unpleasant. Have you opened the post yet, Miss Grant?'

The secretary nodded. 'I've got it here. There's a letter from a Miss Hurst who's looking for a position. She teaches music and history.'

'You'd better write and tell her we have no vacancies.'

'She assumes that would be so at the beginning of the school year. She asks if we would keep her in mind should a vacancy occur.'

The Head put on her spectacles, read the letter and handed it back. 'Keep her address, then. You never know.'

In the midnights of Vivien's bedroom – it was hers now that Robert had moved into the room next door, taking his clothes with their faint aroma of tobacco and man smells with him – she struggled with the emotions his departure had fostered. Telling Mrs Fuller that there was now another bedroom to tidy had been a cause of embarrassment.

'He isn't sleeping well. He disturbs me,' she said, for that was less humiliating than the truth. They still shared the bathroom.

She had stopped having her hair set. The glossy look that had remained constant all her married life gave way to a mild disarray. She bought new clothes, some plain blouses and skirts from Marks & Spencer, flat heeled, sensible shoes and a long beige cardigan. Mud coloured, she would have called it in happier days. She thought it might occur to Robert that after all she was not too different from his responsible mother, who had dressed like this. It came as a shock at first that nobody looked at her in the street, then gradually she accustomed herself to it, as one does to being too warm or too cool, when one has not the spirit to look for a solution.

Kenneth went off to university, but not before becoming aware that his father no longer returned from work at six thirty. He soon forgot. He was starting a new life.

When Yolande asked why Robert was so often late, Vivien explained that he was busy at the office. Yolande recognised it as a lie but, having no experience of parental troubles, did not know what was expected of her. She started to behave badly. Walked heavy-footed on the stairs. Discredited the cook. 'Boiled spuds again!' 'What *on earth* is this?' as she dug critically into some unfamiliar pudding, cooked with love.

Robert frequently returned very late, having eaten out, he said, so as not to bother her. Vivien was helpless as the butt of his sophisticated cruelty. She was not religious but she prayed, every night, that he would come back to her. In the early-morning hours when her exhausted mind emptied itself of the misery of the day, the coral dress, lying unsafely on the river bed, came to haunt her.

She went to the off-licence in the village and bought a bottle of whisky. She hid it, with a glass, under the bed. A few sips helped to lift the weight of the night.

'I never wanted to take another woman's husband,' Alison said. 'I love you, Robert, but I feel guilty when you come here. We must talk about it.'

In the beginning, she had felt no prick of conscience as she indulged her need to mourn her child in the father's arms. But by now there were two of her; the one who loved Robert and felt hopeful she could hold him as father of her twins, and the one who suspected his ill-treatment of his wife was a temporary, petty

115

retribution. That left her as the 'other woman', to be abandoned in due course all over again.

Robert rose and went to the drinks cupboard, which he felt free to rob, having filled it.

'Not for me.' Alison gestured at her coffee cup.

Putting his glass down on the mahogany table he had bought her – an antique that might have graced Folly Hill – he took her hands. 'Is this an ultimatum? Are you saying I should leave my wife?'

'Oh, no! Please, no,' she protested.

He resumed his seat. Sitting forward, swirling the whisky round the glass, he said, 'You asked me that day we met at the Bubbly Hole if I still loved my wife. I have the answer now. I don't love her,' he said.

She suspected he meant he did not love himself for what he had done to Vivien. 'Why did you send Charlotte away?' This was a question she had put to him many times, directly and indirectly, but she felt she had yet to get at the truth.

'I suppose . . .' He started again. 'How should I put it? A sort of palliative madness.'

She thought cynically that he had chosen big words to give weight to what was essentially petty and shameful. 'So you're going to bring her home?'

The answer was there for her to read in the silence, her senses being sharpened by loss. He sipped his whisky, looking down at the floor. She wondered whether he could not go back on his decision because of pride, or because his home, now peopled with warring adults, was no longer a place suitable for children. You war with those you love, hurting them for hurting you. Hating them for giving rise to your hate. Wanting them to exorcise it so that you can go back to loving again.

'We can't mess the poor child around like that,' he said, not knowing she had the real answer in her head.

I think I should go away and give you a chance to get your marriage sorted out.

He took her hands again. 'You gave us such happiness when you gave us the twins.'

She realised then she had not after all spoken, only looked into her heart. Yet she felt she had her answer now and with it, justification for applying for a job at Mountfield Manor School. Better to have some relationship with her daughter than feast on stolen

116

fruit until Robert decided Vivien had been punished enough. If she could get a position at Charlotte's school, losing that brief period with Robert before he went back to his wife was the price she would have to pay.

Chapter Fourteen

'I cannot imagine how you expect us to find a replacement at such short notice,' Miss Wedderburn complained when June Leslie broke the news that her fiancé, an engineer, had been offered a job in Peru and she wished to go with him. Her secretary reminded her of the woman called Hurst who had written last year asking to be considered should a vacancy arise.

Alison sang all the way down to Dorset. She rolled the windows down while waiting at traffic lights, letting her happiness flood over the car roofs and in the open windows. She laughed with the amused drivers. She was full of confidence and joy.

'It's a hap-hap-happy day. Tra-la. Tra-la-la.' She had a good voice, passed down to the twins along with the hair colour that she had relinquished for their sake. She turned off the main road, ran up a lane, went over a cattle grid and saw the school. She pulled up and paused, her chin resting on the steering wheel, eyes devouring the building where her child had been living now for more than a year.

The tawny ochre stone was mottled by lichen predators. Mullioned windows. Flemish type gables. A balustrade with obelisks at roof-level. Niches sheltering statues. Alison breathed a vast, contented sigh. Oh, the wonder of it, the joy, the luck, to be living in this beautiful setting with her beautiful daughter for five, even six years! She felt her heart might burst from happiness.

'She is not yours,' Robert had said, etching the words on her brain. She had been nervous of telling him what she had done, that she had lined them up one against the other, him and Charlotte, and chosen her daughter. To soften the impact, she had made a special dinner for him: his favourite, roast duck and lemon cheesecake. On the coffee table she had laid out smoked-salmon rolls in a forest of parsley, and paté on fingers of toast. She had never gone to this kind of trouble before.

She sent out love to him in rays from her heart, thinking of the long nights without him, wavering over her decision now it was too late. 'Something has happened. I want you to be glad for me,' she said.

'I'll be glad about anything that makes you happy,' he said.

But he was not glad when she told him. 'How wise you were to fill me up with food and wine,' he said. She wondered if he meant he might have hit her if he had been hungry and cold.

'She is not your child,' he said again, labelling Charlotte, definitively, a Godfrey possession. 'You have to accept this, Alison.' Deep lines ran obliquely from nose to chin. 'She – is – not – your – child.' Then he repeated what he had said before: 'You gave the twins away.'

Not her child? 'I sacrificed them because I thought they would have a better life with you. Sacrificed,' she echoed, though she had not thought of it like that before. 'The fact that you let Claire die is reason enough for me to want some part in looking after Charlotte.'

He went over to the mantelpiece. She could tell by the set of his shoulders that he was angry. He picked things up, looked at them, put them down hard. Three wise monkeys carved in cheap stone, an ashtray bought in Spain on that unsatisfactory honeymoon with 'the man Hurst', as Robert called him. When he turned, he seemed to have come to terms with her news.

'So I'll only see you in the holidays,' he said. 'I shall miss you.' He was heroic in defeat. She loved him for it. She thought of saying, 'If you had only shared her, just a little, I might not have had to do this.' But that would have been petty, and besides, it was too late.

Neither did she say, as she knew she ought, that perhaps he and his wife would get back together again.

They showed her to her room, the one June Leslie had vacated. An Art Deco woman was painted on a narrow china strip hanging on the wall. Alison wondered if its owner had felt it might not travel well to Peru. It might have broken, or failed to fit in. She was warmly interested in this woman whom God had moved aside to allow for her heart's desire. Sheet music for *The Mikado* lay on a shelf. 'Miss Leslie had planned to make that our Christmas production,' Miss Wedderburn said. 'Of course, if you would prefer to do something else . . .'

Why should she? Charlotte would make a delicious Yum-Yum.

A man brought her bag. 'Have a good trip down, did you?' he asked, and told her to call him Alfred. He said he was the gardener's nephew and the school handyman. He hoped she would like it here. She said she was sure she would, knew, in fact, that she would, and bestowed on him some of her radiance.

Alfred told her where to find the music room. The piano was a Steinway. She played a few bars of Rachmaninov. It had a beautiful tone. She loved it; she loved everything about the school. She was bursting with love.

Practice timetables were pinned up on the wall. Her eyes scanned the list, looking for the name Godfrey. Mondays 4.30 to 5.30 room number 4. Tuesdays 3.30 to 4.30, room number 1. 4.00 p.m. Thursday was laid down as the time of Charlotte's music lesson. Four o'clock Thursday imprinted itself on her brain.

A head came round the door. 'Hello, are you the new arrival? Miss Hurst? Right. Tea's on in the staff sitting room. I s'pose you know where it is.' The head disappeared.

She still had to find out about choir practice. Charlotte would, of course, be in the choir.

'Did you know we have a child here from your old school?' Miss Wedderburn asked. 'Charlotte Godfrey.'

Alison concentrated on balancing her teacup and keeping her features still. 'Yes, I taught her,' she said. 'I remember she had a pretty voice.' Casually, as though that was about all she remembered. 'She was a twin. They used to sing duets together.' She looked away into the empty fireplace, not wanting anyone to see her eyes had become moist.

'It isn't generally known that she lost a twin, Miss Hurst,' said the Head. 'It was her parents' wish when Charlotte came here that the twin should not be mentioned.' She looked round at the watching faces. 'I must ask you not to repeat what Miss Hurst has said.'

'I'm sorry. I assumed —' Alison stopped, silenced by an upsurge of anger against Robert.

Somebody broke the silence to mention the weather. Other topics flowed.

Out in the corridor, the fragile blonde who had been introduced as Miss Quant, music and English teacher, came up beside her. 'She doesn't sing, either. You had better know that in advance,' she said.

Alison stopped dead. Their colleagues filtered past, casting friendly glances, wearing little smiles, conferring on her secret sympathy, now they were out of sight of the Head, for putting her foot in it. 'Doesn't sing?' she echoed. 'What do you mean, Miss Quant?'

'Isabel. Just what I say. She doesn't sing.'

'At all?'

But Isabel had gone, taking the corner with a gliding movement, her silky hair swinging out behind her.

The tables were set for ten: four girls down each side, one at the foot, and a teacher at the head. 'You're on table six, Miss Hurst.'

Alison sent up a little prayer asking that Charlotte would be assigned to table six. The children streamed into the dining room in the Head's wake. Her eyes darted and searched. 'That's number six over there,' said someone, directing her, not knowing she was looking for a girl.

Nine strangers stood at attention behind their chairs, smiling with shy curiosity. With sinking heart she bowed her head, listened to grace and sat down. She had a job to do; she asked her charges their names, encouraged chat, answered questions and put her own. She dished up the horrible cottage pie, of which every last morsel must be eaten. Every plate cleared, that was the Head's decree. It was an insult to the cook to leave food.

She stopped outside the dining room, waiting for her daughter to emerge. One of the teachers touched her arm – 'Coffee in our sitting room' – and she was swept away.

En route for breakfast next morning she turned and there was Charlotte hurrying along, alone. She waited, her heart bursting with pride and love. How tall she had grown in only a year! Her skin was smooth, with the waxy loveliness of a rose. Then two girls came dashing along the path, shouting, 'Char! Wait for us!'

121

and Charlotte turned to greet them. They came on, the three of them, arms linked, laughing. At the door they released one another to enter the dining room. Only then did Charlotte seem to glimpse Alison out of a corner of her eye.

'Hello, Charlotte,' she said, pressing down at her side treacherous arms that might fly out of control, and hug.

'Hello, Miss Hurst,' Charlotte returned politely.

One of the girls said, 'Come on, Char,' and she darted after them.

There is one thing about being a teacher at a boarding school, Alison said to herself, shivering as she absorbed the shock: there is precious little opportunity for licking wounds. You have to go in and sit at the head of that table, number six, and say Good Morning and supervise. You tuck your humiliation (is that the name of this emotion that has overtaken me?) deep inside you. It is indeed deeply humiliating to love someone who does not love you, but that is only the half of it.

She did not listen to Miss Wedderburn's grace. She was not in a mood to be thankful for what she was about to receive. She was dealing with God in her own way. 'Do you seriously believe,' she asked Him bitterly, 'that such ordeals by fire will make a better person of me?'

Four o'clock Thursday came round. The music-room door opened. Charlotte entered the long room walking straight-backed, holding her golden head erect.

'Hello, Charlotte,' Alison said, aloud. My darling child, her heart whispered.

Charlotte smiled warily, fingering her music book, transferring some emotion to it. Embarrassment? Had a breath of her heart's feeling escaped? 'Now let me see how far you've got.' She made an effort to speak crisply, teacher to pupil.

'Grade six,' said Charlotte.

'You *have* come on.' Careful. Your pride is showing. Speaking in a neutral voice, Alison asked her to start with scales. While she played, Alison's gaze was caught by the way Charlotte's hair lifted at the crown like petals coming from the heart of a flower. Watch the fingers! she said to herself sternly.

When the lesson was over, she commented, 'I was surprised to find you're not in the choir.'

'No.' Charlotte rose from her stool and gathered up her music.

'Why not?'

'They've got lots of good singers here.' She was impatient to get away.

'Not better than you, Charlotte,' Alison protested. 'You have such a lovely voice. I can't believe there are many girls here who sing better than you do.'

Charlotte looked down at her feet.

'Now,' said Alison, bright and smiling, persuasive, 'I'm told Miss Leslie was going to do *The Mikado* this term. I'm going on with it. You'd make a wonderful Yum-Yum. Would you like to think about it?'

Charlotte shook her head. 'No, thank you.'

'Why not?' Alison waited. Began again. 'You must have a reason. After all, that's why your parents chose this school. They intended your voice should have serious attention. Haven't they always said they hoped you would sing professionally?'

Charlotte shrugged. 'Can I go now?'

She left as though a high wind had come in at the open window and carried her off.

'A word,' said Isabel Quant, rather imperiously, Alison thought, for one who must be six or seven years younger than herself. They were alone in the staff sitting room the following day.

'Yes?'

'Charlotte Godfrey. I did tell you she doesn't sing.'

'She does sing,' Alison protested with some indignation. 'Of course she does. She has a beautiful voice. What is this?' she demanded, quite forgetting she had meant to keep her emotions under control. 'What's going on?'

'Just because you taught her in the past, that doesn't mean you can run her life, you know. You have no right to bully her.'

Alison gasped.

Ignoring her reaction, Isabel continued calmly, 'She's asked if she can go on to my roster. I've already spoken to the Head and she's agreed. I'm swapping her over with a girl called Marian West. You'll find her very amenable,' she said, as though she recognised Alison as a fractious and difficult entity to whom only the most undemanding children should be exposed. 'OK?' she asked in that high, falsely bright voice people use when they

123

know perfectly well it is not at all OK. And then she was gone, floating out of the door with her blonde hair swinging.

Alison stood looking at the space where she had been. Her silent shout was dangerously close to sound. 'She is my daughter. My child! My baby! I have come here to be with her. You cannot take her away from me.'

She could not recognise that Charlotte had chosen to leave her, for that way lay pain beyond bearing.

Chapter Fifteen

Yolande, at her own request, departed for Queens in London to do A levels. Her closest friends were going there. It would be hell at school without them. And it was already hell at home without Charlotte and Ken. He had been boarding since he was eight.

'Don't say hell,' said Robert, speaking automatically without looking up from his paper.

Vivien, watching him, thought she had seen a sign of relief in his face, as if he felt he had lived long enough with the unspoken condemnation of his children. What did they know of life and what it could do to you? A man did not necessarily love a child through thick and thin, the way a woman did. Not anyway when she was growing up, growing away. Oh my darling Yolande. Cannot you stay? First Ken, then Claire, Charlotte and now you. Am I to be wholly alone?

Yolande's attention was fixed on her father. 'Well?'

'OK,' he said. It was understandable Yolande should want to be living among girls of her own age. He made no move to consult Vivien. He had blotted her out. He didn't even talk to her about her drinking. It was as though she no longer existed in his mind.

But, 'I do exist,' Vivien said to herself that night in the quiet of her empty bedroom. 'I do.' She looked in the mirror. Turned immediately away. She was no longer the confident mistress of Folly Hill, merely a woman who lived there; whose husband tolerated her staying on because anyway he was seldom at home.

She went with Yolande on a shopping spree to buy clothes to wear at her London school. In her mind's eye she saw an animated, well dressed woman with styled hair sharing this expedition. She didn't know how to be that woman any more and so she hung around in the background, shadowed by the glow and energy of her pretty teenage daughter, until, 'Is that your mother?' the saleswoman asked. 'Access or Visa? Thank you, madam. Sign here.'

The night after Yolande left, Robert came home for dinner. As Vivien saw his car approach she felt a surge of gratitude. So he did care! But he was monosyllabic, and after they had eaten he absorbed himself in television. His personality, his heart, his warm physicality, all were somewhere else, or, she preferred to think, abandoned. By not acknowledging the enemy, you take away her substance. Was there an enemy? He came home the next night. And the next.

She made tremendous efforts to please him. The evening she cooked roast duck followed by lemon cheesecake, his greatest favourite, he looked at her in a way that baffled and frightened her.

He ate the duck as though it was choking him, and refused the cheesecake. She gave it to Mrs Fuller the following day.

She put on a brave face, and set out once more to please. This time she would do a flower arrangement. Would she dare to put on an elegant dress? She postponed the decision as being too fragile to be mixed up with the dinner plans. Her glamorous clothes were still in the wardrobe. The left-hand sliding door had become a shield for garments that signified a way of life Robert had disallowed. She never slid it across.

She knew a shop a few miles the other side of Wylie-under-Lyne where you could buy venison that came down from Scotland.

'It's a long way for you to drive for such a small piece of meat,' the genial proprietor remarked.

She explained that there were only two of them at home, now.

'Last time you came –' he waved his long knife, using its tip to push the white cloth hat he wore in the shop to the back of his head – 'I had to carry it out to the car for you. Anniversary, wasn't it?' He wiped his bloodied hand on the blue-and-white striped apron as he waited for her reply.

'It's not quite the same today, Mr Baker.' She hadn't meant to sound wan, but the memory of the duck and cheesecake was dragging her down.

He nodded. 'Keeping well, are you?' People often asked her these days if she was keeping well. It wasn't that she looked ill, just drab. The drabness seemed to throw them, being neither a serious fault nor an illness. They didn't know what to make of it. She understood they couldn't say, 'Keeping a little less drab?'

'I'm fine,' she said, lifting her voice, jerking her features into a smile.

She set the table with the embroidered cloth bought in Madeira, on a long-ago cruise. They hadn't gone anywhere since Claire died.

Uncertainly, she slid back the left-hand door of her wardrobe and took out a sky-blue silk dress. She couldn't say it was one Robert liked better than the others. He had liked all her clothes. 'Lovely,' he would say when she paraded before him in the old days before their guests' arrival. 'You always look lovely, my dear.'

Every evening she clipped the gold bracelet with the painted enamel flowers round her wrist. It was her reminder to him that he had loved her up to a year ago. He never commented. It looked ridiculous with the plain garments she wore these days. Was she needling him to ask questions? She wasn't sure about motives these days, whether hers or his. But tonight, backed by blue silk, the bracelet glowed.

She was in the process of lifting the roast potatoes with a strainer spoon, placing them carefully round the venison, when she heard Robert's hurrying footsteps on the stairs. She finished her task, closed the oven door and took off her apron. Self-consciously she went into the hall in her pretty dress and high-heeled shoes, smiling.

He was descending the stairs at a good pace, loose knee'd, watching the treads. He had changed out of his city suit. Tweed jacket now. Checked Vyella shirt. Country tie, soft wool. 'Ah, there you are,' he said genially, not noticing the dress, the shoes or her brave smile of welcome. 'I had a ring from Ted Manvers,' he went on. 'Colin and I are to play off. If we're not held up, we'll just about get through by dark.' He hurried down the passage to the big cupboard where he kept his golf bag and folding trolley. 'Don't wait dinner for me,' he called. 'I expect we'll have something at the club.'

She felt her face sliding down. Her leaden heart went also. Her body had become too frail to hold either in place.

'Cheerio, then,' he called from the back door, disappearing with the clubs slung over his shoulder, pushing the trolley ahead.

Yolande called as she ran upstairs, 'I see you're back in your old room, Char,' and Charlotte, swinging her bag turned left on the landing instead of going straight ahead. Her bed and Claire's bed and their dressing table and Dobbin were there where they belonged. She felt as though she had never been away.

Sylvia had been to stay.

'She came for her teeth,' Vivien said. Sylvia had retained her Harley Street dentist and her doctor, though she scarcely visited the doctor at all.

'I'm so healthy, living as I do,' she said, mentioning the fresh vegetables Manuel brought her from the mountains, as well as fruit all the year round, speaking as though in Surrey they lived on bread alone. They conceded she was better off without petrol fumes and stress.

'She asked if your hair had recovered,' Vivien said, running a hand lovingly through the pretty curls. 'Do you remember you came back blonde?'

'I wouldn't wear my hat.' Charlotte had forgotten about being blonde for a while, and the dismay it had caused.

Kenneth remembered. 'You looked just like Marilyn Monroe.'

'Oh, you!'

He laughed and took up a boxing stance, feinting with his fists. 'Are you pleased about your room?'

Silly question. 'Course I am, Ken.' Charlotte skipped to the kitchen door, dug a finger into Mrs Fuller's cake mix, flung a nut in the air, caught it in her mouth. 'You're a good cook, Mrs Fuller.'

The housekeeper beamed.

Vivien was happy with the children at home, all three, though Robert had begun again to disappear on Saturdays and Sundays, for hours at a time. Yolande spent many of her evenings with Oliver Bryant now, driving off in his mother's car. Kenneth passed his driving test and Vivien allowed him to use the Riley. She scarcely went out, wanting to be at home with the children, or whichever child happened to be in.

Charlotte spent an inordinate amount of time in her room. They understood, feeling guilty – though how could they possibly have known how much she would miss it? How had Sylvia known? They assumed the novelty would wear off in time.

They weren't to know Claire was there.

Bonnie was too small and docile for Charlotte now. She wanted to win rosettes. She might have inherited Yolande's Star, but Star had gone. One day Yolande sold her hacking jacket at the second-hand shop run as a convenience by a Pony Club mother and blew the proceeds on dark plum lipstick, white tights and the tiniest miniskirt – guaranteed, Robert said, speaking with equal parts of intolerance and concern, to encourage rape. Star was sold.

Kelly, thirteen point two hands high, with a coat the colour of cobwebs with gunmetal mane and tail, came from a farm in Yorkshire. Robert drove Charlotte up. One glance and she was in love. Kelly's intelligent brown eyes were framed by Minnie Mouse lashes. Her canter was smooth, her mouth soft. A mere touch of the reins brought a response. They trailed her home behind the Citroën. Robert had all his cars (a new one every year, as befitted a successful businessman) equipped with a trailer hitch for towing horse boxes.

'I don't suppose you'll want to come,' he said to Vivien, walking away as he spoke, giving her no opportunity to protest.

Bonnie went to join Posy at the Hallorans' to wait for the little sister to grow out of her Shetland. Robert offered her at a give-away price if they would take her now so the two ponies could be together again. The innocent wrongs they had done Charlotte were gradually being righted.

He did not tell Alison about Kelly, only that he had to go to Yorkshire and would be away that Saturday. Offering news of Charlotte was an acknowledgement that Alison had rights. Sexual gratification became the main issue. Alison felt she had become a mistress, a tart; at best, a lover. She swallowed her pride. At least she had not lost Robert by choosing to join her daughter – the daughter she had lost again.

She wished she could talk to him about that. About the pitiless Isabel Quant taking her child. How she suffered seeing them together, Charlotte's bright face upturned, Isabel's features animated, affectionate. Sometimes Alison thought she should resign her job. What did she see of Charlotte? Twice a week in history periods.

In the distance, a pounding of hooves. Charlotte swung round in her saddle. A boy in T-shirt and jeans, riding like a maniac, dashed past on a chestnut. Kelly pranced sideways.

'Idiot,' she said with a mixture of admiration and disquiet. Why wasn't he wearing a hard hat? She rode up over the top of the hill, down the other side, leaped the stream and there was Max straddling a log, flicking his horse's reins carelessly through his fingers.

'I thought that was you,' he said cheekily, navy blue eyes gleaming, mouth laughing. 'I couldn't stop.'

She laughed too, excited at seeing him. 'I didn't know you had a horse.'

'It's Andy Harverson's Goldie.' In his pronunciation of the name he gave it importance. Goldie might have won the Grand National. Or the Derby. 'Andy's gone to Australia, so I exercise him.' That was grand, too. His friends travelled the world. 'I don't want a horse of my own,' said Max carelessly. 'I'm going to have a Harley-Davidson.'

'What's that?' She had forgotten, or not realised before, just how handsome he was. Black hair flopping over a wide forehead, clear olive skin.

'Get off and sit here by me,' he said, patting the log. With happy obedience, she swung a leg over the saddle and jumped down.

'A Harley-Davidson is a super motorbike,' he said. 'And I'm going to Australia, too. Before university, or after. Back-packing. What d'you reckon to that?'

'Brilliant.' He made it sound like the most exciting thing you could do.

'My father is giving me a thousand pounds for fares and I'll find jobs,' said Max, his eyes flashing. 'Would your father give you a thousand pounds?'

A thousand pounds! She remembered how mean Dr Fosse used to be. Perhaps fathers became more generous as you grew older.

'If I pass my exams,' said Max. 'That's what he wants. Can I kiss you?' Without waiting for an answer, he grabbed her by the shoulders, pulled her to him and kissed her on the cheek.

130

'There you are,' he said, pleased as a puppy.

She felt rich in bliss. As though she was inhabiting another planet where it was commonplace for these things to happen.

'I say, can you jump?' he asked, swinging her back to earth.

'Of course.'

'There's some fallen trees further upstream. They make great hurdles. C'mon.' He jumped off the log. Movement, fluidity was part of him. He held Goldie's reins wide, took aim, circled them neatly over the horse's head, swung himself into the saddle.

'You're supposed to get on the near side,' said Charlotte. Robert, who had taught her to ride, was a stickler for correct form.

'Who says? I can get on any side I like. What's near, anyway? Near to what?' Max laughed merrily as he dug in his heels.

Feeling twice as alive as she had before, Charlotte jumped up on a log and slid a leg over Kelly's back. The pony, responding to the children's excitement, took to her heels before Charlotte found the stirrups and belted along the track through the trees in Goldie's wake. Divots of dry earth were coming like cannonballs from his hooves. Charlotte kept her head down.

They swept through the forest and emerged on a stretch of land where foresters had been at work sawing felled trees into sections. Some of them were still whole, their leaves, huge aromatic sprays of them, green on the ground. Charlotte looked round her with interest. Her exploring spirit had not brought her in this direction before. On one side, green fields ran up into a valley. On the other, the stream she had crossed further up babbled and glittered in the sun.

'Beat you!' Max shouted. He was crouched low in the saddle, already lined up for a jump, energy and purpose in every line of him. She watched him take the logs one after another, admiring his courage but concerned at his lack of skill. A naughty pony would have had him off in a trice.

'Come on,' he called, beckoning her with a generous sweep of his arm.

Kelly, caught up in Max's excitement, dashed at the first tree trunk in their path. Up she went and over. She swung round, took the next trunk in a flying leap, sped ahead, up and over again. Max's enjoyment was a spring that swung them high. Charlotte felt she was riding through the sky.

Goldie shot ahead like a rocket. It was clear Max lacked proper control. Charlotte reined in. His pony was racing, too fast. He leaped awkwardly, seemed to change his mind in mid-air. Charlotte held her breath, waiting for him to go down. Goldie went on to his knees and Max was thrown forward over his mane. The pony gathered himself together and streaked off up the valley. Max clung manfully to the saddle, sliding, sliding.

Charlotte waited only to see that he was clambering to his feet then took the log and gave Kelly her head. Goldie's reins were loose, swinging dementedly from side to side. Charlotte wanted to catch him before they tripped him up. She was gaining ground. She came abreast and reached out. At that moment the gelding went down. She leaped from her saddle and caught his reins as Goldie staggered to his feet.

'Hold on. Hold on.' She talked quietly to him, smoothing his silky nose, and after a while he began to calm. She tied up the broken reins and remounted. Goldie, though prancing and snorting, allowed her to lead him back but he would not enter the region where the felled logs lay. He reared, squealed, showed the whites of his eyes. Max hurried over.

'Did you hurt yourself?' she asked, concerned.

'Me? Hurt myself? No.' He laughed. How absurd!

'What frightened him? He's awfully excited.'

'Something jumped up, I s'pose.'

'What jumped up? A rabbit?'

'No, not a rabbit. I don't know,' said Max, checking the knot in the broken reins.

Charlotte rode over to the log where it had happened. She leaned down, pushing aside scotch thistles and young elder with her riding crop. She could see nothing. And yet Kelly sidled away, flicked her ears, snorted.

Max had seated himself on one of the smaller tree trunks. 'Come and see what I've got.'

She slid out of her saddle to climb up beside him. Using his fingertips, he was polishing the shiny inside of a bit of corrugated bark.

'Look,' he said, speaking as though he had found a jewel, not an old bit of wood. 'Feel it.'

She ran her fingers along the silky surface while he watched her face intently as though her reaction was of the utmost importance to him. 'It's pretty,' she said.

132

A butterfly flew between them. He leaned back to give it space, following it with eyes grown gentle. She smiled at him.

'I could kiss you on the lips now,' he told her.

'You don't have to,' she said, pretending she thought the kiss was a thank you for bringing Goldie back. But all the same she awaited her fate with excitement and dread. His lips were velvety. Navy blue eyes looked into hers. She froze in ecstasy, waiting for him to do it.

Kelly the well-behaved suddenly reared up on her hind legs, showing the whites of her eyes. Charlotte clung to the reins and was dragged off the log. Max leaped to her aid.

'Stay back,' she said urgently. 'Stay back!' She ran with the agitated pony. Pulled her up alongside a flat-topped stump just long enough to slide a leg over the saddle. Kelly shot away. Charlotte found the dancing stirrups with her toes and gathered up the reins, but they were useless. Kelly had the bit between her teeth.

They bolted, across the meadow and into the trees. Several times she thought with fear that she was going to crush a leg against a tree. They came to the stream where Max had waited for her. Kelly leapt across and bounded up the wooded hill.

The track was too steep here for a bolting horse. She slowed to a canter, then to a trot. Eventually, running out of breath, she walked, head down, trumpeting through distended nostrils. Foam from her lips settled like suds on her sweating withers.

After a while Max caught up. 'I expect the meadow's haunted.' He made spooky noises, rolling his eyes.

Charlotte, feeling strange, reached into her pocket for the crystal. She shivered, thinking, I didn't bring it today, yet certain she had. She looked from beneath her lashes at Max, wondering what he had seen.

That evening as she was drifting off to sleep, a voice in her head said, 'I frightened Goldie.'

She fought to regain consciousness. Couldn't. She had gone down too far. Her hand slid under the pillow, felt for the crystal, forgetting it had disappeared. Next morning, in the twilight time between sleeping and waking, she remembered.

'You could have killed him,' she whispered.

'You'd no right to let him kiss you,' said the voice forcefully.

133

'You can't stop me.'

'Can't I? You'll see.'

What Charlotte saw was the gun barrel. Fisherman's Point. She remembered the gypsy was dead. How did she know he was dead? The knowledge surprised her.

She screamed.

Vivien came rushing in.

'I've lost my crystal,' Charlotte said.

Vivien picked it up from the floor. 'Here it is.'

Charlotte held it in her hand and was comforted.

Chapter Sixteen

Max was away visiting his grandmother the day Charlotte got caught in the snow. Of course she shouldn't have gone out or, going, should not have ventured so far, but Kelly was frisky, bursting with energy.

'If the snow does come,' Charlotte told her father, 'I won't be able to ride. Not for days. Weeks, maybe. Months.'

He laughed indulgently, and patted her on the head. 'All right, you go. The forecast did say snow tonight, not this afternoon.'

They galloped, working off the oats: jumped ditches and logs. Max had shown her a new texture to riding. A sensuous interrelation with speed and an ease of accomplishment. She was no longer conscious of sitting correctly, holding her hands on the reins just so, feet here, knees there. Instead, she sat back in the saddle hedonistically free with the wind in her face, reins held loosely, giving Kelly her head.

Riding through the woods on the far side of the common, she missed the gradual darkening of the sky. Didn't notice the silence when the birds stopped chirruping. Kelly's hooves had taken over her hearing. Clip clop, thump, thump on the hard ground, then rustling and shuffling through winter leaves.

They emerged from the forest into an eerily silent world. Daylight was fading, huge flakes of snow were drifting. Green trees caught the snow as it fell, draping themselves in it. Look! I'm a Christmas tree. Look! I'm a ghost. Charlotte was entranced. In the distance, golden glow-worms shone. Was that Forge Green village, far away? No, it couldn't be. She was looking at the Pig and Garter, the pub at Sellick Down. With a sense of shock, she realised that she was miles from home.

Hastily, she reined Kelly round. Kelly shook her head, dislodging fat snowflakes from the long hollows of her ears. 'Hey! We'd better hurry back,' Charlotte said and dug in her heels. She decided to skirt the edge of the forest for she could ride faster on the open heath. She rode with head down, eyes closed against the freezing flakes, cantering fast, keeping close to the trees. She knew a shortcut that would lead them through to Folly Lane, but would Kelly tackle the steep bank that was the only way down into the road? Bonnie had been persuaded once, though she didn't like it and had finished on her bottom. Perhaps not, Charlotte decided reluctantly. If Kelly refused the bank, they would have to retrace their steps to the common and then find their way to the village. She decided to make for Forge Green.

Kelly lowered her head and shook it violently. The jangling bit was loud in the silence. 'You've got to keep going,' Charlotte cried, pulling her round, kicking her heels into the pony's flanks. 'We've got to get home.' Snowflakes slipped into her mouth as she spoke. Snow crept in at the top of her boots, melting down her calves. Snow on the saddle seeped wetly through to her bottom.

'Come on, Kelly!' she said urgently. The pony broke into a sluggish canter. 'Faster!' Kelly didn't seem to like hurrying in the snow. She slowed to a trot, then a walk. Charlotte stood up in the stirrups, peering as though into the distance, seeing only drifting flakes in a world of blinding whiteness. Surely the lights of the village ought to be showing by now? Instead, even the woods had disappeared. She suppressed her mounting panic and urged the pony on.

Kelly moved reluctantly, her hooves squeaking in the dry snow. Charlotte pulled her anorak hood over her hard hat and pushed her woolly scarf closer under her chin. Its folds had filled with snow. When she turned the scarf over, the snow melted against her neck. Water trickled down her back.

Kelly plodded on, blinking the flakes from her long lashes, snorting steam through her nostrils. The snow blotted out her footsteps, covered her hocks. Crept into Charlotte's string gloves. She could no longer feel her fingers. The crop slipped out of her hand and she left it. Hour after hour, it seemed, they kept going, fear endlessly stirring in her stomach. She sensed in their non-arrival that they must be going round in circles.

The snowflakes that had been drifting steadily suddenly took on life, came at her hard and fierce, more like lumps of ice now, than snow. They hit her in the face. She eased her scarf up to cover her nose. She cried with the cold, sobbing into the wet, snow-packed wool. Kelly changed direction, edging round to face the wind.

Charlotte experienced again the frightened, inadequate feeling of being only part of a person. A useless bit of a person, half endowed with knowing, half endowed with strength. If only Claire were here with her, they would find their way out of this. If only Claire hadn't got herself drowned. You could do anything if you were twins.

The wind dropped and the white world fell away. They were in darkness. Kelly's hooves were making a different kind of sound now. Clump clump, instead of squeak squeak. There was a snapping underfoot as of twigs breaking. They were in among the trees again. Kelly shook herself violently to dislodge the snow. She swished her long tail, tossed her head and began to trot with great confidence as though she could actually see a track in the dark. Perhaps she could, Charlotte thought. Did horses see in the dark, like cats?

Leaves brushed her face. She flattened herself along the pony's neck. On and on they went. Suddenly Kelly stopped, gathered up her haunches and dived down a bank. Charlotte shot forward. She pushed hard with the balls of her hands, trying not to go over the pony's head. Kelly was down on her knees, nose buried in snow. She staggered to her feet and Charlotte managed to push herself back into the saddle.

They were in a depression sheltered from the wind, a white wall just ahead. Was it a wall or a bank? Were they in Folly Lane? Oh, please, please let it be Folly Lane!

Kelly shook herself violently, snorting, ejecting snow from her nostrils. Then she began to plough uphill.

A voice. A shout.

Charlotte pulled the scarf from her face to shout back. The words fell just beyond her lips, struck dead by the snow. The shout came again.

It was Robert, moving as fast as a man can when he is up over his knees in snow. And behind him another white figure. 'Daddy!' Charlotte screamed, or tried to. The sound flew back into her throat, pushed by the snow. 'Kenneth!'

'Charlotte! Thank heavens!' Robert was coming towards her, arms reaching. 'Thank God you're safe!'

'Where have you been?' Kenneth croaked. He sounded distraught.

'I got lost. I couldn't see.' Tears of relief poured down her cheeks. She could feel their warmth. 'Kelly found the way,' she said and her father replied, 'Good old Kelly,' in a choked sort of voice. He seemed near to crying, too. He grasped her hand, clung to it. 'Darling, you're frozen.'

She seemed to have gone beyond the cold. Kenneth came up on her other side. 'Give me this hand.' Then, with horror, 'It's like ice.'

They floundered through the barn gate and over to the stables.

'You go in,' Robert said when they reached the yard. 'Take her, Ken. I'll put Kelly away.'

'She's my horse,' said Charlotte, teeth chattering, urging Kelly on to the stables.

'I can deal with her.'

'No, Daddy. No, Ken.' She pushed her brother away as he tried to help her off. Horses knew you didn't care about them if you jumped off and left them after they had saved your life.

'Charlotte!' Kenneth protested. His own teeth were chattering.

'No, I must . . . Let me do it!' She was crying again, with cold and fear now. She was frightened of Robert. That he would carry her inside, leaving Kelly to freeze to death. She slid stiffly to the ground.

'Look at you,' her father said. 'You can scarcely stand!'

Kenneth tried to put his arms round her. She pushed him away. 'I'll help you,' she chattered feverishly. 'It won't take long.' She reached for the brush, but it fell from her stiff fingers and rolled across the earth floor. Her brother picked it up.

'Please, Charlotte,' begged Robert. 'Let Kenneth take you in.'

'No.' With numb hands she knocked snow out of Kelly's mane and tail. Staggering over to the rail, she fumbled for the horse blanket. Kenneth took it from her and flung it over Kelly's back. Robert buckled it, working fast as a whip.

'Bring Peewit in.'

'Oh, Charlotte!' her father cried in despair. Kenneth ran into the donkey's stall and moved her over, pushing her roughly in his haste.

138

'Now come on.' Robert swung Charlotte up in his arms and carried her to the back door, running through the snow with Kenneth following.

Vivien rushed to meet them, making noises of distress. Robert carried her into the hall and put her down. Vivien swiftly took off her boots. Yolande, fussing around, muttering why on earth didn't she come home earlier, removed her hard hat and snow-clogged anorak, her frozen scarf. Vivien carefully eased off the ice-hardened gloves, exposing her poor little red hands.

'Oh, darling!' Robert, anguished, held one of them between his own.

Their faces were imprinted with memories they could not bear. Images of themselves running, running across the meadow with lateness in their hearts. Another sense of lateness had crept close, lining their faces with dread.

Charlotte could sense that the house was warm but the heat stayed outside of her.

'Run a bath,' Vivien said urgently and Yolande dashed away. Vivien held Charlotte close, rubbing her back with warm hands. 'Your jods are wet. Let me take them off.'

'She wouldn't come in. She wouldn't let me deal with the horse,' Robert said, angry with himself now for giving in.

'You should have brought her.' That was the sloughed-off mouse of a wife, reincarnated as a lioness. 'Ken could have dealt with Kelly,' she said as though they could change it now.

'She wouldn't let me.' Kenneth was peeling off his boots and anorak.

Yolande ran downstairs again shouting about cocoa.

'Don't worry yet,' said Vivien. 'Bring a hot-water bottle. Two.'

Charlotte couldn't feel the bath water, couldn't stop shivering. They put her to bed and gave her hot cocoa. The mug wobbled in her hand. Vivien rescued it.

'Are you going to be sick? Shall I get a basin?' Yolande hovered, anxious to help.

She didn't know. She felt strange.

Vivien placed a hand on Charlotte's forehead. Hot. She rushed off to look for a thermometer, but couldn't find it. They were a healthy lot. When had they used it last?

Robert wondered if they should call the doctor. Kenneth ran

139

outside to measure the depth of the snow. He came back upstairs to say that if the doctor came he would have to walk, as if they didn't already know.

'We're probably overreacting,' said Robert. But all the same, a moment later he went into the hall to ring the surgery. An answering machine said, 'If the matter is urgent, you can get Dr Stevenson on this number . . .'

He returned upstairs to check on the urgency.

'It's pointless,' Vivien said. 'Dr Stevenson lives halfway to Wylie. It would take him hours to walk.'

He felt distanced from her. She is not your child, he thought, unfairly. He had become so accustomed to being unfair with her he scarcely noticed it. A picture of Alison entered his mind: Alison with storm clouds in her eyes, saying, 'I sacrificed them because I thought they would have a better life with you, and you let them die.' He felt an overwhelming conviction that she should be there.

He went to the landing rail. Stood looking down into the hall where the telephone stood. Then Vivien was beside him, saying in a frightened voice, 'I think we should at least ask the doctor. He might make it, if he has a four-wheel drive.'

Charlotte never knew whether it was that night, or the next, or the next, that she became aware of Claire's presence in the room. Claire was sitting on her own bed, legs dangling, one hand fingering the crystal.

'It wasn't Kelly brought you home,' she said. 'It was me. You called me, so I came. Don't you remember?'

She did now.

'You're coming with me,' said Claire bossily, and Charlotte felt a pulling in her chest as though the essence of her was being tugged out. And then she was sitting beside Claire, on Claire's bed. The body in her own bed was white and still as a marble statue.

'You don't need her any more.' Claire put her head back and laughed.

Charlotte felt whole again, the way she used to feel before Claire died. A twin. It was lovely. She put her hand in Claire's and they held the crystal together. 'Now you can sing,' said Claire, 'any time you like.'

Their mother was leaning over the white statue. Tears flooded her face. Their father was standing by the bed looking as though he didn't know what to do. And couldn't bear it.

Dr Stevenson was there, too. Yolande and Ken were both crying.

'Easy-peasy, wasn't it?' said Claire.

The doctor put a mirror in front of the statue's mouth, and leaned down to look. 'I'm afraid she's gone.'

Charlotte saw the words written in the air in front of him, like a speech balloon in a comic.

Their mother collapsed, falling across the bed. Their father was trying to pick her up, but she clung to the statue and wouldn't let go. Watching, Charlotte felt a great weight of sadness. The doctor lifted the sheet as though he was about to cover the statue's face.

Charlotte couldn't bear it. She said urgently, 'I've got to go back.' She could see they couldn't do without her, as well as doing without Claire. She let go of Claire's hand.

Claire said, 'You can't . . . really.'

Charlotte could tell by the way she said 'really' that she was trying it on. She longed to stay, but knew that if she did she would suffer the grief on their parents' faces, for eternity.

She slid off the bed. Claire grabbed at her to stop her going. 'You can't! You can't! You can't!' The words splintered through Charlotte's head.

'I've got to. I've got to,' she shouted without making a sound. Kenneth looked straight at them both. Blinked. She flung herself away. Now she was hovering over the statue. It looked cold and abandoned. She looked back with sadness at her twin, ready to say goodbye. Claire's face had gone dark.

Charlotte looked quickly away, then slipped inside the statue like a hand in a glove. Heat and love moved out from her heart, warming it right through. It became a person again. She mustered enough strength to flutter her lids.

The sheet stayed poised in mid-air. Vivien uttered a cry. Robert moved forward with hands outstretched. Kenneth choked. Tears began to rain down Yolande's face.

Charlotte looked over to the bed opposite. Claire had gone, taking their twinness with her, leaving something vengeful and terrible hovering in its place.

'You can take a horse to the water,' said Isabel Quant, 'but you cannot make it drink.' Not having heard Charlotte's voice, she was easy about the child's refusal to sing, and didn't see why Alison was making such a fuss.

The Head was content to let the matter slide. 'She's clever in other ways.'

Charlotte was afraid her singing might bring Claire, the Claire she had wilfully – she thought of her decision as wilful – abandoned that snowy Christmas three years ago. She had appeared only once since, and that for a brief moment at the school swimming pool. Charlotte, having emerged from the water, had paused before a mirror on the wall just inside the door. Claire's face appeared over her shoulder. As quickly, it went. Charlotte held her breath but her twin didn't manifest herself again.

Then Mary Saunders hissed from the entrance, 'Hey! Don't go into the changing room, Miss Hurst's there.'

Charlotte turned, still stunned.

'What's the matter, Char? Don't look so shocked. The staff are allowed to swim because of the heat wave.' The temperature had been in the nineties for weeks. 'I just thought you wouldn't want her to see your bare bosom,' she explained helpfully.

Afterwards Charlotte thought the loving expression on Claire's face meant forgiveness, and she was comforted.

Alison didn't tell Robert of the incident. When you have mulishly gone down your own path, there is not much you can share. She knew what she looked like with her bathing cap on, the dark hair hidden. But how could she know from the back who it was standing before the mirror in the regulation bathing suit until she looked in and saw her child's face? So Alison convinced herself. All the same, she was guiltily aware of having planted something that might grow in Charlotte's mind.

Kenneth got his degree and was off to Australia for a year.

'Did Daddy give you a thousand pounds?'

'What funny questions you ask, little Charlotte.' He hugged her. She and Kenneth had been closer since her illness. She would never forget what he said then, though they hadn't talked about it since. She hadn't dared.

'I thought you had died. I hallucinated with fright. I thought I saw you sitting on Claire's bed. I thought I saw Claire, too. It was a nasty moment.'

At the time she was tempted to tell him the truth, but a voice in her head said no.

'So, did he give you a thousand pounds?' she persisted now.

'Since you ask, yes. About that. It costs a lot for the fare.'

Charlotte knew then that Max wasn't making it up.

'Will you work?' she asked.

'I'll have to.'

'What doing?'

'Whatever I can get.'

Ken's trip sounded ordinary. Max's plans were charged with magic. He was going to work on a sheep station. Learn to be a jackeroo. There were roustabouts and hands, but to be a jackeroo was the best. Max had all the jargon. He would live in a homestead, not a house. He would ride over thousands of acres, camping out for weeks at a time by water holes. He would shoot crocodiles and kill snakes with his bare hands. The way to do it was to pick them up by the tail and flick them round your wrist.

He didn't get his Harley-Davidson, but he passed his driving test and his mother allowed him to use her car. Vivien was afraid when Charlotte went out with him. Robert was more than willing to drive her to parties and collect her, whatever the hour. But she was fifteen now. She didn't want to be thought a Daddy's girl. Max talked them round. At seventeen, he had the confidence to address grown-ups. He would converse with Robert man to man, head up and shoulders square. He gave an illusion of height though as yet he was only about five foot nine.

'I assure you, I'm very careful,' he said to Robert.

He wasn't but neither was he careless. He drove with flair, handling his mother's ordinary saloon like a racing demon, commenting as they sped through country lanes.

'Now we're coming into the second circuit at Brands Hatch. Max Fosse driving the Porsche is in the lead. Look out, Jackie Stewart's coming up behind him. He's passing! He's passing! No! He's fallen back. Fosse is still in the lead . . .'

Max got invited to all the parties. There was a quality to his enjoyment that was infectious. People responded to it, and to him. He was not a good dancer, he was too restless, had too much energy. He would swing Charlotte out of french windows, career down a garden path with her, threaten to toss her in ponds or swimming pools. Every holiday she was newly in love. She had given up riding in gymkhanas: they were slow and boring compared to dashing through the forest and over the heath with Max. He taught her to notice things, to live high, on some sort of brink.

'Look at those trees!' It was September and the leaves were turning.

'Smell that!' His senses were more alert than other people's.

Once, as they sat on a fallen log exchanging sweet, secret kisses, Louisa Waite came walking through the trees with her dog Pip. Charlotte experienced an unpleasant sensation of *déjà vu*. It wasn't so much a memory, more a fox creeping out of the undergrowth, leaving its scent behind. She had had it before on meeting Louisa. Charlotte and Max moved apart, pretending they'd only just met.

'Hello, Louisa,' they chorused. She walked past, head high, curls bouncing, as though she hadn't seen or heard them.

'She's going to be very pretty one day,' Max said.

Charlotte could tell he meant she was very pretty now, which she was, always had been. She tossed her head. 'Baby-snatcher.'

He gave her that navy blue velvet look. Put a hand on her breast, found the nipple with his forefinger, rubbed gently so it was all she could do not to jump off the log. He'd been doing it since he got his O levels.

Chapter Seventeen

Max achieved brilliant A-level passes. Was offered a place at Oxford, reading PPE. He took a year off to go to Australia. In a world that had become grey on his departure Charlotte felt defeated. She didn't want to go to parties without him. Had no desire to ride. The magic had gone out of it.

'I knew you'd get fed up one day,' Yolande, home from London for the weekend, crowed, she who had sold her hacking jacket and never looked back. 'Everyone goes off riding in the end.'

By a curious chance – Charlotte thought it was a curious chance – whenever she went into the little town of Wylie-under-Lyne she ran into William Card. When she came along the High Street he was always standing in the middle of the pavement outside Marilyn's Teashop.

'Hello, Charlotte,' he would say, his pale eyes shining behind his glasses.

'Hello,' she would respond as she sailed by.

One day he moved directly into her path. 'Where have you been? I haven't seen you for ages,' he said, as though there had been a time when he was accustomed to seeing her every day.

She hesitated, nonplussed.

'What are you doing?' he continued eagerly. 'Now, I mean. Would you like to have tea with me?' He indicated Marilyn's.

Charlotte glanced in at the pretty bay window. CREAM TEAS AND CAKES, the sign said. There were people seated at tiny tables. An old lady, holding a china pot, smiled at her through the glass.

'Well?' said William, already half defeated by her hesitation.

She looked up into his pale face, at his spiky hair, like thin cheese straws. She didn't really want to be seen taking tea with him, but her mouth was watering. Fat scones with strawberry jam and cream were outside the range of her pocket money.

'OK, thanks,' she said, and swept inside before someone could step out of a doorway and recognise her. She headed for a table in the far corner. One of the chairs faced the wall. She was making for it when a waitress stopped her. 'Wouldn't you rather sit in the centre?' she asked and pulled out a chair.

Ashamed, Charlotte avoided William's eyes as she sat down.

He was earnest and forgiving behind his glasses. She smiled nervously at him.

'You have a lovely smile,' he said.

His heavy sincerity embarrassed her. She shifted uncomfortably.

'I often think of you and Claire,' William said. 'I've never had a chance to tell you I was sorry about Claire.'

The words were so unexpected they shocked her. 'I always put flowers on her grave on the anniversary.'

She stopped eating and stared at him.

'People do.' He was made awkward by her reaction.

Anniversary? Nobody had ever said anything to her about anniversaries.

'Remember Miss Hurst? She used to teach at your school. I've seen her there. She doesn't know me,' he said, and Charlotte sensed he would not expect people to know him. 'She was crying,' he said.

Charlotte was dumbfounded.

'She cried at the funeral.' William's eyes were kind and grave. 'Have another scone,' he said.

She took one, slathered it in cream and put a huge blob of jam on top. It wouldn't go into her mouth. Embarrassed, she wiped her face with a paper napkin, scraped up the blob that had fallen on her knee, then licked her fingers and reached into her pocket for a tissue. Her fingers closed comfortingly round the crystal.

'I'm sorry,' said William, 'I didn't mean to upset you.'

'I'm not upset,' she said, unstrung at being confronted by the enigma of Miss Hurst. 'She teaches at my school.'

'Did she go there because of you?' Charlotte recognised that she had always known this. William slipped into an older brother/uncle slot in her mind. She leaned towards him across the table. 'Miss Hurst watches me,' she said. 'All the time, she watches me. I can feel her eyes on me. It's creepy and weird. She tried to make me —' Charlotte closed her mouth, aghast at what she had nearly said.

'Tried to make you what?' asked William, genuinely concerned now.

'She's just bossy.' Charlotte tucked the singing inside her, protecting it. 'I talked to Miss Quant about her. Miss Quant is another of the teachers. She thinks Miss Hurst is sick. Unnatural, she says. Miss Quant says she has an unnatural attachment to me.'

'You might be overreacting. Did you like her when you were at Hillcrest?'

Charlotte couldn't remember. 'I was younger then.'

'I'm sure she hasn't done you any harm,' William said soothingly.

'No, when you come to think of it,' Charlotte conceded.

He looked at his watch. 'I must go back to the office. It's been nice talking to you.' He paid the bill.

'Can you wait for me to run you home?' He smiled down at her as they stood together outside the teashop. 'I finish at half past.'

'No, thank you,' said Charlotte politely. 'I'll get the bus.'

He pointed to the upper storey of the building. Gilt letters on a window read: FENTON, LODGE & CARRUTHERS. 'My desk is there,' he said. 'I can see along the pavement. Any time you feel like a cup of tea, stand here and I'll see you.'

She knew then why she bumped into him whenever she came into Wylie-under-Lyne.

Swaying homewards in the bus, dredging in her mind through the events of the past hour, she remembered Claire had been drowned during the summer holidays. So there must be an anniversary about now. She left the bus at the stop by the church.

The white gravestone was still unweathered.

CLAIRE GODFREY 1965–1975. REST IN PEACE.

Rest in peace! Charlotte stared at the inscription, thinking about the fact that Claire was not resting in peace.

Half a dozen posies had been laid side by side on the plinth. At the foot, a bouquet. Charlotte had thought of Claire as growing with her: sixteen, going on seventeen, now. But not here. In her grave, she would never be more than ten. She thought that a little girl of ten would hate that bouquet.

Why had she been excluded from the anniversaries? She bent down to read the card that was attached to the bouquet. 'With deepest love from Mummy, Daddy, Charlotte, Kenneth and Yolande.'

Charlotte? Her discomfort increased.

She turned another card over. The Fosse family! Was this something neighbours did? Did Max know? He never mentioned Claire.

She looked at another card. 'With love from Louisa.' But Louisa wasn't a friend! She couldn't have been more than six or seven when Claire died. Why had they not written 'the Waite family', like 'the Fosse family'? Why should Louisa send Claire a posy? A memory emerged, fuzzy at the edges, but disturbing. Louisa with one of the sweets that had been meant for Claire bulging in her cheek.

William's posy was a circle of pansies with fern. Claire would like that.

Mrs Fuller! 'Love from A. Fuller.' And here was one 'from the staff and pupils of Hillcrest School'.

A voice in her head said, 'Look at the rosy posy.' She picked it up. Rosebuds surrounded by soft, pale leaves. She buried her nose in it, sensing the warm sweetness of love as the perfume of the flowers. The voice said, 'Our mummy put it there.' She didn't properly hear the words, they were in the rustle of the leaves on the big sycamore, in the sound of a jet high up, making for Heathrow.

A cry of 'Pip!' made her swing round. Louisa was wandering down the brick path that ran alongside the church to the lychgate. Her dog saw Charlotte and raced towards her.

'Pip!' Louisa shouted. The dog came to within a few yards, stopped abruptly and backed away, his hair rising. A picture rose in Charlotte's mind of the gypsy's dog at Fisherman's Point. Pip emitted a low growl.

Charlotte and Louisa stared at each other, then Louisa called the dog and went quickly through the gate and into the lane. Charlotte looked after her, clutching the posy.

'Claire,' she whispered, but there was no reply.

Mrs Fuller was coming down the drive as she turned in off Folly Hill. 'Your mother will be glad,' she said when Charlotte told her she had been to see Claire's grave. 'They wonder why you never go.'

'I didn't know people did.'

'Yes, well,' said Mrs Fuller, looking at her sadly. 'I'd tell your mother if I was you.'

Vivien was in the big drawing room, huddled in one of the velvet chairs with an open magazine on her knee. But she wasn't looking at it, she was staring into space.

Charlotte seated herself, facing. 'Why did you put "Rest in Peace" on Claire's gravestone?'

Vivien was taken aback by her question. 'Darling, why not? I like to think of her resting in peace.'

'She isn't. How could she, when you think about it, being drowned when she was only ten?'

An appalled expression reshaped her mother's face.

'I wish I could talk to you about her,' said Charlotte. She thought it might cheer her mother up to know that Claire was alive and well, in her own way.

Vivien reached out with her thin, veined hands – old lady's hands. Charlotte looked down at them with chill foreboding, wondering if she was ill. She took them in her own warm ones.

'I would be so pleased,' Vivien said. 'I think about her such a lot. All the time. I'd love to talk to you about those happy days when we had her with us.'

'I mean now. I mean, where she is now.'

'But we don't know, do we? I mean, she's with God. Resting in God, as the vicar said. Let's get out the albums and talk about . . . everything.' Her face had acquired light. Hope looked out of her eyes. 'I'm sure it would do us both good,' she said, releasing Charlotte's hands, preparing to rise.

Charlotte flinched. Claire was another person now, a wraith of a person with strange and frightening powers. She couldn't think of her as a flesh-and-blood girl. 'No,' she said.

Vivien looked bewildered. 'Oh, well,' she said in a defeated voice. 'I'm glad you've been to visit her grave.'

'I'll make you a cup of tea.' Charlotte headed for the door.

'I seem to be always having tea on my own,' Vivien said wanly when she returned with a tray bearing a single cup.

'I'm sorry. I'm awfully sorry.' Charlotte felt guilty. 'Of course I'll have one with you.' She went for a second cup and then settled in the chair opposite, saying brightly, 'I saw that William Card. He bought me a cream tea. Why don't we, you and I, go into Wylie and have a cream tea together? You could do with some fattening up. And they're truly yum.'

'That would be nice.' Vivien smiled. 'William Card?' she asked, looking at Charlotte with puzzled eyes.

'He's nicer than he looks. He told me about the anniversaries. That's why I went to the churchyard.' She added, 'Nobody told me about the anniversaries.'

'No,' said Vivien. 'Somehow, I don't know ... I suppose we didn't want to upset you. You never seemed to want to visit her grave. I did mention it once or twice in the early days but you brushed it aside.'

Charlotte didn't remember. 'Why did you give her that big bouquet? It was too grown-up. The posy was enough.'

'Posy?'

'The one without a card.'

'Every year there's a posy without a card. It's not mine.'

That just went to show, Charlotte thought, that ghosts didn't always get things right.

Charlotte told her friends about William taking her to tea. She was showing off. Her story raised a laugh.

'Old William Card! He must be a hundred.'

'He's twenty-eight,' said Flora Derwent knowledgeably.

They asked her to point out his window.

'If we stand and stare, and concentrate like mad, he'll look out. Then he'll have to take all of us to tea.'

They waited, breath held. After a while William walked past the window and sat down in his chair.

'Stare! Stare!' Flora hissed.

He turned his head. They panicked then, let out a banshee shriek and streaked away, knocking into people.

That night Charlotte dreamed she was walking towards a small pink house with a bow window. William was sitting there, behind the glass. He took off his spectacles and she saw he was crying.

She wakened in the morning sunk in gloom. After a while she knew it was guilt. The dream had faded but she remembered William's face as he looked down from his window when she was running away. She spent a miserable morning thinking about how kind he had been – paying for her tea, leaving flowers on Claire's grave.

In the afternoon she took a bus to Wylie-under-Lyne. Slowly she walked up the High Street to where he could see her from his window. She stood on the edge of the pavement outside Marilyn's Teashop for ages, but he didn't look.

She bought a choc ice and went home.

Chapter Eighteen

'Dad's got a fancy lady,' Yolande told Kenneth. They were both living in London now. Kenneth worked for a shipping firm, Yolande for a City financier.

It embarrassed Kenneth to think of his father sticking his dick into women. It was bad enough knowing he'd done it with their mother at one time. He couldn't imagine it now, not at their age. Yolande, exercising her sometimes cruel wit, said the fancy lady must be a bitch who came on heat only once in a while. Otherwise, how could you account for Robert's staying at home for weeks on end, then prowling off again. Being brought up with dogs and cats gave you a broad view of the randy male, Yolande said. She knew her father came home in the evenings in termtime because he always answered the telephone when she rang. She was not to know Robert's bitch was away in termtime teaching at Charlotte's school. Charlotte hadn't bothered to tell them that Miss Hurst had followed her. Sometimes Robert wondered why.

The shaming incident that had occurred beneath William's window troubled Charlotte. Sometimes she was tempted to blame her friends but she knew in her heart that she had initiated it. She wanted to make amends.

An opportunity arose when she was in Wylie-under-Lyne looking for Christmas presents. In the High Street, outside Marilyn's Teashop, she paused beneath the windows of Fenton, Lodge and Carruthers, shivering. It was a raw day. The wind hurtled along the High Street. Her ears were freezing. She pulled her anorak hood up against the wind, pushed her hands down into her cosy pockets and decided to give William ten minutes. It was too cold to stand there longer than that. She wished she had enough spare pocket money to treat herself to a cream tea.

A pleased voice behind her said, 'Hello, Charlotte,' and she swung round. 'I thought that was you under the hood,' said William, his thin face drawn into lines of smiles. He was hunched into a dark Crombie, the kind of coat her father wore, and he carried an important-looking briefcase. He had wound a thick woollen scarf round his neck two or three times so that it came up to cover his ears. His pale eyes shone through the metal-framed glasses.

'Tea?' he said.

'Oh, William, I didn't mean . . .' She grinned, embarrassed.

'We need warming up,' he said, and steered her inside.

Charlotte made for the centre table. Even before taking off her anorak, she pulled out the chair facing the door and sat down in full view of the people coming in. That was an apology of a kind.

'I'm so glad to see you,' William said, putting his briefcase down on the floor with such airy carelessness that it tipped over, divesting himself of the heavy coat so ham-fistedly that the waitress had to come to his aid. He couldn't take his eyes off Charlotte. They roved up and down her face as though he had never seen anything so desirable. As though he couldn't believe she had actually come to see him. As though a long-nurtured dream had come true.

'And I'm glad to see you,' she said kindly. She felt older than he. She felt she was doing a charitable deed.

The tea came. 'I'm getting good at this,' she said as she poured. They tucked into scones and strawberry jam.

He put his knife down, dropped his hands awkwardly to his sides and blurted out like a schoolboy, 'I don't suppose you'd like to come with me to my firm's dinner dance?'

She nearly said, 'You're joking!' Yolande went to a dinner dance once, or so she boasted. But she had been nearly twenty at the time. Charlotte's mind leaped to Max, who said you should experience everything, once. 'Yes,' she said recklessly. 'Thanks, I'd like to. What should I wear?'

'It's black tie,' said William.

Black tie! She looked down at her plate so he wouldn't see she hadn't a clue what he meant.

'William Card?' Vivien echoed. Disbelief spread across her face.

Robert said intolerantly, 'Couldn't you find someone your own age?'

'Someone my age wouldn't ask me to a dinner dance.'

Robert, who was sitting by her on the sofa, rubbed her shoulder fondly, looked into her face. 'Don't grow up too fast, my sweet. There'll be plenty of dinner dances later on. And I really don't think an outing with that Card chap is much of a bargain.'

'He's been very kind to me,' said Charlotte.

'What? How?'

'He takes me out to tea. Cream teas with strawberry jam.'

'Oh, that,' said her mother, with a smile. 'Well, you were going to take me, remember? You never mentioned it again.'

Charlotte had forgotten. 'Right, we'll go tomorrow,' she said. 'But please let me go to the dinner dance. Just this once. I won't want to do it again. William said I have to wear a black tie.'

'Oh, darling, you *are* too young,' said her mother, laughing. '*He* wears a black tie. You know how Daddy dresses when he goes to formal functions. He means you should dress formally.'

'Funny way to put it.' Charlotte felt sheepish. 'What would you call formal, for me?'

'At your age, your Laura Ashley would do.'

What had a Laura Ashley granny dress in common with a black tie? She didn't ask. That would be to underline what her mother had said, that she was too young to go to a dinner dance.

They were awkward with William when he came to pick her up. He looked very long and thin, somehow elongated in the black suit. But he was vastly improved. Charlotte thought, Wouldn't Max look smashing dressed like that? He had brushed his hair back tonight. It was running away across his head as though frightened by the smartness of his clothes.

Robert looked hard at them both, first at William, then at Charlotte, as though, being a fair-minded man, he was checking to be sure he had been justified in thinking William was too old to be escorting his schoolgirl daughter.

William turned down the offer of a drink, saying they didn't really have time. Charlotte was relieved. She hurried out to the car, pulling her jacket round her, afraid William might take her arm if it was hanging free. She didn't want him to do that; particularly, she didn't want her parents to see him do it. Their critical reception of him had made her nervous and unsure.

He drove the kind of car wives drive – a small family saloon. She recalled as she slipped into the passenger seat that Max was going to buy a sports Bentley, circa 1935, when he was earning big money. She understood most people had salaries but Big Money was what Max expected to have.

William drove circumspectly, stopping dead according to the rules. Max made nonsense of conventions like double yellow lines, double white lines, NO PARKING signs. 'I'll only be one minute!' he would say to an attendant, holding up a finger, dashing away. He was at ease when flouting the law. He extracted smiles or shrugs from men who treated other people sternly.

'I can't tell you how honoured I am to be escorting you,' William said while they waited at a traffic light for the moment when the orange turned to green.

'I've come this far travelling on orange,' Max would have said. 'I'm not going to change my habits now. What do you bet I can get right across before it turns green?'

Charlotte scrambled through her mind for the sort of jokey comments that came so easily when she was out with Max. Nothing presented itself. She was aware of William's sending quick little glances her way, as though making sure she hadn't disappeared. She turned her head to look out of the window, though there was nothing to be seen in the darkness.

The house where the dinner dance was being held was very grand. William said it had been converted by a consortium who had the money to restore it to its original glory – decorative plaster ceiling, cherubs cavorting among vines. Climbing the impressive staircase, Charlotte became aware of entering a grown-up world where she didn't belong. She glanced down at the Laura Ashley dress and crossed her fingers.

Everyone turned, it seemed to Charlotte, as they entered the room. A grand-looking flunkey in a red coat announced them: Miss Charlotte Godfrey and Mr William Card. The room was full of men in black suits and ties with gleaming white shirt fronts, and glamorously dressed women. Charlotte panicked, certain everyone was asking, 'What's that schoolgirl doing at our dinner dance?' It had been a terrible mistake to come. But William's hand was on her arm and suddenly a big man was standing in front of her, smiling.

'Isn't this Robert Godfrey's daughter?'

William said, 'Charlotte, this is Mr Fenton, our senior partner.'

Mr Fenton's wife didn't wait to be introduced. Looking approvingly at Charlotte's dress – or was it pointedly? – she said, 'Hello, my dear. How nice to see you here,' though clearly she was astonished, too. That she should be here? Or that she should have come with dull old William? Charlotte was uneasy, not knowing whether to be flattered or dismayed.

After dinner, older men took her from William and danced with her, one after the other, just as though William wasn't there. She recognised she had novelty value as a sixteen-year-old. William minded; she could tell by the way his shoulders slumped. Max would have leaped on to the floor with her immediately the band struck up, foiling them, but William didn't have his confidence. Besides, these men were his superiors. They wore an air of being able to do exactly what they liked because William didn't count. She disliked being clasped to their stiff shirt fronts while they pushed her soberly round the room. It was like being propelled by barrels on wheels.

The band suddenly went into an old sixties jive tune, 'Lollipop, Lollipop, oh, Lolli- Lolli- Lollipop'. To her astonishment, William sprang out of his chair and rushed her on to the floor. He swung her out on the end of his long arm and they whirled like dervishes. He lost his steel-rimmed glasses. Seemed not to notice. When the music stopped everyone laughed and clapped; they went back to their seats flushed with success.

Somebody picked up William's glasses, brought them to him, clapped him on the back. He took them carelessly, as though he could very well do without them, anyway. She thought the atmosphere in the room had changed. The onlookers' amusement was tinged with something like respect. Charlotte smiled across the table at him. He put his glasses on very carefully and looked at her like a dog who has peed on the carpet.

When he dropped her at her home, he said earnestly, as she fumbled in her little bag for the front-door key, 'I was so proud. May I kiss you?'

156

She lifted her face politely as she would to an uncle or aunt. He gave her a dry little kiss on the mouth – the kind that belonged on a cheek. You would think the whirling dervish had never been.

In that final year at school, Charlotte put her head down and kept it there.

'You're working too hard,' Isabel said. 'You'll get into Oxford without making a martyr of yourself.'

Isabel didn't know how important it was. That getting to Oxford didn't only mean reading English and history. It meant she would have two years away from home with Max. Bliss that his trip round the world put him one year back. An extra year to share with her. She took the crystal with her when she sat the exams. She confidently expected it to help.

The summer holidays had just started when Max came home. He telephoned.

Charlotte had been pottering in old jeans. She charged up to her room, heart racing, and flicked through her wardrobe, looking for flattering clothes. She pulled out an apple-green blouse and skirt, remembering her mother saying that the colour enhanced the green of her eyes. Her cheeks were hot. Would they be shy with each other? She brushed her hair over her shoulders, grimaced in the mirror, fixed it on top of her head, changed her mind again and brushed it down, tied it with a ribbon at the nape of her neck, then flung the ribbon on her bed and left her hair hanging loose.

On tiptoe with excitement, she went downstairs to wait for him. Would he have changed? Had he fallen in love with an Australian girl? Would he still like her? She went down the drive to meet him. What would he do? What should she do? Would he kiss her? Would they be strangers?

He was ages coming. Folly Hill was only a few minutes from Puddle Lane by car. He'd got a puncture, she thought. Changed his mind. Detoured to visit someone else on the way.

He arrived on his bike, flushed but not out of breath. She remembered he had always been free of shackles. A bike was as good as, and rather more exciting than, the kind of car he had access to. He stared at her.

She stared back at him. The change in him was extraordinary, though he still carried that slightly delinquent look that so charmed people. How tall he was!

157

As though he read her startled, eager mind he said, 'Five foot ten and a half and still growing. Ha! They put fertiliser in your food Down Under.'

Only five foot ten? He gave an illusion of height far beyond that. Radiance spread through her. He was more a man than a youth, now. Marvellously strong-looking, and brown as a hazelnut.

'Same old house,' he said, hands in pockets gazing up at the vine-hung gables, as though getting his bearings. She recognised his emotions, remembered how, on her return from the Canaries, she had found everything strange, though the same. Perhaps being abroad did that to you.

They walked in the garden. She felt as though part of her was skimming the treetops, out of control. He was looking round with intense interest, taking Folly Hill in.

'Did you kill a snake?' she asked, remembering his boast, though that was years and years ago. The experiences that had brought him to five foot ten and a half must have been infinitely greater than that.

He replied, 'No, but I hit one with a spade.'

They went to the little white gate that looked over Farmer Abraham's fields. The hay was drying in the sun. Max leaned on the bar, his eyes sweeping over the valley. 'I'm glad to be back,' he said, and seemed at that moment to put the Australian experience behind him. 'It's Oxford now. Onward and upward.' He spoke as though he could see into a golden future where he would play a distinguished part.

They went through the gate, wandered in the field. Found themselves after a while in Puddle Lane. They went on to the pub and sat in the beer garden, talking, talking. The past year fled away. Coming back up Folly Hill, they moved together like steel to magnet. He kissed her on the lips, the eyelids.

'My God,' he said, and she could have sworn there was a tremor in his voice, 'I've missed you. I was scared rigid you'd go away, or change.'

Oxford swallowed him. She went back to Mountfield Manor to work like a donkey so that she could be certain of joining him the next year. At Christmas she saw little of him. He had taken a job with a wine merchant and was staying in London with one of his undergraduate friends who was working with him.

'What do you do in the evenings?' She was jealous of his new friends who were seeing so much of him.

'When you've spent all day heaving crates of wine, you only want to go to bed,' he said. His eyes twinkled. 'Alone.'

She caught her breath.

He told her about life at Oxford, saying he wished he could ask her to a May ball. 'I won't go,' he said. 'I can't actually afford the tickets.'

'Wouldn't your father pay?' She momentarily forgot Dr Fosse was the meanest father in Forge Green.

'Anyway, I wouldn't let him,' said Max grandly. Charlotte was glad, though ashamed of her gladness, that if he couldn't go to the ball, he wouldn't be taking another girl.

'Do you want to have a year off before university?' Robert asked.

'No. Thanks all the same. Yolande didn't.'

'Yolande didn't work the way you've worked. Secretarial college isn't quite like Lady Margaret Hall.' Robert was indulgent. Immensely proud.

'No thanks. I'm really anxious to get to Oxford.'

'Has this got anything to do with young Max Fosse being there?' asked Robert shrewdly.

'I haven't even told him I've been offered a place,' she said airily. 'I expect he'll be surprised.'

'You!' said Max, pretending amazement. 'What's this lust for education? You're only a woman. Women, historically, are serfs. Men for the use of. What's the world coming to?' She could see he was pleased and proud.

Miraculously, his father didn't make him take a job that summer. He had to work, though, to be sure of passing his prelims. He had to get a first.

Max said, 'I won't, of course. Why should I give up all the fun? A good second will do for me.'

Sometimes his mother lent him her car and they dashed down to the south coast for a swim, or up to London to watch cricket at the Oval, where his father was a member. Once they told their parents they were going to stay with some of his undergraduate friends at a beach house in Cornwall. They didn't. They slept on the beach and talked all night. Talked? Well . . .

159

Halfway through that first night, Max flung himself away and dashed down to the water in the dark. When he came back, dripping and naked, he said, 'My God, Char, you nearly lost your virginity then. I'd better go into Falmouth and visit a chemist. That is, if you'd like to lose it tomorrow.'

She was aware he wasn't persuading her. She reached up and pulled him down beside her. 'I'd have let you,' she said sweetly.

He put his wet arm round her and held her close. 'That way lies great trouble, darling.'

She ran a finger over his dark eyebrows, then slid it down his cheek. 'It has to happen when we can't help it happening,' she said. 'When . . . let it be like it could have been then.'

When he kissed her tenderly, she felt he understood. He disappeared in the town next morning and returned without explanation.

They must drive up to the north coast, he said. He knew a little bay where the surf was wild. He had learned to surf in Australia on Bondi Beach. She told him about Fernando who had taught her how to catch a wave. 'Consorting with foreigners,' he said, frowning, tut-tutting, making her laugh.

'That's all there is on La Gomera. Foreigners.' That night the island seemed a million miles away.

A cool wind sent clouds scudding across the sky, drove the waves roaring inshore. Max met an undergraduate friend and borrowed his surfboard. Charlotte stood on the beach, watching as he swam out to the last wave, then spun in, erect, like a young god.

'He's an expert, all right,' said the friend admiringly. Charlotte glowed with pride.

That evening they met up with some more undergraduates in the local pub. One of them said, 'Come and stay the night with us.' His family had taken a cottage. They said no thanks, they were lodging under the stars.

'Good for you,' he replied enviously.

They said goodnight to their friends and wandered off down the cliff path for a moonlight swim.

The sea had calmed and they floated, looking up at the moon from their watery bed. They kissed with salty lips as they dried themselves on the beach, then ran back up the steps and strolled the half-mile back to the woods where they had left the car in a lay-by.

They took a rug, climbed the slope above the road in silence. They both knew what was going to happen. The bed of leaves was on the edge of a copse. Moonlight shafted in. In silence they spread the rug. A badger, caught in a bright band of moonlight, stared at them with its night eyes for a moment before shuffling away. A cloud crept over the moon. Soft, velvet darkness spread around them. Charlotte slipped out of her jeans and T-shirt then lay down by Max's side. His arm was silky, and tasted of salt when she kissed it. He came up on one elbow, leaned over, touched his lips to hers, caressed them with butterfly wing kisses.

'Remember the first time you kissed me? On the log? I was twelve.'

'Bliss to be alive,' murmured Max. 'At twelve, or eighteen, or twenty.' He put his arms round her, drawing her close. Closer, moving with the whispering ferns and the forest creatures, to become a part of the whole. He was gentle. Possessing without being possessive.

She whispered, 'I love you, Max. I'll never love anyone else.' This was the moment to say it, she thought; to make an affirmation and a promise to the gods. They were both aware of having come a long way, all their growing-up time. They were approaching the top of the highest mountain in the world. The mountain brought them physical rapture in a burst of stars that floated away on their dreams.

Charlotte is aware of the faint crackle of dry leaves and in the distance a sound as of high waves thundering against the shore. She can see a slim figure approaching across the darkened sea. Apricot-coloured hair floating on the wind, filmy garments trailing. She comes closer and Charlotte knows it is Claire, but she can't see her face. The spray obscures her, then clears. Still she can't see the face. How does she know it's Claire? She knows, just as she knows Claire has come on a journey that perhaps she ought not to be taking. She is blowing towards her, bringing darkness in.

Charlotte feels unsafe. Is she on a cliff, about to fall, or jump, or be dragged off? On a rock, to be carried away by the waves? Claire is telling her something she does not want to hear. It is about Max. A threat. 'I won't allow Max and you –' she is saying fiercely.

Charlotte does not listen. She raises her arms and with all her strength she pushes Claire away. Sends her back into the darkness because she cannot bear to hear the vengeful words she is saying.

'Mmn, mmn,' says Max, flinging an arm over her, nuzzling his face into her neck. 'Bad dream?'

'Hold me!' she cries. 'Hold me tight.'

He does, but the unsafe feeling stays.

Chapter Nineteen

Oxford! At last they could see each other every day. Charlotte was jealously aware of the friends Max had made in his first year. He was like a magnet the way he drew people.

Girls hovered like butterflies round a flower. He conferred status on them. Yet the boundary fences were there. The undergraduates leaned on those fences, soaking up his magic, nourishing themselves with it. If you asked what did he do for this adoring public, nothing. He took more often than he gave, but his ease of taking made them feel both magnanimous and favoured.

Charlotte slipped into her special place. Hit P on the computer. Protected. No one, nothing, can dislodge her, even touch her, for she is Max's protected property.

On Valentine's Day the post brought her a Victorian gold necklace exquisitely wrought, each section set with a tiny pearl. 'Oh, Max!' Charlotte felt tearfully emotional as she lifted it from its bed of cream silk. Pushing away her shirt collar, she clasped the lovely chain round her neck. She was deeply touched. He had so little to spend. He worked hard in the holidays but the money he earned was not to be used for pleasure. His father said he must, as far as possible, pay his way.

'Dad thinks it's character-forming to be kept short,' he would say. He was good-humoured about it as though he felt it wasn't such a bad thing to be kept short.

Yet he had saved enough to buy this beautiful and surely expensive necklace for her! She saw it as representing hours and hours of hard labour shifting cases of wine. 'Oh, Max!' she said again, and wiped away an emotional tear.

As luck would have it, she had an opportunity to wear the

necklace that very night. A group of undergraduates were giving a fancy-dress party in a house they shared. Yolande had sent Charlotte a fairy-on-the-Christmas-tree costume she had borrowed from her flatmate. Charlotte was delighted with it. Its white tulle skirt sat like a wobbly button mushroom on her hips, exposing every inch of her long legs.

She hadn't told Max what she would be wearing. He, too, had kept his costume secret. 'You won't know me,' he said, but she knew she would. How could she not?

She went along in a group of girls. It wasn't far to walk. The party was held in a big Victorian villa surrounded by trees in a quiet road. The abundant foliage absorbed some of the music but when they entered the hall, which was already packed with gyrating animals, clowns, witches, kings and queens, the noise was deafening.

'We've warned the neighbours,' shouted a tawny lion who was one of the hosts. 'They've fled to Timbuktu.'

'You've come on your own?'

Turning, Charlotte looked up at one of Max's friends. 'Is this where I step in?' he whispered in her ear.

'Step in for a dance,' Charlotte riposted, wobbling her hips to set the mushroom of tulle shivering like thistledown, teasing him.

'Such legs!' he said. He caught her round the waist and she saw with astonishment how it could be, would be, if Max wasn't there.

'You don't see blokes, do you?' her partner shouted over the beat of the music. 'Have a look at me while you've got the chance.'

'Golly, yes,' she shouted back, opening her green eyes wide. 'I'm noticing you now.'

He leaned closer. 'Can I come to your room afterwards?'

'Sure. Sure,' she shouted back. 'Everybody up to my room. Why not?'

He made a gesture of resignation. 'Ah, well. It'll have to be kidnap and rape.'

Even as she laughed with him, she was aware that you could be lonely while having the greatest fun, if Max wasn't there.

The lights went out, leaving two spots angled down from a ceiling corner. A creeping figure dressed in black moved into the spotlight, carrying a three-pronged fork.

'Who is it?' they cried as his evil form slid in and out of the dancers, snatching at girls, spitting like a cat. Some of the sillier guests shrieked with terror. He put on speed, dived between them, pointed the fork. Stab. Stab. The party disrupted in chaos. He crept into an adjoining room; returned to threaten those sitting on the stairs; then went up to the landing with another spotlight following.

'Turn on the lights! Turn them on!' There were shrill cries from all over.

Charlotte felt a thrill of fear as the creature crept downstairs again. She could tell he had singled her out. Then she saw the colour of his eyes behind the mask. She flung herself away from her partner as the lights went up and waved her fairy wand over the devil head.

'You shall be transformed into a handsome prince,' she cried in ringing tones. He dropped his three-pronged fork, pulled off his hood and mask, and stood erect, the best-looking man in the room.

'Evil is the other side of good,' he said, and kissed her hand. 'Come and get a paper cup of hooch, good fairy.' She went with him, feeling all their eyes on her. Max's friends called out to him:

'Hell of a show, Max!'

'Yeah, you've always been a bit of a devil, haven't you?'

He didn't seem to notice that she was wearing the necklace. She knew that was deliberate, because of its being a Valentine gift, but she wanted to thank him. An opportunity presented itself as they sat on the stairs later, eating spaghetti and tossed salad.

'I love the necklace,' she mumbled and looked away, pretending she hadn't said it.

'What necklace?' He gave it a cursory glance, giving most of his attention to balancing the long strings of spaghetti. 'Oh, that. Where did you get it, spoilt brat?'

'It was a Valentine,' she said, 'from someone who loves me.'

'I'll kill him,' said Max good-naturedly. 'I'll stab him with my devil's fork.'

She laughed and hugged his free arm, loving him fiercely. She thought she was the luckiest girl in the world.

Next day one of her friends said to her, 'You two looked amazing together last night. Clever of you to plan a good-and-evil tableau.'

Charlotte explained that they hadn't planned it together.

The girl looked at her oddly. 'Chance is a fine thing.' She added, 'Max's devil was rather too good. I overheard people say—'

'What did they say?'

'I'm sorry. I shouldn't have brought it up. But I do wonder if you need a warning. You're besotted, aren't you?'

Besotted? She was taken aback by the choice of word. She knew herself to exist on a tide of loving energy. Tides were pulled by the moon. The moon was Max, as well as the sun. 'No,' she said. 'I'm not besotted. That's not right.'

'People were saying last night they thought there was more to Max than met the eye. Why would he want to scare us all out of our wits? The spotlights were his, apparently. I heard he set it all up in the afternoon.'

'He's one for doing things properly,' she said proudly.

'Charlotte, listen to me.'

'I've known him since we were at baby school together,' she said airily.

'Does that make him safe?'

'Who wants to be safe!' She laughed and did a little hop and a skip along the pavement. She understood girls might be jealous of her.

Next time she saw Max, she said, 'You frightened people in your devil's costume. They think you might have typecast yourself.'

'And you,' he retorted. 'Would you, angel of mercy and rich bitch, like to take a poor devil to tea before I starve to death?'

'Delighted,' she said. They broke into a run and didn't stop until they reached the teashop.

'What are you smiling at?' he asked as they tucked into cakes and scones.

'I was remembering my other lover who takes me out to tea. Cream teas, even.' She flapped her long eyelashes at him, teasing.

'I'll kill him,' said Max as he had before, looking fierce, stabbing a cake with his fork. 'Who is he?'

'William Card.'

Max leaned back in his chair and roared with such hearty laughter that he set the other patrons smiling. 'That's my good fairy – spreading light,' he said.

She retorted loyally, 'He's very kind.'

'I'm sure he is. William Card! Well!'

That term, one of the undergraduates asked Charlotte if she would like to join a pro-life campaign. 'We call ourselves pro-life but it's anti-abortion, really,' the girl said. 'There's a meeting tonight. We're organising a rally. If we can get enough people to march we might go down to London and set up something big in Trafalgar Square. Do you fancy carrying a placard?'

Charlotte considered for the first time that the faceless woman who had given birth to her and Claire might easily have had an abortion. She consulted Max.

'It's interfering with people's free will,' he said.

She thought about that night on the beach in Cornwall. Of what he had said when he came back to her after rushing into the sea.

'That was me exercising my free will,' he said, muddling her. 'I wouldn't want you to abort my child. But you shouldn't tell other people what to do with their bodies. Just be ready to help them when what they've done turns out wrong.'

'When they do wrong?'

'I didn't say that. I said "when what they've done turns out wrong".' She recognised in his words his generosity of spirit.

She lay in bed that night gazing at the ceiling, thinking of what she would have missed if she and Claire, as two little seeds, had been scraped out of that woman's womb. She would not have known Max! Yolande and Kenneth. Her parents. But especially Max.

For the first time, she began to think of the woman – she did not see her as their mother for she had never been that – as a real person. Flesh and blood. But faceless still, by choice. Charlotte's choice.

It was possible to accept that a womb which had neither features nor personality could reject them. She thought of it as a nest in which she and Claire had been allowed to mature from embryos to fully formed babies, emerging in the fullness of time to fly to the family who wanted them.

Had the owner of that womb contemplated abortion? Would she and Claire have been little people with features by the time the womb gave its owner the message that it harboured life? She borrowed some books from a medical student and found out exactly how far developed she and Claire would have been when this womb had held them for two weeks, four weeks, six weeks, or months.

She visualised two little people with eyes, ears, arms, legs, a brain even, being scraped out of that womb into a bucket. Heard the whoosh of blood as they went down a drain. She shivered and curled tightly into herself, pulling the blankets round her, feeling unsafe in her imagination.

She decided she would join the pro-life campaign.

After all, Max helped her make her placard. 'Girls are hopeless with hammer and nails,' he said tolerantly. 'If you must run other people's lives, at least I can see you don't smash your fingers.'

She loved him for his tolerance. She didn't tell him what had decided her, what she had worked out in the night. Didn't tell anyone. She used the woman's goodwill in harbouring her and Claire as vindication for, as Max said, interfering in other people's lives.

DOWN WITH ABORTION she painted in large letters on her placard with the black paint the committee was handing out. She was zealous in her campaigning. The picture of two little people flying out of a bucket and disappearing down a drain had etched itself on her mind.

It was the first weekend of Charlotte's summer vacation. Oliver and Yolande were in the Folly Hill kitchen with her, making tea.

A storm had come up, blacking out television. Vivien had gone to her room with a headache. She always got a headache, now, when thunder was in the air. She had put on weight. Her hair was dull and badly needed styling. Charlotte wanted to suggest she go to the hairdresser.

'Mum doesn't care how she looks,' said Yolande, preening in the kitchen mirror.

'Do you like Yol's new hairdo?' Oliver asked Charlotte.

'Love it. It suits her.' Sharp little points on her cheeks, and a soft fringe. Yolande looked very pretty today.

'Oh, thanks,' said Yolande. 'A present from my dearly beloved.' She put her arms round Oliver and hugged him.

Charlotte smiled fondly at them.

'You'd only be rubbing in her plight if you started talking about colour rinses,' Yolande said. 'What's she got to look good for? She doesn't go out.'

Oliver took some biscuits out of a tin and put them on a plate.

'Why doesn't she?' Charlotte poured some hot water into the kitchen teapot and reached for the caddy.

168

'You may as well know now you're a big girl,' said Yolande in her funny way, aiming the plastic whisk savagely, knocking a blow-fly to the tiles, gazing upon it as it lay stunned. 'Dad's got a mistress.'

'*What*!' Charlotte turned so sharply that she caught her foot on the table leg, hurling a jet of hot water across the tiles.

'He's had her for years. I should think ever since he moved out of their bedroom. You'd better get the mop, hadn't you?'

Charlotte was reeling.

'Sorry if I shocked you. You should have noticed yourself – him moving out of the communal quarters, I mean. Years ago.'

Oliver said wryly, 'I'm teaching Yol the soft approach. She'll be into it by next week. Bear with her.'

Charlotte headed numbly in the direction of the utility room. Brought back a mop. Dealt with the water. Tried to remember. Vivien and Robert seemed always to have slept in separate rooms. 'Who is this woman?'

'Who, we don't know. But she lives in Wylie. At 5 Cherry Tree Road, Wylie-under-Lyne,' said Yolande, enunciating the words distinctly, giving them a theatrical discommendation.

'How do you know?' Distress had brought colour into Charlotte's cheeks.

'Oliver just happened to be in that road, Cherry Tree Road, and saw him marching up the path bold as brass. He took a key out of his pocket and put it in the lock. I wouldn't have told you if I'd thought you were going to cry,' said Yolande impatiently, 'but you're nineteen now.'

Charlotte blinked hard. 'I'm not crying.' She was. Crying inside. Recognising with surging compassion what had been bothering her about Vivien for ages. That getting fatter, slower, less interested, more drab, could be a cry for help. She remembered a time when they'd been having a buffet lunch in the conservatory. Two of the uncles were there. Vivien had heaped her plate with food for the second time. Uncle Alan said, 'You're a good trencherwoman these days, Viv.' Yolande, white-faced, with stormy eyes, snatched the plate away and put it on a side table. Vivien didn't react. Robert rose from his seat, crossed with light footsteps to the side table and handed the overloaded plate back to her. Silence descended on the gathering. Then Yolande flounced out. Oliver, looking resigned, went after her to calm her down. Charlotte thought now, Yol's right. He doesn't care.

'Don't interfere in other people's lives, Max would have said, but Vivien wasn't other people. She was her mother. And she minded terribly what Robert was doing to her. Charlotte began asking herself how she could help.

Later, when Vivien came downstairs, Charlotte went to her and hugged her. 'I'm so glad you're feeling better,' she said. She felt close in her contrition, filled with sorrowful love. 'I've got an apology to make,' she said. 'A hundred years ago I promised to take you to have a cream tea in Wylie. Let's go.'

Vivien looked pleased. 'How you exaggerate! Yes, I'd like that.'

'And why don't we buy you a pretty dress while we're there? You need some nice new outfits.'

'I've got masses of them in my wardrobe,' Vivien replied, as though that was all one needed to do with clothes: own them. Charlotte looked at the mud-coloured blouse her mother wore with a baggy green skirt. 'What I wear is suitable for the kind of life I lead,' Vivien said. Charlotte ached for her, understanding she meant the life she led as the neglected wife of a man with a mistress.

During the holidays she took Vivien up to London. To matinées. To lunch with Yolande in the City. They ate jammed together in a restaurant packed with City men.

'It's the best place I know for food,' Yolande said. 'Can't afford it myself,' she added airily, 'but since Mum's paying . . .'

Vivien smiled her wan smile and said she was glad to be of use.

'By the way,' said Yolande, addressing Charlotte, 'that necklace of yours. Did you ever find out who sent it?'

Charlotte's eyes filled up with secrets. 'You don't find out about Valentines.'

'I bet you do know. I can tell by the way you're looking,' said Yolande, digging. 'Was it Max?'

'I told you.' She didn't like Yolande stamping heavy-footed on her hallowed ground. 'You're not supposed to know.'

'Well, I expect it was. I was going to say I saw one like it – anyway, similar – in one of those antique jewellery shops in the Burlington Arcade. It had earrings to match. It occurred to me that yours probably had matching earrings in the beginning. Didn't Victorians wear long dangly earrings with that kind of necklace, Mum?'

'I'm not *that* old, darling.' Vivien was touchy when she wasn't turned in on herself.

'I credited you with knowing your jewellery,' Yolande said, leaning across the table and affectionately shaking Vivien's wrist, making amends for once, though it wasn't her style. 'Come on, give us a smile.'

The idea of looking for a gift for Charlotte seemed to lift Vivien. 'We could prowl round the antique shops,' she said. 'I'd like that.'

They didn't find the earrings, but Vivien seemed brighter for having found even such a tiny mission.

She seemed to enjoy Charlotte taking her out. One day she said, as they walked up Wylie High Street, 'I'm sure you'd rather be running around with your friends.'

'My friends are all working. All one of them,' Charlotte replied, meaning Max was the only friend she wanted to see. 'There's William Card, of course.' It struck her that she always used his surname, as though he needed more identification than other people. She looked sideways at Vivien. 'If we pause under his window, he might notice us. That's what I do sometimes. I mesmerise him into glancing out of the window. He never fails to dash down the stairs and buy me a cream tea. Shall we do it now?'

'Oh, no,' said Vivien hurriedly, but laughing. 'That's very naughty of you, dear. Haven't you been taught never to take unless you intend to give something back?'

'Sorry, Mum.' Charlotte grinned but she made a point of not looking up at the window with the gold lettering, FENTON, LODGE & CARRUTHERS. Nonetheless, William must have seen them, for only moments after they were seated he came through the door like a tall plant being hurled towards them in a storm.

Vivien graciously indicated a chair. 'Do join us,' she said.

William gave her a lot of his attention, but second-hand, scarcely taking his eyes off Charlotte. Vivien said afterwards, tolerantly, 'I suppose he's not a bad sort. But you shouldn't take advantage, dear.'

Charlotte thought she knew her value to William. He was harmless and kind, and saw her as a treat. It didn't hurt her to bring a little sunshine into his solitary life.

Robert and Vivien both, separately, thought it odd that Charlotte should want to invite one of her former teachers to Folly Hill.

171

'If you don't want her to stay here, I could meet her in London,' Charlotte said, looking at her father out of the corners of her eyes.

'No, no,' Robert said hastily. 'Of course we're delighted to have her.'

Charlotte noticed that Robert didn't look at Vivien as he spoke, yet answered for her, as though she had no rights. They were sitting in front of the television, watching a travel programme. Her parents were there because she was there. They both wished to be with her and that meant they had to be with each other. Now that Charlotte knew about Robert's mistress, she was conscious of the silences when she came into a room. She noted every nuance of Robert's behaviour and every reaction of Vivien's. She wanted to do something to bring them together.

'Why don't the three of us go for a holiday?' she suggested, looking directly at Robert. 'Mum and you and me. Italy looks lovely.' She thought she saw a light flare in Robert's eyes.

'Not me,' he said. 'I haven't the time. But do take your mother, darling.'

I'm not your darling, Charlotte thought. Not now I've seen how you diminish my mother. When he put an arm round her she shrugged it away, wishing she could forcibly fix it round Vivien's shoulders.

The subject came up again when Yolande and Kenneth came home for the weekend. The family was gathered in the conservatory at sundown. Robert had dispensed drinks and was now settled in a cane chair. Yolande, dead-heading a summer clematis while holding a gin and tonic in one hand, said, 'Why don't you take Isabel to Italy if Dad doesn't want to go?'

'Can't, Yolande,' said Robert, correcting her mildly. 'Can't.'

She paused behind his chair, looking down on the crown of his head. 'Is business that bad? Are we all going on bread-and-butter rations next week?' she asked, rashly allowing ill-feeling to break through. 'You haven't had a holiday in years. Why not?'

Oliver, crossing the room, squeezed her arm as he passed and gave her a wry, thoughtful look. Charlotte suppressed a smile, remembering him saying he was teaching her the soft approach.

Robert's mouth tightened. Then the telephone rang and he heaved himself to his feet.

'Saved by the bell,' Yolande muttered sotto voce.

'Don't needle him, dear,' said Vivien, showing nervousness in

172

a trembling of her hands, the fingers intertwining, looking at the door he had shut carefully, too carefully, behind him. 'I expect he has business troubles.'

'Did you see a dirty gleam come into his eyes when I suggested the three of you go off to Italy?' Yolande asked Charlotte later as they wandered in the garden. 'Have you noticed his hair? He'll be bald as a coot in a few years.' She was bitter in her satisfaction. 'Dirty old man! I'll bet if you go to Italy he'll be halfway to number 5 Cherry Tree Road with an erection wobbling along in front of him before the plane's taken off.'

Such overt disrespect shocked Charlotte. She could accept, now, that Robert had a mistress, but not the detail. 'I gather you do it with Oliver,' she said crossly, paying Yolande out.

She responded carelessly, 'What do you think? We're more or less engaged. I dare say you do it with Max.'

'No,' said Charlotte, forcefully protecting their precious privacy. 'As you said, I'm only nineteen.' What she and Max had between them was sacred.

Isabel came and with her, torrents of talk. She kept in touch with many of her ex-pupils. Charlotte told her about Oxford, and sometimes a little about Max. But talking diluted people. She liked to hoard the essence of Max when they were apart. Isabel agreed to go to Italy with them. Charlotte took her into Wylie-under-Lyne, ostensibly to show her the town, but in truth to reconnoitre for Vivien's holiday clothes. Stella Bloomingdale said huffily, 'I haven't seen your mother for years. I can't imagine how I could have offended her. Certainly I've got some lovely casual wear that would suit her. Bring her in.'

'Such clothes,' breathed Isabel, closing her eyes against the twin sins of envy and covetousness. Isabel with her squeaky clean blonde hair, slender figure and immense style would look marvellous in Bloomingdale's clothes. She and Charlotte walked up the High Street together.

'I'll take you to Waites,' Charlotte said. 'That's this town's sole department store. They have some nice things.'

Isabel said, 'Nice things will do very well for me.' Now they were no longer constrained by the relationship of pupil and teacher, Isabel gave of herself generously, the fun side Charlotte had not been permitted to see at school.

They went up in the escalator to the first floor. Louisa, wearing a yellow dress, was standing idly in Ladies' Wear. Her blonde curls, ash blonde now, drifted down her back.

'Hello, Charlotte,' she said prettily.

'Hello,' said Charlotte, seeing baby Louisa standing in the long grass, one cheek bulging with a sweet she had bought for Claire. She shut off thought and feeling, turned and walked away.

Isabel called, 'Charlotte! I need your opinion,' but she didn't hear. Wouldn't hear. She went relentlessly on down the stairs.

At the perfume counter she paused, eying expensive gold-labelled bottles, wondering what Vivien would like, thinking she would bring her here to choose. First, Bloomingdales where she would insist on her buying floaty dresses and beach wraps that would disguise her figure. Plans dashed higgledy piggledy through her mind, pushing out Louisa with her bulging cheek.

Isabel, with a plastic bag slung from her wrist, eventually found her. 'What happened to you?'

'I had to retreat,' Charlotte returned with a nonchalant openness that did not accord with what was going on inside.

'Sorry.' Isabel's blue eyes flicked to a sign nearby that said LADIES. She extended the bag held lightly in her fingers. 'I got a beach wrap. Cheap and cheerful it looks after Bloomingdale's. We should have gone there last.'

'Hello, Charlotte.'

She looked up to see Louisa's father standing before her, formal in a navy-blue suit. He asked her how she was enjoying Oxford, and Charlotte introduced him to Isabel.

'We don't see much of your mother these days,' he said.

'I've been sussing out perfume for her. I'll bring her in,' Charlotte promised.

'Louisa's upstairs,' he said. 'In Ladies' Wear. I'm trying to encourage her to come into the business.' He explained to Isabel, 'She doesn't know what she wants to do – only that she doesn't want to work in the family store. But she's a good girl. Willing to try it out for holiday money.'

'Too young,' said Isabel, who could be forthright. 'You'll put her off.'

He shrugged.

'I s'pose he hasn't got a son to inherit,' Isabel said as they left.

'I can't imagine Louisa ever maturing into the kind of person who could run a department store,' Charlotte said savagely.

Isabel glanced at her in surprise. Charlotte looked away.

They were approaching Marilyn's Teashop. 'I want to show you a trick. If we pause here –' She rested a hand on Isabel's wrist. '*Pause*, Isabel. Just for a second. Say something important.'

Isabel was perplexed.

'Just look intense, then. I want a momentary tableau. Now, in we go.' She ushered Isabel across the pavement.

'What on earth are you up to?' Isabel looked baffled.

'I've got a puppet on a string.' Charlotte's eyes danced with mischief.

Isabel looked at her across the table with kind, inquisitive eyes. 'I saw your *bête noire* upstairs in Waites, over in the lingerie department. I don't think she saw me. It occurs to me to ask, have you grown out of that problem? It's Alison Hurst I'm talking about, of course.'

Charlotte fingered a spoon, eyes cast down. 'I have nothing against her now I don't have to see her. She's out of my life. There was something spooky about her coming to Mountfield Manor when I was there, that's all. It got to me.' She couldn't say that Miss Hurst, being the only person who didn't accept that she could not sing, presented a danger to her. It seemed rather silly, now. Except that she still couldn't sing.

'Did you know she left the term after you went?' Isabel asked. 'She said she'd been offered her old job back.'

Charlotte jerked in her seat.

'I shouldn't have told you, I can see that,' said Isabel, and changed the subject.

Charlotte was still stunned when William entered the tea-room. 'I'm so glad you came,' she said, employing social graces she didn't normally use, drawing his net of dull safety round her. 'I want you to meet my friend Isabel. Isabel, meet William Card. Today,' she said, the words toppling and rushing, 'it's my treat. I'm feeling rich. Isabel's broke because she's been shopping.' She could feel Isabel's astonished expression coming at her.

As William sat down, Charlotte allowed herself to realise that this was the first time she had actually given him any encouragement. The dance was experience; the teas were greed. She turned down his cinema invitations because there was nothing in them for her. She felt a salutary sense of shame as she stifled Miss Hurst with emotions connected with him.

'Three cream teas,' Isabel said to the waitress. 'I know you're the hostess, Charlotte, but you seem to have gone into a dream.'

Chapter Twenty

Alison found Robert a lock-up garage in the street behind her flat. His car must not stand all night every night in Cherry Tree Road. Leaving him with a gin and tonic, she went to pick up his suit-case.

'Are you sure you can manage?' he asked, concerned for her. 'I wouldn't have put so much in it if I had thought you were going to have to carry it.'

'I'll run the Mini right up to the garage door. I'll only have to transfer it from your boot to mine. We can't chance your being seen moving in.' She felt as one of her pupils might, bent on mischief. He was like a schoolboy on an escapade, slipping off into Wylie-under-Lyne for these two weeks that his wife and daughter were in Italy.

He was less of a schoolboy now, though, with his head on the pillow beside hers. She had become more dear to him during their termtime separations when she was guarding his daughter, as he thought, though they never discussed it. 'Don't leave me again,' he adjured her, forbearing to mention the dangerous matter of his loneliness, which they both knew could be cured at a stroke. As could that other unmentioned and unmentionable problem, the hostility of his children.

'I'll always be here for you,' she promised. The dark years had taught her a thing or two. Take your happiness where you can get it. Robert still hadn't mentioned a divorce, and she never brought it up. She clung to him and they both in their separate ways clung to the unexpressed hope that Charlotte would be returned to them.

She might have gone up to Charlotte and Isabel in Waites

department store if she had been able to get herself in control. But there is no controlling jealousy of such magnitude. Its jagged edges saw at your heart. Its poison dribbles through your veins. She had caught a glimpse of her face in the mirror separating Hosiery and Nightwear. A stranger. Before she regained her senses she could have murdered Isabel, had a weapon been to hand. Stabbed her through the heart. How dare you take my child! How dare you stand between us! Take that. And that. She had to turn and run.

She pressed her face into the pillow, close against Robert's face, while she fought her longing to spill her hurt. 'She's not yours,' he would say. Even, 'She must be free to choose her own friends, my dear.' Yes, but why did she not choose me?

He had laughed about Charlotte's having her former teacher to stay. 'She seems to have an affinity with older people,' he said, and went on to recount the baffling tale of William, with his dinner dance and cream teas. For once he actually talked about her child. She was not to know his defences had been weakened by Charlotte's rejection of him.

She tried hard not to think of Vivien, Charlotte and Isabel sitting on a foreign beach, laughing together, drinking Italian wines, eating Italian food, the teacher who should have been her, the mother who should have been her. Two thieves who had stolen, and now shared, her child. She gave herself to Robert, spilling her pain and her passion, loving him to distraction. He was all she had.

Yolande and Oliver were to be married that year. 'Lucky you've got back into the habit of buying nice clothes,' Charlotte said to Vivien. 'Do you want me to go with you to find something to wear?'

'Only a hat. I've so many clothes in the wardrobe that I never wear.' But when she tried them they no longer fitted, and besides, they were out of date.

'Good,' said Charlotte. 'Let's send them all to Oxfam and start again.'

Vivien closed her eyes.

'Are you all right?'

'Yes.' Nine years on, Vivien still could not hear the name Oxfam without shock. She seldom went to Wylie-under-Lyne, because the Oxfam shop was there. Of course she could pass on the other side of the street, but the panic, manifest in dizziness and a strangling feeling in her throat, was something she preferred to avoid. That was why her wardrobe was full of clothes she never wore.

'Shall we nip along to Stella Bloomingdale?'

'Let's go to Harrods,' Vivien said. 'I've so enjoyed our trips to London together.'

Charlotte tiptoed down a side lane off the High Street. Turn right, now go straight ahead, now turn left. This path should bring her to Cherry Tree Road. She stood on the corner, looking alertly up and down. Substantial Victorian and Edwardian villas, with biggish gardens. Which way do the numbers go? Discreet little plates, hard to read. She ventured up a drive: 37. Next door on the right: 35. This way, then, for number 5.

It had been raining and might rain again. Dark clouds were scurrying across a bright-blue sky. The breeze shook little showers of raindrops out of the cherry trees on to her hair. She did not know what she expected from this foray into the enemy camp. The idea had been spontaneous, darting into and taking over her mind as she was coming out of Boots.

Number 5 had tall elms, a box hedge and neat, square rose beds. Beside the garage an outside staircase led to the upper floor. A woman was standing at a downstairs window. As though Charlotte's stare had penetrated into her consciousness, the woman looked up. Blonde and middle-aged. Well, she would be blonde, wouldn't she? Paramours, tarts, fancy women, Charlotte judged them all, scornfully, to be blonde. It was their trademark, wasn't it? She looked back boldly. What did she care if the woman knew who she was? 'Your daughter found me out today. I recognised her by the hair. A sort of apricot, you said.' Serve him right. But no, she shouldn't have come. She saw that, now. She had no right. Besides, she had made herself angry.

She swung round, hurried across the road and swept round the corner into a public right-of-way that she could see might lead her back into the High Street. The rain started coming down again. Someone was approaching from the opposite direction, her view obscured by an umbrella. Charlotte dodged. The woman dodged. They collided.

'Sorry.'

'Sorry.'

'Why, Charlotte!' said Miss Hurst, swinging the umbrella aside and gazing on her with pleasure. 'What a nice surprise!'

'Sorry, I can't stop, Miss Hurst. I haven't got an umbrella,' Charlotte said, backing away. 'I'll have to run.'

Miss Hurst touched her wrist and looked at her imploringly. 'No, please, you'll get awfully wet. My flat's just across the road. Do come in until the rain stops. Come and have coffee with me,' she said, begging. 'I would so like that.'

Charlotte experienced a suffocating feeling, the same feeling that had sent her in panic to Isabel to beg for help in changing music teachers. Miss Hurst took her arm, drawing her in to share the umbrella, and together they recrossed the road. 'Number 5,' said Miss Hurst.

As they walked up the drive, the blonde woman was still standing in the window. Charlotte kept her head very straight as though looking directly ahead while trying to see out of the corners of her eyes. What she saw was a prettyish face, the hair swept back from the forehead. She tried to read guilt in the woman's expression.

They climbed the outside steps. Miss Hurst put her key in the door and they made it inside just as the rain bucketed down.

'Lucky we met!' Miss Hurst laughed, shaking the umbrella so that drops splattered the wallpaper in the narrow hall. 'Come into the kitchen while I put the kettle on. Excuse me just a moment while I go and stand the umbrella in the bath.'

They entered a narrow kitchen with a Welsh dresser hung with coloured cups and hand-painted mugs. There were recipe books. *Cooking for One. Vegetarian Dishes.* A row of stained and dog-eared Elizabeth David paperbacks. A sink. A bench. A view down into a small, leafy garden.

'That's mine,' said Miss Hurst. 'I like to do a bit of gardening.'

They took their coffee into the living room. Charlotte was thinking only of the woman downstairs. Who lives here, besides you? Who owns the house? Miss Hurst might ask her why she wanted to know. Perhaps she was herself aware of what was going on. Perhaps she had seen the Citroën and recognised the owner as Charlotte Godfrey's father.

'Do sit down, Charlotte.'

180

She chose a low chair. Put her mug on the coffee table. Miss Hurst manoeuvred another chair with her foot so they could face each other. She sat down, smiling, but not with triumph as Charlotte had warily expected. She looked warm and pleased. 'You must tell me about Oxford,' she said. 'I'm dying to know.'

Charlotte soon found herself relaxing, actually enjoying talking about Oxford. Miss Hurst had been there, too, at Somerville. They grew animated, comparing experiences. For a while they seemed to be in accord, two adults with the same background. There was even a little laughter.

'You could stay to lunch,' Miss Hurst said, bright-eyed and eager. 'Do stay!'

Charlotte replaced her empty mug on the coffee table. 'No, really, thank you all the same. It's very kind of you to offer but I have to get back. I've got such a lot to do.' What had she to do, should Miss Hurst ask? 'My sister's getting married —' She stopped, arrested by Miss Hurst's caught breath and her crest-fallen look. The familiar resentment returned. Did she think she ought to know all the Godfrey affairs just because she had taught the children? Come to think of it, she hadn't taught Yolande.

Charlotte rose quickly, wanting to get away. 'It's stopped raining,' she said, swallowing her resentment and racking her brain for sly and devious ways to find out the name of the woman downstairs. Nothing presented itself. 'I caught a glimpse of the woman downstairs,' she said boldly. 'I thought I recognised her.'

Miss Hurst, looking depressed, gathered up the mugs.

'What's her name?'

'Adrienne Graham. She's a widow. She plays a lot of bridge. If your mother belongs to a bridge club, she may know her.'

'That's probably it,' said Charlotte. 'I'll be off then. I need to get to the bus stop before the rain starts up again.'

Isabel was pleased at receiving an invitation to the wedding.

'Yolande wanted you to come,' Charlotte told her on the telephone. 'We all do.' The whole family had grown fond of her.

The wedding was to be held in the afternoon followed by a reception in a marquee, then supper and dancing. 'We've a problem, though,' she said. 'We haven't got an unattached male on the guest list to partner you.'

181

'I don't need a partner,' Isabel said cheerfully. 'I'm sure one or two of your father's friends will dance with me.'

Charlotte remembered the experience of being clutched to the protruding stomachs of middle-aged men at Fenton, Lodge and Carruthers' dinner dance. Besides, Robert's friends all had wives and couldn't be counted on to spread themselves. She put it to Yolande that William, who was only a year older than Isabel, might be invited.

'Yuk,' said Yolande.

'Perhaps he could come in the evening, then?'

Vivien objected. 'That would be insulting. He'd soon realise he was the only one not invited to the wedding. Hasn't Oliver got any thirtyish friends?'

The answer was no. 'What's the matter with poor old William?' Oliver offered good-naturedly to put him on the groom's list. 'There's no reason why he shouldn't come. I've known him – well, seen him around – all my life. He's probably got more right than some of your father's business friends who don't know Yol at all.'

'Could you bear it?' Yolande asked Isabel.

'I thought he was very nice. We once shared a cream tea.'

Yolande scoffed. 'That's his connection with Charlotte, too. They both like cream teas. Well, he is a neighbour. He'll know some of the guests.'

William was enormously gratified. 'You're a family friend,' said Charlotte warmly, assuaging her guilt for referring to him in a moment of silliness as a puppet on a string. She remembered what her mother had said about paying back. Inviting him to the wedding, she felt, was that.

Max borrowed a car and drove Charlotte down from Oxford. 'Dad's very displeased,' he said. 'He seems to think I should work day and night, weeks and weekends. He's going to shoot me if I don't get a decent pass.'

Charlotte thought it was a very real possibility that he wouldn't get a decent pass. He was not working. He had joined the debating society, the dramatic society, the Labour Party; he wrote for *Isis*; he spent a great deal of time on sports: tennis, rugby, rowing. He was good at everything, brilliant at nothing. 'Too many medium talents and too much energy,' his tutor said.

Charlotte thought it wouldn't be his fault if he failed his finals. Ever since he came up to Oxford he'd been reacting to the fact that his father had not only driven him too hard, but nurtured too great an ambition for him.

'The old boy actually dreams of me being offered an Oxbridge chair one day. Imagine!' Max took his hands off the steering wheel and flung them high in exasperation.

She agreed he would be more at home with a bucking steer.

'Remember how snooty you were about my riding?' He referred to the day Goldie threw him. Now that he had ridden a bucking steer, he could talk light-heartedly about falling off a quiet horse.

'I bet you fell off the steers,' Charlotte jeered.

'Of course. Everyone does, in the end. It's how long you stay on that counts.' He had an honourable scar on his left leg to prove that a steer had had a go at him.

'Do you fight them, like a toreador?'

'No,' he said, 'you run like hell with the crowd cheering you on.'

Yolande's wedding dress was not to be traditional. 'I look ghastly in white,' she said. The dressmaker had shown her some satin that was exactly right.

'Tea rose. Like weak tea that's been stirred with lipstick,' Charlotte suggested, having seen it.

'Poetic you! And I'm having coloured flowers in my bouquet. Tea roses, of course. And stephanotis,' she added. 'That's a bit virginal, if you like. Sorry,' she half apologised, eyes dancing as she saw the embarrassment on the older faces.

Robert and Vivien looked away, separately. Once, their eyes would have met with shared displeasure. 'The very devil,' Robert would have said afterwards. 'She's been to bed with the lad.' They would have agreed, as they used to agree about everything, that it was high time Yolande got married.

'We're old-fashioned,' he said now. 'We like the virginal look but of course you must have what you want.'

'Oh, dear,' said Yolande. 'Hadn't you noticed, virgins went out in the sixties.' She had become more than usually confident since the engagement was announced. She enjoyed putting her parents on trial.

183

Robert was on edge, remembering the yearning in Alison's voice when she said, 'I expect Charlotte will be bridesmaid.' Charlotte would be at her prettiest with flowers in her beautiful hair. He was afraid Alison would take it into her head to come to the church. Did it matter? There were always a few gawpers. Yes, it mattered to him, though he preferred not to look too deeply into the reasons.

Charlotte's bridesmaid dress was to be made of the same material as the brides, though of a darker shade. 'Strong tea,' said Yolande, 'with more lipstick.' She hadn't wanted Charlotte to be bridesmaid, but Robert had talked her round. And Kenneth backed Robert up. He was to be best man. He liked the thought of leading his lovely little sister back down the aisle.

'Nobody has a bridesmaid that's prettier than the bride,' Yolande grumbled.

'A bride is never outshone on the day, old girl,' Robert assured her. 'Charlotte will be hurt if you don't ask her.'

And so, grudgingly, Yolande had asked. Charlotte, not knowing of the hiccup, accepted with pleasure.

Sylvia arrived from her island, delighted that brash Yolande was marrying the gentle Oliver.

A marquee with plastic windows and a beautiful ruched lining in daffodil yellow was set up on the lawn. The snow-white cake was delivered, three tiers. The principal participants went off to dress. Only Vivien was downstairs when the florist's van arrived. She came into the hall calling, 'The bouquets have come.'

Charlotte ran downstairs. Stopped dead. Her nostrils filled up with the scent of the lavender that was intricately woven in among the roses, filling the air with its perfume.

Cold panic. Desolation. A division in her mind. Part of her was in the church walking up the aisle behind Yolande, part following Claire's coffin, smelling the lavender. A scream rose in her throat and rent the air.

'What's happened?' Yolande came running out on the landing, clutching her dressing gown round her.

Robert looked over the balustrade, white shirt-tails hanging outside his striped trousers, one hand holding a stud halfway in a loose cuff. 'What's going on?'

Isabel and Sylvia hurried down the stairs with Kenneth following.

'Charlotte!' Vivien implored, putting her arms round her.

Charlotte broke away, snatched frenziedly at the lavender, tore it out, piece by piece, crushing it in her hands.

'What's she doing?' the bride shrieked, flying down, arms waving like a bat. 'Charlotte! Have you gone mad?' She gave her sister a violent push. Charlotte lost her balance and sprawled on the floor, sobbing, clutching the lavender. Yolande lifted the bouquet, tears spurting from her eyes. 'She's ruined it! She's ruined my bouquet!'

Sylvia drew Charlotte to her feet, cradled her in her arms, then led her away.

'I didn't want her to be bridesmaid,' sobbed Yolande, 'and now look what she's done!'

'Hush, Yolande. Hush,' said Kenneth sternly.

'I don't care! She's ruined my wedding!' Yolande looked balefully after Charlotte's and Sylvia's retreating backs.

Robert said, 'I'll call the florist. It's by no means ruined. It could do with a bit of patching, that's all. There's time for them to bring something else.'

Kenneth retreated silently upstairs to finish dressing. Isabel slipped out to the garden.

'Why did she do it?' Yolande wailed.

'It's time you were dressed. Come on.' Robert escorted her to the stairs then went to look for Charlotte.

She was sitting beside Sylvia on the sofa in the drawing room, rocking to and fro while Sylvia stroked her hair. Robert, exercising tact, turned abruptly bumped into Vivien, set her ungently upright. She wandered aimlessly away, feeling inadequate.

'Come,' said Sylvia to Charlotte in the drawing room, 'I'll help you dress.'

'I can't go.' Charlotte opened her clenched fingers. Looked down at the crushed lavender, not seeing it but smelling it. Seeing instead the little white dress she wore as a ten-year-old. The aisle. Claire at her side.

'You can,' said Sylvia without emphasis. She tipped out the crushed lavender from Charlotte's hand into her skirt, went into the kitchen and dropped it into the summer-dead Aga. Then she took Charlotte upstairs and stood over her while she washed her hands, washing the merciless memories away. The girl looked frail and spent as she dressed.

185

Sylvia knocked on Yolande's door. It was opened by the dress-maker, who had come to arrange her gown and veil. Sylvia slipped inside. 'Charlotte sent me to apologise,' she said.

Yolande, a slender, tawny young animal defending her day, spat at her, 'She can keep her fucking apologies to herself. Tell her she can fucking walk to the church. She's not coming in the car with me. If there was another bridesmaid I'd tell her to get stuffed. She's mad! Mad as a hatter! She did this at Claire's funeral – screamed. What's going to happen when we get to the church? Tell me that? Is she going to start screaming again?'

The dressmaker backed towards the bed, eyes cast down. Sylvia asked her politely to leave them alone and she went, scut-tling out like a frightened rabbit.

Yolande turned on Sylvia. 'Don't you make excuses for her,' she stormed. 'I know you're going to, but this is my day. *Mine.*'

Robert, pausing at the top of the stairs, heard the words coming muffled through the door. He went on to his bedroom, shaking his head, finished dressing and went out to see how things were going in the marquee.

'I put that lavender in the bouquet in memory of Claire,' Yolande said. 'Don't you remember, there was a great thing of lavender on her coffin? A cross or a bouquet. I wanted to have something for her on my wedding day.' Tears of misery, as well as anger, stood in her eyes. 'I thought Charlotte would understand and be glad.' She collapsed on the bed, shoulders heaving.

Sylvia had come in feeling competent and authoritative. Now she crumpled. She put her arms round Yolande, knowing there was no more she could do. 'Life's a bugger,' she managed, she who was not given to swearing. She went into the bathroom and brought a wet flannel to bathe the bride's face. Looking up at the beautiful tea-rose gown drifting from its hanger, she said, 'I've never seen such a wonderful wedding dress.' The words were intended to show affection and admiration, which was what Yolande needed and all, in the circumstances, she could provide. 'You're going to be the loveliest bride.'

'With red eyes.' Yolande, softened by the compliment, looked at her in despair.

'All brides cry on their wedding day,' said Sylvia, making it obligatory, and attractive. Privately, she thought a crushed

Yolande might be demurely fetching. Her usual brash confidence accorded ill with the fantasy of a blushing bride.

Isabel came in from the garden with a bunch of flowers in her hand, shrub roses round as tiny balls, frail ferns from the north wall, mauve clematis nearly, but not quite, the same shade as the lavender. She unravelled the florist's wire and tucked the new blooms into the spaces. Vivien, hovering in and out of her bedroom, saw her and crept downstairs. 'You are kind, Isabel! And clever. One would never know it had been ...' Her voice sounded weary and sad. 'Oh dear, this should have been such a happy day.'

Isabel put an arm round her. 'And so it will be. Let's go and get dressed.'

She stuck her head round Yolande's door to tell her what had been done. Yolande nodded, not gratefully but as though she really couldn't bear to think about the bouquet any more, even that it had been mended. A tear dribbled down her cheek. She angrily wiped at it with a tissue. Turned her back. Isabel went quietly away.

Dressed in her wedding finery, driftwood silk with an enormous matching hat, Isabel emerged from her room. To fill in time, she wandered along the landing, looking at the pictures. She paused before an arresting portrait of a nineteenth-century woman in evening dress: tight waist, low décolletage, hair piled high. Her face had a mannish look only partially softened by the dress and jewelled necklace.

This woman must be an ancestor of Robert's, Isabel thought. The resemblance was there in the square chin and the strong nose. And then she saw the eyes. They looked straight at her, daring her to recognise them. She turned sharply away, embarrassed. She walked to the gallery rail and looked down into the hall. Vivien was standing there in her new blue silk with the unaccustomed hat sitting at not quite the right angle on her head, as though she had forgotten how to be elegant. Or ceased to care. She looked up.

Isabel backed away. Returned to the portrait. I'm imagining this, she said to herself. But surely those are Charlotte's eyes gazing out of the woman's face? Godfrey eyes. And then she thought, Everyone must know. If they wanted to hide the truth, wouldn't they hide the portrait?

187

Sylvia came out of Yolande's room and walked down the stairs. Feeling guilty, Isabel hurried to join her. 'Is there anything I can do?'

'I think it's better the bride and bridesmaid don't go in the same car,' Sylvia said.

Vivien came out of the study. They both smelled whisky on her breath. Sylvia, exercising pity and compassion, squeezed her arm.

Isabel said, 'Why don't we call up Max?' Knowing this was the answer, she did not wait for agreement. 'I'll find Robert.' She ran outside, wobbling in her high heels, holding the shallow crown of her big hat in place with one hand.

Sylvia picked up the telephone book and found the number, handing it to Robert when he came in, black tails swinging.

'What's this?' He wore the expression of a man who is being threatened. 'Max?' he rasped. 'Why should he drive Charlotte?' Hard lines of disappointment and disagreement were etched on his face.

Sylvia slipped an arm through his. She was gentle with him. 'We have to think of Yolande, dear. It's her day.'

Max was standing in the front doorway when Charlotte came down, looking more mature in his father's tails than one would expect at twenty-one. The clothes were almost a perfect fit. Laurence Fosse at forty-six still cut a fine figure.

'Robert thought it would be a good idea,' said Sylvia to Charlotte, shifting the responsiblity. 'It's usual for the bride and her father to travel alone in the wedding car. If there had been more bridesmaids, there would have been another car, but with only one, he thought . . . Anyway, there's been a change of mind. Max is happy to take you. Off you go.'

Charlotte glowed. No one would guess that an hour ago she had been in a state of collapse. She fingered the Valentine necklace Max refused to acknowledge, slipped an arm through his and went with him, walking on springs. 'What's this?' she asked, indicating the highly polished, expensive-looking car that was waiting for them. 'What have you got here?'

'Pa's Merc. He thought Mum's little runabout wasn't dignified enough for a bridesmaid, so he decided to allow me to come in style. For such a mean sod, he's got a fine sense of occasion,' Max said, looking well pleased.

Sylvia thought, You'd never guess it wasn't his. He wore the air of a man who drove, owned, took, only the best. She felt a lump in her throat as she looked at Charlotte in her silk gown with a twist of roses round her head and the apricot curls shining. She was thinking of Claire, looking the same, dressed the same way. Might not two of them have been too much?

Then she thought, and the notion sobered her, would they both have been in love with Max? It was Max's arrival that had brought Charlotte's beauty to its shining, extravagant zenith. She thought it was as well Yolande would not see her little sister until she reached the gloom of the church porch. After that, all eyes should be on the bride.

She shook her head, mutely smiling. Isabel smiled back. Robert had disappeared into his study with the air of a man needing privacy while he came to terms with things.

Vivien looked nervously relieved.

Chapter Twenty-One

Louisa spent most of the autumn thinking of Max. He had danced with her at a party when Charlotte was in Italy. 'You're very young,' he had said, but he had winked at her. The recollection of his look sent shivers up her spine.

The second time he danced with her, he didn't ask. He merely slid an arm round her waist and said in that Richard Burton voice of his, 'Come on, young Louisa. This is ours.' They twirled and whirled, drawing together, swinging apart. Sometimes his face came so close that she could smell his breath – beer and peanuts. His dark-blue eyes were, she thought, smouldering. She longed for him to hold her close as some of the boys were doing to their girls, but he continued to whirl her around.

She had lain awake that night, holding in her memory the softness of his sleeve, the hard muscles of his arm, dreaming about what he might do to her after he graduated when Charlotte was still up at Oxford, out of the way. She didn't believe he was in love with Charlotte. She thought Charlotte had a hold on him.

In the Christmas vacation Louisa discovered that Max was working at Percival's in Wylie-under-Lyne. She persuaded her father to put his Christmas liquor order there. 'I can perfectly well phone it through,' her mother said. When her back was turned, Louisa took the list. She spent half an hour walking up and down the pavement outside Percival's before Max staggered through the door at the back of the shop with a crate of bottles.

She hurried in. Mr Percival, who was standing behind the counter, gave her an old-fashioned look when she walked right past him and spoke to Max. 'I expect you'll deliver it on your way home tomorrow?' she asked, knowing he drove the firm's van.

'No problem,' Max replied.

'Would you give me a lift?'

'No problem there either.' Max grinned cheerfully and tossed the order across the counter to Mr Percival. 'Be here at five thirty.'

Mr Percival was grinning, too, but in a different way. Not that she cared. Some old men were warped.

Next day while her father was eating his breakfast, she slipped out to the garage and stowed her new coat with the fake-fur hood in the boot of his car. It was powder blue, a colour that did wonders for her eyes. She went to work as usual wearing normal gear; school coat and the woolly cap with the big pompom. Her father liked her to be Daddy's little girl, getting experience. Earning pocket money.

At one o'clock, when he went to lunch, she took the keys from his desk, collected the coat from the car and stowed it in the staff room. At five fifteen, when there were no customers left on her floor, she asked Mrs Benson, who worked in Hosiery, to keep an eye on Ladies' Wear. 'And tell Daddy I'm getting a lift home with a friend.'

'Why don't you tell him yourself, dear?' Mrs Benson asked.

She marched off in a hurry, saying, 'I don't know where he is.' Then she went down to Perfumery and drenched herself in Van Cleef & Arpel's First, using the tester spray.

'That's very sexy,' said Mrs Frobisher, the nosy saleslady, giving her a suspicious look. 'What are you up to, young Louisa?'

Louisa tossed her curls and left. After all, she said to herself, I am the owner's daughter. Who are they to question me?

She hurried up the High Street looking at reflections of herself in the shop windows among fairy lights and fake snow. She thought she looked eighteen. Sometimes she thought she might pass for twenty. The sleet had given way to drifting blobs of snow. She hugged herself, not against the cold, but containing the excitement inside.

Mr Percival casually got rid of her. 'The van's not locked. Max won't be long.' She went out through the back door, bridling. He was old, that was his trouble.

Max came, flinging open the door, leaping aboard, filling the cab with a smell of sweat, sawdust and wood shavings. There was snow on his tousled hair.

191

' 'Ave a fag,' he said in pretend cockney, pulling a packet of cigarettes out of his jacket pocket, offering it, leaning close to light up. In the flare of the flame his cheeks were ruddy, his skin a matt olive. 'You shouldn't be smoking at your age,' he said, light-heartedly transferring the responsibility. He tossed the match out of the window. 'Don't throw litter. Well, why not?'

Elated by the way he shared himself and his indiscretions, she smiled the seductive smile she had been practising. He looked down at her appraisingly. When she thought he was about to say how pretty she looked, he sucked in a long breath, blew the smoke out and said instead, 'Lung cancer.' He batted the grey cloud out of the window with his hands. Then he wobbled the clutch and accidentally touched her knee.

Chance or design? Shivers ran up Louisa's spine. They roared out of the car park and joined the road to Forge Green. Wriggling in her seat, she brushed his arm with hers. In the meagre light from the dash she thought she saw his eyes flick her way.

The article in the glossy *Men and Girls* said you shouldn't be shy about letting a man know what you want. Take the initiative, if he's slow, it said. Don't be afraid to touch him. That's how you get your man.

Puffs of snow sped across the windscreen and built up into a pack under the wiper. 'I'll have to stop and clear it,' Max said. 'The wipers aren't doing a very good job.' They were approaching a lay-by in the woods. He braked, pulling the wheel round, undid his seat belt and jumped out. Fumbling, she undid hers but stayed in the cab. He was knocking the packed ice off the base of the windscreen with his fist.

Her heart beat fast as he jumped back in. The interior light was on. Lifting her face, she flicked her lashes and parted her lips, as she had seen on TV. He hesitated a moment, then put his arms round her. He kissed her, then kissed her again, using his tongue this time. 'You're very desirable,' he murmured. 'Mmn-m. Do that again.'

She had tricks up her sleeve from a book lent her by a very knowledgeable friend: seven sure-fire ways to seduce a man. She knew the theory of how to kiss and was intoxicated to find how easily it worked. She moved closer, nudging his knee with hers, and slyly pulled up the skirt of her coat with her left hand. He ran his fingers up her leg. Up. Up. Groaning, he said, 'What are you

192

doing to me?' and took his hand away. 'You're so young, little Louisa. I must take you home.'

'I don't have to go home,' she said breathlessly, heart racing. 'I do love you, Max. I always have.' She put her arms round him, felt his hand on her leg again, closed her knees, imprisoning it.

'You're a forward little hussy,' he said, laughing now, though sounding delighted. 'Do you do this with all the boys?'

'Only you.' Her head was spinning with excitement. Taking the initiative as advised, she forced her tongue into his mouth.

'Yes, I think I had better take you home,' he said, pushing her away, sounding matter-of-fact. He turned the ignition key, put the van into gear and pulled out into the road.

She straightened the skirt of her coat, thinking with triumph that at any rate she had got her message across. She would be nearly a year older next summer when he was finished with Oxford and Charlotte was still there, out of the way. He was bound to stay in Forge Green while he looked for a job. And she would probably be stuck in the family store.

Winter passed and the summer holidays came again. Her mother called, 'Louisa dear, there's something you can do for me.'

What she wanted was any old stuff that was saleable. She was in charge of the odd-and-ends stall at the church fête on Saturday. 'Have a dig round in your wardrobe,' she said. 'And what about your toy box? You probably haven't looked in it for years. Toys don't fetch much but it all adds up.'

Louisa turned out the toy box. One perfectly good rabbit. She held it in her arms, remembering taking it to bed when she was little. Did she really want to part with it? Mightn't she want to give it to her own children? Hers and Max's. There was no doubt in her mind now that she would marry Max. She'd find a way to get rid of Charlotte. She held the rabbit tighter, rubbing it against her breast, setting up delirious sensations while she thought about Max who was down from Oxford now. She had seen him walking in the woods with Charlotte. She heaved a sigh, laid the rabbit down on the bed and began emptying the box.

Four worn-out dolls. Not the kind of thing to insult a charity with. Some jigsaws. A shapeless yellow lump of squashed plastic. What on earth was this? She managed to spread it out flat.

Water wings! Where had they come from? She had never been allowed water wings.

She took them downstairs and showed them to her mother. 'Look what I found in the toy box.'

Margot put a hand to her throat. Swallowed. She said sharply, 'Put them in the rubbish. Here –' she stepped forward with a nervous jerk – 'give them to me.'

Louisa handed the plastic over, mutely curious. 'What's wrong?'

'Nothing,' her mother snapped. 'They're no use to anyone.' She went outside to the big bin though there was a small one, perfectly adequate, attached to the cupboard door under the sink.

Later, walking through the village, Louisa met Crispin Derwent. His appearance triggered a memory connected with the water wings. She recalled him promising that when he was older and allowed to swim at the Bubbly Hole with his brother Dick, he would invite her to join them. No one swam at the Bubbly Hole now. As they walked back down the lane together, she asked him why.

'Claire Godfrey got drowned there,' he said. 'Don't you remember?'

Louisa remembered only that Claire had died. Not where or how.

'Someone took her water wings,' Crispin said. 'That's how. I don't see why we shouldn't swim there. We wouldn't drown.' He kicked a stone with his foot, watched it skim along the road. 'But Dad says no. He won't let anyone.' When Louisa didn't answer, he added, 'I s'pose it might be a bit spooky, come to think of it.'

Louisa felt cold and trembling. 'I'd better go home now,' she said.

She sat on her bed for a long time, trying fearfully to drag old memories out of her mind. Her mother called that she ought to take Pip for a walk. He was old but he still liked to walk. She collected his lead. Without thinking about where she was going, she followed the public footpath that joined the towpath, then took the familiar route that would bring them out just beyond the church. She passed through the lychgate.

She was level with the southwestern corner where the bell tower rose. From here she could see Claire's grave. Someone was

194

bending over it, holding a trowel. She straightened and Louisa saw it was Charlotte. She looked levelly at Louisa, without smiling. Louisa hurried away, dragging at the dog's leash.

Late that night when her parents were watching television, she came and stood in the sitting-room doorway.

'I want to ask you something,' she said.

'Yes?'

Louisa nodded towards the television. 'D'you mind turning that off?'

Her father looked round vaguely for the remote control. 'What's this?'

'The water wings!' Louisa blurted out. 'The ones I found in my toy box. Where did they come from?'

The colour drained out of her mother's face. Her father tried to catch his wife's eye.

'Didn't Maud give them to you? Remember, she was staying with us before she went to Singapore.' Her mother rallied.

Louisa remembered. Remembered it was a lie. Maud had been forbidden to give her water wings.

'Best forgotten,' said her father. He turned back to the television set. 'You should see this, Louisa. A new soap. You'd like it. Come and sit by me.' He patted the sofa.

Louisa read her own guilt in their reaction. She thought she had seen it also in Charlotte's level stare as she looked at her across her twin's gravestone. Without a word, she went back up the stairs to her bedroom and closed the door. The television had gone silent. Her parents' secret voices crept up the stairs. Indistinct words with worry sounding through.

In the hazy twilight between waking and sleeping Louisa saw Claire and Max crossing the meadow towards the Bubbly Hole with Sasha running out in front, racing over the dry grass. She watched them disappear through the gap in the thorn bushes, and saw herself going on down the track towards the towpath with Pip. Entering the woods. Coming out again into Puddle Lane. Then she met Charlotte. Charlotte gave her a sweet.

What happened next? Did Pip run away? She remembered a dry culvert with something yellow wedged into it, half hidden with leaves. Water wings. The wings Claire had been carrying when she met Max.

She brought them home thinking Claire didn't want them any more.

That summer, down from Oxford, Max wasn't at all himself. He had scraped through with a third. His father was giving him a bad time, using words like 'wastrel' and 'ne'er-do-well'. He made Max an object of scorn.

Max was shell-shocked. Demoralised. He couldn't come to terms with the extent of his misjudgement of his own capabilities.

'Things are very sticky at home,' he said to Charlotte, grimacing. '*You*'ll get a first, of course,' he added.

Charlotte, detecting bitterness, worried that she might. She considered the implications of her success. When he said he would look for a job in industry, she put her arms round him and offered to go with him.

'I'll give up Oxford to be with you,' she said, rubbing her cheek along his arm. 'You'll become a big business tycoon and I'll be your sidekick.'

'And I'll get blame from your parents as well as mine,' grumbled Max. 'No, thanks.'

He resorted to proving himself. He showed off, reminding her of the young Max who said, 'Look how high I can climb! How fast I can make Goldie gallop!' He danced with lots of other girls and responded warmly to Louisa Waite's goggle-eyed adoration. Once, Charlotte thought she saw Louisa looking her way with an expression of triumph in her baby-blue eyes.

Dick Derwent told her Louisa had told him that Max's mother had told her mother that Dr Fosse blamed Charlotte for Max's poor results.

She was indignant.

'Mrs Fosse is always pushing other girls at him. Especially Louisa. She's never liked you being his girlfriend,' Dick said tactlessly. 'Didn't you know?'

She hadn't known. She was hurt and astonished.

'Who cares?' said Max, shrugging, thereby confirming the truth. She thought about the posies 'from the Fosse family' that used to appear every August on Claire's grave and was baffled. Besides, hadn't Dr Fosse lent Max his very precious Merc to take her to Yolande's wedding?

196

'That's different,' said Dick, grinning. 'Old Fosse is never backward when it comes to putting on a show.'

It was a painful time.

Charlotte went up to London with Max by fast train. She was to meet Isabel for a visit to the Victoria and Albert Museum. Because Max had another job interview he was formally dressed in a new navy-blue suit. She was casually dressed. Bare legs. String sandals, her hair tied up on the crown of her head with a rubber band. She was tall now, over five foot seven.

'Do you know what I think?' he said, slumping back in his seat as the train sped along. 'I think it was my rebellion against Pa's determination to make me into an academic that's done me in. But I should be able to stand up to him. Why should I let him demoralise me?' He was asking himself as well as Charlotte. 'I've lived with him all my life. I've managed so far. Why now?'

Charlotte said shrewdly, 'He's perhaps never wanted so much of you. He had set his heart on your having an academic career. Did you tell him from the start that you didn't want it?'

'I didn't dare.'

'Are you scared of him?'

'Not scared.' Max looked sideways at her. 'But it's easier to slip round the outside of him than crash head on. It's just dawned on me,' he added, surprised and at the same time sheepish, 'that the reason I didn't tell him was because he wouldn't have gone along with Oxford if he'd known. Funny, the things that hide away in your subconscious.' He sat up, looking surprised. 'I've learnt something new about myself.'

'Learn something new every day, that's Isabel's advice.'

'I'm beginning to think I'd better not mention Oxford when I apply for jobs,' he said, pursuing another train of thought. 'They prick up their ears. Then, when I have to tell them I got a lousy third, a certain look comes over their faces. All those opportunities, they're saying to themselves, and that's all he can come up with – a third!'

Charlotte, never having thought of him as a failure, couldn't take his worries seriously. But it was true that he had had four interviews without being offered a job. Still, jobs were hard to get these days. Young people were leaving university and going on the dole.

'Maybe the people you've seen are just being polite in interviewing you. Maybe they've already made up their minds they're only going to take someone with an honours degree. Maybe you're applying for the wrong jobs. You don't have to start at the top,' she said, though hesitantly, for hadn't he always thought of himself as a top person?

Max said morosely, 'Start out low and stay low.'

'Oh, come!' She tried to jolly him out of his mood. 'You'd make such a success of whatever you took on that everybody would want you. *Everybody*. You'd have them all saying, "He's too good for that job" in no time at all.' She sat up straight on the edge of her seat, face lifted, smiling at him. They had the carriage virtually to themselves. 'Remember how well you rode without a single lesson? Remember the bucking steers? I'll bet you'll be head-hunted before you're twenty-five.' She picked up his hand and rubbed the back of it across her cheek, tickling her face with the soft dark hairs, smelling cigarettes and warm flesh. She turned the hand over and kissed the palm. 'Shall I run off a list of the millionaires who didn't even go to school?'

He put his arms round her and held her tight. 'Don't ever leave me,' he said, emotionally.

She was shocked at the extent of the inroads his father had made on his confidence.

Later that day, Max was not at Waterloo. Charlotte spread her denim jacket over two seats and stepped back out on to the platform. She watched the entrance for a sprinter in navy blue trousers, white shirt, jacket slung over one shoulder, shining black hair flying. Max the tight-rope walker liked to catch trains by the skin of his teeth. His peculiar mixture of charm and confidence would persuade all-powerful station staff to open a slammed gate. The guard blew his whistle. Disappointed, she went aboard.

She told herself that his lateness meant he had got the job. They were keeping him until closing time, showing him the ropes. He would come back on a commuter train. When she arrived back at Folly Hill, there would be a message on the telephone pad saying he would be round later to tell her about it. They would go out and celebrate. He'd have been a lousy lecturer, professor, don, whatever, but he would shine like a star in

198

industry, with her at his side. Always at his side, loving him. Filling that gap where his vulnerability lay.

There was no message on the pad. Her mother called, 'I'm in the kitchen. Yolande and Oliver are coming to eat. You can give me a hand if you like. By the way, there's a letter for you. I put it in your room.'

It was just as well that Charlotte was alone when she opened the blue envelope. One sheet of plain paper. No address, no signature. Large letters printed in black ink:

CLAIRE DROWNED BECAUSE MAX TOOK HER WATER WINGS.

She slumped on the bed and read the words over and over, not taking them in. Her brain had gone into rejection mode. She closed her eyes, listened to the silence, experienced the cold in the room. In the house. It crept round her, went through her, overwhelming her, encompassing her life with its freezing fingers.

A gently exasperated voice from the doorway said, 'Didn't you hear me, Charlotte? I've been calling. What on earth ... ?' Vivien moved uncertainly forward, looking concerned. 'Charlotte? Are you all right?'

She crumpled the paper in her hand, stood up, went through the door and down the stairs like a sleepwalker. Behind her, Vivien's cries of distress grew fainter.

She found herself in Puddle Lane where the gap in the hedge had been. The tough, prickly twigs reaching out unchecked through the years had made it very small. She went down on her knees and crawled through. Across the meadow with its cow parsley, its blood-red poppies, its elder and thorn. Then she was standing on the grass by the Bubbly Hole with its rushing, laughing water, its bubbles and foam.

She stood there as in a holy place, seeking the truth, terrified of what would come. Her eyes went to the ledge to which Claire used to swim with the help of her water wings. Her shocked mind showed her the dream she had had, that first night at Valle San Angelo. Gypsy dancers; Max whirling Claire away. Had she guessed all along?

It's true, said a voice in her head, inflicting terrible wounds.

She looked back at the ledge and there was Claire, sister of her heart, a shadow against the dark rock.

You've got to believe it, said the voice in her head.

No! cried her soul out of the empty darkness. *No!* Max was her lover, her life. She collapsed on the grass, weeping.

A swish of movement in the dry grass. Her head came up. Max was approaching through the gap in the hawthorn. Around him the blood-red poppies, the green bushes, seemed to wither into a strange darkness as though the fountain of life had been cut off. As though eternity had dropped a veil.

Chapter Twenty-Two

'So this is where you got to. I rang. I got the job! But only because my father's a friend of the chairman.' Max flung his towel and trunks on the grass and flopped down beside her.

'You wouldn't think I would end up being beholden to my father for a job, would you?' he asked, spitting out the words. 'He didn't even tell me beforehand, just showed me the ad in the paper. "Why don't you apply?" he said. I would've seen it myself, but of course he had to get in first. He can now say he got me the job. And effectively, that's true,' said Max, explosively.

'The chap who interviewed me didn't tell me either,' he went on. 'But after we'd talked, he said, "You'd better have a word with Mr Dalgleish", and took me along the corridor to this door marked CHAIRMAN. Then I knew – Dalgleish, old buddy of my father's. They went to school together. I should have told him to stick his job,' said Max fiercely. 'I should do it now. Matter of fact, I think I might. At least if I told them to get stuffed I'd have my self-respect back.' He picked a small stone out of the grass at his feet. It skimmed across the water then sank, leaving rings on the surface. 'What do you think?'

She thought she saw Claire in the stone sinking below the surface.

The twilight deepened. The blood red of the poppies had turned black, now. Charlotte looked into the Bubbly Hole. She said, 'You took Claire's water wings.'

Outside the ensuing silence, the noisy water burst over the rocks, foaming.

Max frowned, looking as though something was tapping at his mind.

'I got an anonymous letter,' said Charlotte, choking.

'And you believed it?' Max sounded uncertain. He looked at her, questioning, but the question in his eyes was directed inwardly, focusing on something that was beginning to tell him where the answer lay.

'I have to believe it,' she whispered. Her lost world shuddered.

'No!' Max spoke violently. 'No,' he said, speaking to the truth, pushing it away from him with fear. 'No!'

'It is true,' she sobbed.

'No,' said Max, uncertain again.

She flung herself at him, pummelling him with her fists. 'You killed her!' she cried. 'You killed her!'

'No!' he said again. 'No. No. No,' he repeated, as though by shouting loudly enough he could change the past.

His arms came round her, possessively. She was enclosed within him. They were pushing out what had happened, filling up the space with the strength of their love. She clung to him. The past was over and gone. He was hers. She his. Always had been. They were one.

'Go away,' she said to Claire with the strength of her heart. 'You cannot, may not, separate us.'

'It is you and I who may not be separated,' said the voice in her head. An angry, threatening voice. 'Max has to know he cannot separate twins. No one can separate twins and get away with it. Besides, he was mine first. You shan't have him,' said Claire. 'Never! Never! Never!' A pause, then, 'I'm sorry,' and Charlotte knew that something dreadful was going to happen. That Claire was apologising before she made it happen. 'Sorry,' Claire said again. She thought for a moment that Claire had decided she would make him kill her. That by ignoring Claire's threat she was accountable for her own murder.

'Claire!' she cried, not calling to Claire but to Max, trying to tell him that he must let her go so that Claire would be mollified. Then she felt him pushing himself inside her. 'No!' she groaned.

'Darling,' he whispered. 'My own darling.'

'Let me go!' She wanted to tell him that she was frightened of what Claire might do if they ignored her threats.

'I'll never let you go,' Max said. 'Never.'

'He's raping you,' said Claire cruelly.

'No!' she screamed to Claire. She pushed Max off her and struggled out of his arms. 'Charlotte!' He tried to grab her but she leaped to her feet and ran, running from Claire.

She ran across the meadow, her legs wobbling, threatening every step to cease supporting her. She climbed over the stile; her shirt, hanging awry, caught on the wire. She ripped it away and dragged herself up the green hill where the four-leaf clovers grew. She thrust the garden gate open and floundered into the orchard. In the long grass beneath the old Bramley apple tree, she flung herself down sobbing, with a sense of *déjà vu*.

Yolande found her there.

She, too, experienced that sense of *déjà vu*. Ten years slipped away. She remembered the screaming. The terrible silences. She said, 'Oh, hell!' and signed to Oliver to stay where he was, within the shadow of the trees. She ran through the long grass to where Charlotte lay prostrate, skirt and blouse all over the place, bare legs splayed. Sinking to her knees, she laid a gentle hand on Charlotte's outflung arm. 'What's the trouble, Char?'

Charlotte lifted her head and Yolande saw her swollen eyes, her ravaged face. 'What's happened to you?' she cried in alarm. 'Mum says you got a letter. Was there some awful news?'

Charlotte opened her mouth but could not speak.

'A trouble shared is a trouble halved,' Yolande pointed out tritely.

As though Max's crime could be halved! Charlotte emitted a wounded cry.

'I'm sorry if I've said the wrong thing. But honestly, Char, if it's as bad as that, you've got to tell someone.' Yolande's normal bossiness was softened by foreboding.

After a while Charlotte knew that was so. Her secret was too terrible to suffer alone. 'It was Max . . .'

'Max?' said Yolande, impatient but caring.

'Max who . . .' Charlotte's face worked as she tried to drag out the words that would not come.

'Oliver!' Yolande called. 'Oliver!'

He came running. They lifted Charlotte into a sitting position and supported her. 'What did Max do to you?'

She uttered a raw howl. 'To Claire!'

'What did he do to Claire?' Yolande's words fell harshly one over another in a panicky rush. 'For heaven's sake, Charlotte! What are you saying?'

'Let her cry,' said Oliver. 'Don't tell us if you can't bear to. Shall I say it?' He waited, then asked, gentle within his outrage, 'He drowned her?'

Charlotte's body jerked with convulsive sobs. 'I can't bear it. I can't,' she cried. But neither could she bear to have Oliver say that thing, no less true, but worse. So much worse. She had to put it right. 'No. He didn't. But he took her water wings.'

'Don't scream,' said Yolande in a terrified voice.

The scream stopped in her throat. Oliver and Yolande sat with her in appalled silence, their arms round her. Yolande tentatively straightened her clothes.

'I don't know what to do,' Charlotte whimpered. She wanted to die. She put her hands over her face. Rocked backwards and forwards, suffering.

They were muttering over her head.

'As I see it,' said Yolande, dropping words carelessly in her anger, 'there's not a damn thing you can do this long afterwards. He was only twelve, wasn't he? At least you won't have to see him again,' she added vengefully, 'that's one consolation. He won't be at Oxford next year. And when you come down he'll be off working. Him and his pathetic third,' she said contemptuously. 'I thought he was supposed to be clever.'

'I don't know what to do,' Charlotte whispered again, meaning she could not live without Max. That she dared not defy Claire. 'Help me, Yolande.'

Yolande looked up at Oliver in the shadowy gloom. 'I s'pose the parents have to be told,' she said. 'There's nothing worse than not knowing. I lie awake in the night still, wondering about those bloody water wings. It is a relief to know. And it's only fair to tell them. But hearing will bring it all back, the whole thing. Not only Claire's . . .' even she could not bear to say it '. . . but their problems. That's when things went wrong. Dad blaming her. Oh, damn! Damn! I s'pose we've got to tell them. But I don't think you should be there, Char.'

'D'you know what I think?' said Oliver kindly. 'I think you should nip off to Valle San Angelo, Charlotte, and spend the rest of the vacation with Sylvia. If your father won't pay, I will. As Yolande says, it's not going to help to have you here.'

'Yes,' said Yolande, starting to her feet, sounding relieved, 'what a good idea! Sylvia'll sort you out.'

Laurence Fosse said impatiently, 'What's the matter with the boy? Isn't he happy about the job?'

They were on the south side of the house, in the last of the twilight. Jessica had been pulling up lettuces that had gone to seed and was now tidying the climbers. Laurence was topping up the pond. He suspected a leak.

'I can't get through to him,' Jessica said. 'I don't really think it's the job. I suspect he's fallen out with Charlotte.' She told her husband about the packet that had come addressed to Max in the mail. How he had opened it in front of her, then swiftly thrust it into his pocket. 'He looked angry and upset. I thought it was jewellery,' she said. 'I'm sure I glimpsed gold. And it had a local postmark. Maybe Charlotte was returning something he gave her. Maybe the affair's over,' she said, showing guilty relief.

'A bloody good thing if it is,' muttered Laurence, wondering where Max had got the money to buy jewellery. They both hoped Max would end up marrying little Louisa Waite. They went out of their way to be nice to Louisa, pretty, docile, an only child. Now that Laurence had been forced to accept that Max was not going to be an academic, he could easily visualise him managing, one day owning, Waites' department store.

'I think I'll have a word,' said Laurence. 'It would be damned awkward if he turned round and said he didn't want the job after all the trouble I went to. Phil wasn't all that keen to take him on, but said he'd be happy to find a place for him in the Hong Kong office. Or Sydney. I didn't tell you that because I knew you wouldn't like it. But . . .' He stared into the pond, frowning.

'I would *not* like it,' said Jessica. 'We've seen little enough of him, what with school and university.'

Laurence ignored her implied plea. 'D'you know, there are only five goldfish there now. That marauding cat has been here again. A couple of years abroad could put paid to the Charlotte affair if this is only a tiff,' he said.

'The year in Australia didn't. He hadn't been home five minutes when he was on the phone to her,' Jessica reminded him.

Laurence contemplated her drawn face. She clearly wasn't thinking about the goldfish. He took the hose into the garden

205

shed. When he returned, he said, 'I noticed his trunks on the line the other day. Where's he been swimming?'

Jessica shrugged and picked up the secateurs. 'I don't ask him where he goes.'

'He'd need your car to go into Wylie to the baths.'

'I've said he can take my car any time but he hasn't, lately.'

'You don't by any chance think he's been swimming at the Bubbly Hole?'

'Why would he?' She spoke edgily.

'Because,' said Laurence, looking annoyed, 'as you very well know, he never was one to abide by the rules.'

They were in bed, half asleep, when he knocked on their door. 'Dad?'

Jessica, immediately alert, shook her husband's shoulder. 'It's Max. He wants to talk to you.'

Laurence groaned. He switched on the light and reached for his dressing gown. 'What the hell can he want at this hour?'

She looked at him with apprehension, but did not reply.

The lights were on in the upstairs passage. Max had returned to the ground floor. Laurence found him in the study, standing by the bookcase.

'What's this?' Laurence asked brusquely. 'Are you drunk?'

'No.'

'What's happened?' He shoved his hands deep into his pockets, stared at the knuckles through the thin material. Raised his head, levelled his gaze. Waited.

'Remember that radio I bought when I was twelve?'

'You've got me out of bed to talk about an old radio?'

'I bought it with money I took from Claire.'

Laurence's eyes flickered. In his pockets the fists clenched. 'Borrowed, surely?' He waited for Max to correct his statement.

'Took,' said Max, though indistinctly. 'Then I stole her water wings so she couldn't come after me. She was on the ledge.'

'You've kept it to yourself for a mighty long time,' his father said harshly. 'Why bring it up now?'

'Charlotte's found out.'

'How? Did you tell her?'

Max frowned.

'Well?'

'How could I?'

'I don't understand you.'

'You see,' said Max, 'I'd forgotten.'

'*Forgotten*!'

'You can. You can put things into the back of your mind.'

'Can you?' asked his father, bursting into insulting, bitter laughter. 'Can you really?'

'I was pretty young at the time.' Max was defensive now.

'You were twelve. At twelve you're considered to be aware of right and wrong.'

'How did I know she would . . .? I mean, at twelve, you don't think of these things,' said Max distractedly. 'I was thinking of getting my radio.'

'You can remember that, all right,' said Laurence unfairly. 'You don't remember you left a child to drown but you can remember your goddamn radio.'

Max said, 'I do remember now. It was raining, and there was lightning. I couldn't ride my bike – the man in the shop, what's his name, Franklin, wouldn't let me go because of the lightning. So I sat in the shop and listened to the radio.'

'Settled down to listen to your radio and forgot about Claire, eh?'

Max flushed. Continued stoically as though he had not heard. 'It got to closing time and Franklin shut the shop.'

'Then you remembered?' The cold eyes surveyed him with distaste.

'I did go back to the Bubbly Hole,' said Max angrily. 'At least, I went to the ditch where I'd left the water wings. But they weren't there, so I thought she'd swum across and gone home. She'd have seen the water wings as she came down the bank. They were bright yellow. You couldn't miss them.'

His father looked at him consideringly.

'You don't believe me, do you?'

Laurence did not reply. He went and sat behind his desk, fiddling with his pens. 'I have this problem,' he said, looking up. 'The water wings were never found.'

'I give you my word,' said Max, making a tremendous effort to speak calmly. 'I don't know what happened to them.'

His father was silent for a moment. 'By the way, you know Alan Derwent doesn't allow anyone to swim at the Bubbly Hole,

207

not since . . . I saw your trunks on the line.' He looked into Max's eyes, challenging him to lie.

'Yes, I did go, that day you blew your top about my lousy pass.' Max's humiliation showed in his eyes. 'And don't ask me why,' he added wrathfully, 'because I'll only have to say I didn't think again and you won't like that. And I went there tonight, after seeing your friend Dalgliesh.' He laid bitter emphasis on the word 'friend'. 'But I didn't swim. That's when I met Charlotte. She was there.' His face twisted.

'Swimming?' asked Laurence, his eyes nearly popping out of his head.

'No. That's when she told me she knew.'

Laurence looked down at his leatherbound blotter. When he looked up it was with the air of a man who has made a decision. 'Are you expecting trouble?' he asked. 'Is Charlotte likely to talk?'

'I don't know.'

'You didn't ask her?' He sounded astonished.

'I didn't think of it.' Max turned abruptly so that his back was to his father. He dragged up a deep breath, rested his folded arms against an upper shelf of the bookcase, laid his forehead on the backs of his hands. His mind was boiling with remorse greater than his misdeeds. With what he couldn't, after all, tell this emotional cripple who was his father. Why had he told him about the radio? He knew. Because he couldn't look into those relentless, uncomprehending eyes and tell him what he needed to tell. That now he had faced up to what he had done to Claire he didn't know how he was going to live with himself. That he needed help.

'Let's have a drink,' Laurence said. Max heard a cupboard door open, a tinkle of glass. 'Let's be objective about this. It's the sort of thing—'

Objective! Something shattered in Max's mind. He swung round, saying angrily, 'You took me to stay with Gran. The other kids went to the funeral.'

His father paused, whisky bottle in hand.

'I see now that if I'd been around . . . Talking about it . . . I mean, I wouldn't have put it out of my mind, would I?'

'I remember everything about that evening,' Laurence said coldly. 'I asked you if you knew anything about the water wings. You said you didn't.'

'You didn't tell me Claire was drowned! When I heard, I didn't connect it with taking the water wings. I didn't realise until –' Max's voice broke. Tears stood in his eyes. 'I didn't know until tonight. When Charlotte told me.'

His father put his whisky glass down on the desk. He took a step towards Max. He said distinctly, 'You *did* know Claire was drowned. When I asked you about the money, you said – believe me, Max, the words are etched on my mind – you said, "I can't pay it back, now she's dead." You may have put it into the back of your mind because you wished to forget,' he said cruelly, 'but believe me, Max, you knew.'

A sound from the doorway. Jessica stood there in a pink night-dress and floral dressing gown, her dark hair falling round her face. They looked at her mutely. Laurence put the whisky bottle back in the cupboard, placed the glasses on the upper shelf then walked past her without speaking and went on up the stairs. Jessica looked after him. Then she came forward, reached out and touched Max's arm.

'Can I help, darling?'

'Lend me your car.'

'At this hour? Do you know what time it is? It's nearly mid-night.'

'I have to see Charlotte.'

'No, Max,' said his mother. 'Whatever it is, sleep on it. You can't disturb the Godfreys at this time of night.'

'Then I'll walk.' He strode out of the room and down the passage.

She ran after him, opened the back door that he had slammed. 'Max!'

He did not turn. He walked fast and disappeared into the darkness.

Chapter Twenty-Three

Charlotte gazed on the Spanish villa's white façade. The long windows with their white wooden shutters were closed against the scorching sun. It was so familiar, so dear. The peeling paint she had not remembered. The geraniums were still there in their big stone urns. The smell of hot stone crept into her nostrils. There was the mango tree reaching in over the terrace with its generous golden offerings. It was like coming to a safe haven.

She followed Sylvia into the big white-walled room, shabby now as seen through her grown-up eyes. She looked with affection on the heavy three-piece suite, unremarkable as a set of furniture, but an old friend. She remembered jumping on the bed, sinking into its deep safety. Remembered the geckos. Where had they gone, those silent spectators of her days and dream-filled nights?

She turned and looked through the open door at the great somnolent giant of a mountain. She embraced its greatness in her heart. Experienced its benevolent blessing.

Carmina, fleshier all these years later, came to offer her own garrulous welcome. Incomprehensible Spanish words toppled one over the other. Sylvia's translations were left behind. How Charlotte has grown. A woman now! '¡Que hermosa!' How beautiful she was! She must wear her hat in the sun. 'Sombrero.' Carmina mimed putting it on her head, a big one, pulling down the brim. Such pretty hair must not be allowed to lose its colour again.

She had brought a papaya in a basket, yellow as a buttercup. 'Es la papaya mas grande', it is the biggest. She was proud of having grown it, and prouder still to be giving it to the guest. She would leave them to talk. She went off down the steps triumphant in her ability to give.

That night, after a meal of goat stew and mangoes, they settled on the long cane chairs, side by side. Over the stone balustrade, the mountain with its moonlit promontories, its shadowed folds, smiled down on them.

'There's something I need to tell you,' Charlotte said.

'Take it gently. There's all night. And all the tomorrows. Is it a blood-letting, or do you want advice?'

'A blood-letting.' Sylvia's antennae found exactly the right word. 'I have to tell you who caused Claire's death.'

'I know,' said Sylvia. 'I've always known. And so have you.'

Charlotte waited to be knocked senseless by Sylvia's disclosure. Felt the knowledge creeping out of its hiding place in her mind. Old knowledge that she had not allowed. The dream. Gypsies dancing. Max stealing Claire away.

'The mountain gives of itself, but it doesn't ask that you accept,' Sylvia said. 'When I saw you with Max at Yolande's wedding, I understood you couldn't.' She reached out a hand and Charlotte gripped it.

'I love him, Sylvia.' She had not been able to say that to Yolande and Oliver. How could you? they would have demanded, baffled and indignant. He killed Claire and you say you love him!

Sylvia spoke, 'This is your testing time.'

Time to bind herself to her love? Or give in to Claire? Charlotte contemplated the empty desolation of life without Max. She knew, had known since that day Goldie threw him, that Claire, the rogue spirit, wanted revenge more than she wanted peace in paradise.

That night as she lay in bed looking through the moonlight at the mountain, she felt Claire was near. 'Go away,' she whispered.

'He raped you,' said Claire.

'No,' Charlotte told her in reply. 'He did not.' Something had happened to her because of Claire accusing him, but not rape. Max loved her. 'Max and I were born for each other,' she murmured into the night.

'You and I were born for each other,' Claire said, 'but Max only wanted you. He has to understand he can't have one without the other.'

'Go away!' Charlotte wept. 'You don't know what you say. Go away,' she whispered with fear.

Fernando owned a part share in a restaurant. He seemed not to have changed, though grown taller, certainly. His brown smile gleamed with white teeth. He had learned English and German in Frankfurt at a language school while also learning the restaurant business. It was mostly German tourists who came to the valley. He and Charlotte swam and sunbathed on the beach together in the mornings as they used to do when she was ten.

'Why did you need English?' she asked him. 'You don't get English tourists here.'

'I learnt it for you. I wait for you to come.' He reached out and touched her damp hair. Ran his fingers through the tips. 'Always I want a blonde wife.'

'And I'll do? Thanks.' She snatched the hair tips away, laughing. 'You must have lots of Frauleins and señoritas after you now you're a man of substance.' He threw a handful of sand over her. She might never have been away.

One morning she reached into the pocket of her shift and brought out the crystal. 'Remember this?'

He held it in his palm, turning it this way and that so that the sun shafted off it into rays of pink, green and gold. 'It has brought you luck?'

'Not luck, no. But it has helped to hold things together.' She lifted a handful of sand and let it speed through her fingers, sliding like silk.

He unzipped a tiny pocket in his trunks and slid the crystal in. She was about to protest, then stopped.

'I will keep it for us,' he said. 'If you need it, it will find you. Look out!' He leaped to his feet, snatched up their clothes and towels. There was a whoosh as the water swirled round them on the sand. They stood in it, ankle deep. Watched it retreating leaving a white line of salt. They moved further up towards the stone retaining wall, the tide's ultimate deterrent. The sun had risen higher in the sky. It burned down on their heads. They would have to go in soon.

'I know you have been to Italy for holidays,' Fernando said. 'Why did you not come here? Why not stay here now and help me in my restaurant? Always I want a blonde wife.'

212

'What a tease you are, Fernando!' She crinkled her eyes at him.

'Come and see my restaurant.'

They rubbed the sand off their bodies, slithered over stones worn smooth by the running tides, pulled on their scanty garments and crossed the dusty road. Inside the restaurant's palm-filled garden tourists idled at little wrought-iron tables dipping into *tapas*, sipping wine or cool Spanish beer.

'You like my English lawn?' Fernando asked, gesturing. 'I water it every day. You know about the wells in the valley?'

She had seen how the water rushed through the banana plantation, running along open canals. She remembered racing with the spectral Claire at her side and he, a sturdy boy then, not too fleet of foot, bringing up the rear.

'If I am to keep an English wife,' he said, 'I must give her something to remind her of home.'

She grasped his hand and smacked it, then held it to her cheek with affection. 'It's lovely to be with you again, Fernando.'

They crossed a palm-thatched courtyard and went into the main part of the building. The whitewashed walls were green with climbing geraniums and red with their blossoms; great pots disgorged exotic blooms on long stalks.

'It is a very old villa,' Fernando said. 'Built one hundred years ago. Accommodating, you say, to a restaurant?'

'Yes, I would say that.'

'Only three rooms now we have taken some walls down. And the kitchen, of course.' That was at the back, looking into the banana palms.

He introduced her to his partner, who kissed her hand and complimented her on her beauty – '*Es exquisita*' – and poured them long glasses of sangria.

Charlotte had an idea. 'Look, I don't want to impose on Sylvia,' she said. 'I'll come and work here. You can pay me in dinners.' Work would keep problems at bay, she thought.

Fernando's black eyes glowed. 'And the señora – she will have to chaperone you, of course. We'll give her a special table. The best,' he declared, throwing wide his arms, enveloping the concept of Sylvia.

'A chaperone! I like that.'

Sylvia agreed. Decorative in bright kaftans, she settled each

213

evening in a palm-decorated corner and was given the freedom of the menu. The staff paid court to her. She chatted to old friends and made new ones.

Jesús came to see her, but he was no longer Sylvia's helpful boy. Five years in Madrid had made him sophisticated. He was twenty-nine now and aware of Charlotte no longer as a child. He bowed over her hand and looked her appreciatively up and down.

Perceiving him as predatory, Fernando did not make him welcome. 'There are other restaurants around. *?Porqué no probar lo de Francisco?*' Why don't you try Francisco's? he snapped, eyes flashing. Charlotte related the story of how she had told her parents she met Jesús in Valle San Angelo. That they had not been amused.

'*Vaya lavar los pies de alguien.*' Go and wash somebody's feet, said Fernando, waving him off with a curt flick of the hand.

Around midnight, Fernando escorted his waitress and his guest along the narrow track through the whispering banana plantation and up the steps to the villa. Sylvia worried just a little about the dinners coming free.

'You're not getting food free,' he protested. 'You are on duty, looking after important staff. The dinner is nothing. *No es nada.*' He flipped the concept of cost away with his hand. 'I pay you in *pesetas* if I can afford.' He was grave and courtly in his dealings with Sylvia.

'Besides,' Charlotte added, 'Fernando says you're good for business. People come in because you're there.'

Sometimes Carmina came, not to dine, but to sit for a while at Sylvia's table chatting, drinking a glass of wine. Fernando's brothers and sisters came too, shook hands with the new waitress and passed the time of day. The dining room, the courtyard and the lawn were busy with their comings and goings, noisy with their good will and laughter.

Then one evening, Charlotte threw up. The fish dish could not have been to blame, because the restaurant bought only from the most trusted fishermen. The next morning, before she could get out of bed, she threw up again. Her period was three weeks overdue.

Since she had gone to work in Fernando's restaurant, she had been too busy, too involved with newness, with people and

214

excitement, to think. But now she could no longer turn a blind eye. She had hoped that the problem would go away.

It hadn't.

'You can abandon Oxford and marry him,' said Sylvia, having no knowledge of how this seed had been sown.

Charlotte remembered Yolande saying, 'Sylvia'll sort you out.' There could be no sorting out without knowledge, and no telling when the truth would cut your heart to pieces in its speaking.

'You say he's got this job. Is it well enough paid to keep a family? Or you can have an abortion. It's not up to me to comment on that.' As a Catholic, she meant. 'Or you can have the baby in secret, if you wish. You're very welcome to stay with me, and if you want to have it adopted, no one at home will be any the wiser.'

Except Claire. She had not gone away as Charlotte begged her, that first night of her arrival. Charlotte felt Claire's eyes on her, was aware of her predatory presence in the darkness of the night. She knew now that good spirits, like Carlos, wait to be invited in. The bad ones, the mischievous ones, slip into the void when the heart is empty. She was afraid to bear Max's baby in the valley where Claire was so near. This had not been Claire's plan for her, she was certain.

Last night Charlotte had dreamed again the dream that came to her on her previous visit. She was on the flat roof of Sylvia's villa, looking up. The terrace above, where Max had stood, was empty, though the people whom she had seen down below were there as before, swarming about their business. 'We can't help you,' they said, repeating what they had said before.

Where was Max?

She told Sylvia about the 'pro-life' campaign and the crude banners she and her undergraduate friends carried through the streets of Oxford.

'Since he helped you make the banner, it would appear he agrees with you.'

'Life was simple then,' said Charlotte, angry now with that girl of eighteen who didn't know what the hell she was doing, carrying a banner telling other people, as Max said, what to do. 'I was looking at the matter from a different perspective,' she said. 'I was grateful that Claire and I had not been aborted. Now I'm seeing it from that woman's viewpoint.' She wondered if that

215

woman also had been racked with indecision. It must have been so.

'Woman?' echoed Sylvia, not at all certain she understood. 'Do you mean your mother?'

'My mother,' said Charlotte ferociously, 'is Vivien Godfrey. *That* woman gave me away.'

Sylvia took a moment to answer, then she said, 'You seem to have crossed off one of your options.'

Had she? 'I suppose I have.' Then she thought of another one. 'Fernando proposed to me. There's an option.'

'Oh, no!' Sylvia leaped to Fernando's defence. A red-blooded Spanish boy would kill his bride if he found she was carrying another man's child. Spanish bridegrooms, especially those brought up in the old-fashioned way of remote islands, were hot on virginity.

'I was only joking,' Charlotte said feebly. She no longer knew what she really meant.

Time to go home. Time to return to Oxford, except that she could not. Sylvia offered to accompany her.

'I have to do it myself,' Charlotte said. Sylvia did not enquire what she had decided to do.

On the plane Charlotte made her decision. She took the memory of what Louisa had told her out of its hiding place in the back of her mind, and sent it like a spirit missile through the double plastic window of the plane. She watched it disappear as a shadow over the Atlantic Ocean, bearing the burden of Max's culpability for Claire's death that was now half her lifetime away. Time to forget. She wished she hadn't sent the necklace back.

They were in Charlotte's bedroom. Vivien, wanting to be close, was sitting on Claire's bed watching her unpack. It was still Claire's bed for nobody ever slept in it.

Robert had come alone to the airport, answering Charlotte's questions with 'I came straight from the office' and 'Your mother scarcely drives these days. I suspect she's lost her nerve.' Charlotte had been quiet with him, intimating displeasure. He could have nipped down off the motorway and picked Vivien up.

When she saw Vivien, unsteady on her feet, crumpled rejection in her expression and the way she stood, shoulders drooping, she

216

felt murderous. Not only on her mother's behalf, but because Robert had caused her to turn against him. She put her arms round Vivien, willing strength into her. You can die of a broken heart if someone you love doesn't care. I care, she said with her warm, close arms. Listen to me. I care.

Vivien said fretfully, 'You haven't left yourself much time to get your things together. We expected you at the beginning of the week.' She had put on more weight. Her drinking problem showed in the coarseness of her skin and the trembling of her hands.

Yolande, on the telephone, hinted at serious disturbances: broken china, hurled abuse; gin found hidden in the Aga oven, which was not used in the summer. Robert had emptied his drinks cabinet, but that wouldn't stop her. She had her caches.

'The situation's dire,' Yolande said. 'We went down last weekend. Dad wasn't warned – deliberate on our part, I have to say. We found Mum sitting in the study, staring at the wall. He didn't appear. He looked embarrassed next morning when he found us there.'

Charlotte was full of anguish and compassion, as well as regret that she had run away. Forgetting how Oliver and Yolande, wanting to spare Vivien, had rushed her to the plane, she felt she might have stayed. She had not thought that Robert would be off seeking comfort from the blonde at 5 Cherry Tree Road. But of course. Of course.

She turned with a loving smile and her eye fell on a small packet lying on the dressing table. 'What's this?'

'It came in the mail,' Vivien said.

A Wylie postmark. Under the soft packing something hard. Before going to La Gomera she had posted just such a packet as this. Charlotte felt a glow start in the centre of her, experienced it spreading out through her body. A smile came up from her heart and drew her mouth into an upward curve. Max had refused to take the necklace back. He was ready, as was she, to start again. With a nail file, she slit the end of the packet, took out the necklace and put it round her neck.

Vivien smiled. 'It doesn't go well with jeans. What was it doing in the post?'

'Secrets,' said Charlotte. She took the necklace off again. 'I'm going now to visit Claire's grave.' She lifted her head, confident in the knowledge of what had to be done. She went through the door and dumped her empty bag on the landing. Later she would take it up to the attic. 'D'you feel like a walk?'

'Yes, I'll come.' But her steps were uncertain as they crossed the lawn. She was not looking where she put her feet. The second time she tripped, hitting her toe on the edge of a paving stone, she said pathetically, 'I don't think I'm wearing the right shoes.' Then she added in a sad little voice that begged for relief, 'I took some flowers up on the anniversary.'

'That's OK,' Charlotte replied. 'I'll go alone.' Perhaps it was as well. She could speak aloud when there was no one to hear.

The ancient church lay somnolent, etched against a cloudless sky. She went into the churchyard through the east gate and crossed the grass to Claire's grave. For some moments she stood looking down at the fading posies. The rosebuds and lavender were there again, with no card.

'Goodbye, Claire,' she said, speaking kindly but firmly. She pointed to the words on the gravestone. 'That's what you must do now: rest in peace.' She felt a great deal wiser and tougher than that girl who had protested so vociferously about the inscription.

'Goodbye,' she said again.

She stood still and alert in the silence, looking round the churchyard. Not a leaf moved. There was no sense of a ghostly presence. No disturbance. 'Claire?'

Footsteps on the brick path. She looked up and saw Louisa with her old dog Pip.

Louisa looked away. Quickened her steps. Memories crowded into Charlotte's mind. Louisa's look of triumph when Max danced with her. Jealous people lied. There was the anonymous letter that she now perceived as containing a lie because she would not have it true. Perhaps Max had told Louisa there was no hope, no love in his heart, for her. That he was going to marry Charlotte.

Quick as a flash, she intercepted Louisa on the path. 'Hello.'

Colour flared in the other girl's cheeks as though some hint had come to her of Charlotte's intention.

'I had an anonymous letter,' Charlotte said. 'I'd like to know who wrote it.' She added, looking squarely into those baby-blue eyes, 'Perhaps it was you.'

Louisa flipped her pretty curls over her shoulders, first with one hand, then the other.

'It concerned Max,' said Charlotte, watching Louisa's face for guilt.

'Then you'd better write and ask him about it,' Louisa snapped.

The words crept into Charlotte's mind, not making sense.

'Didn't he tell you he was going back to Australia to live?' she asked. Those blue eyes glittered with cold triumph. 'He's already gone.'

Charlotte did not see her walk away with her dog, She stood staring, transfixed, at the place where they had been.

Chapter Twenty-Four

They saw her coming up the garden path, saw the dejection.

'I'll deal with it,' said Laurence, stepping back from the window.

He wandered casually out on the lawn and looked up at the sky. When he heard her voice, he turned, looking surprised. 'Charlotte!'

Her face was empty of all but distress. She asked in a quivering, voice, 'Is Max at home?'

Laurence could see she knew Max was not at home. Was indeed far away. 'Hrumph,' he said. 'Did he not tell you he was going to Australia?'

'He didn't know he was going when I saw him last. Didn't know,' she repeated with a beaten air.

'I expect he did.' Dr Fosse took on the manner of a lecturer facing a foolishly troubled student. 'I expect he wasn't ready to talk about it. And then you went away, I understand. You didn't leave an address.' He laid the blame firmly on her, smiling.

'Could you tell me where I can get in touch with him?'

Laurence considered. 'I wouldn't want to give you his address without his consent. I understand you'd had a row. You accused him of something . . . well, let's not go into it.' He made a pretence of showing her friendship though she scarcely deserved it. 'You're both very young. You've a long way to go. I know your father is expecting great things of you,' he said encouragingly, then added with sadness, 'which indeed we were of Max. I don't want to be hard, Charlotte, but we do blame you for his third. We expected a first followed by an offer of a lecturership. I'm sure you know we intended he should have an academic career. I'm sorry to say it but we believe you put paid to that.'

She looked at him as though he had landed from another planet. Spoke Martian which she did not understand. She thought, Now I know why Max was so demoralised.

Laurence adopted a brusque voice. 'He's got a great opportunity now, in Australia. You wouldn't want to hold him back, would you?'

Her face had gone hollow, as though his words had emptied her out. She made a thin protest. 'He wouldn't go without getting in touch. Leaving a message. Something . . .'

'I don't know about that. Have you asked your parents?' He reached out to pick two dead heads off a rose bush.

'I've only just heard,' she said. 'Louisa told me.'

'Ah, yes. Louisa.' He smiled, conferring status on Louisa. 'Yes,' he said, 'she knew. They saw a good deal of each other before he went. Well . . .' He half turned away. Jessica was watching from a window, looking strained. 'There's really no more to be said. I'd ask you in but my wife's . . .' He broke off, stood watching Charlotte as she retreated.

She disappeared behind the hedge into Puddle Lane. He picked up a pair of gardening gloves that were lying on the grass and took them to the shed. When he went inside, Jessica was still standing at the window. Now she had her back to it, waiting for him. Her face was drawn with distress.

Suddenly he felt deeply ashamed. 'Bloody kids!' he said. 'Let's have a drink.'

'Yes, he appeared,' said Robert. 'I gave him short shrift, I have to say. Knowing what I knew, I had trouble keeping my hands to myself. I told him he could do with a horsewhipping. I was blunt,' said Robert. 'I sent him on his way. I told him not to show his face here again. I made it very clear how you felt about him.'

Charlotte saw her father as a stranger. You're so good at getting rid of people, she thought. You got rid of my mother – short shrift describes rather well what you've done to her. She wanted to leap at him, claw his face, tear his hair.

I'm going mad, she thought. In her fevered imagination, Claire laughed. That'll teach you to love the boy who took away my life.

'To think he could murder Claire and expect to carry on a friendship with you!' Robert said. 'It beggars belief. Still, as you say, he's gone to Australia. Perhaps he had merely come to say goodbye. Running scared,' he said with cold contempt. 'We could have made Forge Green too hot for him. He knew that. So he's fled to safety. Good riddance!'

She went upstairs, moving automatically, aware not of her feet, only her brain which had become unhinged and was flapping around in her empty head. In her room she thought, I must get rid of that bed. What's the point of having Claire's bed here when she's dead? Dead and gone and buried.

She flung the duvet on to the floor and took a look at the bolts that held the bed frame together. Ran down the back stairs, across the dusky lawn, into the garden shed for a spanner, and back again. Heaved the mattress up, slid it against the wall, unscrewed the bolts, top and bottom.

Out! Out! she muttered as she staggered up the attic steps with the headboard. She left it leaning against the wall. Returned, panting, for the foot. Out! One sprigged duvet, Liberty print. Pillows, neat cotton squares edged with frills. Out! She lugged the mattress across the room. Out! Next, the little twin lamp with its blue frilled shade, and the twin bedside table.

Robert looked up from the hall, frowning. 'What on earth are you doing?' He hurried up the stairs and saw the mattress and furniture. 'What *are* you doing, Charlotte?'

'I need to get these things out of my room,' Charlotte said through clenched teeth.

'All right.' He was baffled, but reasonable. 'Why tonight?'

'Could you help me?' She went back into the room and pointed to the sprung base lying flat on the floor. 'Pick up that end,' she said. 'We can carry it between us.'

'But we don't need to,' he protested. 'I'll get O'Brien in tomorrow. It's far too heavy—'

'Tonight,' she said.

He rubbed his forehead in that way he had, looked at her mad eyes and made a decision. 'All right,' he said. 'I'll take the front. The back end may be easier for you.' They edged it round the bend in the stairs. Robert said, 'Hold it this way. Now that.' They reached the attic. He leaned it against the wall. Charlotte ran back for the mattress.

Vivien was standing in the middle of the room, looking bewildered. 'What's going on?'

'Exorcism,' said Charlotte.

'Now come on,' Robert said authoritatively. 'I can cope with the rest of this tomorrow.'

Vivien bent down to pick up a piece of paper from the floor. 'What have we here? A note for you?'

Charlotte took it from her and read, '*I did not give this to you. You should know I cannot afford such things. Max.*'

'It must have fallen out of the packet when you opened it,' Vivien said.

Charlotte began to pack her bags. Back to Oxford, pregnant by a man who did not want her. Who had never sent her a Valentine's Day gift of an expensive necklace. Who had raped her. Who had killed her twin. Who was in the long run a coward. Cowards run away.

Vivien came and stood in the doorway, glancing with sad eyes at the bags. 'I miss you so much when you're away.'

'Only one more year,' said Charlotte cheerily.

'Then you'll be off to London. You won't want to stay here.'

Vivien looked so lonely standing there, arms hanging by her sides, that Charlotte went over and folded her in her arms, wanting to say, 'There's going to be a baby soon. You'll love that.' Something held her back.

'Yolande says when I was small you were the smartest woman in Forge Green,' she said, noting in her mind that only yesterday she would have said 'when we were small'. She felt she had moved one step ahead.

Vivien's voice emerged down beat and quivering as though she was about to cry. 'I had so much to live for, then.' Her desolation was palpable.

'Claire has been dead for ten years,' said Charlotte robustly. 'It's time to forget. You've got a great deal to live for now. Three children who love you. I expect Yolande'll be having a baby soon. There's an excitement!' She recognised she had hit upon the way to lead up to telling Vivien about her own pregnancy. Two babies, she would say. Yet still something held her back. A phantom warning hand.

'I can't see Yolande having a family for years,' Vivien said. 'She and Oliver have taken on a huge mortage. I was so glad when she got married. I was terrified for years that she would get pregnant. I knew she was sleeping with Oliver.' Vivien smiled affectionately. 'You're such a good girl. I've never had to worry about you.'

'How did you know?' Charlotte's voice snapped like an elastic band. 'How did you know she was sleeping with Oliver?'

'Girls take on a different look. They get – ripe, I suppose, is the best way I could put it.'

Ripe! Did she look ripe? Charlotte cast a swift, covert glance at her face in the mirror. No, she did not look ripe. The memories that marked her face were bleak and cold.

'I know there are a lot of foolish girls having babies these days outside of marriage, and perhaps some parents condone it,' Vivien said, 'but Robert was brought up in the old-fashioned way. Victorian, almost. He never moved with the times. If Yolande had got pregnant he would have thrown her out.'

'*What!*'

'Yes, truly. Your father is a hard man,' said Vivien, looking down at the carpet. 'Unforgiving. And as you know, very much for keeping up appearances. You can't blame him, I suppose. His mother was the hardest woman I ever knew.'

'Victorians,' said Charlotte distinctly, 'kept mistresses tucked away. Victorians were hypocrites.'

Vivien said in a bright, brittle voice, 'Oh, yes. You could say that. But brushing the dirt under the carpet isn't such a bad way of keeping things tidy.' She lifted her head and went out of the room, walking as though she had suddenly found dignity in the way she lived.

Charlotte recognised that she had been adopted by surely the only family in the country who couldn't cope with the thought of an unmarried, pregnant daughter.

There was no future in returning to Oxford. She would have to make plans.

She saw history repeating itself. Was this the route by which she and Claire had come to Folly Hill? For the first time a breath of sympathy stirred. Had that girl who gave birth to them been thrown out? She remembered the misery of thinking she had not been wanted after Claire's death. The sheer despair of rejection. Of living through that terrible first term at Mountfield Manor, clinging to Isabel, cherishing the hope that someone might take her home for the holidays and keep her.

224

Would Yolande give her a home? She already knew Yolande would say, 'Why the hell should my life be disrupted by your so-called standards? Go and get an abortion like everybody else. Oliver will pay . . .'

Would Kenneth allow her to share his tiny flat at the wrong end of Wandsworth? Imagine him taking her to hospital in labour! How? On his bike?

Oh, why had she driven Max away! What did it matter, ten years later, that he had taken Claire's water wings? A childish trick that went wrong. Claire was dead, dead, dead. It was the living that counted.

Ideas, like gnats, flew through her mind. Could she borrow enough money for her fare to Australia? How would she find Max when she arrived?

But he didn't want her.

The next day she took the bus into Wylie-under-Lyne.

'Employment agencies?' William repeated. His glasses shone in the sunbeam coming through the library window, blanking out his eyes. 'What are you looking up employment agencies for?'

'I need a job. What are you doing here?' Charlotte asked brightly, turning the tables.

'I'm looking up a newspaper report of a recent case at the crown court. What about Oxford? Haven't you got another year to go?'

Shrugging, she turned over a page and scribbled something in her notebook, really too busy to talk to him.

William sat down opposite, leaning his elbows on the table. The librarian, coming up beside him, said, 'I've put the papers over there,' and pointed.

William said, 'Thanks.' To Charlotte he went on, 'I thought—'

She broke in impatiently, still looking down at the page, 'Oh, yes. Everybody did. But when Max left Oxford, I discovered I wasn't really all that interested. It was fun being there with him.' She flipped over another page, looking down concentratedly at the print.

William said, speaking very carefully, 'I heard he'd gone to Australia.'

'Yes.' She ran her finger down the page, absorbing herself to show how uninterested she was in Max's going to Australia.

'So it's . . .'

225

'Hum,' she said and made another note.

William tried again, 'It's off?'

'Oh, yes,' she said casually. 'Quite off.' She laughed, saw with horror that a tear had plopped on to the page. Swiftly she brushed it with her sleeve, pushed her chair back.

William reached across the table and clamped his fingers round her wrist. She collapsed back into the chair. His face was swimming before her eyes. The tears splashed on her arms, on the desk as she thrust the book away. She was aware of being in a public place. Of people staring.

Gently, William wiped her face with a clean handkerchief. He said, 'My car's outside.' As he rose, the hand that gripped her wrist slipped down until he held her fingers. Tightly. With his free hand he picked up her shoulder bag and they walked, close together, he moving in front to shield her from curious eyes, out of the door and down the stairs.

'I'm sorry. I'm sorry,' Charlotte sobbed, squeezing William's big white handkerchief between her palms. 'I'm terribly sorry. I can't imagine . . . I can't think why . . . Oh, hell.'

He opened the car door and helped her into the seat. She slumped, jamming the wet handkerchief against her eyes and her mouth in a fruitless attempt to block the pain. She was aware of the car moving, slow, fast, revving, swinging round corners. Then they had stopped and she was in William's arms, sobbing into his shoulder, saying, 'I'm sorry. I'm so sorry,' apologising for making a fool of herself.

'Don't be sorry,' he said, kind and gentle. 'Cry as much as you like.' She was aware of kisses on her forehead, and then, as she calmed down, on her lips. She drew away, confused by the unreason of William kissing her.

Like that.

'Oh, you are a good Samaritan,' she said with an embarrassed laugh, feeling like an idiot, recognising that the kisses could not be undone, not knowing where to look, how to apologise.

She felt she owed him an explanation. 'I was upset, of course,' she said, attempting a sensible tone. 'I bottled it up. They say you shouldn't do that. Though why it should come out in the library, I can't imagine. I'm so sorry to do that to you. You're very kind,' she babbled. 'It's just that . . .' She felt herself crumpling again. 'I didn't know what to do.'

'You could marry me.' He was gazing at her with an expression of longing.

She thought she must have misheard him. Or was it a joke? Wryly, she said, 'You don't have to marry every girl who makes a scene in the public library.'

'I mean it.' His face was grave and yet somehow lit up. 'I've always meant to marry you,' he said, sincerely, 'ever since you were a little girl. I'd have told you long ago, but you were so obviously in love with Max. You can't do much when a girl is in love with another chap,' he said.

She stared at him. It was like looking at a stranger. Not a stranger, a friend with a stranger's heart and mind.

'It was terrible, watching you and Max.' She saw his eyes fill with suffering, saw what he said was true. 'Ten years I've waited for you.' He put his arms round her again. 'Don't go away to London,' he said, pulling her so close she almost lost her breath. 'Stay here and marry me. You're old enough now,' he added, as though that was the qualification he had been seeking.

Chapter Twenty-Five

She did as she was told. She kept secret what William planned for her.

She hid the beautiful emerald ring. Having lived with his parents all his life, he'd had no cause to spend money. He had a lot of it stacked up, he said with pride. Their engagement was a very easy secret to keep because it did not seem real. You didn't talk about matters of the imagination.

On the day before Charlotte was due to return to Oxford, which was also the day before the one William had chosen to start his holidays, she went for a long walk down through the fields behind the house and up the other side. She took in huge lungfuls of air. Deep breathing was supposed to calm the mind.

Entering the woods, she seated herself on a log. Aloud, she said, 'I can end this tomorrow. Yolande would know how to get an abortion.'

Out of her memory leaped that picture of Claire and her, two little people, flying into a bucket, aborted.

No!

She visualised herself alone in London, living in one room, working to pay for Max's child, whom she would not see in the daytime because some stranger would be looking after him. What was the point of keeping a child if you had to give him to strangers for most of his waking hours? Keeping a child should mean giving it safety. Parents and a home. William had offered a home. She said aloud to him, 'I am pregnant with Max's child.' William's face slid out of her vision and disappeared. She said to Robert, son of the hardest woman Vivien had ever known, 'I am pregnant,' then fearfully took the words back. 'I am still in shock,' she said, speaking to herself.

She contemplated asking William to give her time, but knew he would not. He had made all the arrangements.

She slid down off the log and trailed wearily home.

In her bedroom she took a sheet of writing paper and wrote: 'I love William, I love William, I love William,' until she had filled up the page. Writing things down helped you remember. She turned the sheet over and wrote 'I love William' on the back. When she reached the bottom of the page she felt she had established the fact that she loved William.

She wrote a card to Isabel. *Please meet me at Chelsea Register Office Saturday at 11 a.m. Keep it secret. Love, Charlotte.*

She asked herself why she was doing this but all that came to her was the fact that there was nothing secret about post cards. She put it in an envelope and biked down to the village newsagent to buy a first-class stamp. She asked also to see gift wrapping. She chose pink with silver stars, then bought a reel of silver ribbon. That evening she put all her negative feelings about William into the gift wrapper, folded it carefully and tied it up. There was no one around when she lifted the lid of the Aga, which Robert had lit the day before because autumn was on its way. She dropped the packet into the flames. As they licked round the paper, consuming it, she remembered that pink was for love. Shaken, she watched it shrivel and die.

In bed that night she closed her eyes and conjured up gratitude. She filled herself with it until it overflowed; until the room vibrated with it. She didn't need a psychologist to tell her what the mind can do. She remembered what Sylvia had said about testing times. This was the test of her goodness, she said to herself. She must be grateful to William for marrying her.

'She wanted me to come and see you,' said Isabel, looking nervous. 'It was her wish and I'm honouring it. I'm sorry you should feel like this, Yolande. You must understand, there was nothing I could do.'

'When did you hear?' That was Robert, his face set in grim lines. Vivien had collapsed on the sofa, giving way to shock.

'When I came back to the school from visiting a sick pupil who had been whisked off to hospital, the letter was there in my room. It was eleven o'clock.'

'You could have rung at eleven o'clock,' flared Yolande.

229

Robert made calming movements with his hand. Oliver put an arm round her.

Yolande refused to be quietened. 'You could have rung someone.'

'No one could have stopped her.' Isabel felt sorry for them. Would have liked to talk to them, but that would be disloyal. In her opinion, Charlotte hadn't known what she was doing, but even so, there was no stopping her doing it.

'I caught an early train. I was on the steps of the register office long before eleven. They turned up dead on the hour. There was no opportunity to interfere,' she said. 'We had to go straight in.'

Their faces were set, stuck in the mould of certainty that she could have done something. What they didn't know was that the William Card of this morning knew exactly what he was doing. Knew, too, that Charlotte did not. Like a donkey, William had a carrot dangled in front of his nose and he was going to eat it, he who had never been offered a carrot before. He didn't care that it might not be good for him. He wanted what he wanted and he intended to take it now because he knew damn well that by next week the carrot might not be there.

She could have told them . . .

How he straightened when he saw Isabel standing waiting on the steps. How fast his shock receded. How his eyes took on a fighting look, as though he saw her arrival as an interference with his destiny. Charlotte's interference – for who else could have summoned her? Isabel could have said, 'This wasn't the wishy washy man, the silently yearning man that I danced with at your wedding, Yolande, while his eyes sought Charlotte in the crowd.' She'd have needed a knife to cut him away.

'There was nothing I could do,' she said helplessly,

She had known when she saw her that Charlotte desperately needed her, but she couldn't tell the Godfreys that, either. Why, they would want to know, hurt, did she not need *them*? Though their eyes told her they had faced the question in their minds and knew the answer.

'They'll be in the air now,' Isabel said. 'The plane was due to take off an hour ago.'

'Where have they gone?'

'Charlotte didn't know. William wanted to surprise her.' She had hoped Charlotte might have rung her parents from the airport. 'If it's any comfort to you, my heart was touched to see William's happiness,' she said, understanding their need for comfort. In fact, it was triumph rather than happiness she had seen. 'I'm sure he'll bend over backwards to make her happy —' She stopped herself just in time from saying 'too'.

Yolande picked up the hesitation. 'And what about her?' she asked ungraciously. 'Was your heart also touched by Charlotte's happiness?'

Oliver gave her a reproving look.

Neither did Isabel answer. It would do nobody any good to say that Charlotte had looked desperate.

'And you knew nothing about it? Before receiving the letter, I mean,' Robert asked.

'I thought it was Max she was marrying.'

Deadly silence. She looked round the room. 'Why William?' she asked in a small voice.

They had to tell her, then, things they would rather not. 'Rebound,' said Kenneth dully.

Robert, employing careful courtesy, asked her to dine with them. Vivien wanly suggested she stay the night. No, she said, no thank you, she was expected back at school. It was good of her to come, they said. Robert took her to the station. She had travelled all the way from Wylie by taxi – a great expense. He handed her a cheque, signed but not filled in. 'You must allow me to recompense you,' he said. 'Don't think we're not grateful. We're just a bit shell-shocked.'

'Of course. But no, thank you.' She tried to brush the cheque away.

'I do insist.'

'Thank you.' She took it and put it into her bag.

There wasn't much more either of them could say.

Oliver, Yolande and Kenneth returned to London. Robert was now free to run away to Cherry Tree Road. He wanted the comfort Alison could give even though that meant telling her what Charlotte had done. Meant offering her another opportunity to say that if she had not given the twins away, this wouldn't have happened.

'The poor child must be pregnant,' she said, pointing up the worth of a real mother, experienced in the matter of love, compassionate, quick off the mark. 'How could it be otherwise?'

She listened to the story of Max which had not been vouchsafed to her because Charlotte was not her child and therefore she had no claim to be made privy to her affairs. 'You don't suppose she's pregnant by him, do you?' She knew handsome Max Fosse with his winning ways. Had taught him until he went off to his prep school. She hadn't spoken to him since but had glimpsed him from time to time. A young Caesar, she thought, a conqueror. She wasn't surprised Charlotte had been in love with him. She was wretched at this further exclusion from Charlotte's life.

'Impossible!' Robert asserted. 'If you had seen her when she discovered he was the cause of Claire's death!' he said. 'She was beside herself.'

'Caught off guard, and in a panic,' she said, 'a girl might grab any man who offered.'

'What sort of girl?' Robert asked with scorn. He thought he knew his daughter.

There are some questions you don't answer. Alison asked, 'Are you going to announce the marriage in the paper?'

'Good God! Do you think we want to advertise it?'

She said, 'Very sensible. And when people ask, keep the date vague. When did Max go away?'

'While she was in La Gomera.'

'I didn't know,' she said, feeling forlorn at having been left out again. She had wondered why, ever alert for a glimpse of her child, she hadn't seen her in Wylie during the holidays. 'When did she go?'

'Near the beginning of the summer vacation. We thought it would do her good to get away. She's very close to Sylvia,' Robert said. He was whirling the whisky round in his glass, concentrating on not spilling it. Alison could tell by the way his lids came down and his mouth straightened into a line that it had been someone else's idea that Charlotte should look again to Sylvia for comfort. She counted the weeks swiftly on her fingers. History has a habit of repeating itself. She ached with sympathy.

They will have to live locally because of William's job, she thought. She knew William worked for Fenton, Lodge and Carruthers; she had seen him taking tea with Charlotte in Marilyn's Teashop, glimpsed him later in the High Street carrying a briefcase, followed him, watched him go up the stairs. When you excluded people from their rights, you made them into spies.

Hermione Card, whose nose was sharper than most, would have smelled a rat had she been aware of the liaison between Charlotte and Max, for she knew he had gone almost immediately to Australia after coming down from Oxford. That was common village gossip. Not knowing Charlotte and he had been in love – there was no reason why she should for her social path did not cross that of the local young – she had no hook on which to hang the mystery of her plain, unimaginative son winning Forge Green's most eligible daughter. She didn't know about the cream teas. And she never saw the Godfreys these days. She had telephoned during the summer to ask for a cake for the church fête. Mrs Fuller had answered. The cake was delivered direct to the vicarage on the day, though by whom nobody knew. The village had accustomed itself to the withdrawal of the Godfreys. Her mind, dancing round in circles, tripped on a memory.

Her husband put his head round the door. 'Is tea in the offing?'

'Yes, dear. It's all ready. Drawing.' She fitted a tea cosy purporting to be a crinolined lady over the pot and stilled its wobbling china torso with careful fingers. 'Do you recall going to Claire Godfrey's funeral?'

'Yes.'

'Do you remember my telling you what William said as we came away?'

'Do I remember what the boy said one day ten years ago? I don't remember what he said yesterday,' Jack muttered.

Hermione struck an attitude at the kitchen bench. 'He said he was going to marry Charlotte,' she said.

Jack Card's mouth fell open.

She put the curl of lemon rind on the saucer and picked up the tray.

Jack followed her into the lounge. 'I must say,' she said, 'you're taking it very calmly.' She set out the cups and saucers on the folding table. Carefully placed the tea pot on a cork mat to protect the veneer. All the furniture was modern. Had been new when they married. Hermione couldn't abide anything old.

'Why not? We've acquired a lovely daughter-in-law. I'm grateful.' Jack Card had never seriously entertained the thought that his son was what he called a fairy, but you couldn't be sure of anything these days. William went to parties alone. Came home alone. Without consciously thinking about it, he'd have said the best they could expect of a daughter-in-law was one of those spinster type women. Skinny. Bespectacled. Colourless. Clever, maybe. Stringy hair. He realised he was describing William in his mind.

'I'd just like to know when and where the courting took place,' Hermione said, worrying at the theme. 'She's been up at Oxford. He hasn't been anywhere without us. He's never mentioned Charlotte. Not since that day at the funeral.' She straightened, touched her dark-dyed hair and gave a forced little laugh. 'It looks as though we've got a son who plays his cards close to his chest.' She handed Jack his cup. 'You've not got much to say.'

'For God's sake, Hermione, you're like a dog with a bone. Pack it in.'

She was hurt. 'I'm only trying to solve the mystery. I do think it's a pity if we can't have an ordinary discussion once in a while.'

'Why don't you ring up her mother?' He sipped his tea, reached for a biscuit.

'Tricky,' she said, meaning that if she rang up, gushing, 'How pleased we are to have Charlotte in the family,' and her good will received a cool response, it would be dreadfully embarrassing. She had been hoping ever since the post card arrived that one of the Godfreys would ring them. She picked it up now and squinted at the stamp. 'Where's Skiathos?'

'It's one of those Greek islands. In the north. Gets a lot of rain and mist at this time of year. I should have thought they'd have done better to go to Crete.'

Chapter Twenty-Six

William had chosen a converted artisan's cottage, built in 1790 or thereabouts, for them both to live in. Its overgrown lawn ran all the way down to the steep riverbank. There were tangled shrubs, rioting holly and some neglected flower beds. Beyond the yew and apple, trees that grew close to the house at one side, there were the neighbours' conifers. Beyond them, one or two chestnuts, and a couple of hundred yards away the church spire, rising to the sky.

William's firm had the deeds of this little pink house. The owner couldn't afford the necessary repairs, and no one wanted to rent it until the repairs were done – an impasse of the greatest convenience to William. In the last-minute rush of bringing his holidays forward and making his plans, he had found time to persuade the owner that empty properties run down fast. The sale was hurried through by one of his colleagues while they were on honeymoon.

'It's old, of course,' he said apologetically, 'but we can modernise it.'

Standing on the front path, Charlotte experienced a sense of *déjà vu*. Why? She had never come this way before.

'Cuckoo Lane,' said William, innocent and unaware.

And what do cuckoos do with their eggs? Avoiding knowledge, feigning nostalgia, Charlotte said swiftly, 'The bay window reminds me of Marilyn's Teashop.'

'Happy memories.' William squeezed her hand.

It was less painful to remember the teas than the cold and damp honeymoon.

'It's always like this in the autumn,' the ferryman told them, heading out from mainland Greece into blanketing mist and fog. 'You ought to go south at this time of year.' He suggested the Peloponnese, not knowing William had been unable to ask advice. Hadn't had time to study latitudes and weather. Had picked his honeymoon venue in secrecy and haste. Greek islands are romantic and sunny. The brochures say so.

And then there was William's love. Ten years of dammed-up emotion had flooded incontinently over her. He couldn't have enough of her. She would waken in the night to find him straddling her, half asleep, ramming his tired little thing into her. He infringed her privacy, encroached on her space. He reminded her of a child guzzling cream cakes lest they run out. He talked of babies. Hoped she would become pregnant as soon as possible. In his moments of uncertainty – she was aware of them – she thought he was afraid she might come to her senses and in that event a child, his child, might keep her from running away.

She held gratitude in her hands, used it to light up her eyes when she looked at him, to give strength to her arms when she enfolded him as she must in return for safe shelter.

The little pink house was not a home. How could it be? Without the benison of love there is only a shell contrived of bricks and mortar. Charlotte would have liked it to know that, in withholding her love, she was saving it from the sorrow and pain of her going – for in her darkest hours she saw William throwing her out bag and baggage when the baby arrived early, and looking like Max. She comforted herself with thoughts of sanctuary at Folly Hill, returning not as a daughter with a love child in tow but in the acceptable guise of a woman whose marriage had failed, as marriages regretfully, but acceptably, do.

Robert had the piano sent down. It stood in the small sitting room, taking up too much space. 'It's a pity it's so big,' William said, critically.

'Why don't you exchange it for an upright, dear?' That was Hermione.

'Because it's mine,' Charlotte snapped.

Hermione looked away, tight-lipped. Jack said heartily, 'Of course.'

William, in the nervous manner that came upon him when the frightened Charlotte burst out of the case of goods marked 'Mrs

236

William Card, wife', said, 'I don't want to get rid of you, but I've brought some work home.'

William always referred to the little pink house as home and that was how Charlotte saw it. His home. Her refuge. A refuge is something one can abandon in a hurry, when the time comes. After Hermione and Jack had gone, Charlotte went to the piano and ran her fingers lovingly along its shiny surface. Robert had bought it for Claire and her when they were six years old. It held memories she could not bear to abandon. And besides, it was a comfort in these awkward days while she was settling in.

'I hope your parents didn't think me rude,' she said, apologising to William. 'Do you think it takes up more than its share of room?'

'We'll see,' said William and she did see, that he was thinking she would soon realise her piano was too big.

They had bought the house furnished. Chunky oak chairs with curved backs. An oblong slab of a table. A rocking chair. 'Wouldn't you like new?' Hermione had asked. 'Brides usually want new things. I'm sure William wouldn't begrudge you.'

Charlotte ran her hands over a sturdy oak tabletop, polished from generations of elbows, invested with centuries of table talk. 'No,' she said. 'I'm happy with this.'

Hermione's voice lifted magnanimously over her disappointment. 'Our son is lucky to have found a wife who is so easy to please.'

The previous owners had used the smaller room next door as a dining room. Charlotte suggested William should make it into a study but, 'I want to be with you in the evenings, dear,' he said. 'Darby and Joan.'

Charlotte felt herself being dragged towards mediocrity, feet bogged in wet clay. 'Even if I'm playing the piano? Won't that disturb you?'

William said he loved to hear her play.

He was flattered, but puzzled, when she deferred to him in the choice of colour schemes and curtains. The soft furnishings that came with the house were so badly worn and faded that they had to be replaced. Hermione, exasperated by her daughter-in-law's indifference, had samples of material sent to William's office.

'I like them all,' Charlotte said to William, 'but you must make the final decision. It's your money.'

237

'Our money,' he corrected her, but not for long. The spirit of affirmations, like that of houses, easily dwindles and dies.

The little living room had a rustic fireplace with a fireback stamped '1797' and a duck's-nest grate. There was a two-seater oak settle where you could sit with legs stretched over the fender, toasting your toes. Charlotte imagined flames licking a great pot of stew or soup as it swung from a metal chain. A vast kettle with a head of steam. A tin bath standing on the hearth. Thursday night – bath night. Everybody down to the Spade and Shovel, the pub on the corner, while Gran has her tub.

'What an imagination you have!' William looked at her with affection as at a quaint little person, a garden gnome perhaps. 'I had thought of blocking the fireplace in. We could buy one of those gas fires that send up flames. They're clean and you'd scarcely know them from the real thing.'

Charlotte said he must do as he wished. The part of her that could not always be controlled wanted to embrace the house with love. She went into the heart of the house and apologised for the possibility that its lovely fireplace was going to be banished behind clean gas flames. She apologised also for not loving it. 'But I can't stay,' she said. 'You must know.'

The kitchen was adequate. A plain wood bench. Deep porcelain sink, ugly green linoleum, a lovely old iron-framed window looking out on the rampant garden. A robin came and perched on the sill, head cocked, eyes curious. 'Hold on,' she murmured, quiet so as not to frighten it. 'I'll get you some crumbs.'

William asked from the doorway, 'Did you say something?'

She pointed, whispering, 'We have a robin.'

William adopted a wry expression. She tore off the end of a loaf, broke up the bread, opened the window and carefully distributed the crumbs.

'There's a kitchen designer at the bottom of the High Street,' William said. The robin, startled by his voice, flew away. 'We could get them in.' He stepped past her, tested the loose catches on the ill-fitting cupboard doors one after the other, then shook his head.

'Not yet,' said Charlotte. She pulled an excuse out of her brain. 'They take ages to put kitchens in. Two weeks, they say, then spend two months on it. I remember getting a new kitchen at Folly Hill. The workmen were there for ages. Let's settle in first. I don't want a house full of workmen and nowhere to cook a chop. Not for a while, anyway.'

William wandered away leaving her thinking of fine lines and razors' edges. Choices. Pleasing William now inevitably meant to incur blame when the balloon went up, as Max would say.

The next morning, while folding away the holiday clothes, she felt something hard in the pocket of a skirt she had not worn on the Greek island. Had not, in fact, worn since her return from La Gomera. Her crystal. 'If you need it, it will find you,' Fernando had said. She wondered if her sudden departure from the Valle had led Fernando to suspect she was going to need it. She took it to the window and held it out, offering it to the sun's rays, but at that moment the sun went behind a cloud. She pushed it into the pocket of her jeans, experiencing the familiar sense of comfort it brought.

Charlotte busied herself in the garden in those autumn days, chopping back green-smelling and ebullient growth, sweeping up golden leaves as they fell. Living with William brought an impoverishment of the senses. Dealing with nature helped to replace her heart energy. 'I'll get a man in,' he offered, but she wanted to do the work herself. When her mind was full of the earth's impulses there was no room for matters she preferred not to face. Not yet.

She forked the beds on either side of the front door, watching the soil shift and reform. She befriended snails and earthworms, moving them to safety while she dug. 'Stay there,' she cautioned them. 'I'll put you back later.' She made little beds for them in the dug soil. She felt an affinity with creatures at the mercy of good or bad will in others. She made friends with Sid, the young Rottweiler next door. 'I love dogs,' she told Mrs Penrose, his owner, remembering Sasha. The family had never replaced her. Couldn't bear to. Now, she thought she would get a dog of her own. She was offered a border terrier, one year old with a golden face and round jet eyes shining with mischief.

'Hello, scraggy,' said William in a half-hearted attempt at friendship, though without leaning down to pat her. 'Where did this come from?'

'She's a she, not a this.' Charlotte gave William a smile to soften her automatic indignation. 'She came from Mr Abrahams who farms Folly Hill. His old collie was jealous.' She was aware of always making small explanations, William being unfamiliar with so much of her background. Max it was who had frolicked with Claire and her in the loose hay, played with the dogs, and climbed the haystack when the farmer's back was turned.

'I'm going to call her Maggie,' she said, shouldering William's insult. 'It rhymes with "scraggy."' She offered him a very gentle smile, understanding that he saw without pleasure some of her attention slipping away to the dog. He had never had pets. Somewhere he had heard Rottweilers were dangerous, especially if they weren't properly exercised.

'Do they take that brute next door for runs?' he asked. 'I've never seen it out. We had better keep the side gate shut. It could eat your mutt.'

'Dogs know when you don't like them,' she said.

'I could take it or leave it alone.'

Maggie enjoyed playing with Sid. He burrowed a hole through the hedge so he could visit her.

'I agree with William,' Vivien said one day. 'That dog doesn't get enough exercise. You said the woman is out at work all day? That's not fair on a dog. You know, he is rather rough with Maggie.'

Inevitably, Maggie got hurt in a game. She was only a quarter the size of Sid.

'He wouldn't have nipped her deliberately,' Eileen Penrose said defensively. 'He's a pussycat, so long as he's kindly treated.'

William repeated what Vivien had said, that it was unkind to leave a dog alone all day. They didn't like that. Mrs Penrose snapped back that plenty of dogs stayed at home while their owners went out to work and were none the worse for it.

William asked them to mend the fence.

'If you don't want him in your garden, then you'd better mend it yourself,' Trevor Penrose retorted.

William, not being good with people, told them categorically where the responsibility lay. 'I'm a solicitor,' he said.

The fence was mended and the early buds of friendship shrivelled, then died.

Vivien was not at all well. She easily caught colds and they all went down to her chest. Her hearing had deteriorated. She was

240

pleased to be losing weight. Losing weight was one thing, however; wasting was another.

'I'll take you to see Dr Stevenson,' Charlotte said.

Vivien went obediently and was referred to the Wylie hospital for tests. Leukaemia was diagnosed.

The family gathered at Folly Hill, all except William, who hadn't wanted to come. Charlotte never pressed him. He said he felt uncomfortable with Robert and Yolande. Robert's cool, impersonal courtesy acted on William like a cold draught. Yolande's sharp honesty scared him.

'It's Dad's fault,' Yolande burst out acrimoniously, walking with Charlotte and Kenneth in the garden. 'Happy people don't get cancer.'

Charlotte knew you had to be strong to make happiness work. Vivien was not strong; never had been, in her memory. 'Would you fight back if Oliver got a mistress?' she asked, then immediately realised she knew the answer. Yolande had inherited Robert's strength. Of course she would fight.

'Oliver wouldn't,' Yolande replied with a grin. 'He's got more than enough on his hands looking after me. Dad wouldn't have got his beastly mistress if Mum had stood up to him in the first place. If she had refused to take the blame for letting Claire go to the Bubbly Hole alone.'

Charlotte's face twisted and her eyes filled with tears. She cried easily these days. 'It's lucky you're living nearby, Char,' Kenneth remarked.

'Lucky she gave up her degree,' Yolande said malevolently, kicking at a stone on the path. It was unfortunate that when Yolande lashed out at fate people got in the way.

'I'll look after her,' Charlotte said. 'I don't have to work. William is perfectly able to keep me.' Why had she said that? Apparently pointless statements were continuously coming out of her mouth. Afterwards she knew they were not pointless. They were part of her covering-up. There was safety in letting the family think she had married William on the rebound.

'So we don't have to wait for drink to get to her liver. She's going to die anyway.' Yolande started to cry. 'I wish Oliver would hurry up. I hope he g-gets here in time for supper. I need him to stop me clawing Dad's eyes out.'

'Very ancient Greek,' said Charlotte. The shock of seeing

Yolande collapse had restored her sense of humour. Yolande's saving grace was her deep love for and dependence upon Oliver. 'We must try to make Mum laugh,' Charlotte said. 'Did you know that laughter releases endorphins that can put cancer into reverse gear?'

'A fat lot she has to laugh about.'

Robert was truculent with his children that night, conscious that they avoided his eyes and did not address him directly. He escaped immediately after pudding, refusing coffee, saying he had some matters to attend to in his study. He looked unhappy, but they didn't mind that. What they didn't like was the anger behind his eyes. Against them for judging him? Against Vivien for contracting an illness that stirred his conscience? They felt that he had no right to be angry when he was in disgrace.

Vivien went obediently to a clinic to be dried out. Charlotte wondered if her gentle acquiescence came with the shock of discovering her days were numbered, or whether she saw there was more dignity in dying of a disease of the blood rather than one of the liver.

'Now, with two daughters married, I want to last long enough to see my grandchildren,' she said on her return, looking better than she had looked for years.

'You'll last for ages,' Charlotte told her robustly. 'I'll bet you make it to ninety. And as for grandchildren,' she added, tentatively testing, 'my curse is late.'

'Oh, Charlotte! Are you saying that to please me?'

'No, it's true.'

They talked about grandchildren. Vivien's eyes began to shine. 'Can I start knitting?'

'Why not?'

'What's that thing you're always stroking?' William asked one day.

'A crystal.'

He picked it up and turned it over. 'Quartz.'

'Yes.'

'It's not much of an ornament for the mantelpiece,' he said, putting it down again. 'We don't seem to have any ornaments.' He looked round the room. 'There's a good china shop in the High Street. Why don't you buy some plates and arrange them along there?'

She said she would.

Vivien brought O'Brien down in the car. She had acquired a tentative confidence. Enough, anyway, to drive again. While he dug the garden, she took Charlotte to a nursery where they bought shrubs and tulip and daffodil bulbs for the spring.

'Good stuff, this,' O'Brien said on their return, looking down on the rich brown earth he had turned over, leaning on his spade. 'Loamy.'

They showed him the plants. 'It's going to look lovely,' Charlotte said. This was something she could leave for William when he threw her out. A house would be more marketable with its garden in order.

'I said I'd get someone in,' said William on his return, looking dispossessed.

'I'm sorry.' She recognised too late that they had overridden his rights.

'I'll get someone tomorrow.'

'There's no need now. The work's done.'

'Oh, well,' said William, shoulders sagging.

She put her arms round him in an uprush of pity and guilt, hugged him hard, and after a while he stood erect again.

Lying awake in the night after William had taken his greedy helping of her, worrying about Vivien, Charlotte thought of a bold and audacious plan. An unforgivably meddling plan.

She would ask the bitch on heat – her father's mistress – to perform an act of sacrifice: to give him back for just as long as it took Vivien to die.

She acted on it the next day, before she could change her mind.

'I'm Charlotte,' she said, standing bright-faced at the front door of 5 Cherry Tree Road. She held one foot poised to shove in the crack should Mrs Adrienne Graham, attractive blonde widow, attempt to shut the door in her face. 'My father is Robert Godfrey. May I come in? I'd like to talk to you.'

An expression of faint curiosity passed over Mrs Graham's face as she moved aside, but Charlotte noted a singular lack of dismay. She swept into the room, eyes flicking with surprise over the worn carpet, which looked as though it had suffered the onslaught of dogs and small children in its time. There were comfortable chairs in faded loose covers, with hand-stitched tapestry

243

cushions. Hard to see it as Robert's illicit love nest. What had she expected? Purple velvet?

'Do sit down,' said the bitch. 'Can I get you a cup of coffee?'

One of Charlotte's hands indicated that this was not the kind of call where she would expect coffee. She perched on the edge of an upright chair and began breathlessly, 'It's about my father.'

She said in rapid sentences what she had come to say, though not in the way she had intended. The woman's detachment had unnerved her. 'My mother . . . going to die . . . leukaemia. We don't know how long . . .'

Mrs Graham broke in long before Charlotte had finished. 'I'm sorry, my dear, this has nothing to do with me. I'm afraid you've got the wrong woman. It's my tenant upstairs that your father visits – Alison Hurst. Not me.' She added kindly, though Charlotte scarcely heard, 'It is possible for people to live with leukaemia for twenty years.'

244

Chapter Twenty-Seven

Charlotte was appalled. All her recollections of Miss Hurst took on a new and obscene meaning. She remembered history classes, Miss Hurst sitting at her desk watching. Waiting for Charlotte to look up, then smiling as their eyes met. *I am watching over you, who will be my stepdaughter when your father and I have driven your mother into her grave.* She wanted to throw up.

She recalled the surprise – shock? – on Miss Hurst's face when Charlotte had mentioned Yolande's wedding. *In my capacity as Yolande's stepmother (once I have willed my lover's wife into her grave), I would expect an invitation.* And William had said that he had seen Miss Hurst crying at Claire's grave. Even the dead were not safe from her!

That afternoon, Charlotte walked in the woods with Maggie, trying to come to terms with her discovery. Should she tell Yolande? Kenneth? What does it matter, they would say, who his mistress is? It's the fact of his having one that's the problem. Miss Hurst was nothing to them. Why should you be so concerned? they would ask.

Something clicked at the back of her mind. Something so unacceptable that she crushed it, suppressed it so brutally that it could never rise again. Picking up a stick of beech wood, she began to run. 'Here, Maggie, chase this!' She flung it far ahead. Maggie dashed away, then brought it back. Charlotte tossed it into the river; Maggie took a flying leap, swam in a circle and snatched up the stick in her teeth. They ran again, in and out of the trees, Maggie barking excitedly. They played until Charlotte was too tired to go on. Too tired to think.

That night, in her dreams, she cried again for her mother. She saw Miss Hurst as an insect with long legs, backing towards a dark hole in the ground, carrying Vivien in its mandibles, taking her to oblivion.

William's voice. 'Darling one, what's the matter? Why are you crying?'

'I don't know,' she sobbed, only half awake. 'I don't know why I'm crying. I think I may be pregnant – I think I must be.'

William put his arms round her and held her close, but the insect that was Miss Hurst didn't go away. Clinging to its booty, it backed further and further towards the dark hole in the ground.

William was over the moon with delight. He agreed to call the baby Tom. 'Can I name her if she's a girl?' he asked with humility. Charlotte agreed. She knew Max's baby wouldn't be a girl.

Lucy was the name William favoured. He was humbled by this great luck bestowed on them from on high. That was how he saw it. He pictured the angels up there watching, assessing his virtues. Sorry we've overlooked you. Now your turn has come.

Hermione was tight lipped. Smelling a rat. She had been poking her nose into things. All those silent people with whom she played bridge were full of information. They had just been waiting for the signal to spill it out. Did she not know Max Fosse and Charlotte had been close since childhood? They went to all the young people's parties together. (Knowing looks.) And they were up at Oxford at the same time. Why did Charlotte come down a year early without her degree? Not to marry William, that was certain. Meticulous in her research, Hermione discovered that Max had skipped off to Australia while Charlotte was in the Canaries.

Jack, well pleased, said, 'Fancy that! A grandchild,' and slapped his knee. He was approving of his son these days. Never mind the hows and whys, plus the fact that the Godfreys kept their distance, William had given them a lovely daughter-in-law and now it looked as though he might even have been up to a bit of nooky in the woodshed. Well, well! Maybe they'd misjudged old William.

Hermione knew better than to share her suspicions with her

husband. She attempted to waylay Jessica Fosse in the village, but she ran like a rabbit.

'It had to be that,' Yolande said to Oliver. 'She had to be pregnant. Why didn't she come to me? I'd have helped her with an abortion.'

Oliver reminded her that Charlotte was fervently against abortion.

'All that twaddle! I should think it's different when it actually happens to you. If it's a choice between marrying William Card and having an abortion, I'd've thought the most active anti-campaigner would settle for getting rid of it. I hope Max Fosse roasts in hell. Why didn't she go after him?' Then she remembered Max had killed Claire, and burst into tears.

Vivien spent a good deal of time at the little pink house, talking to her daughter and playing with Maggie. 'I've seen so little of you over the years, what with boarding school and Oxford,' she said. She never spoke about her illness; it might have gone away or never been.

Charlotte telephoned her mother at least once a day. 'Come and watch my efforts at decorating the dining room,' she suggested one day. 'That should give you a good laugh.' She had cheeriness down to a fine art.

Vivien said anxiously, 'You shouldn't be doing that. You might fall off a ladder. And you mustn't stretch. Stretching could bring on a miscarriage.'

Charlotte considered the possibility of losing Max's baby and told William she had changed her mind.

'I'll get decorators in,' he said, looking at her fondly. 'You choose the wallpaper and paint,' he said. 'That's enough for you in your condition.'

'Condition!' she snapped. 'I'm not a horse.' She hardly ever spoke unkindly to William. Struck now by remorse, she flung her arms round him. Charlotte was aware, every hour of the day, that William had saved her bacon.

He put the explosion down to her condition but never used the word again. Once he said hesitantly, 'Why don't you have friends in sometimes?'

'My friends have all flown the coop, that's why.' The girls she knew before boarding school had scattered. They had become army wives; got jobs in London; some were students in termtime, backpackers in vacations to India and beyond. Old girls of Mountfield Manor wrote, 'I hear you're married! Whatever happened to Oxford?' She did not invite them to stay, not wishing to see their surprise and disappointment on meeting William. He had been good to her. She imprisoned herself with him in the little pink house, allowing only the family in.

'You're always fingering that bit of quartz,' William said. 'I thought you were going to buy some plates to put up there.'

'I'm sorry, I forgot.' Charlotte slipped the crystal into her pocket. 'I don't really like spending your money.'

'That's your Scots blood,' said William, adoring her.

'You forget, I'm adopted.'

He looked surprised. 'Funny, I never think of it.' Suddenly he was animated. 'Why don't we look up your real mother? I could help you there.'

'Vivien Godfrey is my mother,' she said.

William looked disappointed. She felt she knew what he was thinking. He didn't fit in well at Folly Hill; another mother would be unbiased about him, as the Godfreys were not.

'I'll look round some antique shops,' Charlotte said, mollifying him. 'I'll see if I can find some interesting plates.'

'No need to skimp,' William told her affectionately. 'I can afford new.'

'First babies are sometimes late,' the doctor said. Hope rippled through her. How late? 'Don't worry. We'll induce if you get uncomfortable.'

'I wouldn't want that,' said Charlotte hurriedly, hiding her pink face, reaching for her vast pregnant-lady's pants. 'I'd want it to run full term.'

'Full term? I don't think we need to worry about that,' said the doctor vaguely, speaking over the rush of hot water as he washed his hands at the gleaming white sink in his consulting room. 'They tend to come when they're ready. Doesn't your husband want to know whether it's a girl or a boy either?'

'No,' she said.

She decided she would somehow keep Tom in her womb until

long after the due date. She stopped taking Maggie for walks, exercising her instead by throwing a ball from the garden seat William had bought for her. She lay down on the bed for hours at a time. Sleep, little baby. Sleep. She was prepared to suffer any amount of discomfort in order to save William's pride.

She told him first babies often come early. She had become careless with the truth. Truth was not suitable as a survival weapon. More than that, it could upset William terribly. Intentions had become muddled in her mind. She recognised that the plan to go back to Folly Hill when William threw her out was too pat. He had become her husband, now.

She made up a song to the tune of 'Frère Jacques' and sang it to Tom as she rested:

> 'Stay where you are, stay where you are,
>   Sleep, sleep, sleep,
>   Sleep, sleep, sleep.
> Little Tommy Fosse, Little Tommy Fosse.
>   Dear good boy. Dear good boy.'

She was no longer afraid of Claire. Claire had forfeited all rights by what she had done. 'Go to hell,' Charlotte would retort if she turned up saying, 'You can't sing without me.' Claire didn't turn up, but there were times when Charlotte felt her shadowy presence in the room.

249

Chapter Twenty-Eight

Nobody questioned the date of the baby's expected arrival. William out of ignorance. The others? There was a frailty to the silence that shrouded Charlotte's existence. She thought of herself as being holed up in a house waiting for a crime to be committed. She scarcely went out now, except to shop. She had lost touch with everyone.

She felt dreadfully alone. Only Vivien treated her normally as though, having serenely abandoned the cares and problems of the world, she could look forward to her final luxury, a grandchild.

The winter had been mild. Spring was quiet. The daffodils came early, as did the bluebells on the bank running down to the river. Charlotte was not at ease with this burst of life. Time was passing too quickly, Nobody remarked that the baby seemed far advanced. Not even Yolande, who could always be counted on to speak her mind. Charlotte preferred not to go to Folly Hill now when Yolande was there. Her silence had a cutting edge; she felt the blade hovering.

Sometimes she stood leaning against one of the big old trees on the bank at the back of the garden, looking down at the water quietly flowing. That was when she felt really safe, with the trees enfolding her and the unchanging pace of the river.

One day Jessica Fosse, in Wylie-under-Lyne to do her big monthly shop at the supermarket, saw Charlotte searching along shelves containing washing powder, dish cloths and scourers. A serene young madonna coming innocently closer with the vast bulk of her unborn child holding wide the front opening of her coat. Jessica felt small hairs standing up on the back of her neck. She spun her trolley round into the next aisle, where she took out and deposited cat crunchies, toilet paper and Vermouth among flour and baking powder because she couldn't go back the way she had come. Daren't pause at the check-out.

She rushed on, still carrying some unwanted fish, agonizing. You can't leave packets of frozen haddock on a shelf displaying cakes. You can, if you're desperate enough. She sneaked a look to right and left. No one coming. She dumped them too, then shoved the trolley into its bay, and ran through the NO EXIT gate. When she got to the car, the key would not go in the lock. She pushed and shoved. No wonder. You can't drive a car using the key to the back door of your house.

She drove home, weeping. When did Charlotte marry the Card boy? She remembered the shock of first hearing the news. Laurence had talked carelessly of rebound. 'So she's OK,' he had said with satisfaction. 'Be grateful.'

Jessica knew exactly how long Max had been in Australia, for she mentally ticked off every week, looking at the calendar, longing for his return. It was exactly eight and a half months now. If that girl she had seen in the supermarket wasn't eight and a half to nine months pregnant, she was a Dutchman.

Should she write to Max? Should she ring him?

Only after she had put the car away did she realise there was no supper. She burst into tears again thinking not of the food but of her grandchild growing up in another family. She was out of control by the time Laurence came home. She attacked him ferociously as he appeared in the doorway, seeing in her mind's eye Charlotte's face, vandalised by his articulate weapons of rejection, turning away from him in the garden last summer.

'Look here –' He put his briefcase down and grabbed her arm. 'Calm down, Jessica.' He led her into the kitchen, where she collapsed into a chair.

He said curtly, 'Now look here,' again. 'I'm not going to take all the blame for this. You didn't want Max to marry her in view of . . . in view of . . .' Even now he couldn't say out loud what Max had done.

'What did he tell you that night? What made you ask Ron Dalgleish to banish him to the Sydney office? Did you tell me the truth?'

'I did,' Laurence said. '*He* didn't. Claimed he hadn't remembered Claire being drowned.'

'Are you quite, quite certain he didn't say Charlotte was pregnant?'

'*That*,' said her husband, 'I would have remembered.'

'What are we going to do?'

'Nothing.'

'We can't do nothing,' she cried in distress. 'This is our grandchild.'

'It's William Card's child.'

'It's not! It can't be!'

'How can you say that? She's married to him.'

'The baby's due any moment. *Any moment*, Laurence.'

'Even if you're right,' he said, unconvinced, 'the girl was on some bloody island in the Canaries, wasn't she? How do we know what she got up to? They're all into one-night stands. That's what they go on holiday for. Sex,' said Laurence.

She looked up at him with red-rimmed disbelieving eyes.

'Say it is Max's child – then what? After what he did to her twin, there's no way she would have married him. No way her parents would have allowed it, either. Little bastard!' he said venomously, having forgotten Max now stood two inches taller than himself. 'Australia is a bloody good place for him. Let's hope he stays there.' He patted his wife's shoulder and smoothed her hair. 'Go and tidy yourself up,' he said, though kindly. 'Let sleeping dogs lie. She's married to young Card. If what you say is true, it's bloody awful, but it's his problem. What you need is a stiff drink.'

'Oh, God!' She twisted away from him. 'Do you really think a drink solves everything?'

'No. But it helps.'

Almost as though she knew, Hermione dropped by on the day that was to be avoided at all costs: the day the doctor had given Charlotte for Tom's birth. She brought a cake, William's favourite, made with four eggs, as she was pleased to announce, and a quarter of a pound of cherries. Always there were four eggs in her cakes. If she was providing cake for the church bazaar, that was a different matter. Three eggs would do and no one any the wiser.

'I do wonder if you're getting enough exercise, dear,' she said, eying Charlotte's vast, egg-shaped front like a horse dealer examining a mare. 'I was just saying to Jack the other day, I don't think that girl gets enough exercise. Why don't you take a little walk with me along the riverbank?'

On walks, lulled by the gentleness of nature, the sweetly flowing river, confidences may be too easily drawn by the strong from the weak. Charlotte pictured Hermione pulling the truth out of her, saw herself cravenly asking pardon for this terrible deceptism she had inflicted on Hermione's son.

'If you wouldn't mind taking Maggie in the car,' she responded, nervously pleading, 'I'll come as far as Dewberry Pond with you and walk back along the towpath.'

Hermione stayed silent for long enough to let it be known that was not the answer she expected. Then, staring critically down at the terrier, she said, 'I've never actually considered putting a dog in my car.'

Gazing hopefully up into Hermione's face, Maggie thumped her tail.

'She's awfully good in cars,' said Charlotte.

Hermione picked up her keys. 'There is the smell,' she said, looking critically, consideringly, at Maggie, then with an air of having decided against her better judgement to indulge a pregnant woman, she added, 'But it's mild today. We could leave the windows open, I suppose.'

Charlotte picked up Maggie, whispering apologies in her hairy little ear. She offered to take the dog on her knee.

'I don't think you've got much knee,' said her mother-in-law, not smiling. 'Perhaps you would be more comfortable if she went in the back. I just hope she won't tear the upholstery.'

Charlotte settled awkwardly in the low passenger seat.

'See what I mean?' said Hermione, looking grimly at Charlotte's knees peeping out from beneath her distended stomach. Weighing up evidence. Charlotte read in her eyes that she had proof of what she had long suspected. This foetus was many weeks too far advanced to be William's child. 'I don't know how you're going to get on with this seat belt, I'm sure,' Hermione said, delivering her verdict in inches.

'You're right, it's not quite my size,' said Charlotte bravely, though close to tears. 'I'll hold it. It's not far to the common.' Maggie jumped from the back seat to the floor. Poking her head between the seats, she found Charlotte's hand and licked it. Hermione started the car.

Neither spoke as they drove up the road and turned into the small common by the pond. Hermione braked, heaved herself out and went round to Charlotte's side. 'Swing your feet out first,' she said. She took Charlotte's elbow in a firm grip and levered her up. 'Are you all right?' she asked, not without concern. 'I don't know that I ought to leave you here alone.'

Charlotte said, 'I'm fine.'

Hermione gave her time to change her mind before saying, 'I'll be on my way, then.'

Charlotte sat down on a wooden bench. Maggie raced for the water, swam to the centre of the pond, swung round and came back to the edge. She dashed up the slope, panting, and shook herself all over Charlotte's skirt. Charlotte smiled at her. 'Pig!' She remembered Claire had called her a pig the day she died. She was overwhelmed by loneliness.

A car pulled in beside her bench. She looked round. A head of blonde curls hovered over the passenger seat as the driver leaned across to open the door. A dog jumped out. Pip! The curls lifted, exposing a face. Louisa. Maggie hurried to welcome Pip, nose to nose, tails wagging. Charlotte turned hastily back to face the pond. She picked up a stone and threw it. Maggie dashed after it. Pip, ears lifted, followed slowly, showing his years.

'Oh, hello,' said Louisa, carefully keeping her eyes above the huge bulge of Charlotte's stomach. 'Pip's a bit old to be chasing things now, but he still likes his run. I've been to the store to see Dad. Mum lets me have her car now I've got my driving licence.'

Charlotte recognised Louisa was chattering through the shock of finding her nine months pregnant on a bench on Wylie common. 'I'm going down to the towpath,' she blundered on. 'Pip! Pip! Hurry up. Hurry! Lovely day. See you.' She walked a few steps, turned. Her face had dispensed with the shock. It was smiling. There was triumph in her eyes. 'By the way, I've had an invitation from Max. I'm going out to Australia for six weeks.'

That was when Charlotte felt the first pain.

She sat very still after Louisa had gone, holding Tom with both arms clasped across the little sac that held him, thinking of Max. Not believing that he had invited Louisa to visit him. She attempted to put the wicked lie out of her mind.

Out. Out.

It wouldn't go.

Oh, Max! she cried in her heart. Max, my life, my love!

'But it's not due for another six weeks,' said William, looking frantic.

'I must have walked too far,' she said.

For an hour now she had been lying on the bed, willing the pains to go away, silently beseeching Tom to stay where he was. Sensing with fear his first disobedience. 'It's quite a long way from the common.' A helpful memory surfaced, helpful to William's peace of mind. 'And I stretched up to reach for some wild flowers off the bank. You're not supposed to stretch. You can bring things on early.'

She began to cry, not from the pains but because the time had come for William, who did not deserve it, to be cruelly hurt.

'Don't,' he said, taking her hand. 'Don't cry. I'm sure it'll be all right. Shall I ring for an ambulance, or do you think it's safe for me to drive you? Hadn't I better phone the hospital first?'

'No, don't,' said Charlotte, heaving herself into a sitting position. 'If I just turn up, they'll have to take me.'

'But what if there isn't a bed?'

She looked into his kind, concerned, unsuspecting eyes. 'They'll find one,' she said. 'They'll have to.'

'A fine baby boy,' said the doctor heartily. 'Eight pounds and seven ounces.'

'Is he going to be all right?' asked William anxiously.

The doctor looked puzzled. 'Why on earth not?'

'He's so early. And small.'

The doctor scratched his head. 'What?' he asked at last.

'I mean, he's six weeks early,' said William. 'Premature.'

'What on earth made you think that? He's full term.'

'He's not,' said William. 'We've only been married seven and a half months.'

'Oh,' said the doctor reflectively, after another long silence. He rubbed the side of his nose, sizing William up. 'You'll be able to go in and see your wife in a few moments.' He began to move away. Came back. 'I'll be around if you want to talk to me,' he said. He gripped William's upper arm before turning to go on his way.

Charlotte looked up at William as he came through the door, walking slowly. She was lying with her beautiful hair spread across the white pillow, her eyes soft with love and pride, something in the crook of her arm. William glimpsed a brush of black hair. He gazed at his wife. Into her green eyes, so soft and gentle now with the fear gone. He recognised that it had been fear he had seen before, that had puzzled him.

He leaned down and kissed her on the lips, his beautiful madonna. His icon. His dream. Kissed her again while he could, in case the dream shattered in an immediate future that he sensed was already unfolding. He lowered his long thin body on to the chair by the bed, reached out and took her free hand between both of his. Held it like a precious jewel.

'I'm sorry,' he said with humility, eyes cast down, crushed beneath the weight of their collective sins. His eyes swivelled towards the bundle in the curve of Charlotte's arm. Swivelled back. 'My own fault —' his voice broke. 'It was big-headed of me to expect – I didn't think . . . I'm sorry,' he said again. He went on looking at her, devouring her beauty, as though storing it against the bleak, cold days that he saw stretching ahead. 'I'm sorry,' he said for the last time. 'It was presumptuous.' He let go of her hand, removed his glasses, wiped his eyes.

She said, 'William?'

Unsteadily, he pushed the chair back. 'I think I'd better go home,' he said. 'I'll come in tomorrow.'

He was backing towards the door when it opened. The doctor entered, paused tentatively, looking concerned. Suddenly, untidily, William was gone. The doctor closed the door behind him. 'Anything I can do?' he asked gravely.

Charlotte looked down at Max's beautiful raven-haired son. 'Thank you, but no.'

'Be kind to each other,' she heard him say.

Robert drove to Cuckoo Lane and walked up the path to the little pink house. 'Hello, old chap,' he said when William opened the door, not looking directly at him. 'Mind my dropping by?'

'Come in,' muttered William, backing away. Robert followed

him into the sitting room. William went to stand with his back to the window. Dusk was falling.

Robert cast around for something to say. 'That's a great fireplace,' he remarked as if he had never seen it before.

William said, 'We were going to block it in and get one of those gas things with flames.'

'Whatever for?'

'We didn't anyway.' A long, uncomfortable pause. Then, 'Would you like a beer?' he asked.

'Beer? Yes, please.' He noted that the piano lid was open. 'Does she still play a lot?'

'Yes, a lot.' William spoke from the kitchen, facing the open fridge.

'Good. I'm glad she's kept it up. Pity about the singing.'

'She sings a bit.'

'Good.'

William brought one bottle and two glasses. Set them down on the oak table. Levered the cap off. Poured carefully while Robert watched. A clamour of bells came in over the trees. 'Bell-ringing practice, Thursday,' said William.

'Oh? Bell-ringing. Oh, yes. Thanks, old chap.' Robert took his glass.

'Cheers,' said William.

'Cheers.' Robert glanced out of the window. 'Daffodils were early this year.'

'Yes.'

He sat down on the oak settle. 'Do you get any foxes down here?'

'Sometimes.'

They emptied their glasses, listening to the bells. Robert stood up. Hesitated. 'You all right, old chap?' He allowed his concern to show.

William nodded.

Robert clasped his upper arm, much as the doctor had done. Gave it a squeeze and a shake. 'I'll be on my way, then. Cheerio.'

Vivien lay back in the deep chair in Robert's study looking at the pictures on the walls. Photographs, mainly. Essentially Robert's. School rugby teams, class photos in black and white. But also Kenneth at Henley in his grandfather's striped blazer; Yolande

257

with her hockey team. The twins were not represented. Brownies, princesses in little school plays, that sort of thing went into albums. Charlotte had not shone at games but there was one of her receiving a prize on speech day, tall and slender in her school uniform with her lovely hair swinging down her back in a pony tail.

There had been a beautiful photo of Vivien on the desk, head thrown back, laughing. In a panicky gesture of self-defence, in the aftermath of Claire's death she had removed it. Or perhaps because at the time she could not bear all that laughter. In the last hour, since the phone call came from the hospital she had become sanguine about the past. Colours had faded. Corners smoothed out. Pain softened. A grandchild. A *raison d'être*. She smiled, deeply content.

'I won't have you talking like that,' said Jack Card angrily. 'You don't know what William would or wouldn't do.'

'I know my son. We've brought him up decently. He's not one to sleep around—'

'Stop it, Hermione!'

'I've seen the baby,' she cried shrilly. 'It's got black hair. Black as the ace of spades.'

'Your own hair is black,' he observed.

'Dyed black, as you very well know,' she said rancorously. 'I've a good mind to have this out with the Godfreys. Why should our son have to bring up—'

'I wouldn't if I were you,' said her husband, issuing his directive in the form of an unspoken threat. Then he left the room, shutting the door behind him.

Chapter Twenty-Nine

There was no confrontation. William brought Tom and Charlotte home from the hospital, then went back to work. Returned at the usual time. Five-thirty. When Charlotte was attending to Tom, William concerned himself with other matters, or merely waited. Tom hid in his own silence when William was close by. She thought he bore an air of waiting, too.

Charlotte accepted that William was sacrificing without complaint a part of their marriage to someone who did not concern him. First the dog, then the child.

She made allowances for him and she made promises to herself. She would love William in exchange for his loving Tom. But he did not love Tom. Had no intention of it. She was chilled when he talked to her while looking over the head of the child on her knee. She did not look ahead, but sometimes, in the night, she was afraid. She feared that his unexpected show of self-knowledge at the time of Tom's birth was unlikely to survive the daily irritation of the baby's presence in the house.

Miss Hurst came to visit one evening in the summer when Tom was three months old. William answered the door.

'I'm Alison Hurst. I'm sorry I didn't ring,' she said. 'I was on my way home and I had this in the car –' she held out a box prettily tied with a blue bow – 'so I thought I'd take the chance of finding Charlotte at home.'

William said, backing away, 'You'd better come in. She's in the garden.' He led her through the living room, skirting the piano, then out of the french window. 'Charlotte!'

Charlotte was sitting on a rug on the lawn with Tom tucked

into his tiny rocking chair. She looked up, recognised – something, not Miss Hurst. What did she recognise? She did not rise from the rug, though knowing she should. She sat watching the visitor come nearer.

'I taught her at school,' she heard Miss Hurst say. Then she was standing looking down at Charlotte on the rug. 'I've brought a present for the baby,' she said. Smiling.

'That's kind of you.'

'Do sit down,' said William, proffering one of the garden chairs.

'Thank you.' Miss Hurst bent down and handed the parcel to Charlotte. Charlotte untied the ribbon, unfolded the paper and took the lid off the box. A teddy bear gazed up at her. 'Tom will like that,' she said, holding back another Charlotte whose furious tirade beat through her mind. You are not my ex-school teacher. You are my father's mistress. Breaker-up of homes. Killer of mothers and wives. You have no right to come here making excuses with teddy bears.

'He's lovely.' Alison was looking down at Tom with that proprietory air Charlotte recognised, with fear now, from her first day at Mountfield Manor.

After a while – Charlotte never knew how long it was or remembered what was said in that time – Miss Hurst said in a forlorn voice, 'I'd better go.' She waited, as though hoping to be asked to stay. 'I'll show myself out.'

Did she say goodbye? What Charlotte remembered was that suddenly Miss Hurst wasn't there.

'What's the matter?' asked William, emerging from the french windows carrying a bottle of lemonade and some glasses on a tray. He looked from the empty chair to Charlotte sprawled face downwards on the rug. 'Why did she go?'

Charlotte lifted her head. Her eyes blazed. 'Because she knew she wasn't welcome.'

'Why ever not?'

'Just because you teach someone at school, it doesn't follow that you can bring her son presents,' Charlotte said.

'Good Lord!' William looked baffled. 'Isabel sent him a present. You didn't seem to mind that.'

All through that day and the next Charlotte fretted, feeling unsafe, until Vivien came.

She came every day, bubbling with happiness. This morning she was wearing a well-cut denim jacket and an expensive looking silk blouse she 'just happened to see' in Wylie-under-Lyne. 'What an extravagant grandmother!' Charlotte felt choked with emotion, seeing what Tom had done for her.

Vivien delighted in the novelty of bringing lunch for her daughter: a quiche made with young spinach from the Folly Hill garden; salad and a special dressing she had concocted herself with aromatic herbs, also from the garden. She would wash the Baby-Gros and the dishes, dust the living room, clean ashes out of the fireplace – chores the cleaner did at home. She returned again and again to hover over the sleeping Tom, her face soft, her eyes shining.

'You're willing him to wake up, you naughty old granny,' Charlotte pretended to scold. Vivien agreed, without guilt.

'He's got all night for sleeping. There, he's awake.' A triumphant whisper. 'He's opened his beautiful blue eyes. Such dark eyes for a baby.'

Max's eyes.

'Look, Charlotte, he's smiling at me. May I pick him up?'

'Of course.' She watched them together gazing into each other's eyes and felt tears prick behind her own. Vivien was taking on a cherished look that stirred memories of Charlotte's childhood, before things went wrong. She brought Tom little presents – mobiles, rattles, a tiny hair brush with a Mickey Mouse transfer on the back.

'Remember those Mickey Mouse T-shirts?' It was as if the miracle of Tom's birth had enabled Vivien to speak of Claire with serenity at last.

'It was a long time ago.' Charlotte did not wish to be reminded. Sometimes, when she held Max's child close to her heart, singing lullabies, she would become aware of Claire randomly and darkly present in the room. 'Go away!' she would whisper. She had known for some time that the mischief created at the Bubbly Hole was punishment for loving Max. It had certainly not been meant to bear fruit. 'I love you, I love you, I love you,' she sang defiantly to Tom, driving the malevolent spirit of Claire away with the strength of her love.

Maggie, too, adored Tom. When she thought no one was looking she crept close to his wooden rocking chair and licked his tiny fingers. As Tom grew stronger he would tug at her ears and her shaggy brows but she forgave him, moving with obsequious little bows just out of reach, then creeping back when something else took Tom's attention.

One evening in September, Charlotte went up to her bedroom, leaving them together, Tom safely strapped in his chair, Maggie on guard. Moments later she heard a scream and staccato barking. She flew down the narrow stairs. William was standing, briefcase under one arm, looking down at Tom. He seemed unaware of either the child's screams or the dog's agitation. Tom, who was rigid in his chair, relaxed at sight of her. His mouth widened into a red-gummed, toothless smile. William also smiled. His smile spread thinly over his face like butter covering a slice of bread.

She approached him warily. 'Hello darling,' she said. 'You're early.'

In the recesses of her consciousness she was aware there was something that needed dealing with. She felt she no longer knew this man who used to buy her cream teas and adore her. She thought the presence of Tom in his house had unleashed something in him. Later, when they were retiring for the night she recognised that he had to be defused. Made safe.

'How about a daughter?' she asked, tossing her nightdress in the air and catching it. 'A girl for you, a boy for me. How does the idea of a daughter grab you?'

William stood stiffly at the foot of the bed, fingers hesitating on the top button of his cardigan. 'Isn't it too soon?'

'I don't think so.' She forced a smile. 'I think I can manage two.'

'Yes,' said William. 'All right.'

In April, when Tom was nearly a year old and Charlotte had not yet become pregnant, Max walked up the path and rang the bell. His head was bare, his hair shining like jet. His eyes, which Tom had inherited, sparkled. In his confidant demeanour there was certainty of welcome.

This figure in trainers and jeans, a loud check shirt open at his sun-bronzed neck, the kind you would expect a cowboy to wear, could not be Max, Charlotte thought. She went cold all over, thinking she must have materialised him out of her unvoiced longings and fevered dreams.

262

'Hello,' said Max, and smiled.

The word reverberated in the stillness. Then something inside Charlotte gave way and she fell into his arms.

'Oh Max! It is you!'

'Who else?'

A triumphant crowing pierced their idyll. Max released her and strode through the door into the living room. Tom had pulled himself into a standing position. He was clinging precariously to one of the round-backed chairs, wobbling back and forth on his fat little legs. His face wore the astounded expression of one who has achieved the impossible. Maggie sat back on her haunches, watching with pride.

Then Tom saw Max with astonishment and toppled over backwards on to the floor.

He swept the baby up, held him at arm's length, gazing, gazing.

Charlotte staggered backwards drunkenly to the oak settle. The log fire sent up a shower of sparks. Don't burn the apple wood, William had said. It spits. But he had left it lying beneath the tree and she disobeyed, stored it in the garden shed for the perfume was ambrosia. It surrounded them now.

After their last, fateful encounter at the Bubbly Hole, Max had been to Folly Hill that night, but Robert had threatened to call the police. A court order would be sought, Robert said, if he didn't leave Charlotte alone.

Safe in the haven of his sheltering arms, she told him about being bundled off to La Gomera. 'Before I knew about —' She nodded at Tom on his hands and knees, gazing intently up into Max's face.

Why hadn't she answered his letters begging her to follow him to Australia? Or cashed the cheque he sent to pay her fare?

She was chilled with the knowledge of what Robert had done to her. No wonder he came seldom to the little pink house. Such a burden of guilt to have to bear.

'I thought it was the best thing for both of us,' Max said, 'that I should take up this offer. Of course I knew who engineered it and I didn't have to accept, I could have told them to stuff their job, but I suddenly saw a way out. A new life was offered to us, just the two of us. That's what emigration's all about. Getting a new life when you need it.'

'There was no way back, then,' he said. 'Not with you ignoring my letters and never answering my calls. Your father insisted you never wanted to see me again. How was I to know he wasn't telling the truth? Some of it was the truth. I'd done enough damage, he said. I had.'

He turned his head. Tom had keeled over on the floor and lay fast asleep; Maggie, too, with her chin resting on his legs.

They couldn't stay together. Not in William's house. Max had come in his mother's car. They took Tom and Maggie to Folly Hill. Max stayed in the lane outside, keeping his head down.

'How lovely! I can have him all day?' Vivien wasn't interested in the excuses Charlotte proffered for dumping Tom.

Max and Charlotte drove to the forest where she had been caught in the snowstorm. Here they were unlikely to meet anyone who was known to them. The trees were in spring leaf; beeches and chestnuts, ash, and a good deal of holly.

'I missed the holly at Christmas,' Max said. 'I was homesick in the heat. I missed everyone then.'

Charlotte remembered Louisa's boast that day they met on Wylie Common. She filled up with pain. 'How could you ask Louisa to visit you?'

Max looked astonished. 'Oh, no! Did she really tell you that? The minx! I didn't invite her. She came to Australia and called me up. I took her to lunch, once or twice. She was staying with the owners of a big department store, working there. Her father had sent her to get experience; you know he wants her to take over Waites eventually. Her hosts asked me round but I was crewing on my boss's yacht at weekends, and working on it, very often, in the evenings. I'm a great deck hand and barnacle scourer,' Max said, boasting. 'I wield a mean scrubbing brush, too. I didn't have any free time. She told you I had invited her!' he repeated. 'That girl needs her fat little bottom smacked.' He grinned at Charlotte. She could see he was telling the truth.

'Who told you about Tom?' she asked softly.

'My mother.'

'Your *mother*! How did she know Tom was yours?'

'She can count,' Max said.

Charlotte kicked into the thick layer of leaves on the track. Musty, earthy scents filled her nostrils. 'When did your mother tell you?'

264

'A month ago. She'd known for ages but—' He sobered. 'She has my father to contend with, you know.'

She did know. She brushed the memory away.

'And you didn't hop on a plane that very minute, leaving rent unpaid? You've grown up, haven't you?' She hopped, skipped and jumped through the pulpy leaves, silly with happiness.

'Actually, I rang British Airways, then swiftly packed my bag. I suppose it was lucky for me a friend dropped by. He flung the bag out of the window.'

'No!'

'True. They do that kind of thing in Australia. I dashed down the stairs and there it was lying in the gutter. Half the passers-by were yelling I was a danger to the community and threatening to call the police, and the other half were helping themselves to my clothes.'

The old Max, larger than life. She rubbed up against him, yearning. She never wanted to let him go.

'You'd have loved Australia,' he said. 'I wish – never mind. It's too late now. Anyway, when I'd staggered back up the stairs with my gear, this interfering baboon was ringing up everyone we knew. They trooped round and we drank your health and Tom's in Foster's lager. We got horribly drunk,' he said, and she could well believe it. 'Next day I boringly and very decently handed in my resignation, which meant I had to fume through four long weeks. Does that prove anything?'

Wordlessly, she hugged him.

'Look!' said Max, pointing. 'There's that woodman's hut! We camped here once, with the Boy Scouts.'

It was derelict, and the door had come off its hinges. A stately owl blinked at them from the rafters. 'Ssh! Don't disturb it,' whispered Max, and she remembered how he had once leaned back to allow a butterfly to go by.

In the silence she felt her heart expanding as though her soul was filling it up. She forgot she was married to William. They were swept away by an undertow of emotion as they sank into each other with tenderness. The owl sat watching them, unblinking.

Much later, something caused her to look at her watch. Four thirty! William would be home at half past five! She panicked. 'What are we going to do? I can't go home. Not to William. Not now, not after . . .'

'Darling, we should have talked. Tomorrow we'll do that.'

'Yes.' She looked round for her clothes and hurriedly pulled on her jeans. 'They're full of leaves!' She was laughing, crying, buffeted by alternately soaring happiness and craven guilt. The owl, with a flurry of wings, shot out of the open doorway.

'We'll talk tomorrow,' Max repeated. 'We'll work something out. Bring Tom. With him here we may be able to think.'

She couldn't bring Tom, for he had developed a cold. She took him back to Vivien on the following day. 'I'll keep him warm, don't worry,' she said. 'What a busy girl you are, and how lucky for me!' She didn't ask what Charlotte was doing that she needed a baby sitter again, all day. Didn't notice that she walked with a spring in her step and stars in her eyes. The luxury of Tom's presence was an opiate for her curiosity.

They went back, inevitably, to the hut in the woods. Charlotte had brought a rug, cushions and sandwiches. She didn't really want to talk. Was afraid to. She nuzzled into Max's neck, kissing his collarbone, fast little kisses along the length of it. She was hungry for his love.

'What's that?' Sitting up, Max noticed something lying among the leaves on the edge of the rug. He answered himself before she could tell him it was hers. 'It's a crystal!' He held it to the light. 'What a thing to find!' He stroked it with his fingers. 'I can feel the power in it. I read somewhere that researchers in Central America have seen visions from ancient civilisations in crystals they found there. Hundreds of thousands of years of knowledge can be stored in a crystal. Did you know they beam energy, and travel on their own beam? And perform miracles. Do you think this one brought us together?'

'Perhaps it'll perform a miracle for us,' she said.

'The good people of Atlantis knew all about them,' Max continued, holding the crystal out so that the light from the door struck it, setting it glowing. 'They did wonderful things with them. But the perverted ones created an imbalance with their crystals and blew themselves out of the world.'

She shivered.

On the third day Tom's cold was a little better, so they took him with them. Max carried him on his back in the Dream Rider she had bought when she thought William might take him for walks. Maggie came too, diving into tree-trunk crannies, digging with her sharp little claws, barking.

They made plans as they walked, keeping to safe paths well away from the unsafe woodman's hut. Tom, snug in his woolly hat and coat, sang his own little songs. He wore cute boots that Vivien had bought for him, with bunnies on the toes. Max announced that he would go to London, find a flat and look for a job, in that order.

In Charlotte elation alternated with despair.

'Do you want me to talk to William?'

'No.' She saw Max with his laughing blue eyes, his all-conquering air and pictured William injured, bitter. Diminished. She had to find a way to spare him as far as possible. 'I'll talk to William,' she said. She would need time, a day or two – a week. Two weeks . . .

'Hug a tree,' said Max.

She erupted in laughter.

'If you don't feel strong enough, hug a tree. Here's a nice old one. Old trees are strong and benevolent.' He paused beneath an enormous beech, leaned against the trunk. Tom, sandwiched between his back and the bark, looked astonished, then pained. 'There's life spirit in there,' Max said.

Charlotte stretched wide her arms to embrace the trunk. She thought she could sense the sap coursing, root to tip, seventy feet or more. Thinking of William, she prayed to the tree that she could somehow manage to do this cruel thing without hurting him too much.

'Tom,' said Max confidently, 'will be able to walk now. He has tree strength in him.'

They walked on to the edge of the forest and stood looking out on the rolling common land. 'I'll easily find a job now,' Max said. 'I could climb Everest in bedroom slippers if I had to. Give me ten years with you at my side and I'll be driving a Rolls-Royce. Make that seven. Ten to be a captain of industry. Twenty to be Lord Mayor of London. What a splendid lady mayoress you'd make!'

She loved his confidence, his wonderful optimism. 'You really haven't changed.'

'I wouldn't dare,' he said, his fingers tightening on hers. 'You didn't like – I'll re-word that: you were critical of me when I was down.'

'Never!'

'Critical in your heart.'

She remembered being turned away from Poplar Cottage. 'I didn't know then what your father could do to people,' she said.

'What anyone can do to anyone, for that matter. One thing I've learned,' Max said, 'people are capable of anything when they get screwed up. But you know that,' he added, looking into her eyes. 'You married William Card.'

'I've decided to forgive you,' William said. They were seated at either side of the oak table, their coffee cups before them. He had waited until supper was over before making his considered statement. He took off his glasses and wiped the lenses on his handkerchief. His eyes were smaller without the magnification. 'I've given this matter a great deal of thought, you'll understand,' he said. 'I'm prepared to bring the child up as my own, paying for his education and . . .'

Loving him? Charlotte might have asked last week but it wasn't last week. Did William know by some strange osmosis that she had been with her lover on a bed of blown leaves in a hut in the forest?

With the father of this child he proposed to educate. Whose mother he had decided to forgive. She began to tremble.

William was talking. She knew because his lips moved. Her mind had become a cinema screen, presenting a whirl of pictures. Tom on Max's back in the Dream Rider which William had never used. Maggie, with whom William never played, rummaging in the bushes, huffing and puffing with excitement, scattering after the source of intriguing smells and noises, ears pricked. She dragged herself back to the little pink house that her kind husband had provided for her. Listened to him as he sat, stiffly upright, in his curve-backed chair. 'You are my wife,' he was saying. Relentlessly.

She put a hand to her head. 'Yes.' That was a fact, all right. She lifted her eyes. Thought he might look like this in court, glasses set squarely on his nose, his cheese-straw hair perhaps tidier, delivering well researched evidence on behalf of the prosecution. She dug in her mind for the least cruel words with which to tell him that the shelter he had given her was no longer necessary; that it was good of him to forgive her but she had no further need of him now. She felt sick to her very soul. Shivering, she pulled her cardigan close.

William looked at the fire. 'I see you've run out of logs. That enormous fireplace,' he said, damning it as always, 'takes such a lot of wood.' Then he smiled. 'Why don't you go and have a look at some gas fires? I'm sure if you did you'd come round to my way of thinking.' A gas fire, in return for this forgiveness I am offering – no – thrusting upon you. He rose from his chair and went out through the kitchen door carrying the log basket. She could hear sounds outside. Blocks of wood being thrown into the barrow. William being good. Providing for the fire he so disliked. Too big. Too extravagant. Too old. There was nothing big or extravagant about William. She wanted to take her tree strength and make a leap into the future with Max, taking her baby with her, while it was still safe to go.

Clutching her empty coffee cup, she listened to William's slow footsteps approaching on the concrete path outside.

Chapter Thirty

It was a pity William had that spat with the neighbours about the fence. A pity, too, that Hermione, usually punctilious about telephoning to ask if she might visit, should have called on a whim. Eileen Penrose, who had a day off work, was in the front garden next door as Hermione stepped out of the car.

'Mrs Card isn't in,' she said, snipping at the box, the lilac, the buddleia all growing in a line from the front of the house to the fence, bringing herself to within a few yards of Hermione where she stood on the pavement locking the car door.

'Thank you.' With a brusque nod Hermione turned away, delving into her handbag where she had already dropped the keys. She knew about the problem with the Rottweiler and had no intention of making friends with this awkward woman. Out of the corner of her eye she could see the animal standing in the front doorway, handsome and alert. A good watchdog, she'd no doubt. Scarcely a pussycat, as the woman said. She retrieved the key from the bottom of her bag.

'Don't expect her back until a half-hour before her husband's due,' said Eileen Penrose shrilly. 'She's out with the boyfriend again.'

Hermione straightened, keys jangling.

'That'll teach her stiff-necked son to throw his weight around,' Eileen Penrose said to herself, snipping viciously at the buddleia as she watched the car roll back down the lane. The fence he had insisted they erect to keep Sid in had cost them their holiday in Spain. And a fat lot of good it was going to do him. Did he think she was going to confine Sid to her back garden? He could jump his own front fence and run down the side of their house from the road any time he liked. She went back inside, well pleased with herself. What a God-given opportunity that had been to exact revenge!

Hermione, driving back stern-faced across the bridge that would lead to the Forge Green road, dimly perceived that Max Fosse could have returned from Australia. As luck would have it, she happened to be carrying with her the means to find out. She pulled into a lay-by, opened the glove box and took out some envelopes held together by a rubber band. She slid one envelope free, laid it on the passenger seat and replaced the rest. Then she signalled that she intended to pull back into the traffic.

Puddle Lane.

At Poplar Cottage she climbed out of the car, jerked her skirt into place and pleating her lips marched up to the front door.

Jessica answered the bell. Hermione gave all her attention to reading the expression in her eyes. Tom's eyes, she realised with renewed shock. Recognition turned her from an investigative, protective mother into an avenging mother-in-law.

'I'm distributing these,' she said angrily, thrusting the envelope under Jessica's nose. Jessica took it, looking down at the words stamped across the front: HELP THE AGED.

'I don't know if you would like to give me a contribution now or drop it in the post,' Hermione said.

'Just a moment,' Jessica replied. Her voice was scarcely audible. Turning, she tripped on the mat, recovered herself and disappeared.

Hermione's discovery took on a nightmare quality.

By the time Jessica returned to the door – 'Had to search for my purse,' she said wanly – Hermione had lost control.

'I hear Max is back,' she blurted out accusingly. She had intended to ask casually how he was getting on in Australia.

'Yes.' Jessica licked the envelope and handed it to Hermione, avoiding her eyes, backed away. 'Sorry I'm in a rush. I'm in the middle of . . . Sorry,' she said again, and began to close the door.

Her panic reaction had the effect of dissipating Hermione's anger. My fault, she conceded, strutting back to the car. She sat with her key in the ignition trying to make up her mind whether to telephone William at his office now, or wait until five.

William, who returned from work at precisely the same time every day, was late. It had been a warm, sunny day, the kind that can mislead one into planting out seedlings that may be struck down in a few days' time by frost. Charlotte looked out through the open glass doors. Tom had left his baby walker and was staggering freely across the grass. He looked up, saw her, crowed with triumph and fell over.

'Clever boy,' she called as he struggled to his feet again. She thought, I too have tree strength. I'll talk to William tonight. After supper, when Tom has settled down, I'll talk to him.

Why was William late, tonight of all nights? By six o'clock she felt a touch of apprehension.

I will work up to it gradually, she decided. But how can you be gradual about telling a husband who has been kind to you, given you shelter when you needed it, that you are leaving him?

I have lived with William for one year and seven and a half months, she said to herself. Nineteen and a half months, all told. He has spent money on me. Made me safe. Treated me with kindness.

Six ten.

She caught a glimpse of herself in the mirror. She was wearing a green shirt that matched her eyes. She thought of William's pride in her beauty, rushed up the stairs, hauled off her blouse and skirt, pulled on an old black cotton jumper and a pair of tatty jeans that she used for gardening. She dragged her hair back. Plaited it tightly. Fixed the plait with a rubber band, looked in the mirror again. She turned away not wanting to know she didn't look all that plain. Only redesigned.

The chimes of the quarter hour from the church clock filtered into the room. Why was William three-quarters of an hour late? The house had become silent. She listened. The silence was telling her something. What was it saying?

She went to the piano and began to play an old Beatles song. Sang it softly.

There were whispers in the room. A corona of light came in through the glass doors from the setting sun.

You can't sing without me, said a dangerous voice in her head.

She looked down at the keys, rejecting the vision of Claire standing before her. There was something dreadful in the way her lips curved, the way her eyes shone. They were not green any more; they were so dark Charlotte couldn't read them.

Her fingers dashed across the keys. In and out of the flats and

272

sharps, *prestissimo*. Three octaves high and back again, *sforzando*. Foot on the pedal. Crash the chords. 'I have to live a life of my own,' she said. *Forte*.

Twins do not have a life of their own. The words came as a threat. Charlotte pressed down on the pedal again *fortissimo*. 'I'm not a twin now,' she cried. 'I'm not! I'm not!'

No one can get rid of one twin and keep the other, said Claire. A twin is a twin is a twin.

Charlotte's fingers flew, *energico*. The music swirled round the room. Great chords filled it, hitting the ceiling, pressing against the walls. 'I love you, Claire,' she said distractedly, 'but you're not here for me any more and I love Max beyond anything.'

I *am* here for you. I'm here when you need me.

'I've needed you when you didn't come,' Charlotte said, remembering having to send for Isabel to come to the register office. Isabel, who had anyway been powerless to save her.

I wouldn't have stopped you marrying William, said Claire. William did me no harm.

'And you won't stop me from going to Max,' said Charlotte, *molto vivace*. She sang the words at the top of her voice, touching high C. 'You will not stop me now-w-w. I will go to Max, go to Max, go to Max.'

I'm sorry, said Claire, but Max can't have you without me. So sorry. Her voice crept through the music, eerie and threatening, filling the room with evil. You will see. Charlotte's fingers scurried and thumped, blotting the words out, keeping the evil at bay. She had the strength the tree had given her.

'I can sing without you,' she sang. 'I can do anything I want without you-u-u-u-u.'

She could not hear the front door open, but she felt the draught on her bare ankles. Her fingers went limp. In the silence she heard William's footsteps.

His pale eyes were a little mad behind the shiny spectacles. He strode into the room, his anger leaping in front of him. She felt the force of it lifting her out of her seat, She staggered beneath its weight and power, caught her heel, staggered again and fell.

He bent down and grasped her wrist, jerking her to her feet. She knew he was shouting from the way his mouth opened and shut, but she couldn't hear the words for Maggie's barking. Maggie was jumping up, clawing at her legs. Her barks were screams. She caught Charlotte's jeans in her teeth. The denim ripped. Then she swung away, raced outside, still screaming.

But the screams were not coming from her. They were coming from Tom.

Charlotte sped out of the door. Sid the Rottweiler had Tom in his jaws and was shaking him like a rag doll.

They all came to the hospital except William.

Vivien, too, in spite of her heavy cold that she had caught from Tom. Her illness had taken away her resistance to germs. Yolande and Oliver had dashed down by car, picking up Kenneth on the way. They gathered in the passage outside the room where Tom lay, talking in low voices. They were allowed to go in one at a time. The doctor who had attended to Tom's wounds came and joined them. Babies were tough, he said, and the bites were not extensive. Concussion and shock was the issue. He felt the child would pull through. 'But I'm a little concerned about the mother.' He looked from Oliver to Kenneth to Robert with puzzled eyes. 'The father . . .?'

'He's not here,' said Yolande in her straightforward fashion, making no excuses. 'I'll see if Char wants us to fetch him.' Gently she opened the door to Tom's room and went in. Charlotte was seated on a straight-backed chair, leaning over the cot. All Yolande could see of Tom was his little pale face; his arms and head were bandaged. She put a hand on Charlotte's shoulder and whispered, 'Do you want us to get Max?'

Charlotte looked up, her face drawn with grief. At Yolande's question, her expression changed to one of fear. A tear broke free and ran down her cheek. 'No! No, Yol, please, no!'

Yolande waited a moment in case she should say she wanted William, but she didn't.

Robert entered. 'I think the others ought to go home soon,' he said to Charlotte, 'but I'll stay the night. I'll be in the waiting room. Don't hesitate to call if you need me.' He kissed her cheek and then bent over the cot. 'Hang on, little chap,' he murmured. His eyes returned to Charlotte. In shock she had a strange look. No wonder the doctor was worried about her. Robert felt, with fear, that if Tom died she might slip away at his side, clinging.

It must have been midnight when Charlotte realised Claire was in the room. She jerked forward, leaning protectively across

Tom's little body. 'Tom is not your child,' she spat at Claire. 'You can't have him! He's mine!'

You wouldn't have had him but for me.

Charlotte had always known that Max had not raped her by his own will.

You were told what he did to me, and still you loved him, said Claire bitterly. You kissed him and held him as though you didn't care about him taking my water wings. You forgave him. Didn't you think I would react?

'You didn't give me Tom,' Charlotte said forcefully, ignoring Claire's question. 'Max gave him to me. Max,' she repeated. 'He was Max's gift, and nothing to do with you.'

Claire's eyes narrowed to dark slits. Charlotte looked into them and panicked. 'I won't see him again if you will go away and leave Tom with me. I promise,' she whispered.

Claire sat still as a watching bird. He might have been mine, she said bitterly. I have lost everything. I have none of this joy and fulfilment that you—'

Charlotte had stopped listening. You have to close your ears when there are words being spoken that will break your heart in two.

It was three days before Tom regained consciousness. As he opened his navy-blue eyes, he saw Charlotte looking down at him, and smiled. Charlotte's happy tears fell on his face.

Yolande, who was taking her turn to sit with Charlotte, rushed out to call the doctor, as well as to leave them for a few precious moments alone. And to ring Oliver. And Robert. And Ken. 'It's not like me to cry, is it?' she asked, coming back into the room wiping her eyes. 'Not my form.'

Somebody had to go and see William. The Godfrey family, reassembled, were all wondering why neither he nor his parents had been in touch. It was Saturday morning, so they presumed William would be at home. In the event it was Kenneth who volunteered.

He drove up Cuckoo Lane in his father's car and parked outside the little pink house. As he removed the key from the ignition, in the side mirror he saw Mrs Penrose hurrying purposefully down her garden path. 'Blast!' he muttered and remained seated. Perhaps she wouldn't recognise him. He glanced again in the mirror, saw that she was coming towards him, groaned and proceeded to climb out.

'You're Mrs Card's brother, aren't you?' Eileen Penrose stood square in his path.

Kenneth nodded.

'The little boy – is he all right?'

'I believe so. He's conscious now.'

'Thank God! All the same,' she said, her face twisting, 'I don't suppose it's going to make much difference to Sid. The fact that the child survived, I mean. I've not been able to talk to that brother-in-law of yours. He's not answering the door.' Eileen Penrose's face crumpled. 'The police have been here and taken Sid away. They're threatening to put him down.' Her voice trembled. 'He's only a pup. He's got ten or twelve years ahead of him.'

'I'm sorry,' said Kenneth. 'This is a matter, as you said, for the police. I don't see that William could do anything.'

'He could say it was his doing.'

'*What?*'

'Yes, it was his doing,' she said forcefully. 'I saw him striding up the road. He was furious, I could tell. I knew, as soon as I saw the expression on his face, he'd discovered what his wife was up to. Sid ran to him, friendly as a puppy, and he lashed out. Well you shouldn't kick a dog. Especially not a Rottweiler.' She looked at him, pleading for understanding. 'I've got to go to court and I think that precious brother-in-law of yours should come along and admit his guilt. Sid's not a dangerous dog. He would never have done it if he hadn't been kicked.'

'Oh, God!' Kenneth muttered, passing a hand across his eyes.

'And I'll tell you another thing, for what it's worth,' the woman went on, fired by Kenneth's shocked reaction. 'If he says he didn't know Sid was in the garden, I can tell you he did. Sid went ahead of him, straight down the side of the house. He knew all right.'

Kenneth thought he saw a shadow on the front window of the little pink house, as of someone surreptitiously watching. He returned to his car and drove back to Folly Hill.

'What good would it do to tell Charlotte?' asked Oliver, conciliatory as always. They'd been about to sit down to lunch when Kenneth returned with his news.

276

'Eat up your meal,' said Vivien tiredly. 'There's time to think about it. Yolande dear, no one can run another person's life.'

'William has had a bloody good try at running hers.'

'I'd rather you didn't use such language at the table,' said Robert. 'Could someone pass me the salt? I think it would be inadvisable to condemn William on these facts. How was he to know Tom was in the garden?'

Vivien, who knew Tom was nearly always in the garden after tea, thought it would be unwise to say so.

By evening they were in agreement. Charlotte was going to find out about William's having kicked Sid whether they told her or not. The local paper carried human-interest reports from the magistrates' court, where it would seem Mrs Penrose was going to be summoned for keeping a dangerous dog. Robert volunteered to convey the bad news.

Charlotte listened in silence, so calmly that Robert wondered if she was taking the facts in. As he finished, she lifted her eyes to her father's face. 'I'll go and see him,' she said.

'Do you want me to go with you?'

'No, thank you. I'd like you to stay with Tom. Can I take your car?'

'Of course.' Robert fished in his pocket for the keys. 'But wouldn't you like someone to go with you? If not me, then Kenneth?'

She managed a wry smile. 'William's not going to eat me. There won't be a row. I'm not going to blame him.'

'Even if he admits—'

'I don't blame him,' said Charlotte distinctly.

Her father eyed her in baffled silence. Then, 'I'll recommend you for sainthood,' he said.

'It was good of you to say it wasn't my fault,' said William, sagging inside his loose jumper in the middle of the room. His voice took on a bleak, defensive tone. 'How was I to know the child was walking? I'd never seen him do it, had I? How would I expect him to be in the garden, by himself, *walking*?'

'No,' she said, 'you wouldn't.'

His eyes shifted round the room. 'What do you want me to do?'

'I want us to stay here,' Charlotte said. 'I know it wasn't your

277

fault. Nor was it Sid's. It was Claire. Claire sent Sid to attack Tom.' Yet even as she said it she remembered Tom's stillness, and his air of waiting, when William was at hand.

William seemed to rock on his feet, without moving. 'Were you going away with Max?'

'William.' She went to him and took his hands. 'I want you to know I can never see him again.'

'But you will,' he said, looking with pale, distrusting eyes at her unhappy face. 'Girls like you don't marry dull fellows like me,' he said, the words drip, drip, dripping from his twisted lips, falling into the silence of the room. 'I had this dream. I'd had it for so long. But I don't suppose I thought there was going to be a miracle. Not really.'

'William,' she began, aching for him.

He didn't seem to hear her. 'Then the cream teas started, and I thought it could happen. I lived for those teas. And that night you came with me to the firm's dinner dance – I'd never been noticed before. You don't know what it's like to be a man like me,' said William, bewilderment and acumen flowing freely with his words. 'People don't look at you. You go through life invisible.

'That night went to my head. I couldn't get it out of my mind that it might be possible to marry you. I used to lie awake dreaming about it. About us walking down the aisle with you looking like an angel – as you looked at Yolande's wedding – and everyone envying me. I thought if I concentrated hard enough it could come true. So when you—' He took his glasses off and rubbed his eyes. 'When I saw you in the library, I thought – I thought – I thought I'd brought it about.' He dried up with embarrassment. 'I thought I'd brought it about by being positive,' he said in a small voice.

'Oh, William!'

He looked down at the floor. 'You won't want to stay here,' he said.

'I particularly want to stay here.' As Charlotte said it she knew for all this raw-edged exposure of his fantasy William had thought of her as no more than a beautiful ornament who could bring a kind of glory to his hum-drum life. She saw how she had taken him into her light and his little world had woken up and seen him standing there. She felt a deep ache of pity for him and wished it could have been love.

But the house . . . In that moment she became aware of what had been true for a long time, although she had not remarked it. Since Tom's arrival it had become a home.

'Perhaps you would like a cup of tea. I could do that for you,' said William, dully acknowledging the fact that an outpouring of one's life story is not the same as turning the key that unlocks the universe.

Max telephoned. Charlotte did not want to remember what she said to him, shouted at him, screamed at him. Claire put the words into her mouth. Words that, God willing, would never emerge in her memory.

Brave little Maggie, who had attacked her friend Sid with such enormous courage, came back from the vet's with her forelegs bandaged. By the time Tom returned from hospital, the bandages were off and she was running round again. Her delight on greeting him came close to ecstasy.

The three of them went often to the woods together, Tom on Charlotte's back, Maggie diving and digging, chasing real and imaginary birds and insects, Charlotte searching out trees bigger, stronger and therefore wiser than the rest. She leaned against them thinking of the sap rising, from root to topmost branch, until she sensed strength seeping into her. She held Tom and Maggie against the tree too. They all needed strength.

One day Charlotte came across the woodman's hut. She put Tom down and went inside, thinking to perform a sort of exorcism. She leaned against the rickety wall and closed her eyes. She could hear Tom running his little hands through the dry leaves. A tear slid out from beneath her closed lids and rolled down her cheek. then another. There is no exorcising Max, she said to herself. We were made for each other. 'Claire,' she whispered. 'Claire?'

After a while she knew that Claire was not there. She had taken Charlotte's promises and gone.

She sank down on the leaves and wept.

Tom scrambled on to her knee. 'Look!' he said, holding out what seemed to be a stone.

She wiped her eyes, took it in her hand, recognised the familiar shape. 'You've found my crystal,' she said. She rubbed it on her

279

jeans, but could not get it clear. It looked as though it had taken to itself a thousand years of misery. She thought of it coming from the golden rock strata of the mountains and travelling to her on its own beam. Now it looked as though it had given up.

'I'm sorry,' she said to the crystal. On the way back she washed it in a puddle but still it did not shine. She felt it knew she had disowned it.

Vivien was back in hospital. The cold she had caught from Tom had gone down to her chest. It had taken her hearing away. They were doing something with her blood. Cleansing it? Changing it? Treating it? Charlotte didn't want to listen to details. She became Vivien's guardian, a wall that would keep out Miss Hurst, the predator who crouched, waiting to spring. Waiting to be Mrs Robert Godfrey with two daughters and a son. If Charlotte kept Vivien happy, she would live and Miss Hurst would not be able to come in.

'I went to the hospital and had a sperm count,' said William, speaking formally as though giving evidence in court. 'I thought we might as well know. It's very low,' he said, looking over Charlotte's head, focusing on the opposite wall. 'It's unlikely I could father a child.' Into the silence he repeated, 'I thought you might as well know.'

The previous week she had told him she might be pregnant. A girl for you!

Charlotte became very calm. She smiled and said, 'Unlikely. Not impossible.'

'It may not be my child,' said William.

'It is your child,' she said, speaking to Claire who might be in the room, listening. 'It only takes one little sperm, as I understand, provided it teams up with the right egg. You only need one.' She went to him. Put her arms round his neck. 'Come on, William! Let me kiss you.' In the end she had to move away. You cannot touch a man who has gone beyond reach.

'Did you notice the plates? Nice modern ones,' she said, gesturing towards the mantelpiece where half a dozen Royal Staffordshire treasures were lined up in a gleaming row. 'I bought them today at that new shop, Chinacraft. And I'm sure you'll be pleased to know I had someone in today to value this,' she said, moving back to the piano and fingering its shining black surface. 'You're right, it does take up too much room.' She gathered up her tree strength and smiled at him again.

'Good,' said William. 'And now that we've got those plates, perhaps you'll throw that old bit of quartz away. I can't imagine why you should think it's ornamental.'

She put the crystal into her pocket and kept her fingers there, touching it. Then she saw William's eyes were on her knuckles, little mounds in the denim of her trousers, and she took her hands out.

'I've looked at gas fires,' she said, lifting her head, speaking in a bright, bright voice. 'I've chosen one. Perhaps you know some-one who could put it in.'

'I do,' he replied.

She knew then that he had begun to hate her as well as Tom, but she did not accept it. She was tree-strong. She would work and work on him, striving to please him, until she won him round.

Robert had the piano collected and put back into the drawing room at Folly Hill.

'I missed it,' said Vivien in the wan way that she had adopted again. 'Such memories it holds. All those Christmases when you were small. You and Claire singing carols. And those duets you played. I often dream—'

Charlotte cut her off. She did not like Vivien dreaming about the past which was becoming the future. Feeling close to Claire. Being with Claire again was part of Vivien's will, now. She felt Vivien was slipping away. Sliding through the fingers of her mind.

Yolande said bluntly, 'You're pregnant, aren't you?'

'No,' said Charlotte.

Yolande glanced meaningfully at Charlotte's waist, which was not as slim as it had been. 'I saw Max the other day. He and Louisa were lunching together.' She waited.

'Good,' said Charlotte. 'His parents would be happy if he mar-ried her. That's good. I'm glad.'

Yolande said, 'You could have fooled me.'

That night Charlotte dreamed Max was in court, charged with

281

murdering his wife. She was on the jury. She came into the court, shuffling along the row with the other jurors. Max was in the dock.

A voice. 'You, Max Fosse, the names you are about to hear are the names of the jurors who are to try you. If you object . . .'

She waited for him to say he wished her to be dismissed. That he was her lover, the father of her child. She was the woman he could not live without and for whom he had disposed of his wife.

He smiled at her, trustingly. Her hand went towards the Bible and she swore that she would faithfully try him according to the evidence. She sat down and looked into the well of the court. Miss Hurst was there. She was wearing the Victorian earrings Charlotte and Vivien had not been able to find. In Miss Hurst's face was Claire. Claire was looking at the prisoner in the dock with venom to shrivel the soul. 'You are to find this man guilty,' she said, speaking to Charlotte. Looking at Max.

'Will the foreman of the jury pronounce the verdict?'

She stood up and said in a ringing voice, 'We find the prisoner guilty, m'lud.'

She woke up, weeping.

'Nightmare?' asked William. 'You woke me. Again.'

She asked, 'Did you ever send me a Valentine gift?'

'What a question to produce in the middle of the night! No, of course I didn't. Go to sleep.' She knew from his tone that William truly hated her now.

Next day she moved into Tom's room. He slept so soundly, she was free to rise in the sleepless night and stand by the window looking at the stars. She listened to the church clock striking the night hours, moving the time on. Sometimes in the stars she searched for Claire. Perhaps she could bargain with her.

The child within her stayed small and still. Was it afraid to come into the world, as she was afraid to bear it? She did not give it a name or guess its sex. They had no contact, she and this reluctant little being. She put her crystal on the dressing table and asked it for help. After a while it came to life and began to shine again.

Chapter Thirty-One

'It is true,' she said distinctly. 'Max and Louisa are to be married.'

William looked stunned. 'Did he tell you?'

'You must know I haven't seen him.' What she saw in his face was a plan, hurriedly formed.

'If you haven't seen him, how do you know?'

'Yolande told me.'

Was Yolande trying to goad her into making a move, not knowing Claire had disallowed it? 'Oliver and I saw Max and Louisa at the theatre last week,' Yolande would say. 'They looked very happy.' Or, 'Oliver and I went to a dinner party and Max and Louisa were there. They're getting married, had you heard? On the twenty-first of December.'

'On the twenty-first of December,' Charlotte said now, smiling with her lips. 'Did I tell you he and Andy Harverson have started up in business? Something to do with computers, I understand. They're doing amazingly well. That's why he's getting married at Christmas, because he can actually afford to honeymoon in Australia. In the sun. On the firm's profits.' She smiled directly at William. Or bared her teeth. That's what it felt like with her face staying frozen. 'Isn't that nice?'

Give me ten years with you at my side and I'll be a captain of industry, Max had said. Would he become a captain of industry with Louisa at his side? Twenty to be lord mayor of London. Had he decided Louisa would make a better lady mayoress than she?

William rose and left the room. She knew then he had seen right through her defences, thin as tissue paper. Limp with unshed tears.

He returned, wearing an air of purpose, carrying a hammer and some tiny hooks. She watched as he set about attaching the telephone cord that had broken away from the wall.

'I'd like to ask Isabel for Christmas,' Charlotte said, enunciating her cry for help very carefully. 'What do you think?'

'After Christmas, perhaps,' said William. 'You might like her to come after Christmas.' He smiled down at the hammer as though something had settled in his mind.

On Friday evening, the twentieth of December, it occurred to Kenneth to wonder whether there was any connection between Tom's call to the hospital for an overnight check-up and Max's marriage to Louisa the following day. Had Charlotte wanted to be free on this particular evening? And if so, for what reason?

Life is full of coincidences, he told himself. Hospitals, in his experience, did not give you a choice of dates. But still his mind remained troubled.

After supper he said to Robert, 'I think I'll go over and see Charlotte.' No one ever said, 'I think I'll go and see Charlotte and William.'

Robert's face fell, but he recovered himself quickly. 'What a good idea. I'd thought . . . Yes, better you than me.'

Kenneth wasn't taken in. He knew Robert's way of dealing with Max's marrying Louisa in the morning would be to nip over to Wylie for a bit of comfort. So, he couldn't go now, Kenneth thought with satisfaction. Somebody had to stay with Vivien.

He went upstairs, carrying a distressing image of Robert and his mistress talking about Vivien, wondering when she was going to die. Were they already having discussions on how long they should wait before openly shacking up together? Unlike Yolande, Kenneth never visualised them rolling round, embarrassingly, in bed.

He tapped, then cautiously opened Vivien's bedroom door. The form in the bed was still. He listened to her breathing, decided she was asleep and went back downstairs again. He took the keys from the hall table, knowing she wouldn't mind. It was a mere courtesy to ask for the use of her car. A pretence that she still held the reins in her hands.

Robert was wandering restlessly. As he passed, Kenneth said, 'Are we still not mentioning the pregnancy?'

'That's the way she seems to want it.'

284

'Yol has decided it's a phantom. Apparently women can have phantom pregnancies and blow up like a balloon.'

'That's what your mother thinks.' Robert spoke brusquely. Kenneth could see he did not wish to discuss Charlotte. But he did. He was worried about her. She was strange these days, with an air of being on guard. Guarding what? Or guarding herself from what?

'I never thought of William as much of a stud,' said Kenneth, 'but at least if it is a baby it has to be his. Max came back in April and I'm quite sure she hasn't seen him since Tom's accident. When she was eight months gone with him, she was enormous.'

'I'd rather not discuss the matter.' Robert's tone was final. 'And I hope you won't bring it up with Charlotte. I hope you'll behave as though nothing—'

'Trust me.' Kenneth strode into the brilliant flood of the security lights, rattling the car keys, glad to get out of the house. How can a house feel so empty when there are three people in it? He knew why his father didn't want to talk about Charlotte's behaviour. It was too like his own.

'Out walking, at this hour? Bloody hell, it's pitch dark.' Kenneth was indignant that William should have allowed Charlotte to go. 'And freezing. Where's she walking to?'

'I don't know. She likes to walk. Perhaps she's gone to visit a friend.' William's face took on a haunted look.

'What's the matter? Have you had a row?' Kenneth asked bluntly.

'No. No, of course not.'

Kenneth looked down at the clutter on the floor. A knife, some thick rope, a hammer and screws. 'What are you doing? A bit of DIY?'

'There's always something needing doing,' William muttered. He lifted his gaze to Kenneth's face. His eyes behind the glasses seemed desperate, in a way. 'Would you like to stay for a while? Have a coffee or something?'

Kenneth recognised the invitation as a plea. So there had been a row! It looked to him as though William would like him to be there when Charlotte returned. He thought of his little sister out walking in the cold night and hardened his heart. 'I think I'll drive round and look for her, thanks all the same.'

There's something going on here, he thought. Maybe not a row, but something. He decided that when he found Charlotte he would take her back to Folly Hill for the night. At the door, he asked, 'Where's Maggie?'

Again that haunted look. 'With Charlotte. Are you sure you won't stay?'

'No.' Kenneth left by the front door, banging it behind him.

He drove up and down the byways adjacent to Cuckoo Lane, then further afield, driving slowly with his lights on full beam. Surely she wouldn't go into the woods at this hour? All the same, he went down a side road from which he guessed he would have access to the towpath. Climbing out of the car, he went to the edge of the trees. It was pitch dark there and he hadn't brought a torch. He cupped his hands and called, 'Charlotte!'

There was no reply. He climbed back into the car and continued his search. At half past eleven he drove back up Cuckoo Lane. The little pink house was in darkness. She must have come home. So at least they weren't sitting up arguing. He drove home.

Charlotte walked with her hands in the pockets of the voluminous coat she had bought when she was pregnant with Tom. This quiet little, still little baby could be hidden under one of her ordinary coats but she had chosen this one anyway because it was warm and it had a hood. She wore gloves and wool-lined boots but still she was cold. The cold was coming from inside her, pushing out to meet the hard frost descending. Maggie trotted along at her heels.

She traversed the ill-lit lane by the church. Its clock struck midnight. She stood leaning against the old stonework, listening to the silence that came in the wake of the chimes. Around her the big trees stood black in the moonlight. Frost had begun to form lace on the ground. She shivered, hugging her coat close.

It is the twenty-first of December now, she said to herself. Today is the day that Max will marry Louisa.

The moon went behind a cloud. Came out again. She said, 'Claire, Max is getting married today. So that's all right, isn't it? There's no reason why I should ever see him again, even by chance. They'll probably live in London. And the piano has gone so I won't want to sing. And this is William's baby I'm carrying. You know what I'm saying, don't you? I want you to promise to leave us alone now.'

286

There was a rustle in the bushes. A badger, perhaps, or a fox? Maggie leaned against Charlotte's ankles, comforting her.

'It is not Max's baby,' she said distinctly, looking all round, looking up at the stars, and the moon, huge and golden now in the sky. 'It is William's. William's.'

The night became uneasy. The shadows disappeared and darkness spread around. Suddenly she was very, very frightened. Maggie, at her feet, whined. Something was going to happen, she could feel it.

She thrust her cold fingers down into her pockets, looking for her crystal. They store knowledge over hundreds of thousands of years, Max had said. So they know the patterns. It was not there. She began to run, with Maggie running at her side.

The road was dark, for the lights of Wylie went out at midnight. The cloud eased its way back from the moon and she could see again.

They hurried up the lane. All the lights were off in the little pink house. She searched frantically in her pocket for the key. It was not there. She rang the bell and waited. The silence was profound. She ran down the alleyway between the house and the fence, on the path Sid had taken when he came to get Tom. The door of the shed, normally locked, stood ajar. She hauled out the ladder. The light was off in her room, the curtains drawn wide. Because the wall below was encumbered with the bare winter branches of a climbing rose, she put the ladder up against William's sill. They had been sleeping in separate rooms for some weeks now.

She put her foot on the bottom rung of the ladder, stepping carefully, holding on tightly with her hands, thinking of the silent, still little baby that lay under her heart. She reached the window, easily pushed it up, and put a leg over the sill. The room was empty, the bed, William's bed, still neatly made up. She went out of the open door and stood on the landing. Looking at what the moonlight revealed.

William had left, abandoning his bones and what flesh there had been on them, his cheese-straw hair, his old jumper and jeans that he wore to do jobs round the house, leaving them strung from a rope in the middle of the narrow stairs.

Chapter Thirty-Two

Charlotte leaned out of the window. She could see Maggie looking very small on the lawn below. I can't go back down this ladder, she said to herself, trembling. And I can't go down the stairs.
Without touching, she meant, the abandoned thing that hung
there. She felt herself imprisoned with William's terrible deed.

But she had to go down – to telephone, and to let Maggie in out
of the cold.

Keeping her eyes averted, she went to her own room, hers and
Tom's, on the other side of the stairway. The light was on there,
too. Looking at Tom's empty cot, she felt a great wave of relief
that he was not there. She took a scarf from a drawer, folded it
and tied it round her eyes. She felt her way to the head of the
stairs. Sucking in her breath, leaning back so that she might not
touch that thing she had to pass, she started to descend, step by
careful step. She felt no sense of William's proximity as she
would have expected from a living person as one passed by.

At the foot of the stairs, she took the scarf off. The hall was in
darkness. The whole house was in darkness now. She wondered
how she could have seen William's body in the dark. When she
opened the front door, Maggie was crouched on the step, shivering. She slipped in and scurried past in search of warmth.
Charlotte followed her.

She felt she couldn't go on. Someone would have to come and
save her for she did not know where to begin saving herself.

Numbly, she went into the living room. Maggie was hunched
on the hearth, close to the fading embers of the fire. She pulled
her warm coat round her and collapsed beside the dog, burying
her face in the rough hairs.

After a while she sensed a subtle energy in the room. 'Claire?' She thought she heard a breath like a distant sigh. 'I so need you now, Claire,' she whispered piteously. 'Forgive me. Forgive me for sending you away.'

There was the sound of the front door being crashed back on its hinges. Then, a few minutes later, 'Holy shit!' Kenneth staggered into the room, retching. 'I came back,' he gasped.

When he had recovered a little, he said, 'We'll have to cut him down. We can't leave him there.'

'The police . . .?'

'No. We can't leave him like that.' Kenneth went to the kitchen and returned with a knife. 'Don't look,' he said. 'Stay here.' He went into the hall, shutting the door behind him.

Charlotte put her hands over her ears so she would not hear the sound of William's body falling. Then she took them away again. After all, he had wanted her to experience his death. She listened to the terrible silence until it was broken by an undramatic, muted thud. But then William had not, on the whole, been a dramatic man.

When Kenneth came back he was holding something in his hand. 'This fell out of his pocket. Isn't it your crystal?'

She remembered then what Max had said, that some perverted Atlanteans had used the power of crystals to destroy, and destroyed themselves.

'You can't go back to Cuckoo Lane after what happened there,' Robert protested. 'It's morbid.'

Charlotte did not see it that way. The little pink house was where William had found freedom, in the end, from an intolerable circumstance into which his mistaken belief had led him. At least he had had something out of the marriage. People had noticed him, several times.

After Hermione took his clothes away, it was as though he had never been there. Maggie seemed untouched by his departure. He had never talked to her. Never patted her. Since Tom came out of hospital he no longer wore the air of waiting. Charlotte wondered if he had foreknowledge of William's hand in the dog's attack. Since his return man and baby had ignored each other.

Kenneth felt bad about having refused William's invitation to coffee, and having failed to recognise the possible significance of the rope. But Charlotte knew that nothing Kenneth might have done would have made any difference. In staying to have coffee with William he might have changed the pattern, but the end result would have been the same, for once suicidal energies accrue there is no stopping them.

'Stay with us,' Robert pleaded after the muted celebration of Christmas and the funeral.

'I must go home,' Charlotte told him. 'I intend to finish my degree with the Open University. I need quiet to work.'

'This house is not quiet?' Robert was quizzical.

'Kenneth has volunteered to live with me for a while. And it'll keep Mum going, having somewhere to visit. She could help with the shopping. That's what mothers are for, aren't they? To help.'

Vivien's sharp decline that came at the time of Tom's accident, had halted. She was in remission, the doctor said. She had responded well to treatment, she was happier, and anyway, leukaemia was essentially unpredictable.

Charlotte went up to the landing. Instead of going to her room to collect Tom, who was having his afternoon sleep, on a sudden impulse she crossed over to the picture of the great-grandmother from whom it was said in the family that she and Claire had inherited their green eyes. Robert climbed the stairs. She turned. His eyes were kind, more gentle than she ever remembered them.

'Kenneth told me you're my father,' she said. 'I should have seen it myself but so much has happened, there hasn't been time to pause and think about things like that.'

'It's quite important.' Robert looked wry. 'You might have found the time. How did Kenneth know?'

Kenneth saw ghosts, too. Saw Claire on his windowsill at night, smiling at him. He told Charlotte that Claire had sent him to her aid on the night William died. But Charlotte knew Robert couldn't handle ghosts. Sylvia said he wasn't ready.

'Ken thinks it makes sense,' she said. 'I'm glad you wanted us. And thank you.' She put her arms round his neck and sweetly kissed him on the cheek. 'Is that why you put the portrait there? So that the green eyes would gradually sink into our consciousness? Did you want us to know?'

He surprised her by replying, 'Perhaps.' Then, more true to himself he added, 'Anyway, if I had removed the portrait Vivien would have wondered why . . . Do you want to know who your real mother is?' he asked suddenly.

At this, she turned hard. 'My real mother, who brought me up and looked after me to the very best of her ability in difficult circumstances, is your wife. I would never want to know the person who gave me away. Never!' She thought she had made herself clear.

Robert went to his study to think. To face the possibility of a rift with Charlotte. For ten years he had thought of her as Alison's child, and his. He now saw his effort to bring mother and daughter together as foolhardy, as well as disloyal. And he knew there was a decision to be made. With Max married and William dead, one baby to look after and another on the way, Charlotte needed him. There was no longer any doubt in the family's collective mind that she was pregnant and William's suicide, they had reluctantly agreed, proved Max was the father. Robert rested his head on his hands. He thought of Max on honeymoon in Australia with Louisa and considered their return with bleak dismay.

He made his decision, rose and went towards the big drawing room. Through the half open door he could see Vivien watching television. She looked small, She looked small, frail and very much alone. He went in, sat down beside her and tentatively took her hand. For an instant she appeared startled.

Then she smiled.

The little pink house was haunted in the days that followed. Claire became playful. She flicked soapsuds into Charlotte's face while she was washing Tom's clothes. She moved things round in the kitchen.

Where was the sugar? Charlotte felt distracted. She was making Kenneth's cocoa. She heard soft laughter, whirled round and there was the sugar basin, teetering on a shelf above her head. 'Stop it!' she scolded. 'You're not a poltergeist.'

'I am what I am,' said Claire. 'You'll see.'

'At any rate you're grown-up,' Charlotte retorted, saving the bowl and dumping a large spoonful of sugar in the cup. 'You're the same age as me.'

But Claire continued with her mischief, hiding Tom's shoes, banging doors if Charlotte was cross with her.

Sometimes she was helpful. One morning there was a recipe book open on the kitchen bench. Claire's see-through body leaned against the cupboards in its filmy see-through dress. 'You

291

might make cottage pie tonight,' she said. 'Ken likes cottage pie. I'll push Mum along to the supermarket to get you some minced beef.'

Then Vivien arrived, saying she suddenly had a great longing for cottage pie and had brought extra minced beef for Charlotte in case she and Kenneth would like one, too. 'I don't know what came over me,' she said. 'I was looking at some very nice steak, then suddenly I switched. Look out!' She dived across the room.

Tom had staggered to his feet, taken a few steps towards the low windowsill, reaching for a glass that Kenneth had carelessly left there the evening before. As his fingers were about to make contact, the glass slid out of reach. Tom looked astonished, then collapsed backwards on the floor.

Vivien picked the glass up and the moment passed. 'Funny,' she said, 'I'd never noticed the sills here are on a slope.'

'Thanks a lot, Claire,' said Charlotte. 'You know, that's one of my best glasses.'

'What did you say, dear?' Vivien asked.

'Talking to myself.'

Vivien said gently, 'It comes of being so much on your own. Why don't you come shopping with me? Or we could go for a drive.'

'Too busy,' said Charlotte. She was not yet ready to risk running into people who knew that Max had married Louisa the day William died. She imagined the village was humming with gossip. She put the local paper in the bin without opening it, not wanting to see a picture of the bride and groom.

Claire, in her mischievous moments, teased Tom a lot. She tweaked his hair, provoking a squeal and a look of surprise. Tom talked to her in his baby jargon, and offered her sips of milk or orange juice from his mug.

'I think he's got an imaginary playmate,' Vivien said one day. 'It's quite common.' She went on to name several people she knew who had had them. 'They grow out of it after a while.'

'Imaginary playmate?' repeated Sylvia, whose comforting presence was only a telephone line away. Sylvia believed that babies sometimes brought friends with them from the spirit world to comfort them during their early years in the harsh reality of life on earth.

Maggie did not find Claire imaginary. Though her hair no

292

longer bristled when the ghost came into the room, she would rise from the floor, look warily in Claire's direction, then go quietly to whichever door was open and settle down just out of sight.

Sometimes Claire sat on the opposite side of the table while Charlotte ate her lunch. 'Have some more fruit,' she said one day, sliding the bowl nearer. 'It's good for the child.'

Charlotte held her breath. Was Claire going to allow her to have Max's child now Max had gone? She dared not ask.

Sometimes in the depth of the night she wakened, thinking, If this is what she wants, then she has won. She felt it might make sense in Claire's scheme of things to live with her twin and Max's children. She saw herself as being possessed by the dead.

'I think you should get the piano back,' Claire said one day. 'We'll sing together.'

Kenneth often brought work home. That evening when he was sitting at the table surrounded by his papers and she by the fire knitting a jumper for Tom, he said, 'It occurred to me today, why don't we get the piano back?'

Charlotte put her knitting down on her lap.

'Why are you looking at me like that?'

Charlotte swallowed. 'What made you think of it?'

'Dunno. The idea hit me. I rang Dad. He's going to have it sent down. Sorry to appear to go over your head, but I thought you might have a mental block about it. That's why I didn't ring you. OK?'

'OK,' said Charlotte. She needed to go out of the room to talk to Claire. 'Shall I make us some hot chocolate?'

Kenneth nodded. His head was down over his work again.

Claire was in the kitchen. 'Can you make people do what you want them to do?'

'Sometimes. That one was easy because Ken knew you wanted the piano. Some people are hard to move.' Claire sighed.

'Did you bring our parents back together?' In the past few days Vivien and Robert had seemed easier with each other.

Claire said, 'He did it himself. It's right for the time.'

'What do you mean?' Charlotte opened the fridge and took out the milk.

'It is all about timing,' said Claire. 'This is Vivien's time.'

Why had she called their mother Vivien? Charlotte felt a down draught. A sense of change to come. 'Did you send Ken to live with me?'

'I can't run the world,' said Claire peevishly. 'People do things for themselves.'

Charlotte found it odd and unnatural to be keeping house for her bachelor brother. She was puzzled that he seemed so content in her company. Why was he not taking out girls? Why did he not stay in his flat in London occasionally and go to the theatre? She carried the hot chocolate back into the living room.

Kenneth looked up. 'Since we're talking about mental blocks, Mum thinks you ought to see your doctor.'

Charlotte was frightened when she thought about doctors. The baby still hadn't moved. If it doesn't move, it's dead, the doctor might say.

Without replying, she went back to her seat by the fire and picked up her knitting.

Kenneth said, 'I only ask because some people think you're going to have a baby.'

Charlotte dropped her needles. 'I wish you wouldn't talk to me when I'm concentrating,' she said crossly. 'I've lost a stitch.'

The next afternoon when Vivien dropped in, Charlotte asked if she would like to take Tom home. She felt on edge, blaming Kenneth for bringing up the subject of the doctor. She said she wanted to be alone for a while.

Vivien was delighted. 'Come with Granny?' she asked, holding out her arms.

Tom understood more and more words each day. He scrambled to his feet, was lifted up, then leaned over her crooked arm looking for the dog. 'Mag, Mag!'

'Yes, we'll bring Maggie too.' Vivien took him off to get his outdoor clothes.

That afternoon the snow began to fall. It came drifting in across the garden, holding the light. Charlotte sat down in a comfortable chair by the french windows, watching the leafless trees gradually lose their stark outlines. Nothing moved. There was not a sound to be heard.

Claire came and sat in the chair opposite, watching with her in the stillness. 'Remember when you got lost in the snow and I brought you home?'

What Charlotte remembered was being pulled out of her body. Sitting on the bed with Claire in her other dimension, holding hands. In those few moments she had felt like a twin again.

294

She had a feeling of drifting to another shore.

She opened the glass doors and breathed in the cold air. Extending a hand, she captured a snowflake. 'What is to happen now?' she asked. She felt very close to Claire.

'I will be with you always,' Claire said.

Charlotte heard a sound of ringing as of a lone bell. She stayed listening, hearing the silence of the garden. The bell came again, more insistent this time. The dread that had been with her for so long started floating away.

'Something is happening,' she said. A moment passed and then she saw a figure coming towards her across the snow-white grass. A tall young man with broad shoulders and dark hair. A grown-up Tom. She was being drawn into the future.

'Hello.' The voice was real, and achingly familiar.

She stayed suspended in time and space.

There was a whisper from Claire and there she was standing between them, lit by a glowing light. The vision faded and Charlotte felt her breath catch as the little baby within her moved, rolled over, and came alive.

Max entered the room, bringing the snowflakes with him, and held her in his arms.

Sitting by the fire with the scent of apple wood drifting in the room, Max reached out and laid his hand on the child lying under Charlotte's heart. 'Why didn't I know about this?' he asked, his eyes full of love and bewilderment.

'She didn't seem to be there,' said Charlotte. 'But she's there now all right. Jumping around like fun. Claire could be her name.'

'I thought I glimpsed Claire standing by you as I came across the garden. It seems like an omen. Charlotte and Claire Fosse,' he said, smiling. 'Mmn, I do like that.'

So there was, after all, a way for them all to be together. Claire had found it, in the end.

'You're supposed to be in Australia,' Charlotte said.

Max looked troubled at the memory. 'There was no wedding. Ken telephoned Louisa at five o'clock on the morning we were to have been married. He got her out of bed and told her what William had done.'

Ken! All the breath seemed to leave Charlotte's lungs. So that was what his presence in the little pink house was about! He was taking responsibility for what he had done.

'He thought it would be best if Louisa saved face by jilting me,' said Max. 'I got a call from her when I was dressing to go to the church. Last-minute stuff.' He looked wry.

There are some things, Charlotte thought, to which there is no solution. Vivien's illness. Louisa's obsession with Max.

'I didn't get in touch because – how could I, in the circumstances? I dived into work. Kept my mind occupied. My mother understood, and my father was happy for me to stay away. But this morning I seemed to be in a vacuum. My brain wouldn't work. The fax machine churned out a couple of messages that didn't make sense. The phone kept ringing with wrong numbers. I shredded a couple of statements that were waiting to go out in the mail.

'It was weird,' said Max. 'I felt light-headed. I sat down and tried to focus and found myself focusing on you. I had this compulsion to go and find you. I couldn't resist it. So I locked up and got into the car and drove down here.' He gripped her hands tightly.

'When I arrived and you didn't answer the bell, I decided I was just going mad. I turned round to go back to the car. Then I remembered there was a path running down the side of the house.'

The bell! She had thought it was a part of the magic. She looked into the flames flickering in the great fireplace and thought with wonder of the miracle of a child bringing its parents together. She remembered what Claire had said about timing. If Max had come before, before Claire was ready, she would have been afraid to let him in.

She thought about William's timing, too, and hoped Kenneth's intervention might save him from going on with vengeance in his heart.

She thought of Sylvia, who had been with her through the long, long wait, and immediately she felt a warmth that did not accord with the snow drifting against the glass outside. She had a sense of skimming with the little sharp-winged birds across the canyon at Valle San Angelo, she and Claire, with their love flying between them, following the path of the sun.

296

The very best of Piatkus fiction is now available in paperback as well as hardcover. Piatkus paperbacks, where *every* book is special.

The prices shown above were correct at the time of going to press. However Piatkus Books reserve the right to show new retail prices on covers which may differ from those previously advertised in the text or elsewhere.

Piatkus Books will be available from your bookshop or newsagent, or can be ordered from the following address:
Piatkus Paperbacks, P.O. Box 11, Falmouth, TR10 9EN.
Alternatively you can fax your order to this address on 01326 374888 or E-mail us at books@barni.avel.co.uk.

Payments can be made as follows: Sterling cheque, Eurocheque, postal order, (payable to Piatkus Books) or by credit cards, Visa/Mastercard. Do not send cash or currency, UK and B.F.P.O. customers allow £1.00 postage and packing for the first book, 50p for the second and 30p for each additional book ordered to a maximum charge of £3.00 (7 books plus).

Overseas customers, including Eire, allow £2.00 for postage and packing for the first book, plus £1.00 for the second and 50p for each subsequent title ordered.

NAME (Block Letters)—————————————————

ADDRESS ————————————————————————

I enclose my remittance for £ ——————————

I wish to pay by Visa/Mastercard Card.

Number ☐☐☐☐☐   ☐☐☐☐☐☐☐☐☐☐

Card Expiry Date ————————————